ALONE
WITH
YOU
IN THE
ETHER

ALONE WITH YOU IN THE ETHER

a love story

OLIVIE BLAKE

TOR

A Tom Doherty Associates Book
New York

ALONE WITH YOU IN THE ETHER

Copyright © 2020 by Alexene Farol Follmuth

A Tor Book
Published by Tom Doherty Associates
120 Broadway
New York, NY 10271

www.tor-forge.com

Tor® is a registered trademark of Macmillan Publishing Group, LLC.

Library of Congress Cataloging-in-Publication Data

Names: Blake, Olivie, author.
Title: Alone with you in the ether / Olivie Blake.
Description: First Tor edition. | New York : Tor, 2022. |
"A Tom Doherty Associates book."
Identifiers: LCCN 2022034860 (print) |
LCCN 2022034861 (ebook) | ISBN 9781250888167 (hardcover) |
ISBN 9781250891501 (signed edition) | ISBN 9781250888174 (ebook)
Subjects: LCGFT: Novels.
Classification: LCC PS3602.L3476 A79 2022 (print) |
LCC PS3602.L3476 (ebook) | DDC 813/.6—dc23/eng/20220725
LC record available at https://lccn.loc.gov/2022034860
LC ebook record available at https://lccn.loc.gov/2022034861

Our books may be purchased in bulk for promotional,
educational, or business use. Please contact your local bookseller
or the Macmillan Corporate and Premium Sales Department
at 1-800-221-7945, extension 5442, or by email at
MacmillanSpecialMarkets@macmillan.com.

First Tor Edition: 2022

Printed in the United States of America

0 9 8 7 6 5 4 3 2 1

to the old you,
from the old me

ALONE
WITH
YOU
IN THE
ETHER

A HYPOTHESIS

There would be times, particularly at first, when Regan would attempt to identify the moment things had set themselves on a path to inevitable collision. Moments had become intensely important to Regan, more so than they had ever been. Considering it was Aldo who had altered the shapes and paths of her thinking, it was probably his fault that she now considered everything in terms of time.

Her own hypothesis was fairly elementary: There was a single moment responsible for every sequence thereafter. Regan wasn't the science enthusiast Aldo was—and certainly not the genius he was, either—but her view of causality was methodical enough. Everything was a consequence that rippled out from some fixed point of entry, and it had become a game of hers (probably stolen from him) to expose the genesis from which everything else had sprung.

Had it begun the moment Aldo met her eye? Was it when he said her name, or when he told her his? Had it been the moment she'd told him Get up, you can't sit there, or did it have nothing to do with him at all? Could even that moment have been the product of something begun days, weeks, even lifetimes prior?

With Regan, everything came down to sacredness. She liked, in the time between docent tours, to wander her favorite parts of the Art Institute, which she typically selected to match the religiosity of her moods. Which was not to say she gravitated to religious art specifically; more often she aimed to match her private longings with the god (who was sometimes God, but not always) being worshipped through a polished frame. In early Catholic paintings, she looked for awe. In modern work, for sleekness. In contemporary, the vibrancy of dislocation. Deities themselves had changed over time, but the act of devotion had not. That was the torment of it, of art, and the perpetual idolatry of its creation. For every sensation Regan could conjure, there was an artist who had beautifully suffered the same.

The wandering was a foregone conclusion—a constant, as Aldo would say—but the armory, that day, was not. When Regan had chosen to visit the armory in the past it had been because it stood for the sacredness of purpose: There was no frivolity here. Instead there was the irony of peace; empty shells of weaponry, garish red walls, fossils of conquest. It reminded her of a time when people still committed their violence eye to eye, which gave her a paradoxical sense of gratification. It was intimate because it was not. It was religious because it was not. It was beautiful because, at the heart of it, it was twisted and soulless and ugly, and therefore it mirrored something masochistic in Regan herself.

Her choice of the armory that day implied Significance; it had the ripple effect of Consequence, cosmically so. But then what had been the cause? Had she met Aldo there because fate had willfully intervened, or because they already possessed such similar forms of rumination? Was it contrived, god descending from machine, or was it because she had been vacant where he was vacant, and therefore both would inevitably seek to be filled?

Did it matter where it started, and would it matter where it would end? Either yes, it mattered very much, because everything was a consequence of something and therefore what became of them was somehow predetermined, or no, it did not matter at all, because beginnings and endings were not as important as the moments that could have happened or the outcomes that might have been. Either it was everything to know the whole story, to look back and see the shape of it while standing along its periphery; or it was nothing, because things in their entirety were less fragile and therefore less beautiful than the pieces within the frame.

By the end, Regan would know the answer. Having turned a corner from where she'd been, she would come to recognize that it was less a question of when everything had happened and more a surrendering to when there had been no turning back. It was always a matter of time in the end, just as it had been in the beginning.

Because for once, in a moment that was either everything or nothing, there would be someone else in Regan's universe, and from there everything would be as it was, only very slightly different.

PART ONE

BEFORES.

The day before was nothing special. It was special only because of how unspecial it was, or perhaps by how unspecial it would very soon become. Things were always stranger in retrospect, which was a funny little consequence of time.

Aldo, who was called less frequently by his surname, Damiani, and even less commonly by his birth name, Rinaldo, had rolled a joint five minutes prior to his episode of silent meditation. He was twirling it between his fingers, staring into nothing.

> **SCENE:** The air that afternoon has the crisp, weatherless quality that only happens in Chicago for about a week in mid-September. The sun is bright overhead, and the leaves on the tree above him are mostly undisturbed.
> **ACTION:** ALDO raises the joint to his lips, saturating the cigarette paper.

The joint was unlit, because he was thinking. He'd come out to this park to sit on this bench to solve something, and he had been sitting there for ten minutes, thinking for nine and a half, rolling for four, and now fake-smoking for a good thirty seconds. Muscle memory, Aldo had always thought, was the key to unlocking any door that wouldn't open. The act of solving something was, for him, as superstitious as anything.

> ALDO glances at the audience. Noticing nothing amiss, he looks away.

The mechanics of his ritual were simple: Raise the joint to his lips, breathe in, breathe out, let his hand fall. This was the formula. Formulas he understood. He brought the joint to his lips, inhaled, and exhaled into nothing.

> A BREEZE slides through the leaves overhead.

Aldo's right thumb beat against his thigh, percussive to the rhythm of Grieg's "In the Hall of the Mountain King,"

Cue soundtrack.

which then infected the rest of his fingers. They drummed against the threading of his jeans, impatient, while his left hand continued the motion of faux-smoking.

Aldo was thinking about quantum groups. Specifically, hexagons. It was Aldo's firm belief that the hexagon was the most significant form in nature, not purely because of his fondness for the *Apis*— commonly known as the honeybee—but not entirely unrelated. Many people were typically unaware of how many kinds of bees there were. The bumblebee was slow and stupid enough to be petted, which was sort of sweet, though not quite as interesting.

THE NARRATOR, AN AGING, ARTHRITIC MAN IN POSSESSION OF MANY BOOKS: We interrupt your perusal of Aldo Damiani's intrusive thoughts to provide some necessary academic insight. The great Kurt Gödel, a twentieth-century logician and friend of Albert Einstein, believed that a continuous trajectory of "light cones" toward the future meant that one could always return to the same point in space-time. It is Aldo Damiani's essential thesis that these cones travel methodically, perhaps even predictably, along hexagonal paths.

Hexagons. Quantum groups. Symmetry. Nature loved balance, especially symmetry, but rarely managed it. How often did nature create perfection? Almost never. Math was different. Math had rules, finite and concrete, but then it just kept going. The problem and the thrill of abstract algebra was that Aldo had been studying it in depth for over seven years, and he could study it for seven million more and still understand almost nothing. He could spend infinite lifetimes studying the mathematical basis of the universe and the universe would still not make sense. In two weeks it might snow, might rain sideways, and then this park would not be available to him. He could get arrested for not-smoking or die at any moment, and then he'd have to do his thinking in jail or not at all, and the universe would remain unsolved. His work would never be done, and that alone was tragic, exhilarating, perfect.

Right on schedule,

FROM ALDO'S POCKET: a vibration that prompts the audience to reach instinctively for their own pockets.

his father called.

Aldo tucked the joint into his pocket and dug out his phone. "Hello?"

"Rinaldo. Where are you?"

There was a long answer and a short answer, and Masso would probably insist on both. "Working."

"You mean school?"

"Yes, Dad. I work at school."

"Mm." Masso already knew that, but the asking was another ritual. "What are you thinking about today?"

"Bees," said Aldo.

"Ah. The usual, then?"

"Yes, something like that." There was never an easy way to explain what he was working on. It was nice of his father to ask, but they both knew that anything Aldo had to say was mostly lost on him. "Everything okay, Dad?"

"Yes, yes, fine. How are you feeling?"

There was a right answer to this question and many, many wrong ones. This question, much like quantum groups, did not get any easier the more times Aldo was asked. The more times he ran the scenarios, in fact, the more the variables changed. How was he feeling? He had been bad before. He would be bad again. It would cycle and fluctuate the same way the weather would. It would rain in two weeks, he thought.

THE WIND picks up slightly, tendrils of it slipping through the leaves.

"I'm fine," Aldo said.

"Good." Masso Damiani was a chef, a single father, and a worrier, in that order. Masso thought about the universe often, the same way Aldo did, but differently. Masso asked the universe how much salt to boil in the water, or whether this vine or that one would provide the sweetest fruit. He knew when the pasta was done without looking, probably because of the universe. Masso had the gift of certainty and did not require any superstition.

Aldo's mother, a lively Dominican girl too young for motherhood and too beautiful to stay long in one place, had never been very present. If she had ever asked anything from the universe, Aldo imagined she'd probably gotten what she wished.

"Rinaldo?"

"I'm listening," Aldo said, though what he meant was *I'm thinking*.

"Mm," Masso said. "Did you try the museum?"

"Maybe tomorrow. It's nice out today."

"Is it? That's good. Rare."

SILENCE.

Masso cleared his throat.

"Tell me, Rinaldo, what are we doing today?"

Aldo's mouth twitched slightly. "You don't have to keep doing this, Dad."

"It helps, doesn't it?"

"Yes, of course, but I know you're busy." Aldo checked his watch. "It's nearly lunchtime there."

"Still, I have two minutes. Or so."

"Two minutes?"

"At least."

ALDO hums to himself, thinking.

"Well," said Aldo, "I think maybe today we're on the ocean."

"What year?"

He considered it. "When was the Trojan War?"

"About . . . twelfth century B.C.?"

"Yes. That."

"Are we fighting, then?"

"No, we're leaving, I think. Journeying."

"How is the wind?"

"Poor, I suspect." Aldo took the joint between his fingers again, rolling it slowly. "I think we may be at sea quite a while."

"Well, I suppose I'll just have to find out again tomorrow, then."

"You don't have to, Dad."

ALDO says this every day.

"True, maybe I won't."

So does MASSO.

"What's the special today?" Aldo asked.

"Ah, porcini. You know I like to mark the season with truffles."

"I'll let you get to it, then."

"Okay, good idea. Are you going back now?"

"Yes, I have to teach soon. At three."

"Good, good. Rinaldo?"

"Dad?"

"You are brilliant. Tell your mind to be kind to you today."

"Okay. Thanks, Dad. Enjoy the fungi."

"Always."

Aldo hung up, tucking the phone back into his pocket. No answers today, unfortunately. Not yet. Maybe tomorrow. Maybe the next day. Maybe not for months, years, decades. Luckily, Aldo was not a "right now" sort of person. It had once been a quality that frustrated the other people in his life, but he'd gotten rid of most of them by now.

He glanced over his shoulder at his bike,

PROP: a 1969 Ducati Scrambler.

which slid easily through traffic and pedestrians and, as far as Aldo was concerned, through time and space as well. Why anyone would own a car rather than a bike was beyond him, unless they were opposed to the possibility of accidents. He had broken his arm once, scarring up the side of his shoulder.

If he were a "right now" sort of person, he'd probably get on his bike and drive it directly into Lake Michigan, which was why it was probably best that he wasn't. Aldo was a "maybe tomorrow" sort of person, so he tucked the joint back in his pocket and picked up his helmet from the bench.

ALDO rises to his feet and inhales deeply, thinking about hexagons.

Turns, he thought. One of these days he'd hit a corner and there'd be something else on the other side; something very like this, only 120 degrees different. He mimicked a boxing pivot to the left, struck a left hook, and then kicked a little at the grass.

Maybe tomorrow, everything would be different.

————

Regan, meanwhile, had begun the exact same day by shooting upright in bed.

SCENE: A lavish master bedroom. Shoes have been mislaid. Articles of clothing have been flung. Whatever has happened here, no mother would approve.
ACTION: REGAN squints at the clock, which reads an abysmal 2:21 P.M.

"Well, fuck me entirely," Regan announced to the room.

Beside her Marc rolled over with a groan, managing with great difficulty to expel a series of unintelligible male sounds. Regan presumed them to be a version of "I'm sorry darling, explain?" and answered accordingly.

"I'm going to be late."

"For what?"

"My fucking job, Marcus," Regan said, sliding her legs out from beneath the duvet and stumbling upright. "You know, that thing I do from time to time?"

"Doesn't the Institute have those . . . what are those things," Marc grumbled, shoving his face back into his pillow. "You know, the little . . . radio things. For people who can't read placards."

"The audio guides?" Regan said, pressing a hand to her temple.

Her head spiritedly condemned her poor decisions with a decisive throb. "I'm not a walking audio guide, Marc, I'm a docent. Astonishingly, people might notice if I'm not there."

THE NARRATOR, A MIDDLE-AGED WOMAN WITH A BRISK INTOLERANCE FOR NONSENSE: Charlotte Regan has a degree in art history and would likely say that she has dabbled in art herself, which is in many ways an understatement. She graduated college at the top of her class, which had been no surprise to anyone once upon a time; except maybe her mother, who considered the top of a liberal arts program to be the equivalent of being, say, the winner of a dog show. Among the things Charlotte Regan was not was her older sister Madeline, who'd finished at the top of medical school, but that is of course not relevant to the subject at hand. Presently, Charlotte Regan is a docent at the Art Institute of Chicago, a coveted role at one of the oldest and largest art museums in the United States. Charlotte's mother would say it's a glorified volunteer position rather than a job, but that, again, is not relevant at this time.

While many things made Regan *#blessed,*

THE NARRATOR, DISAPPROVINGLY: She is being sarcastic.

primary among them was her hair, which was characteristically perfect, and her skin, which was generally resistant to the consequences of her lifestyle. Genetically speaking, she was built for waking up late and rushing out the door. A swipe of mascara would do the trick, and maybe a rose-tinted lip stain for the high bones of her cheeks, just to make her look slightly less dead. She pulled out one of her black sheath dresses and a pair of black ballet flats, twisting the claddagh ring on her finger. Then she reached for the earrings she'd stolen from her sister's room after college graduation: the little teardrop garnets that made her ears look like they were slowly weeping blood.

She paused to eye her reflection with something of a honed ambivalence. The dark circles were getting notably worse. Luckily her mother had given her the East Asian genes for eternal youth and her father had given her a trust fund that made people think twice about rejecting her, so it didn't really matter whether she slept or not. Regan pinned her name tag to her chest, pricking her thumb only once in the process, and stopped to eye the finished product.

"Hi," she said to the mirror, practicing a smile. "I'm Charlotte Regan, and I'll be your guide to the Art Institute today."

"What?" Marc asked groggily.

"Nothing," she said over her shoulder.

They'd fucked last night to moderately successful results, though Marc never got particularly hard when he'd done that much cocaine. But at least she'd gone home with him. At least she'd gone home at all. There had been a moment when she might have opted not to; when a stranger standing in the corner near the back of the room might have been the more interesting choice, whereupon she might have hazarded a little sashay his way. All it would have taken was a breathy laugh, a sly *Take me home, Stranger,* and then wouldn't it have been so easy? There were a million spidery webs of possibility in which Regan had not come home, had not slept with her boyfriend, had not woken up in time for work, had not woken up at all.

She wondered what she was doing out there in all those mirror-shards of lives unlived. Maybe there was a version of her who had woken up at six and gone jogging on the lake path, though she doubted it.

Still, it was nice to consider. It meant she possessed creativity still.

This version of herself, Regan calculated, had fifteen minutes to get to the Art Institute, and if she believed in impossibilities she would have believed it to be impossible. Fortunately or unfortunately, she believed in everything and nothing.

She fingered the bloody tears of her earrings and pivoted sharply, eyeing Marc's shape beneath the sheets.

"Maybe we should break up," she said.

"Regan, it's seven in the morning," Marc replied, voice muffled.

"It's almost two thirty, dipshit."

He lifted his head, squinting. "What day is it?"

"Thursday."

"Mm." He burrowed his face in his pillow again. "Okay, sure, Regan."

"We could always just, I don't know. See other people?" she suggested.

He rolled over with a sigh, propping himself up with his elbows.

"Regan, aren't you late?"

"Not yet," she said, "but I will be, if you want." She knew he wouldn't.

"We both know you're not going anywhere, babe. All your stuff is here. You hate inconvenience. And you'd have to use condoms again."

She made a face. "True."

"Have you taken your pills?" he asked.

She glanced at her watch. If she left in five minutes, she'd probably still make it.

She considered what she could do in five minutes. *This isn't working, I'm not happy, it's been fun*—that would take what, thirty seconds? Marc wouldn't cry, which was something she liked about him, so it wouldn't be terribly inconvenient. Then she'd have four and a half minutes to gather up the things that mattered and throw them into a bag, which would really only require about two. Which would then leave two and half minutes. Ah, but thirty seconds for pills, she kept forgetting. Five seconds to take them but twenty or so to stare blankly at the bottles. Which . . . what could she do with the remaining two minutes? Eat breakfast? It was nearly two thirty. Breakfast was out of the question, temporally speaking, and besides, she wasn't sure she could eat yet.

Motion from the clock suggested that Regan's five minutes for flight had dropped to four. There'd be such a terrible restriction on her time now unless she recalculated, rescheduled. Changed her priorities.

"I have to do something," she said suddenly, turning away.

"Are we breaking up?" Marc called after her.

"Not today," she told him, snatching the orange bottles from their usual place beside the fridge before making her way to the bathroom. She set the pills aside and pulled herself onto the sink, hiking one leg up to rest her heel atop the marble counter, and slid her hand under her seamless thong, unlocking her phone with her free hand. She'd never enjoyed porn, finding it kind of . . . upsettingly unsubtle. She preferred mystery—craved it like a drug—so she pulled up a password protected note on her screen.

THE FIRST PHOTO is a grainy shot of a nondescript masculine hand under a short skirt, positioned lasciviously between the slim curves of feminine thighs. The second is a black-and-white image of two feminine torsos pressed together.

This, Regan determined, was worth it. This was the better decision. She could have ended her relationship, true, but instead she had these four minutes. No, three and a half. But she knew her physicalities well, and therefore knew she'd need only three, tops. That left at least thirty seconds.

With the remainder of her time, she could do something very Regan, like tucking her underwear into Marc's jacket pocket before she kissed him goodbye. He'd find it later that evening, probably while he was schmoozing with some bespoke-suited exec, at which point he'd sneak into a bathroom stall and take a picture of his dick for her. He'd expect something in return, probably, but in all likelihood she'd be sleeping. Or maybe she wouldn't have come home at all. What a mystery, her future self! The possibilities were fascinatingly mundane and yet, somehow, perfectly endless, which was close enough to elation itself.

She came, biting down on the sensation, and exhaled.

Forty-five seconds.

REGAN reaches for the bottle of pills and says nothing. She wonders how long it will be until she feels something again.

———

Aldo was getting his PhD in theoretical mathematics, which meant a broad variety of things depending on who he was saying it to. Strangers were typically impressed with him, albeit in a disbelieving sort of way. Most people thought he was joking, as people who looked like him did not typically say the words "I'm getting my doctorate in theoretical mathematics" unironically. His father was proud of him but blindly, having been bewildered by most things Aldo had done or said for the majority of his life. Others were unsurprised. "You're one of those brainy fucks, right?" Aldo's dealer used to say, always asking about the chances of winning this or that, and though Aldo would remind him that statistics was a practical application, i.e., *applied* math, his dealer would simply shrug, ask something about life in outer space (Aldo didn't know anything about life in outer space) and hand him the items he'd requested.

Aldo's students detested him. The truly gifted ones tolerated him, but the others—the undergraduates who were taking calculus to satisfy requirements for study—positively loathed him. He lent very little thought to why, which was likely part of the problem.

Aldo was not an especially good communicator, either. That was what the drugs had been for to begin with; he was an anxious kid, then a depressed teen, and then, for a brief period, a full-blown addict. He had learned over time to keep his thoughts to himself, which was most easily accomplished if his brain activity was split into categories. His mind was like a computer with multiple applications open, some of them buzzing with contemplation in the background. Most of the time Aldo did not give others the impression he was listening, a suspicion that was generally correct.

"Exponential and logarithmic functions," Aldo said without preamble, walking into the poorly lit classroom

SCENE: A university classroom.

and suffering the usual itch to dive out its institutional windows. He was exactly one minute late, and, as a rule, was never early. Had he been any earlier to arrive, he might have had to interact with his students, which neither he nor they wished him to do.

"Did anyone struggle with the reading?"

"Yes," said one of the students in the second row.

Unsurprising.

"What exactly is this used for?" asked a student in the back.

Aldo, who preferred not to dirty his hands with application, loathed that particular question. "Charting bacterial growth," he said on a whim. He found linear functions banal. They were mostly used to simplify things to a base level of understanding, though few things on earth were ever so straightforward. The world, after all, was naturally entropic.

Aldo strode over to the whiteboard, which he hated, though it was at least less messy than chalk. "Growth and decay," he said, scrawling out a graph before scribbling $g(x)$ beside it. Historically speaking, this lecture would be extremely frustrating for all of them. Aldo found it difficult to focus on something that required so little of his attention; conversely, his students found it difficult to follow his line of thought. If the department were not so hard-pressed for qualified teachers, he doubted he would have been promoted to lecturer. His performance as an apprentice had been less than stellar, but unfortunately for everyone (himself included), Aldo was brilliant at what he did.

The university needed him. He needed a job. His students, then, would simply have to adapt, as he had.

For Aldo, time in the classroom regularly slid to a crawl. He was interrupted several times by questions that he was required by university policy not to remark were stupid. He enjoyed solving problems, true, but found teaching to be more tedious than challenging. His brain didn't approach things in an easily observable way; he unintentionally skipped steps and was then forced to move backward, usually by the sound of some throat-clearing distress at his back.

He knew, on some level, that repetition was required for some base level of learning—extensive boxing training had been part of his self-inflicted rehab, so he knew the importance of running the same drill over and over until his head pounded and his limbs were sore—but that didn't stop him from lamenting it. It didn't keep him from wishing he could walk out of the room, turn a corner, and head in an entirely different direction.

Theoretically speaking, anyway.

———

The first of the day's tours included an elderly couple, two twenty-something women, a handful of German tourists, and what Regan furtively ascertained (having made it a custom to check for rings whether she was interested in the outcome or not) to be a married couple in their mid-thirties. The husband was staring at her, poor thing. She knew that particular stare and was no longer especially flattered by it. She'd started using it to her advantage as a teenager, and now simply stored it among her other tools. Phillips-head, paint-brush, saturation scale, the attraction of unavailable men; it was all the same category of functionality.

This particular husband was good-looking, sort of. His wife had a pretty but unremarkable face. Likely the husband, a "catch" by virtue of what Regan guessed to be a practical job selling insurance, saw the Chinese mixing with Irish in Regan's features and consid-ered it some sort of exotic thrill. In reality, she could have been the genetic combination of half the Art Institute's current occupants.

"I'm sure many of you will recognize Jackson Pollock's work," Regan said, gesturing to the *Greyed Rainbow* canvas behind her.

THE NARRATOR, A TEENAGE GIRL WHO IS BARELY PAYING ATTENTION: The piece *Greyed Rainbow* by Jackson Pollock is basically just a black surface covered with splotches of grey and white oil paints with, I don't know, some other colors at the bottom. It's like, ab-stract or whatever.

"One of the most remarkable features of Pollock's art is how tac-tile it is," Regan continued. "I encourage you to step forward to wit-ness the painting's depths up close; the layers of paint have a distinct solidity you will not find elsewhere."

The Wife stepped closer, eagerly eyeing it upon Regan's sugges-tion, and the others followed suit. The Husband hung back, hover-ing in Regan's eyeline.

"Amazing they even call this art, isn't it? I could do this. Hell, a six-year-old could do this." The Husband's gaze slid to hers. "I bet you could do it much better."

Regan estimated his dick to be average-sized, and while that wasn't necessarily problematic, the fact that he probably didn't know what to do with it was. A pity, as he was handsome enough. He had a pleasant face. She guessed that he was unhappily married to his college sweetheart. She would have guessed high school girlfriend, given how that was relatively standard for people with his Minnesotan drawl, but he seemed like a late bloomer. She caught the faint pitting from acne scars on his forehead, which was a detail that most people probably missed—but they wouldn't have missed it in the tenth grade, and Regan didn't, either.

She had a couple of choices. One, she could fuck him in a bathroom stall. Always an option, and never not worth consideration. She knew where to find privacy if she wanted it, and he seemed like he'd probably strayed once or twice already, so there wouldn't be a lot of easing his conscience beforehand.

Of course, if she wanted mediocre dick, that was deplorably easy to find without picking *this* mediocre dick. The fact that Regan was his object of choice out of all the things in the museum on which to focus his attention said far more about him than it did about her.

It could be a diverting ten minutes. But then again, she'd had more fun in less.

"Jackson Pollock was highly influenced by Navajo sand painting," Regan said, her own gaze still affixed to the painting. "With sand," she explained, "the process is just as important as the finished product; in fact, more so. Sand can blow away at any moment. It can disappear in a matter of hours, minutes, seconds, so the process is about the moment of catharsis. The reverence is in *making* art—in being part of its creation, but then leaving it open to destruction. What Native Americans did with sand, Jackson Pollock did with paint, which is perhaps an empty rendition of it. In fact, he never openly admitted to adopting their techniques—which makes sense, as it's far closer to appropriation than it is to an homage. But could *you* do it?"

She turned to look at The Husband, sparing him a disinterested once-over.

"Sure, maybe," she said, and his mouth twitched with displeasure.

The art is always different up close, isn't it? she thought about saying, but didn't. Now that he knew she was a bitch, he wouldn't bother pretending to listen.

Eventually the tour ended, as all tours did. The Husband left with The Wife without having fucked any docents that day (that she knew of, though the night was still young). Regan readied herself for the next tour, feeling a buzz in her blazer pocket that meant Marc had found the underwear she'd left for him.

Everything was so cyclical. So predictable. At one point, Regan's court-appointed psychiatrist had asked her how she felt about being alive,

THE NARRATOR: That whole thing was honestly so stupid.

and Regan had wanted to answer that even when it was never exactly the same, it seemed to follow a consistent orbit. Everything leading to everything else, following the same patterns if you happened to look closely enough. Sometimes Regan felt she was the only one looking, but she'd given the doctor a more tolerable answer and they'd both gone home satisfied, or something. Mostly Regan had felt thirsty, a result of her recent lithium increase. Dehydrate even a little and the pills would gladly offer her the shakes.

"*Saint George and the Dragon,*" Regan said, pointing out the painting to the next tour. A visiting family's teenage son was staring at her breasts, and so was his younger sister. There's no rush, Regan wanted to tell her. Look how warped the medieval works are, she wanted to say, because there's no perspective; because once upon a time, men looked at the world, took in all its beauty, and still only saw it flat.

Not much has changed, Regan thought to assure the girl. They see you closer than you are, but you're further from reach than either you or they can imagine.

———

Aldo lived in a building of lofts that had once been occupied by a printing company in the early twentieth century. Initially he'd lived closer to the University of Chicago, on the city's south side, but restlessness had driven him north to the South Loop, and then slightly east to Printers Row.

SETTING: Printers Row is a neighborhood south of the Chicago downtown area known as the Loop. Many buildings in this area were once used by printing and publishing businesses but have since been converted to residences.

It was warm this evening, the air still playing host to remnants of summer's humidity, and Aldo opted to take advantage of an evening run. He didn't live particularly far from the lake path

THE NARRATOR, AN OVERZEALOUS CUBS FAN: Nowhere in the city of Chicago is ever too far from the lake path!

but he often preferred to run on city streets. The beat of his stride against pavement was too similar to a pulse sometimes. Without interruption, it was disquieting. Made him too conscious of his breathing.

That, and the path was often occupied.

After his run was shadowboxing, bag work, occasional sparring. Aldo wasn't training for anything, as such, but he supposed he was ready if it came. He'd always been naturally wiry and thin

THE NARRATOR: One of them skinny little shits like my cousin Donnie, eh?

and lacking much in the way of ego or temper. Generally speaking, Aldo was unlikely to get into any sort of street fight, much less a formal boxing ring. He just liked the reminder that, from time to time, he retained the option of adrenaline and pain.

After three or so hours he'd come home, locate a couple of chicken breasts, probably some spinach, and definitely some garlic, for which he didn't use a press. (Diced garlic was an outrage, as his father had told him many times, an abomination for its lack of taste. When it came to garlic, Masso said, it would have to be crushed or whole—no exceptions.)

Few people ever came to Aldo's apartment, but the ones who did had commented without exception on the sparseness of his possessions. It was an open-air loft with red Ikea cabinets and modern stainless-steel appliances, and Aldo owned exactly one pot and one pan. Two knives: a santoku knife and a paring knife. His father had always said that was all anyone ever needed. Aldo did not own a can opener or an ice tray. He *did* own a pasta maker, though he preferred to make ravioli or tortellini the way his nonna had insisted. Adalina

Damiani had taught both her son and her grandson to cook, but while Masso found cooking to be a religious experience, Aldo considered it something best reserved for special occasions, or homesickness. Though, in his experience, most people considered religion precisely the same way.

On nights when Aldo couldn't sleep (i.e., most of them), he would head up to the roof to light whatever remained of the joint still languishing in his jacket pocket. He specifically chose the type of marijuana reserved for bodily aches and mindlessness, soothing the prattling going on at the back of his head. His bones would cease their frantic motions for the evening, and inevitably his body would buzz, searching for something new to fill its vacancies.

AND NOW, LADIES AND GENTLEMEN, we are proud to present . . .
Aldo Damiani's thoughts!

Buzz. Bees. The honeybee's wings flapped 11,400 times per minute, which was what created the buzzing sound. Bees were known for industriousness and organization; see also, the phrase "worker bee." That, plus determination; a beeline. Aldo was similarly single-minded, even if he was many-thoughted. He floated out on an exhale, adrift and out to sea.

He would have to try something different tomorrow, since his problem solving had not been particularly fruitful that day. He had a number of favorite places within the hive of the city, and typically bounded around between them. The top floor of the public library was an atrium called the Winter Garden, though Aldo couldn't understand why. There was no particular season involved, but there was a pleasing vastness, a certain proximity to the heights and the heavens, and it was frequently empty. The concrete beams lofting up the glass ceiling would descend on him in hexagonal shadows, and if he positioned himself correctly beneath them, perhaps something new would occur to him. Otherwise, there was always the Lincoln Park Zoo, or the art museum. It was often quite busy, but to the right eye, it still contained places to hide.

THE NARRATOR: Foreshadowing, baby!

Aldo exhaled the taste of burning, the film of it coating his tongue, and then put out the smoldering end of the joint. He had as much of a buzz as he needed, and sleep felt pointless for the night.

Aldo disliked the sensation of being asleep. It felt something very close to being dead, which was an uncomplicated and therefore troubling state of being. He wondered if bees felt that way when their wings stopped beating. Though, he wondered if they ever did. He wondered what a bee would do if it knew its life's work was contributing to the ecosystems of fancy toasts. Would that be enough to compel it to stop?

Doubtful.

Aldo made his way back to his apartment and fell onto his bed, staring up at the track lighting overhead. He alternated between opening one eye, then the other. He could read, maybe. He could watch a movie. He could do anything, really, if he wanted.

11,400 beats per minute was really something.

He closed his eyes and let his mind wander, settling into the buzz of his thoughts.

"So, Charlotte—"

Regan fought the urge to flinch and ultimately managed it, opting instead to tuck one ankle behind the other and angle herself slightly away, facing the window. She itched to cross her legs—to fold in on herself entirely—but some habits couldn't be unlearned, and her mother had taken her social cues from Queen Elizabeth: no legs crossed. Regan suspected she would have been forced to wear pantyhose, too, if anyone had ever bothered to make it in her skin tone.

"How are your moods lately?" the doctor asked. She was a nice enough woman; well-intentioned, at least. She had a comforting, matronly air to her and the sort of bosom Regan imagined grandchildren nestling into. "You mentioned during our last session that you sometimes feel restless."

Regan knew enough about the practices of clinical psychology to recognize that "restlessness" in this particular space was code for "mania," which was in turn code for "falling into her old ways"—at least, if her mother were here to translate.

"I'm fine," Regan said, which wasn't code for anything.

In fact, she *was* fine. She had enjoyed her walk here from the Art Institute, passing Grant Park as she aimed herself toward Streeter-ville. The streets were buzzing with people, which was why she liked it. It felt very alive and full of possibility, unlike this particular room.

Regan often opted to take a meandering path on her way to her bi-weekly appointments, passing contemplatively by all the doors she might have entered while the shops were closing and the restaurants were starting to fill. She had been thinking about what she might want to eat that evening—pasta sounded good, but then again pasta always sounded good, and either way prosecco sounded better—and whether or not she'd make it to yoga in the morning when she'd suddenly recalled that she had yet to check her phone.

THE NARRATOR, A BELOVED KINDERGARTEN TEACHER: Regan's consistent unreachability was once a carefully honed practice that had gradually become a habit. When Regan was younger, she had coveted the prospect of a call or a text; it meant, primarily, attention. It meant that she had filled the vacancy of someone else's thoughts. Then, after a while, she began to understand that there was power in devaluing her worth to others. She started to place limits on herself; she wouldn't check her phone for ten minutes. Then for twenty. Eventually she'd space hours between, making a point to direct her thoughts elsewhere. If others were forced to wait for her time, she thought, then she would not have to owe so much of herself to them. Now, Regan is so very talented at being completely unreliable that people have started to call it a weakness. She takes some pride in their misconceptions; it means people can always be fooled.

"How are things with your boyfriend?" asked her psychiatrist.

On Regan's phone had been the expected dick pic from Marc; he was wearing the white Calvins that Regan had bought for him some weeks after they'd moved in together.

THE NARRATOR: Marc Waite and Charlotte Regan met at a bar about a year and a half ago, back when Regan was planning a gallery opening with a friend. She'd selected the venue, determined the artists and the pieces, and then she'd met Marc. He'd been going down on her in the bathroom of the Hancock Signature Room—in Regan's opinion, the best view of the city was from the women's restroom on the ninety-fifth floor—when she received a voicemail from her father listing the ways that her subject of choice, The Fraught Lies of Beauty, was inappropriate for someone who had only narrowly avoided federal prison for white collar crime. "There's candor, Charlotte, and then there's hubris," he'd ranted into her voicemail. She had not actually listened to the message until close to three days later.

"What's your boyfriend's name? Marcus?"

"Marc," Regan said, which he preferred. "He's fine."

Which he was, generally speaking. He was something-something hedge funds. He didn't ask for very much from Regan, which was ideal, because she didn't typically give very much. If they tired of each other, they simply didn't speak. They were good at occupying each other's spaces. She often thought of him as an accessory that matched with everything; some sort of magical mood ring that adapted to whatever persona she had currently filled. When she wanted silence, he was silent. When she wanted to talk, he was generally apt to listen. When she wanted sex, which she often did, he was easily persuaded. Eventually she would marry him, and then everything she was would vanish into his name. She'd attend parties as Mrs. Marcus Waite, and no one would ever have to know a thing about her. She could shrug him on like some kind of cloak of invisibility and vanish entirely from sight.

Not that he wanted her to. If there was one thing Regan would willingly say about herself, it was that she was an ornament, a novelty, a party trick. She was the center of attention when she wished to be, quick-witted and charming and impeccably dressed, but those types of girls grew dull when there were no eccentricities or blemishes. The world loved to take a beautiful woman and exclaim at the charm of her single imperfection; Marilyn Monroe's mole, or

Audrey Hepburn's malnutrition. It was the same reason Marc took no issue with Regan's past. He didn't mind that she had once required reinvention; she doubted he'd take an interest in her if he couldn't elevate himself with her flaws.

"You've been getting along lately, then?"

"Yes," Regan said. "We're fine."

They always got along, because getting along required the least of their energy. Marc would consider a fight to be a poor use of his time. He liked to smile at Regan when she argued, preferring to let her tire herself out.

"And your family?" the psychiatrist asked.

Regan's phone had contained two voicemails: one from her psychiatrist asking if she could come to her session an hour earlier (she hadn't received it and had come at her usually scheduled time, it was fine, nobody died), and one from her sister, earlier that evening.

"I know you won't get this for like, a month," Madeline said, "but Mom and Dad want you home for their anniversary party. Just let me know if you're bringing someone, okay? Seriously, that's all I need. Just text me back a number. One or two, but zero is not acceptable. And don't just send me a cryptic series of gifs again, it's not as funny as you think. Are you going to wear that wrap dress you just bought? Because I was going t—ah, hang on, Carissa wants to speak to you." A pause. "Honey, you can't tell me you want to speak to Auntie Charlotte and then refuse." Another pause. "Sweetheart, please, Mommy is very tired right now and you're going to lose your good behavior stickers. Do you want to talk to Auntie Charlotte or not?" A long pause, and then a shrill giggle. A sigh, "Okay, fine, whatever. Carissa misses you. Though, I can't believe I have to say this, but please do not buy her more chewing gum, that peanut butter trick only does so much. God, she's just like you as a kid, I swear. Alright, bye Char."

Regan thought about Carissa Easton, who was probably wearing a lace headband, perhaps with bows, and a velvet dress whose washing instructions demanded dry cleaning; not simply "dry clean," which was the best method, but "dry clean *only*," which was the exclusive method, and which was a distinction that Madeline Easton, née Regan, would know.

THE NARRATOR: In reality, Carissa was not much like Regan. Her mother adored her, for one thing, and she was an only child, or at least a future oldest child. Carissa would be more like Madeline one day, which was precisely why Regan made a point to send her chewing gum.

"They're doing very well," Regan said. "My parents are having an anniversary party next month."

"Oh?" asked the psychiatrist. "How many years?"

"Forty," Regan said.

"That's very impressive. It must be very beneficial to have such a stable relationship in your life."

THE NARRATOR: Regan's parents had slept in separate bedrooms since she was ten years old. In Regan's opinion, marriage was very easy to do if you simply operated in totally separate spheres. If she were to chart her parents as a Venn diagram, the only three things in the center would be money, Madeline's achievements, and what should be done about Regan.

"Yes, it's wonderful," Regan said. "They're made for each other."

"Is your sister married?"

"Yes. To another doctor."

"Oh, I didn't realize your sister was a doctor."

"She is. A pediatric surgeon."

"Oh." It was an *Oh, how impressive,* as it usually was.

"Yes, she's very smart," Regan said.

Sibling rivalry was nothing new, though Regan didn't exactly feel the need to disparage her sister. It wasn't Madeline's fault she'd been the more pleasing daughter.

Regan touched her garnet earrings, thinking about what she'd say when she called her sister back. The last thing she wanted was to bring Marc home, and certainly not for this party. Her parents hated him, but not in a fun way, and certainly not from a place of concern. They hated him because they didn't particularly like Regan, either, but also there was a very palpable sense—to Regan, anyway—that their opinion fell somewhere along the lines of: *At least Marc is sufficiently rich.* He wasn't after her for her money, and that, they exhaled, was a relief.

Madeline thought Marc abrasive, but Regan thought Madeline's husband passive and uninteresting. He was all the worst things about doctors; all diagnosis, no bedside manner. Marc, on the other hand, was bedroom eyes and gregarious laughter, and had he ever told you about the time he lost a goat-milking competition to one of the locals in Montreux?

So, yeah. In Regan's experience there was always room for disagreement.

"Anyway," the psychiatrist said. "How is your volunteering going?"

"It's fine," Regan said.

The doctor meant the docent job, which had at least put Regan within the realm of art, even if she was no longer studying or creating it. Every now and then she looked around at the pieces and thought about picking up a brush, or possibly rushing out to buy some clay right after work. She had hands that itched to be busy, to be occupied by something or another, but it seemed every time she sat down lately, her mind simply went blank.

"Have you thought about what you'll do next?"

Next. People were always thinking about what to do next. Other people were always planning their futures, moving ahead, and only Regan seemed to notice how the whole thing was just moving in circles.

"Maybe art school," Regan said. A safe answer.

"That's a thought," the psychiatrist said approvingly. "And how are you adjusting to your new dosage?"

Beside the fridge lived five translucent-orange pill bottles. Regan took three in the morning and three at night (the lithium she took twice). One of them, a name she would probably never remember, was relatively new, and about as difficult to swallow as certain aspects of her personality. Taken with too little food, she got incurably nauseated. Taken too late at night, her dreams were so vivid she woke without any concept of where she was. She usually grimaced at the bottle before finally conceding to open it, placing the pills on her tongue and swallowing with a gulp of flat champagne.

"In my professional medical opinion, Charlotte Regan is unwell" was the diagnosis by the psychiatrist that her lawyers (or more aptly, her father) had hired. "This is a young woman who is well educated, intelligent, talented, and raised in a secure and loving home, and who has the capacity for great contribution to society. But it is my professional belief that her bouts of depression and mania make her easily led astray by others."

The pill typically went down with the chalky, bitter taste of repetition. Regan was a spontaneous person who was now tethered to the mundanity of a routine—morning and night, plus the monthly blood tests just in case the pills that made her well decided to poison her instead—though she didn't necessarily resent the doctor for that, either. Resentment seemed a pointless task, and was, like most things, far too much effort to conjure.

Later that night, Regan would take that pill and the rest of her pills and then wander into the bedroom she shared with Marc. The apartment was his space, full of his things and designed to his taste—he'd already owned it when she moved in and Regan hadn't bothered purchasing anything since her arrival—but she could see why he wanted her inside it.

THE NARRATOR: Regan believes there are two ways to manipulate a man: either to let him pursue you or to let him pursue you in a way that makes him feel he's the pursuit. Marc is the latter, and he loves her the same way she loves art, which Regan considers a pleasing form of irony. Because even when you know everything about how a piece is made, you're still only seeing the surface.

"I feel much better," Regan said, and the psychiatrist nodded, pleased.

"Excellent," she said, scribbling something down in her notepad. "Then I'll see you again in two weeks."

Regan would go to bed before Marc returned home that evening, which was (unbeknownst to her) the occasion of her last normal day. She would pretend to be asleep when he curled naked around her. She would also leave for yoga before he woke up, and the day would proceed as it always did: with pills, water, a meager breakfast, and then to the museum. She would wander, eventually, through the variations of whitewashed Jesus in the medieval corridor to the end of the European exhibition. The armory contained red walls, unlike the neutral tones of the other rooms, and featured a bodiless knight in the center, frozen in time as Regan and everything else continued around it.

Everything would be the same in there, precisely as it always was, except for one thing.

That day, there would be someone else inside the armory.

———

For the record, Regan wasn't the only one to speculate on the causality of it all. Aldo was a chronic wonderer, compulsive with his pondering, and therefore crises of meaning and sequence were fairly commonplace.

But unlike Regan, whom he had not yet met, Aldo could be patient with the concept of nothing. Emptiness repulsed Regan, filling her with abject terror, but the concept of zero was something that Aldo had come to accept. In his field of expertise, resolution was difficult (if not fully impossible) to come by. Answers, if they were to arrive at all, took time, which was why Aldo's specialty was constancy. He had a talent for persisting, which his medical records would confirm.

The night before he met her, Aldo had resigned himself to the fact that an epiphany might never find him, or that it wouldn't matter if it did. That was the risk with time, that knowing things or not knowing them could change from day to day.

On that day, Aldo believed a certain set of things wholly and concretely: That two and two were four. That of the lean proteins, chicken was most accessible. That he was trapped within the constraints of a maybe-hexagonal structure of space-time from which he might never escape. That tomorrow would look like yesterday; would look like three Fridays from now; would look like last month. That he would never be satisfied. That in two weeks, predictably unpredictable, it might rain, and therefore in changing, everything would remain the same.

The next day he would feel differently.

THE NARRATOR, A FUTURE VERSION OF ALDO DAMIANI THAT DOES NOT YET EXIST: When you learn a new word, you suddenly see it everywhere. The mind comforts itself by believing this to be coincidence but it isn't—it's ignorance falling away. Your future self will always see what your present self is blind to. This is the problem with mortality, which is in fact a problem of time.

Someday, Regan will tell Aldo: It's very human what you do, and at first, he'll think, No, not true, because bees.

But then eventually he'll understand. Because until that night, Aldo had been comfortable with nothing, but he would eventually learn because of her: It isn't constancy that keeps us alive, it's the progression we use to move us.

Because everything is always the same until, very suddenly, it isn't.

THE NARRATOR: If I'd known I would meet Charlotte Regan in the morning, maybe I would have gotten some fucking sleep.

In the center of the room was a young man sitting cross-legged on the floor. He was sketching something in a notebook. Regan was initially distracted by his activity (painstaking) rather than his appearance (obscured from her position in the doorway), but one thing led to another and eventually it became unavoidable to conclude he'd been given a sublimely terrible haircut. His hair, a brown-black salute of thick curls, exceeded poor management and elevated, in Regan's mind, to institutional failure: a flaw in the construction. He kept sweeping parts of it back from his face, which struck Regan as a reflex of annoyance rather than pretension.

Remembering herself, Regan stepped further inside.

"Excuse me, you can't sit there," she began to scold, and then faltered, having lost her train of thought upon spotting whatever the man was drawing. Even from a distance, she could see it was a tight, precise geometric pattern, parts of it shaded or blocked out entirely. The whole thing was drawn with lines so consistent and deliberate that the ballpoint tip had dug into the pad below, leaving behind shallow channels and curling the leaf of the page.

"What are you drawing?" she asked him, and he looked up.

His eyes were a hazel dominated identifiably by green, a stark contrast to his skin. They were also slightly vacant, as if he were having some trouble dragging his attention away from something else.

"Hexagons," he said, and then, with very little pause, "You don't look like a Charlotte."

She glanced down at the scripted lettering of her name tag. "I don't go by Charlotte. Why hexagons?"

"I'm working on something." He had an interesting voice; sharper than she'd expected, and slightly drier. Regan guessed that if he were to tell a joke, most people in the room would fail to catch it. "Is it even your name?"

"Yes," she said. "Why would I lie? Also," she repeated, "you can't sit here."

"I don't know why you'd lie. I just know it doesn't seem right."

She opened her mouth to answer, then closed it. She'd always hated giving other people the sensation of being right.

"Why hexagons?" she asked again.

"I'm trying to solve something." It was a slightly better answer than he'd offered before, though still not particularly illuminating. "It works better if I do something with my hands, and they're easy to draw. And relevant. I'd smoke," he remarked tangentially, "but I think that'd be frowned upon in here."

"Cigarettes are extremely out of fashion. And they're bad for you. And you can't sit here."

"I know that. Not cigarettes." He looked up, squinting into something, and reflexively, Regan stared in the direction he was facing—looking for what he was seeing, which was almost certainly nothing—before collecting herself, turning her attention back to him.

"What are you trying to solve?" she asked him.

"Time travel," he said, and she blinked.

"What?"

"Well, time. But Eternalism suggests we could return to the same place in space-time," he said, neither patiently nor impatiently. He must have been asked the same question in the past, though he didn't appear to care much what she thought of his answer and probably hadn't before, either. "People disagree, but from a purely theoretical standpoint, there's some viability to the concept. Not that you could ever move faster than time," he told her, or the air around her, "that's out. You'd be shredded to pieces. But wormholes, that sort of thing, that's plausible for argument's sake. The most common theory suggests that a continuous trajectory of light cones, if there is one, would be circular, but that's highly unlikely. Perfect circles do not exist in nature. Hexagons, on the other hand, appear quite frequently."

He tore his gaze away from the opposite wall, dragging his attention to her.

"Bees," he said.

"Bees?" Regan echoed doubtfully.

"Yes, bees," he said. "Hexagons. Time."

He didn't *sound* insane, but he didn't not, either.

"You think bees know the secret to time travel?" she asked him.

He seemed to find that highly unreasonable, possibly even offensive. "Of course not. Their brains aren't designed to wonder. A useless evolution," he muttered to himself, "but here we are."

He closed his notebook, rising abruptly to his feet.

"If you don't go by Charlotte, what do people call you?" he asked her.

"Guess," she said.

"Charlie. Chuck."

"Do I look like a Chuck?"

"More a Chuck than a Charlotte." He didn't seem to be teasing her, though she couldn't decide if that made it better or worse.

"What's your name?" she countered, and then, thinking better of it, "No, wait. Let me guess."

He shrugged. "Go for it."

"Ernest. Hector. No, I bet it's something totally normal, like David," she said, feeling vaguely combative, "and you hate it, don't you?"

"I don't hate it," he said. And then, "What's your last name?"

She hadn't intended to answer any personal questions, but as of the last two minutes he had established a talent for catching her off guard. "Regan."

"Ah." He snapped his fingers. "That's it. That's your name."

"Are you naming me?"

"No, but that's the name you use," he said. "The way you use it, it's very comfortable. You can see the variables fitting together."

"You can?"

"Yes," he said, and it wasn't a boast. He said it the same way he might have recounted how he'd had the flu once, and in a similar way, she believed him. "I'm sure other people can."

"Tell me your name, then," she said.

"Rinaldo," he replied.

She narrowed her eyes.

"That's not it," she said, and his mouth twitched a little.

"No," he agreed. "I go by Aldo."

Ah. He was right. She could hear the difference. "Rinaldo what?"
"Damiani."

"Are you as Italian as you sound?"

"Nearly."

"Nearly, but not entirely." Regan noted the features of his face, the texture of his hair and the shade of his skin, categorizing him by layers of portraiture. Italian origins naturally required a different pigment than, say, Northern European, but for Aldo, Regan estimated she'd need something much more saturated than even the darkest shade of Mediterranean olive. If she were planning to paint him, which she wasn't, she'd require a sienna overlay, or a distinctly reddish color burn.

"My mother's Dominican," Aldo said, which explained it.

"And she had no problem with your father giving you that intensely Italian name?"

"She wasn't there to stop him," he said.

That, too, was matter-of-fact. The sun had been out earlier that day. His mother had left him when he was an infant. He was maybe probably some sort of genius. He was . . . Regan estimated 5'10", 5'11". Not overly tall, but certainly not short. He was also wearing a lot of leather for someone who was currently drawing hexagons in the armory of a fine art museum.

"What's your deal?" she asked him. "Why time travel?"

"I like to keep a long-term problem going," he said.

"What, like a computer program?"

"Yes." She'd been joking, but he clearly wasn't.

"You're some kind of math dude?"

"A specific kind of math dude, yeah."

He raked his fingers through his hair, which was definitely too long on top.

"I hope you didn't tip much on that haircut," she remarked. "It's not very good."

"My dad did it the last time I was home. He doesn't have a lot of free time."

Well, now she felt like a dick.

"Why are you drawing in here?" she asked him.

"I like it here," he said. "I have an annual membership."

So he wasn't a tourist. "Why?"

"Because I like it here," he repeated. "I can think in here."

"It gets crowded," she pointed out. "Noisy."

"Yes, but it's the right kind of noise."

The longer she looked at him, the more attractive he got. He had an interesting jawline. He didn't sleep well, that much was obvious. The bruising beneath his eyes was violently purple. She wondered what kept him awake at night, and what her name was. Or his name. Or maybe they were all nameless. He was a mystery, which was interesting. He never quite did or said what she thought he was going to, though that could become its own kind of predictable after a while.

He had a nice mouth, Regan thought. She glanced down at his pen, which had bite marks along the side. She would have guessed as much. She imagined the plastic getting caught between his teeth, his tongue slipping over it.

She shivered slightly.

"You work here?" he asked her.

"I'm a docent," she said.

"You look too young to be a docent."

Everything he said was astutely informed, clipped and certain.

"I'm older than I look," she informed him. It was a common mistake.

"How old are you?"

"Three years past my arrest," she said whimsically.

He indulged his curiosity; she'd wondered if he would. "Arrest for what?"

"Counterfeit. Theft."

He blinked, and she preened in his hitch of hesitation.

Then he glanced down at his watch.

"I should go," he said, registering the time, or possibly the concept of time itself, which she had recently learned was a thing he thought a great deal about. He reached for the bag she hadn't noticed at his feet, which had a motorcycle helmet strapped to it. The existence of a motorcycle explained the leather, even if it didn't explain anything else. He closed his notebook and placed it in his bag, which was a nondescript backpack that had suffered moderate abuse. There was a textbook inside, a thick one, like *Janson's History of Art*, and Regan shook her head.

If she were to paint him, she thought, nobody would even believe her.

She didn't say anything as he slung his bag over his shoulder, though he paused for a moment just before he moved to pass her, toying with a thought.

"Maybe I'll see you again," he said.

She shrugged. "Maybe you will."

She meant it, of course—the "maybe" of it all. It seemed they were both saying that logistically speaking, it might happen again. Clearly their spheres of occupation had a tendency to intersect. That would technically be a coincidence. If and when it happened, Regan would have an actual reason to recognize him. (Rather than what she had now, which was just a sensation.)

He had such defined brows for someone with so many messy features. That, of course, and his mouth, which was unmissable. There was a defined dip on top, a crooked sort of slant to the shape of it, making it seem as if he were regularly caught between expressions. He definitely had some sort of oral fixation, Regan confirmed, watching his hand rise reflexively to his mouth. He'd said that he smoked, and that seemed right. Of everything she'd noticed about him, that seemed like the most (and perhaps the only) fitting detail. He seemed like the sort of person who liked having something between his lips.

He moistened them once, eyeing something that wasn't quite her face, and then his teeth scraped lightly against the swell of his bottom lip.

"Bye," said his mouth, and then he was gone.

Regan turned to the vacancy where Aldo had been, frowning to herself. Suddenly the room seemed less quiet, buzzing with disturbance, and she felt her mood adjust to the new frequency, deciding to opt for something else. Contemporary art, maybe. Pop art. She could stare at the bright colors of commercial vacancy for a while to find her footing. She had at least ten minutes left of her break, she thought, checking her watch and reacquainting herself with time.

Then she turned and walked out, the moment temporarily over.

Aldo had considered the prospect of the multiverse many times, given his work, but regularly felt there was something unnecessarily cerebral about it, and also slightly unsatisfying. For example, if, in the armory, he had been holding the innumerable threads of what could come next—if he had simply chosen one of them while other versions of him carried on relentlessly elsewhere—then time remained forcefully linear. What good was choice if he could still only have one outcome at a time? No, the better option wasn't multiple Aldos talking to multiple Charlotte Regans. It was one Aldo, and one Charlotte Regan, and both of them encountering each other on some sort of geometrically predictable loop.

His phone buzzed in his pocket as he left and he slid it from his pocket, pausing on the steps of the Art Institute.

"Hi, Dad."

"Rinaldo," Masso said, "where are you today?"

"The museum." Aldo glanced over his shoulder, eyeing where he'd been. "The armory."

"Ah. Productive today?"

Aldo considered it.

It wasn't as if Charlotte Regan had *interrupted* him, necessarily. She had, of course, but not in any sort of obtrusive way. She was actually very quiet. Not her voice (she had a perfectly audible one) but her motions, her questions. He supposed some people might have called it elegance or poise, but he had never really understood those terms. It was more like there was a sliver of space between him and the outside world and she had unassumingly filled it, less like a piece fitting into the vacancy of another and more like liquid being poured into a cup.

"About average," Aldo said.

"Well, it's Friday, Rinaldo. Are you doing anything today?"

The gym was always quieter on Friday nights, which Aldo liked.

"Just the usual. Class this afternoon, and I have some work to do this weekend." Exams to grade, which was never as bad as the outcry that followed. He'd also have to prepare a lecture for the following Monday.

He doubted his father actually thought he was going to do anything out of the ordinary; more likely, Masso was doing him the favor of reminding him what day of the week it was. All of this was Masso's way of checking up on him, and Aldo did his father the favor of needing it. It calmed them both.

"And where are we today, Rinaldo?"

Aldo thought of the slope of Charlotte Regan's hips. Her dress had an asymmetrical hem, full of sharp, neat lines. It suited her, seeing how she was also tall and full of lines. She reminded him of the buildings that had been constructed along the river. They were mirrors of the landscape, beautiful and sleek and discreetly reflective of the water itself.

"In a city," Aldo said.

"A big city?"

"Yes."

"And are we lost?"

"No." Just dwarfed. "Hey Dad," Aldo said, suddenly remembering something. "How long do people usually go to prison for counterfeit?"

"What, like bills? Counterfeit bills?"

He hadn't thought to ask that, but he assumed so. "Yeah."

"I don't know," Masso said. "Hard to imagine people still manage it."

"True." Masso sounded distracted. "Everything okay over there?"

"Ah . . . yeeeees, nothing to worry about."

Aldo put on his helmet, throwing a leg over his bike. "Yeah?"

"Just . . . a shipment didn't come this morning." Masso barked something at someone, then returned to the phone call. "Where were we?"

"Dad," Aldo said, "if you're busy, you don't have to call."

"I know, I know. I like to."

"I know you do." Aldo looked up, a shadow coming over him. "I better go, Dad. It's going to rain soon."

By the time Masso and Aldo said their goodbyes, a few sprinkles had started. A Chicago autumn typically meant that sprinkles would rapidly become torrential rain. Aldo, who had grown up in the suburbs of Los Angeles and hadn't known until moving to the Midwest that rain was something that could occur horizontally, was never adequately prepared. Maybe in the world where he'd asked Charlotte Regan to have coffee with him (something he didn't drink and probably wouldn't enjoy), he had also taken the bus.

This was why the multiverse was so unsatisfying, Aldo thought. He couldn't step laterally into a version of himself who was prepared for rain, but maybe somewhere, in some other corner of time, he would've happened to plan this differently.

He was soaked through by the time he got to class.

"Exponential equations," he said without preamble, his jeans clinging to the tops of his thighs. He turned to the board, picked up the marker, and shivered slightly.

THE NARRATOR, A STUDENT WHO HAS JUST ARRIVED: You can never prepare for weathering anything in Chicago.

———

"Regan. You coming?"

She looked up, reflexively obscuring her phone screen. "Where?"

Marc gestured over his shoulder. "Bathroom."

It was too casual an invitation to be for sex. He must have meant drugs.

"You go ahead," she said, and he nodded, leaning forward to kiss her forehead.

"What are you doing?" he asked, gesturing to her phone.

"Nothing. Instagram."

He shrugged, giving her a wink and disappearing with one of his friends.

She waited until he was gone before unlocking her phone again, leaning back in the booth and glancing down at the Google results for Rinaldo Damiani. He didn't have any form of social media as far as she could tell (there was a LinkedIn page that listed him as a student at the University of Chicago, which made sense given the textbook) but what had caught her attention had been the results on a page called ratemyprofessor.com.

Rinaldo—Aldo—had deplorably bad results. His overall rating was a 1.4 out of five, with a 7% "would take again" and a 4.8 level of difficulty. His tags were abysmal: "get ready to suffer," "tough grader," "impossible to understand," "incredibly unsympathetic."

The reviews were even more vitriolic: "Damiani is a dick," said one student, describing how flippantly Aldo had dismissed his request for an extension.

"You're better off with LITERALLY ANY OTHER T.A.," said another.

One mildly flattering review said, "Damiani is really fucking smart and probably a lunatic. Good news is he grades strictly to the department-mandated curve, so statistically speaking someone will magically wind up with an A."

The best of them, which had awarded him three stars, said, "Damiani likes argumentation, or at least seems to respect it in like, an ADHD kind of way. Even if your opinion is bullshit, he'll like you more if it's thoughtful enough."

Regan took a sip from her drink, entranced. She hadn't guessed Aldo was a teacher, though it was pretty obvious he wasn't a very good one. Strangely, she found herself with a grudging sort of respect for him. It took someone painfully ambivalent or blissfully ignorant (or both) to be this out of touch with his students, and either way, she admired it. She found it interesting, which was certainly the highest praise she could offer anyone.

Eventually she ran out of material on the internet, finding herself somewhere between relieved Aldo didn't have a Twitter and disappointed she hadn't dug up anything particularly good. She wasn't sure what she'd been expecting, really. She just found the whole thing very strange, and he'd stuck in her brain a little bit, embedding himself there like a thorn. Like something on the tip of her tongue or hovering just at the edge of her periphery. She half expected him to be inside every room she entered, or to be the footsteps just behind her on every set of stairs. She kept turning him over and over, analyzing the angles she could see and wondering what else she might've missed.

If she ever saw him again, she thought, she'd have to ask him some questions. She started compiling a mental list, though she couldn't quite get past: Who are you? and, perhaps less flatteringly: *What* are you?

In her experience, curiosity about a person was never a good sign. Curiosity was unspeakably worse and far more addicting than sexual attraction. Curiosity usually meant a kindling of something highly flammable, which wasn't at all what Regan wanted from this. Sure, she thought about leaving Marc from time to time (Marc's primary business partner was always about one beat-too-long glance away from proposing a sordid tryst) but certainly not for something serious. Not for something prolonged. Having been in relationships that failed (and failed, and failed, and failed), Regan wasn't looking for anything enduring. The only thing she'd be willing to leave Marc for was freedom, but that and curiosity about a man did not usually go hand in hand.

Still, he was intriguing.

"Regan," Marc said, having returned, at which point she accepted the hand he offered her. Likely they'd grind a little on the dance floor, stay out too late, wake up partway through the afternoon. This was a life of no expectations, which was the safest kind of life. Regan always felt most secure in the hands of a man with no misconceptions of her flaws, because for better or worse, he would not be swayed by the possibility of their resurgence.

Regan suspected that Marc *liked* her a little broken; he liked expressing concern for her health, because caring for her made her grateful to him and therefore secured her as one of his treasures. She didn't see herself and Marc in their matching rocking chairs when they were old and grey, no—but she *did* see them having polite affairs with other people at some point in their forties, bribing a waitress to come home with them after yoga had kept Regan fit and money kept Marc advantageous.

It wasn't *not* love. She didn't *not* love him, and he was enamored with her precisely the way she liked: no rousing speeches, no undue pedestals, and nothing promised beyond what he could keep. He was a perfect complement to her—something as difficult to find as a match—which was why, curiosity or not, Regan had no plans to speak to Aldo Damiani again.

THE NARRATOR, CHARLOTTE REGAN: Though if he speaks to me first, it would probably be rude to refuse.

PART TWO

CONVERSATIONS.

It wasn't that Aldo was looking for Charlotte Regan, because he wasn't. Not that he spared much consideration for the imprecision of statistics (truly, the con artist of math) but as a matter of probability, it wasn't inconceivable their paths might cross a second time. They'd already established that their lives intersected in at least one place: the art museum.

So really, this was purely coincidental.

"Regan," he said, and she looked up the way strangers do: with surprise, and then a brief sense of dislocation. She had just finished a tour, and she glanced down at her watch before making her way over to him.

"Aldo," she said, and then, "right?"

He suspected the addendum had been for her benefit, not his.

"Yes," he said, indulging her. "How was the tour?"

"Oh, you know." She waved a hand. "I'd say about half the people on any given tour are there against their will, so it's mostly about playing to the most enthusiastic audience."

"Makes sense." Teaching was a similar experience.

"Yeah." She tucked her hair behind her ear, which was a girlish sort of motion. She had a definite doe-like quality to her; wide eyes, a narrow tulip nose, with a heart-shaped face and a sense of tremulous vulnerability to the shape of her mouth. Her eye contact, though, was hawkish and exacting. Because she was so close to his height, it was impossible to miss.

"How's your quest for time travel going?" she asked, and he shrugged.

"Depends how you look at it."

"Poorly, I'm guessing, seeing as you're still here."

"Who says I'd want to use it if I solved it?"

Half a laugh slipped from Regan's lips. "True, then you'd have to pick up some new hobby. Curing cancer," she suggested. "Knitting. Crochet."

"Maybe the other two, but I certainly can't cure cancer," Aldo said. "I don't know anything about it. It's a mutative cell degeneration, and those can't be predicted with math."

"Well, I guess we're fucked, then," she said.

"Something has to kill us," he agreed. "We already live far longer than our peak reproductive years. After a certain point we're just overusing resources."

"That's—" She fought a smile, or a grimace. "Bleak."

Was it? Probably. "I guess."

Regan glanced over her shoulder and then looked back at him. "I've been thinking about that thing you said, actually."

"Which thing?"

"About perfect circles not occurring in nature." She paused, and then, "I feel like that can't possibly be true."

"Have you thought of one?"

"Well that's the thing," she said, brow furrowing, "I haven't. Planets aren't circular, and neither are their orbits." She tilted her head, considering it. "Eyes, maybe?"

"Spheres are different than circles. And eyes aren't perfectly spherical, either. Plus insect eyes are packed hexagonally, which only further proves my point."

"Bubbles," she suggested.

"Spherical, and they become hexagonal in groups," Aldo said, as she frowned to herself. "I've been thinking about something you said, too, actually."

She looked up. "Really?"

"Well, you said you were arrested."

"Oh." She didn't seem overly pleased that this was the thing he remembered, though he felt quite certain she must have known it would stick in his brain. Maybe she was the sort of person who resented being proven right; he could understand that.

"Well, I just . . . I sort of need to know how you did it," Aldo admitted, and she gave him a look that suggested he'd better make his point. "Counterfeit is . . . well, hard to get away with, isn't it? It couldn't have taken very long to get caught, seeing as people are always checking big bills. You could use small ones, but mathematically speaking, in order to be worth it that would take—"

"I didn't make American bills," she said, interrupting him. "I'm pretty good with digital art," she explained, "or I was, at one point. I designed foreign bills and took them to exchanges for American currency."

"That," Aldo said, "is . . ." He paused. "Very smart."

"Not very, actually. A mistake of my youth."

She didn't look particularly contrite.

"Can you do something for me?" Aldo asked, and Regan blinked.

"Depends," she said.

"A small favor, probably," Aldo said.

"Is this a 'small favor' that only I can do?"

"Yes."

She swept a wary glance over him. "Just don't be gross. Is it gross?"

"No, it's not gross. Do you think I'm gross?"

"*Are* you gross?"

"No. Or at least I don't think so. I just—" This was getting away from him. "Look, I'd just like you to lie to me."

She blinked. Then frowned.

Then she sighed.

"What does that even *mean*, Aldo?"

(The first time she'd used his name, she'd been pretending at unfamiliarity. That time, though, he could hear the way it had previously crossed her mind.)

"You're obviously a very good liar," Aldo said, to which Regan seemed to have to fight a laugh. "Science requires a control group. A *known* lie," he clarified, "to compare against possible lies."

"And why would you need a control group?"

Seemed obvious to him. "Because I want to know when you're lying to me."

She opened her mouth, then closed it.

"If I *were* a liar," she said, "wouldn't my lies be extremely valuable currency to me?"

"Probably," he said. "Though I already know you have no moral opposition to counterfeit."

Her doe eyes widened, then narrowed.

Then, having decided something for herself, she glanced again at her watch.

"Hungry?" she asked him, looking up.

"Not especially," he said, since it was rather between meals. "I usually eat after I go to the gym, so—"

"Aldo." She stepped closer. "I'm asking if you want to go somewhere with me. You know," she added, "to talk."

He watched her face for a second, examining her eye contact, the dilation of her pupils.

"You're lying," he guessed, and her mouth quirked.

"Am I?" she asked.

"I think so," he said, and then, upon further reflection, "Do it again." He didn't have enough evidence; he'd have to compile it further.

"Aldo," she sighed, "that's not how this works. But you can come with me while I get something to eat," she suggested, "and who knows, maybe I'll lie to you again." She seemed perfectly aware that she was offering him something he wanted; she struck him as the sort of person who had a very clear idea what other people hoped to get. "Or maybe I won't," she added, bolstering his theory.

"But either way," she concluded, "I'm leaving."

He considered it. He hated to have his schedule interrupted, but it wasn't as if he had anywhere else to be.

"What do you want to eat?" he asked her.

"Thai," she said, too-quickly.

He frowned.

"That was a lie," he guessed.

"Hm, I wonder if this will get old," Regan mused to herself in reply, turning away. "I just have to get my purse," she tossed over her shoulder, rooting him in place with a glance. "Don't go anywhere."

"I won't," he said, and couldn't imagine why he would. The prospect of having something new to puzzle out was mildly enthralling, so he watched her as she took a one hundred and twenty degree turn into a corridor. Her stride was premeditated and unhurried, as if she'd mapped out a path defined by ambivalence and then followed its projection to the inch.

He tucked it into a new file in his mind; one he'd opened without realizing it.

REGAN, it said, and within the subsection marked *LIES,* he filed the sound of her footfall while she was walking away from him.

————

Regan took Aldo to a hotel bar across the street, settling into a booth at the back of the room. It was barely five, still early, and there was a pianist setting up, but not much other source of noise. She ordered a Nicoise salad with a glass of wine and sat back, watching Aldo request a glass of water.

"You're just going to watch me eat?" she asked, amused. Not that she typically ate much these days, and the pills had helped with what appetite she did have. The first month on this particular cocktail of medications had made her so sick she'd dropped an effortless ten pounds, the feeling of hunger gradually becoming preferable to the putrid sense of rotting from the inside out.

"Will that bother you?" he asked.

"No," she said, shrugging, and took a sip of her wine. "Okay, so. What's your story?"

He fidgeted a little, clearly made uncomfortable by the question. He seemed intensely uninterested in talking about himself, which was half the reason she'd brought it up. She'd spent enough time looking too closely at things to know when she was the one being clinically observed.

"I'm getting my doctorate in theoretical math," he said, which she already knew, though she wasn't going to tell him that. "I'm from California. Only child." He took a sip from his glass of water. "No major arrests."

"No *major* arrests?" she echoed, arching a brow.

"No arrests," he amended quickly, and she scoffed.

"Well, there's obviously a story *there*," she remarked, tapping her fingers on her glass. "Something in your juvenile record?"

"I had problems in the past. 'Illicit substances,' I believe is the term." She hid a blink of surprise and he took another sip. "I'm fine now."

"Rehab?" she asked, finding the thought mildly amusing. He wasn't exactly Kurt Cobain.

He shook his head. "My dad asked me to stop."

She waited, but he didn't elaborate. "That's . . . it?" she asked, a little underwhelmed. "You had a drug problem, your dad said, 'Hey, quit that,' and then you just . . . stopped?"

"Well, yeah." He drummed his fingers on the table. "I, ah." His gaze cut away from hers for a second, then rose again. "Well, I overdosed. My dad was upset."

He said everything with precisely the same degree of unambiguous fact that he'd used to address everything else. It scarcely registered, really, before dissolving into the small collection of data that Regan now possessed about him. She wondered if she should tell him she was familiar with the concept of medication (or self-medication, which his seemed to be) but his tone of blithe dismissal felt distinctly separate, as if he were referencing an amputated limb.

"It's my understanding that people tend to not like it when their children almost die," Regan commented, opting not to focus on the doom and gloom of it, and in response, something pulled at Aldo's mouth, alighting near the corners.

"He was sitting next to my bed when I woke up," Aldo said. "He just said, 'Never again, okay?' and I thought . . . yeah, sure, okay." He shrugged, lifting his glass of water to his lips and discarding the mood entirely. "So I stopped."

"That's," Regan began, and shook her head. "*Supremely* unlikely." Not that she had much experience with addiction, but her understanding of the world suggested that his story was incomplete. It wasn't as if people typically woke up with perfect resiliency, or that something could be made to vanish without leaving traces in its place.

But he'd lost interest in the subject; she could tell. His gaze hadn't technically moved, but the spark of focus in it had receded.

"Time travel again?" she asked, and he blinked, catching himself.

"No, actually," he said, in a way that suggested the answer was usually yes. "I was thinking about your counterfeit scheme again."

"It wasn't a scheme." It was definitely a scheme.

"Did you need money for something?"

"No," she said. "I just . . ." She trailed off, calculating what was worth saying. "It wasn't long after college," she decided. "My boyfriend at the time was an artist, and it was mostly his idea."

Aldo paused with his glass midway between his mouth and the table.

"Lie," he said.

She caught herself pausing mid-breath and reached for her wine, exhaling.

"You don't believe me?" she asked neutrally.

"Of course I don't believe you. I bet you've never gone along with someone else's idea in your life." Aldo's glass resumed its path to his lips. "I think it was your idea," he said after a pensive sip, "but I can't figure out why you'd do it." He scanned her again, the effect of it intensely asexual and certainly aromantic. "You seem like you have plenty of money."

"Do you actually believe that people only do things because they need to?" she asked, though as soon as she said it, she figured he probably did. He'd needed to kick a habit, so he had. He seemed to see the world through some lens of necessity, as if everything was purely reflex.

"I think you needed something," he assured her. "I'm just pretty sure it wasn't money."

The waiter arrived with her salad, which was convenient timing. She spread the napkin over her lap, delicately spearing part of an egg and an olive with her fork. Then she placed them in her mouth, chewing thoughtfully.

"Tell me more about your father," she said after a moment.

"He's a chef. He owns a restaurant."

"Oh?" She took another bite. "Can you cook?"

"Yes."

"Huh." She set her fork down temporarily, glancing at him. "Do you like it?"

He shook his head. "Not really."

"Well, makes sense," she said. "I don't think we're really capable of loving the things our parents love. I always wonder about father-son athletes, you know?" She picked up her fork again. "If my dad were Michael Jordan there's no way I'd ever pick up a basketball."

"You're from Chicago," Aldo noted aloud, and she rolled her eyes.

"Can you make this less like an interview, please?" she sighed. "You're making me feel like a zoo animal."

"I like zoos," Aldo said.

"Everybody likes zoos. That's not the point."

"I'm pretty sure you're wrong," he said.

"About what?"

"People take issue with zoos."

"People take issue with everything," she assured him, taking another bite. "The point is, you're observing me too closely."

He eyed her for a second, then half smiled.

"Truth," he judged.

She glared at him, just to try it out, and his smile broadened.

"Fine. Where are you from?" he asked her, and she sighed.

"Here," she conceded, earning herself a little smug glance. "Well, Naperville. My dad's in finance."

"And you're a thief?" he asked, still smiling.

"I wanted to be an artist," she said, and then corrected herself. "I was trying to be." She picked at an olive, separating it from a leaf of lettuce. "But yes." She sat back, giving up on her food and redirecting her attention to Aldo. "I was formerly a thief."

"Suits you," he said.

For some reason, she wanted to believe him.

"So," she said after a pause. "Did you get the lies you came for?"

"I don't think so," he said. His water glass was empty, and he tapped his fingers lightly against its side. "I think you pretty much told me the truth. Except for the thing about the heist not being your idea."

"It wasn't a heist," she said.

"It was basically a heist," he said, "and you're definitely the one who thought of it. I just want to know why."

She picked up her glass of wine, giving it a pointed swirl. "Perhaps I'm very vain," she suggested, "or too clever for my own good. Too interested in causing my parents grief."

"Those," Aldo said, "sound like lies. Or possibly someone else's truths."

They were. Her mother's, specifically.

"You said you wanted to be an artist," he prompted.

She waited for the statement to resolve to a question, but no such luck. "Yes, and . . . ?"

"Well, what's your . . . you know. Medium? Aside from crime." His smile quirked.

She opened her mouth, then closed it.

"Technically I just studied art," she said. "I have a degree in art history."

"Do you have a favorite painting?"

She took a sip of her wine. "No, not really. I like certain styles," she said. "Certain themes. But having a single favorite piece feels juvenile, somehow."

"You're lying," he said, and she gave him a dispassionate glance.

"You seem to think very little of me," she remarked, and he shook his head.

"I don't think there's anything wrong with a lie."

"Unless it's a lie for the sake of lying?" she guessed, unimpressed.

"No." Another head shake. "I think it's unrealistic to expect truth all the time. I just want to, you know, sort out the equation." He shrugged. "Why you lie, I guess."

"You want to puzzle me out like a math problem," she said dully. "How flattering."

"If it helps, not too many people are all that difficult to puzzle out, comparatively."

"I find that difficult to believe."

"Most people are a very specific set of variables. You know, goals, motivations, flaws, varying degrees of psychological trauma—"

"No," she corrected, "I meant I find it difficult to believe I'm in any way complex."

He stopped for a moment, tilting his head.

"You don't really mean that, do you?" he said.

"Crime doesn't make a person complex," she pointed out. "Everyone has a history."

"Sure," he said, "but that's not what's interesting."

He leaned forward, shifting to accommodate the worst possible thing: curiosity, which again Regan realized must have become mutual at some point while she hadn't been paying attention.

"Why," Aldo said slowly, "did you mastermind a heist?"

She stared at him. Things had clearly gotten away from her.

"I have a boyfriend," she decided to announce.

"Doesn't answer the question," he replied.

She opened her mouth, then closed it.

"Anything else?" asked the waiter, prompting her to jump.

"Just the check, please," she said quickly.

By the time the waiter had gone, Aldo had raised one hand to his mouth, observing her from his vantage point across the booth. The other hand was resting on the table, forearm tensing while he drummed his fingers in silent agitation.

"So," Regan said, "if I answer this question, you'll leave me alone, is that it?"

Aldo's mouth twitched. "Probably not," he said. He tapped his fingers on the table again. "Do you want me to leave you alone?"

"I asked you first," she countered even though she hadn't, and he shrugged.

"I thought maybe we could be friends," he said. "Or, if that sounds like too much work, then maybe we can have five more conversations."

She might have said yes to being friends, even just to be polite, but the follow-up offer was too strange not to question.

"Five?" she echoed. "That's very specific."

"Yes."

"Why five?"

"Seems like a reasonable number."

"Is that supposed to have some sort of mathematical significance?"

"I think theoretically the mathematical factor would be compiling the sum of your parts."

"Which you think you can do in six total conversations?" she asked, and then blinked, registering what she'd just said. "Ah," she murmured, shaking her head at him. "Bees."

His mouth was most crooked when he was pleased; one side of it lilted up in concession while the other fought to remain in place. "You can refuse, of course."

"You know I won't, though." She sipped the rest of her wine. "Was that just a guess?"

"Oh, yes," he said, "absolutely."

"The check, whenever you're ready," said the waiter, reappearing at Regan's side, and she paused him, reaching for her credit card before sending him scurrying off again.

"Alright. Six total conversations," she agreed slowly, returning her attention to Aldo, "but you have to tell me what you learn about me each time."

"Fair," he said. "Will you do the same?"

She shrugged. "If you want."

"What did you learn today?"

"That you don't have very many friends."

His smile broadened.

"And you?" she asked. "What did you learn about me?"

"That you're so bored you'll agree to six meaningless conversations with a stranger," he said.

She smiled at him.

He smiled back at her.

"Thank you very much," the waiter announced, handing Regan her card, and she looked down.

"What's the tip?" she asked Aldo, maybe-testing him. "Since you're some sort of math genius."

"I always over-tip," he said, reminding her, "my father owns a restaurant."

She glanced up at him, considering it.

"Next time," she said, "either neither of us eat, or we both do."

"Noted," he said. "And doubling the tax is probably sufficient."

She did as he suggested and rose to her feet.

"Next time," she offered, which he accepted with a nod.

"Next time," he agreed, and then she walked out the door, adjusting her earrings before hiding a smile in the curve of her palm.

———

"I was wondering when you were going to turn up again," Regan said.

She had tucked her hair neatly behind one ear, angling herself toward him as he approached her. She had a way of doing that, Aldo thought; of inviting him into the geography of the conversation. He wondered how quickly in life she had learned that people wanted to be invited in.

"I had you pinned for either immediately or never," she continued, "though your timing isn't great." She gestured to the meeting point behind her. "I have an Impressionism tour in five minutes."

"Yes, I know," Aldo said, holding up the museum's pamphlet. "I'm signed up for that Impressionism tour."

She blinked, half a laugh escaping against her will. She seemed to only laugh unexpectedly or not at all, from his observation. As far as Aldo could tell, any outward show of amusement by Charlotte Regan was either staged or a mutiny, no in-between.

"Well, this counts as one of the six, then," she told him. "You can't go around wishing for more wishes."

He shook his head. "It counts," he agreed, "*if* we have a conversation. Otherwise it's just me observing fine art."

"It's cheating is what it is," Regan said. "You're gaming the system."

"If you consider your company a prize to be won, then yes," he said. "But if it's a hypothesis to be tested, then I'm just performing the necessary research."

She frowned at him, looking suspicious. She seemed deeply suspicious of him in general, which he liked. He wasn't often suspected of much that couldn't be confirmed or rejected within the first five minutes of meeting him.

"What are you doing?" she asked him, and he shrugged.

"I want to see what you see," he said. "How will I do that if I never observe you in your natural habitat?"

"This is a job," Regan said, "not a habitat."

"One you choose to do for free," Aldo pointed out, and she opened her mouth.

"Excuse me," interrupted someone on his left, "is this the area for the Impressionism tour?"

"Yes," Regan and Aldo said in unison.

Regan gave him a silencing look.

"Yes," she confirmed to the other person, a tourist with a Boston accent, and then she turned back to Aldo, arching a brow that seemed to indicate that he should behave himself. He shrugged in reply, innocent enough.

He'd told her the truth, after all. There was something very strange about her, and in order to ease his need to simplify a complex problem, he'd split her up into distinctive areas of study. The first of these was her relationship to art. She had once been both an artist and a criminal, according to her, and if he couldn't observe her being one, then he would have to find a way to make sense of the other.

Mostly, Aldo was waiting for an epiphany of some sort. He felt confident that there would be a moment when all the disjointed parts that made Charlotte Regan so incomprehensible to him would form a recognizable shape, and then he would understand the basis of the problem.

Everyone, in Aldo's experience, could be quantified by the things that mattered to them. Take his father, for instance. Masso was made up of an abandonment complex, a reflexive protectiveness, a love of great food, and a weighty sense of responsibility. Thus, Masso required habit, reassurance, and a certain degree of shielding from the truth. Aldo, who understood this and could predict his father's behavior to a reliable degree of precision, was therefore able to concentrate on other things.

Regan, however, remained a series of unknown qualities, and also seemed to be popping into Aldo's brain uninvited. He was frustrated to find that her Impressionism tour, which was certainly informative enough, wasn't particularly enlightening. She was filling the role of Art Historian, which was like a coat she'd shrugged on rather than any recognizable version of herself. There was nothing introspective about the way she spoke about art; from time to time Aldo thought she might reveal some personal connection to the art or the artist, but even Regan's most enthusiastic observations stopped just shy of passion.

"Hi, excuse me," he said, raising a hand and startling her. "I have a question."

"About Degas?" she asked doubtfully, gesturing to the painting of the dancers behind her.

"No," he said, "about you."

She gave him a prim look of impatience.

"You can have one question," she allowed.

"What's your favorite painting in the museum?" he asked her.

"Sir, this is the Impressionism tour," she said. "You'll have to limit the scope of your question."

"Fine," he said. "Your favorite painting on this tour, then."

She hesitated a moment, then conceded, summoning their group further into the room. "This one," she said, gesturing to a rendition of a sunset over a water channel; even to Aldo, who knew nothing about art, the colors suggested it had been painted at dusk. "This is *Nocturne: Blue and Gold*, by James McNeill Whistler. It's part of a series he painted in the evenings and named after musical pieces," Regan explained. "It's considered a forerunner of modernism's abstractions."

"Why?" Aldo said, startling her before she could move on.

"Well," Regan said, "because it isn't illustrative or narrative so much as—"

"No, sorry. I meant why this painting?" he clarified.

"I said one question," she reminded him.

"Hardly seems fair," he replied. "This is just a subset of the initial question."

"Are you saying my first answer wasn't complete?"

"Not especially," he said. "Not satisfactorily, anyway."

She bit down on something. Possibly a smile, or a shake of her head.

"Sir," she said sternly, "this is a tour, not a private conversation."

"Why does it need to be private?" he countered, waving a hand. "It's a conversation you're having with us. You know, publicly. Pseudo-publicly," he amended.

"All art is private," she said. "The first question was about the collection, but now you're asking me to reveal something personal about myself."

"If all art is private, then it's the same question," Aldo argued.

"That's a very loose interpretation," she replied.

"Most of art is a loose interpretation."

She seemed to disapprove. "You think there's no precision to art?"

"Certainly not to Impressionism," he said, which he felt was obvious.

"Only if you're looking for the truth in an object," she said. "But if you want to identify an emotion, or a sensation, then there is nothing more precise than art."

"What's the precision in this painting?" he asked her.

"Well, that assumes I like it for its precision, doesn't it?" she replied.

"Do you?"

"Absolutely not," she said, and he blinked.

"Then what do you—"

"Whistler intentionally did not paint specifics," she said, appearing to have incidentally tripped and fallen into an answer. "Many people mocked his work. They thought his pieces lacked emotion because he told no story. But he wasn't trying to tell a story—according to Whistler, art should stand alone from context. Art was simply art," Regan explained, "with inconsequential specifics. The year? Unimportant," she answered herself. "The place? Close to irrelevant. What you're seeing before you is a single intake of breath—*one* moment. It is the beauty of the world in its most objective state, because the artist isn't expressing any meaning. He isn't trying to define you or teach you or tell you what space to occupy, he's just—"

She exhaled sharply, turning to look at the slowly fading sun behind her.

"Look at the colors," she said, her voice less insistent now and more imploring. "Look how somber it is, how lonely. He named his paintings after music so that none of the senses would go unsatisfied. You can see the lights," she added, gesturing to them, "to prove he's not alone in the world. It's going on around him in a slow, incoherent fade, but there's nothing to connect you, the observer, to this moment. Nothing rooting you to anything except for this single intake of breath, sitting over the English Channel just before the sun goes down. It's art because it's art, which is circular in its way," she said, and then blinked, that same half smile lingering at the edges of her mouth when she turned to face him. "A perfect circle, if you will," she said, "because it is and it was and it will be, all at once."

"That's a cycle," he said, "not a circle," but he understood what she meant.

She nodded once, concluding the exchange.

"Anyway," she said, leading them to Monet, "moving on."

Aldo said nothing else until the end of the tour, though he waited until he was the last to remain.

"So," Regan said, her gaze sliding to his to invite him back to her space of consideration. "What did you learn about me?"

"Not as much as I thought," he said. "But also quite a bit more."

"Helpful," she said drily. "Anything specific?"

"You tell me," he suggested, but then, "What did you learn about me? Because if the answer is nothing, then it wasn't a conversation," he pointed out. "Doesn't count if you didn't learn anything."

She opened her mouth, then stopped.

"Let me ask you something," she said. "How many people were on this tour?"

He thought about it. "Four?"

"Fifteen. Did you notice the girl looking at you?"

"What girl?"

"Right," she said, "exactly. Also, are you aware that you've worn the same clothes all three times we've seen each other?"

He glanced down. "They're clean."

"That's not what I asked," she said briskly. "What about the couple next to you?"

He tried to conjure an image of the group and summoned only the sensation of overcrowding. "What about them?"

"They were *glaring* at you." She looked delighted.

"I don't see how any of this is relevant," Aldo said, and then, to his surprise, Regan's expression contorted in unbridled laughter, the sound of it dancing up to the ceiling and ricocheting back with a surprising warmth around his ears.

"Let's just say I learned you're very single-minded," she told him, shaking her head. "You were very fixated on sorting out whatever it was you were trying to sort out," she explained, "and I think at least half of the group wanted to murder you."

That wasn't out of the ordinary; Aldo had learned over time to ignore that sort of thing. Regan glanced at him for reciprocation, obviously expecting his answer to the same question—she seemed a person highly dependent on reciprocation—but he was unsure how to put it in words.

"Out with it," she said, and he sighed.

"Well," he said, "I learned something. I just don't know what it is yet."

He'd learned a particular expression on her face that she hadn't made before.

"When you were talking about the painting, the *Nocturne*," he clarified when she arched a brow, waiting. "I learned . . . something."

She wasn't impressed. "I don't think it counts as learning it if you don't know what you learned."

"Well, I observed something that I suspect I'll understand later. Maybe around conversation number four," he guessed.

She watched him for a second, contemplating something, and then held out her hand.

"Give me your phone," she said, and he dug it out of his pocket, settling it in her palm. She glanced down, shaking her head. "No password, huh?"

"Not too many secrets," he said as she pulled up his contacts.

"Doubt that," she murmured, and typed in what was ostensibly her phone number. "There," she said, handing it back to him after calling the number she'd inputted. "This counts, by the way," she added, glancing at him. He'd noticed that her expressions were more disarming the less thought she seemed to put into them, and this one was more reactionary than most. "This was conversation number two."

"Right," he said. That was fair. They'd both learned something, which met the necessary parameters.

"I don't like surprises," she told him. "I want to know about the next one in advance."

That, too, was an understandable impulse.

"Why don't you pick the next one?" he suggested.

She considered it.

"Tomorrow night," she said. "Meet me outside? Around eight."

He mentally rearranged his schedule, forming the usual points of mundanity around a new apex.

"Yes, I can do that," he said, and she nodded, turning around.

"See you tomorrow," she said, wandering away from him again.

———

"You really don't like crowded places, do you?" Regan asked Aldo, watching him uncomfortably take a seat. He was wearing the usual black jeans with the worn leather jacket, which made slightly more sense now that they were in a cocktail bar in River North instead of the museum. He hadn't brought his backpack, thankfully, but the curls of his hair were tousled and twisted in complete disarray, helmet-shaped. She guessed he'd ridden over immediately after a shower.

"I don't love crowds," he said, "but no one does." He glanced around before picking up a menu. "What are you drinking?"

She typically liked to be a mirror of whoever she was with. "Not sure. Any thoughts?"

She figured beer, maybe hard liquor. Or maybe he was the sort of Italian who exclusively drank negronis. "The bottle selection is better than the glasses," he said, gesturing to the wine list. "Have any interest in splitting one?"

"What did you have in mind?"

He scanned the list, his gaze darting briefly to the side as someone passed his chair, and then he shifted closer to Regan, somewhat unsuccessfully. "The Barbera," he said, passing the wine list toward her.

Red wine. Interesting.

"Sounds perfect," she said.

"You're lying," he noted. "You prefer white?"

She did.

"The red is fine," she said, and his mouth twitched slightly.

"We don't have t—"

"It's fine," she repeated. "Besides, maybe I'll learn something about you by drinking it."

More importantly, a bottle meant they'd be there a while. Considering his current discomfort, that had a more tangible guarantee than a glass.

"True," he permitted, nodding.

She was gratified he didn't say *you'll like it.* That was one of her least favorite phrases; it was always unwisely assured. She hated all scenarios preceding the assumption that someone could predict her taste. Either they thought it universal enough that she could be lumped in with masses or they thought (usually incorrectly) that they understood her *specific* needs, and she wasn't sure which crime was worse.

Ultimately, though, she thought the wine was good. She didn't know the proper words for it, but was relieved that Aldo didn't offer any. He merely took a sip, glancing with that same degree of discomfort over his shoulder.

She wondered if he resented her for taking him there.

"How's the time travel research going?" she asked, and he let the wine linger on his tongue for a moment before answering.

"It's not really research," he said. "More like problem-solving. I know the solution, but I don't know how it works."

"I don't think that's how science works. Aren't you supposed to hypothesize and then test it?"

"I'm a theoretical mathematician," he said. "I hypothesize and then prove."

She tucked that away for later use.

He glanced over his shoulder again, then back at her. Or, more accurately, at something that existed inside his head in approximately the place she was sitting, but not quite her.

"I've lost you," she noticed.

"I was just thinking," he said, "how the more harmful the sting of a honeybee, the less effective it tends to be at its job. The more the bee has to protect its hive, the less honey it produces."

He took a sip of wine, and Regan said, "Tell me more about bees."

"You don't actually want to know about bees," Aldo said warily, which was a hypothesis that Regan was happy to disprove.

"Don't I?" she countered. "Besides, maybe bees for you are like art for me. Maybe it'll teach me more about you than it does about bees."

"Are you interested in me?"

It seemed to be a neutral question despite the phrasing, which in her experience usually meant something else. In general, Regan's previous experiences were proving unhelpful when applied to Aldo.

"I'm here now, aren't I?" she reminded him. "I don't typically do things I don't want to."

He considered it, gaze dropping to the stem of his glass and then rising to hers.

"If I tell you about bees," he said, "then you have to tell me about the heist."

She already knew he was single-minded. She added "transactional" to her mental list.

"That wouldn't be an even exchange," she said. "One is personal."

"Maybe they're both personal," he replied.

She thought about it.

"Maybe," she determined in answer.

"Maybe?"

"Yes, maybe," she confirmed. "You tell me about bees and maybe I'll tell you about—" She broke off before saying *the heist,* nearly shrugging on his interpretation of it. How easily she let other people take ownership of her story, she thought. "About what happened."

"Okay," he said, and thought about it. "Some honeybees have stingers incapable of penetrating human skin. So they make all this honey, right?" he said rhetorically, and she nodded. "But obviously people take it from them, and they just keep on making honey anyway."

This has to be a metaphor, Regan thought.

"That's not a metaphor," Aldo said.

"Of course not," Regan agreed.

"Some hives are more . . . hostile, I guess. More lethal." He sipped his wine. "The more they're able to defend their hive, the less honey they typically produce. Also, queen bees are interesting," he went on tangentially. "The queen can choose whether or not to fertilize certain eggs."

"What happens if they don't get fertilized?"

"They're drones," Aldo said. "Male bees."

She blinked. "I'm sorry, what?"

"Yes," he said to her general sense of surprise, "and male bees only have one job."

Regan set her glass down. "Don't tell me it's to fuck the queen."

"It's to fuck the queen," Aldo confirmed, taking a sip. He eyed his glass. "Grippy," he remarked, his concentration wandering back to the wine, and Regan gave his foot a nudge.

"Keep going about bees," she said. "What happens after the male bee fucks the queen?"

"Well, his penis gets ripped out," Aldo said.

Regan blinked.

"Yeah, he only has one shot. Bees mate in flight, right?" he said, and she nodded like that meant something to her; as if the mating rituals of bees had ever crossed her mind before. "Right, so, the drone bees have bigger eyes to see the queen coming. They mate one time, and then—"

"He . . . dies?" Regan cut in.

"He dies," Aldo confirmed. "His only purpose in life is to reproduce. Not unlike other species."

"That's—" She blinked. "So wait, how does the queen become the queen?"

"Well, she's more developed than the rest of the bees," Aldo said. "If an egg isn't fertilized, it becomes a drone. If it is, it becomes a worker bee—female," he clarified, to which Regan nodded again, "and then they feed it bee proteins, which have a limited supply. Eventually, they transition to feeding the larvae nectar. But if they choose to feed one of the larvae more of the bee proteins, it eventually becomes the queen. It develops more," he explained, "and can make more worker bees."

"So who chooses the queen?"

"The hive. The worker bees. They usually do it when the current queen dies, or if she seems to be getting weaker."

"So they choose the next queen," Regan said, and then corrected herself. "No—they *make* her?"

Aldo nodded, taking another sip. "Yes."

The opposite of divine right, Regan thought; a godless society of women. A true patriarchal nightmare. The thought inflamed her temporarily with a reverential delight.

"But—" She picked up her wine, shaking her head. "But some of the bees," she said slowly. "You said if they're more protective of the hive, they make less honey?"

"Yes," he repeated. "The more time the bee spends defending the hive, the less honey it produces."

"So, somewhere out there, there's a hive of lady bees killing people for vengeance instead of doing what they're supposed to do?"

"Yes," Aldo confirmed, "probably."

"That's—" Encouraging. Invigorating, even. Temporarily mesmerizing. "Interesting."

He nodded, glancing up at her with half a smile as he brushed a loose curl out of his face.

His haircut was unfortunate, Regan thought again. There was a certain degree of conventional handsomeness to him that went unrecognized beneath a layer of enigmatic fog. Or maybe not, she amended internally, recalling the girl who had been looking at him during her Impressionism tour. Maybe that girl had looked past the undereye shadows and the terrible haircut and the too-thin look of his cheeks and seen something else. He had those eyes, Regan supposed, and that mouth, and for better or worse, he had all the strangeness that fell out of it. Part of Regan irrationally resented the girl for not knowing that Aldo Damiani was closest to handsome when he was talking about bees.

"So," he said. "Can I know about the heist now?"

She wanted very badly to retort that the details of her personal history could not possibly amount to the same sort of knowledge she would have gotten from a Wikipedia page—which was, after all, what the bee factoids had been—but she did feel she owed him something.

His transactional nature was rubbing off on her.

"It wasn't a heist," she said.

He seemed amenable to a discussion on nomenclature. "What was it?"

"Complicated, but not a heist."

"Why not?"

"Because a heist implies . . . I don't know. Theft." She sipped her wine. "Which it was, ultimately," she admitted, "but that wasn't really the goal."

Aldo looked unsurprised. "I was already pretty sure the goal wasn't money."

"No, not really. Sort of." She tapped her glass. "My boyfriend needed the money," she admitted. "That part was true."

"Let me guess," he said. "Your parents didn't like him?"

They never liked anyone she dated, which was probably why she chose the people that she did.

"He was a sculptor," she said. "Not with ceramics, or at least not exclusively. He had access to a lot of different materials."

"So he was resourceful?" Aldo guessed.

"Yes, very," Regan said. "I met him while he was working on an installation that involved different types of metals. He was a blacksmith in his spare time," she added. "That was his only real source of income, which wasn't a lot."

"You're telling his side of the story," Aldo pointed out. "I asked for yours."

"They kind of intertwined at this point," she said, shrugging, though she was mildly pleased he could make the distinction. "So he was forging at the time, right? And he had this idea to make fancy swords and daggers and things, you know. Like, to sell at renaissance faires."

"Right."

"And I watched him re-create these swords and I thought . . . I could do that, but more efficiently." She felt herself leaning forward before she realized she'd planned to do it. "He was making these fake swords for money, right? But I," she mused, reaching over to refill her glass, "figured I could probably make fake money if I wanted to, which seemed like a quicker way to get things done. Cut the middleman, you know? I could do the designs well enough, and he had access to materials. I thought about it, but just like, for fun. I was just turning it over in my head, at first. But it was just like . . . once the thought had occurred to me, I—" She cleared her throat. "I couldn't shake it."

Aldo nodded. "Hexagons," he said, and she smiled weakly.

"Bees," she agreed, and shrugged. "Anyway, it wasn't like I'd left a lot of room for myself to do other things. Specializing in art wasn't exactly leading me to any career in particular. I don't like to teach, and I wasn't interested in academia—"

"You said you're an artist," Aldo interrupted. "Digital art?"

"I said I *wanted* to be an artist, yes, but I'm not one. I tried working as a graphic designer," she said, "but I didn't like having clients. Nobody knows what they want, not really. 'Oh, change it, I don't like it,' but then they can never explain what they want me to change. I've never liked dealing with other people's tastes."

"Understandable," Aldo said, fingering the stem of his glass. "And I don't enjoy the necessity of having to predict how other people think."

"You're doing it now, aren't you?"

He shook his head. "I'm not trying to predict you. I'm trying to understand you."

"Couldn't you predict me if you understood me?" She felt sure she'd caught him. Why else was he doing any of this?

"Seems like a question better suited to our inevitable robot overlords," he demurred with a sip, "which is not a philosophical meandering I have any expertise in, to be clear."

That, she thought, was the sort of conversation Marc liked to have when he was high, along with how he planned to survive the zombie apocalypse. But she agreed with Aldo's position that not every hypothetical situation was worth pursuing.

"Why choose to fixate on bees?"

"Hexagons," he said again. "I'm not an entomologist. Or an apiarist."

"Why a mathematician, then?"

"I took an algebra course my first year of college because I thought I might need it for my major."

"What was your major?"

"Undecided," he replied, "but I did well in that class, so I just kept going. I left for two years, came back, had to pick a major. All of my credits were in math, so I just kept going." Another sip. "I started working with some grad students and got asked to stay on in the doctoral program. I haven't left, as you can see," he said with a smile floating somewhere between wry and grim, and then he added, "so I guess I'll just stay until the university tells me to leave."

The sentence rung with familiarity. Regan wasn't sure how to identify what specifically had struck her as relatable, but she felt certain that whatever mental space Aldo had just occupied, she had been there before herself.

"Well," she said. "That's something." She eyed her glass, remarking, "I suppose I learned a little of your history today."

"So did I, sort of, though it still doesn't really answer my question."

"What, the one you had about the heist?"

"Not a heist," he said, and she permitted a fleeting smile. "It was . . . a fixation, I think. At least partially."

"Partially?"

"Maybe I'll figure out the rest another time," he said. "During one of the other three conversations."

"Maybe," she said.

They both paused, sipping from their respective thoughts.

"I like it," he said.

"What?"

He loosened the wine from his lips. "Your brain."

Three conversations, Regan marveled, and she already understood that was the highest compliment in Rinaldo Damiani's arsenal. Clearly he was onto something with his rule of sixes.

"Thanks," she said, and toasted him, permitting her glass to chime in synchronicity with his.

———

He glanced at her name on his screen and answered on the second ring.

"Wave patterns," she whispered.

He squinted at the clock. "It's four, Regan."

"I know. I couldn't sleep."

He dragged himself upright, leaning his pillow against the wall that lacked a headboard, and shifted to sit up. He reached over for the unlit joint on the nightstand, considered it, and then changed his mind, directing his attention back to Regan.

"What about wave patterns?"

"When you drop something into water," she said, "and it ripples out. Those are circles."

Ripples of consequence.

"Our eyes perceive them to be perfect circles," he said. "There's no telling whether or not they are."

"Still, it sort of counts, doesn't it?"

He figured he'd let her have that one, or at least part of it. "It's not the most compelling contradiction but it counts, yes."

"Crop circles," she said. "Fairy rings."

"Those aren't natural," he said. "They're supernatural."

She hummed a little in thought. "Do you believe in the supernatural?"

"I think I'd be irresponsible not to," he said. "I'm sure there are explanations. I just don't have time to consider them."

"True. Not with time travel to puzzle out."

"Right," he agreed. "Only one impossibility at a time."

Regan was silent for a moment. He didn't feel the need to fill it. Instead, Aldo leaned his head back and lingered in the quiet contemplation that swung between them.

"Rainbows," she said.

"What about rainbows?"

"They could be circles," she said. "That arc is, you know. Circular, right?"

"Could be. But symmetry is only implied, and symmetry doesn't often happen in nature, either."

"True," she sighed. "We did some facial compositions with symmetry in one of my drawing classes and they were terrible. Disturbing, even."

"Yes," he agreed, glancing at the still-dark sky outside. "Why are you whispering, by the way?"

"My boyfriend is sleeping."

"Ah," he said. "And you just figured I'd be awake, or did you plan to wake me?"

"I wasn't really thinking about you, to be honest."

For whatever reason, he smiled.

"Anything else going on in your mind?" he asked her.

Evidently yes. "Why hexagons?"

"Patterns, mostly," he said. "Kept running into them, especially in math. They're the basis for quantum groups."

"And they occur in nature?"

"Yes. William Kirby called bees 'heaven-instructed mathematicians.'"

"But that's wrong," Regan said, sounding distressed. "Bees are godless."

Aldo cupped his hand around a low laugh. "Well, Darwin conducted experiments to prove that it was instinct related to evolution."

"Oh, good." She sounded relieved. "Better."

Aldo reached over, turning on the lamp beside his bed. Clearly he wasn't going to be doing any more sleeping. "What did you do tonight? Or last night, I guess."

"Nothing. Nothing interesting. You haven't been to the museum lately," she added as an afterthought.

He hadn't wanted to overwhelm her. It was feeling less and less like an accident that he was associating the two of them in his mind.

"It's one place I go," he said, "but not the only one."

"Where else?"

"Outside, if I can. That's ideal."

"Oh." He heard the sound of movement on her end, like she was taking something out of the fridge. "What do you do during the day?"

"Go to class. Teach. Go to the gym." He glanced around his sparse apartment. "Not much, really."

"Huh." She seemed to be thinking of questions. "Who's your best friend?"

"I don't know," Aldo said. "My dad?"

"Yikes."

He laughed. "Who's yours?"

"I don't know. Not you, obviously. You're a stranger."

"True," he said. "Excellent point."

"My niece is pretty cool," she said.

"Niece?"

"Yeah, my sister's daughter."

"I didn't know you had a sister."

He heard a door closing. "Yeah," she said, her voice rising above a whisper now. "Older. She's a doctor."

"Does she also go by Regan?"

"No, she's exclusively Madeline; definitely not Maddie, our mom hates that. People only started calling me Regan because of her, actually. In high school everyone just called me 'Little Regan' or 'Regan Junior,' and then eventually it stuck."

"Is she much older?"

"She's four years older."

"And she has . . . a baby?"

"A toddler. Her name is Carissa. I call her Cari when Madeline isn't listening."

"I didn't pin you as the type to enjoy the company of children." He certainly wasn't that particular type himself, though the thought of Regan influencing a child's development was charming in a way. A slightly troubling, very amusing way.

"Well, it's . . ." She trailed off. "You're going to hate this."

"Am I? Seems unlikely."

"Madeline's just . . . she's, you know, perfect. It's—fuck," Regan sighed, "this is so cliché."

"I like clichés," Aldo said, seeing as he occasionally was one. "Got nothing against them, anyway."

"Well, fine, just don't—okay, whatever," Regan muttered, speaking mostly to herself. "The point is Madeline never did anything wrong. She went straight to Harvard Med, met her doctor husband, got married when they both got residencies here. Then, out of nowhere, she's pregnant—and it's her *first year* of residency, right? She's been married for about five seconds and boom, she's pregnant. My sister the surgical genius can't operate birth control, and for the first time, like, *ever,* she's freaking out." Aldo heard Regan laughing to herself on her end. "Anyway, it was the first time I ever felt like it was Madeline and me on the same team. She was so nervous to tell our parents and . . . I don't know, it was just—it was kind of fun, I guess. Seeing her mess up." She gave a low groan. "Anyway, I'm terrible."

"Well—" Aldo curved a hand around his mouth, laughing. "I mean yeah, kind of."

"Oh, *thanks,* Rinaldo—"

"So you like your niece," he pressed her, and she sighed.

"Yes," she admitted, "I do. She's a good kid. And she drives Madeline crazy, so that's a fun bonus."

Aldo laughed. "I like this."

"What, me being petty?"

"No, the idea of you being doting."

"I don't dote," she said with an audible grimace. "I just think the trick with children is to treat them like adults."

"How do you treat most adults?"

Silence.

"Probably poorly. So maybe you have a point."

He smiled.

"So," she said. "Got any more hexagon things?"

He thought about it. "There's some Babylonian stuff."

"God, of course there is," she said with a laugh. "What Babylonian stuff?"

"Well, the Babylonians were very into astronomy. They gave us our current concept of time. And circles," he added. "They did everything in units of sixty. Sixty seconds in a minute, sixty minutes in an hour—"

"There's that six again."

"Exactly," he said. "So we really only see time the way they intended us to see it, which suggests there might be another way to see it."

"Which would be?"

"Well, quantum theory seems to indicate a multiverse," he said. "Where all times and possibilities and outcomes exist in tandem."

"In hexagons?"

"Probably. Maybe." A shrug. "But we can't actually identify the shape of the multiverse, seeing as we don't know which universe we exist in ourselves."

"Why try to solve time travel instead of multiverse travel?"

"Well, the idea of the multiverse is that you wouldn't travel," he said. "You exist in all things at all times, so in terms of it being something you could actually *experience,* then—"

"Oh, hi," she said, clearly speaking to someone who wasn't him. "Sorry, did you need to . . . ?"

Aldo quieted, listening to the male voice on the other end.

"Yeah, no I was . . . I couldn't sleep, so—yeah. Sorry," she said, this time to Aldo. "One second—no, it's fine, I'll just . . . yeah, okay, go ahead."

He heard the sound of her leaving wherever she'd been.

"Sorry," she said. "Marc needed to use the bathroom."

"You were in the bathroom?"

"Yeah, well, you know. It has a door. I was sitting in the bathtub."

Briefly, Aldo was reminded of Audrey Hepburn in the claw-footed bathtub couch in *Breakfast at Tiffany's.*

"That can't have been comfortable," he remarked.

"Well, it's fine, I'm gone now. What were we saying? Babylonians? No—time travel."

"Both, I guess."

"Do you *want* to travel in time?"

A good question. "I think I'd mostly like to figure out how it would work, but I don't expect to."

"Kind of an odd fixation, isn't it? If you never plan to use it."

"Well, if I figured it out, then fine, maybe I'd use it. But—" He hesitated. "Well, there's a reason mathematicians sort of stop at a certain point when developing theories," he explained. "If there's no capacity to understand the math moving forward, then there's no reason trying to figure it out. We'd all just lose sleep over it, trying to sort out our own existence."

"But *you're* willingly losing sleep over it," she noted.

"I . . ." It was difficult to explain. "Yes, because—"

"Because if you don't have something to figure out, then you have no reason to keep going?"

Or maybe it wasn't that difficult to explain.

"Yeah," he said. "Basically."

She was quiet for a few beats of time.

"So this is how you did it," she said.

"Did what?"

"Kept going. After . . . you know. What happened to you."

"Ah." He wasn't sure he wanted to discuss it; other people tended to treat the resurrection of his mental stability as some sort of dramatic event, but for him, it was simply historical. "I guess."

"No, it totally is. You gave yourself an impossible problem so you'd never be able to stop thinking about it. It's brilliant, actually." She sounded close to impressed. "Other people probably think it's crazy, don't they?"

"My dad sort of plays along. He doesn't get it," Aldo admitted, "but every day he asks me where in time we are. I make it up, obviously, and he pretends it's new and interesting every time, but I think it's his version of 'how are you,' basically. Checking in."

She was quiet again.

"That's sweet," she said. "I like that."

He wondered what expression she was wearing.

"Do you want to do something later?" she asked him, her tone shifting to something crystalline and urgent. "Or, I don't know. Now, I guess."

"I have something at seven," he said, "but I guess if you wanted t—"

"What are you possibly doing at seven on a Sunday morning?"

You're going to hate this, he thought, wincing a little.

"I'm going to church," he admitted.

"What? No." She sounded bewildered. "You're religious? But—"

"Not really," he said quickly. "Not at all, actually. But I used to go with my dad, and then it became a routine. I like the early masses because they're quiet, and—"

"Mass. You're Catholic?"

"Yes," he said, wondering vaguely if her tone might mean she had some eccentric argument stored away for rebuttal to the essence of Catholicism; some opposition to the Medici family, maybe. Probably not, though, if she liked art. "But if you wanted to do something aft—"

"Can I come with you?"

He blinked, taken entirely by surprise. "Really?"

"Yeah. I haven't been to church in ages, and I only ever go with my parents, you know, on Easter and Christmas. Would it be okay if I went with you?"

He doubted there was any mental space he could occupy that Regan would disrupt. In fact, he felt the place he usually reserved for rote mechanization and the occasional wandering thought would be vastly improved by her presence.

"Sure," he said. "I go to Holy Name, the cathedral in Streeter-ville."

"Oh, that's really close to me, okay. Seven?"

"Seven," he confirmed.

"That'll be a different conversation from this one," she told him. "Just so you know."

"Naturally," he agreed. "What did you take from this one?"

"Mostly? That you go to church," she said, and he laughed.

"Fair," he said. "Most of what I got out of this was that your best friend is a toddler."

"Well, try to get a little bit more out of the next one," she suggested. "There's only . . . what, one left after that?"

"Yes."

"Well, better not waste it."

None so far had been a waste, he thought.

"See you at seven?" she asked.

"Sure." It was five, which meant he could get in a morning workout. *Or.* "Or I could keep talking about the Babylonians," he suggested.

"Mm. Tempting," Regan said. "What else did they do?"

He wondered what she believed in. Probably most things, or nothing. "Astrology?"

"Ooh, yes, okay," she said quickly, settling in. "Tell me about the Babylonians and the stars."

———

He was waiting for her on the steps of the cathedral, wearing a long-sleeved shirt with the cuffs pushed up and a pair of chinos that were a step up from his usual jeans. His hair was, for once, swept away from his forehead, though that appeared to be more a consequence of wind than anything sartorial. Autumn was well underway, and Chicago was a sweeter version of its blusteriest; a light suggestion, probably, to those who couldn't stand the harshness of winter that perhaps they ought to seek the door.

"Did you walk?" Regan asked him, and he nodded.

"You look nice," he said.

She'd worn a midi-length skirt and a pair of heeled oxfords, her long blazer paired sensibly with a low bun. She felt like she was in costume as a Good Girl, though that wasn't necessarily a bad thing. She was usually in some sort of costume, one way or another. The thing about women and clothes was, in Regan's mind, that nothing was ever a permanent expression; it wasn't any sort of commitment to being this type of girl or that one, but purely *today, I am.* It was just whichever version of herself she wanted to project for the time being. When attending mass for the first time in at least a year with a sort-of stranger, she'd aimed for somewhere between neutrally well-intentioned and blatantly puritanical.

"Thanks," she said, and they walked inside.

The relief of Catholicism was that very little ever changed— geographically, temporally, or otherwise. There was a consistent

Baroque devotion to grandeur in every Catholic space Regan had ever entered, and Holy Name was no exception. It was its own kind of imposing from the outside, an island of squatty, stone-washed brick and steeple beside its high-rise cousins of industry, while the interior featured an eclectic mix of the things Regan considered very On Brand, papally speaking. Bronze cathedral doors boasted a tree of life; from afar, a suspended crucifix sobered the brazenness of luxury. Gothic revival dominated the schema of the space, the ceilings high and vaulted, and the lofty sense of violence and idolatry poured in through color-stained rays of light.

It wasn't unlike the Art Institute, which made sense. She understood why Aldo opted to surround himself with it. It was like bathing in opulence, only colder, stiff with authority. Churches were their own kinds of museums—with their devotion to ritual, at least, if not to God—and to exist inside of one was to dwarf oneself with inequity.

She understood the compulsion to seek out more space. To lessen to a speck of nothingness.

Aldo picked a pew somewhere in the middle, gesturing her in first and genuflecting before he sat. It looked like a motion he performed out of habit rather than deference. She'd noticed he had a different set of expressions for thinking and for routine, and this one came with a notable blankness.

She wondered what he looked like when he did other things; when he taught, for example, which her cursory Google search had indicated he did without much devotion. She wondered how he looked when he slept; when he dreamt; when he came.

She shook herself, shuddering a little.

"Cold?" Aldo asked.

Something like that. "It's very . . . austere, isn't it?"

"That's a cold word," he noted with half a smile. "And yes, it is. I find it sort of refreshing."

He leaned forward, picking up one of the paperback missals from the chair in front of him. He wore no jewelry, she observed. He was notably unornamented. He didn't bite his nails (Regan did, sort of, but painted them regularly to keep herself from it). Instead, Aldo's fingernails were neatly trimmed, possibly even filed in addition to clipped. They contained those little pale half-moons she rarely saw on her own fingers. He smoothed his hand over the cover of the book, setting it squarely on his lap, and promptly commenced his fidgeting.

He fidgeted a very specific way. It wasn't knee-jiggling. It was closest to a finger-tapping, though it transitioned very quickly to what Regan thought at first was aimless drawing but then realized was purposeful writing. Scrawling, actually, in numbers. Math equations? Probably. He moved with a sequential rhythm from tapping to drawing to scribbling. She nearly missed it when they were supposed to stand, occupied as she was with her attempts to translate his motions.

Mass was familiar, the words and refrains all the same. The psalm that day was about wings; Catholicism yearned for flight as much as it championed a healthy sense of fear. The institution was particularly human that way.

At some point during the homily, Regan returned her attention to Aldo, who was definitely thinking now. His lips were a different shape when he was considering something, almost as if he were on the brink of mouthing it aloud to himself. His fingers fluttered, then stilled for a moment, and then returned to drawing. A hexagon, she noted. He drew the same shape, over and over, and then paused.

He turned his head, looking at her.

Caught, she registered with a grimace.

His mouth quirked up with a question, accompanied by a furrow of his brow. All the energy he'd expended on whatever problem he'd been solving transferred to her, and she felt the impact of it like a blow, landing squarely in her chest. She tried to think what it was that made his mouth so appealing and couldn't.

She reached out, tentatively, and every inch of him went still.

He was skittish, she realized, half-charmed, and she considered retracting her hand, only she'd never been the ease-in sort of person. Instead she rested her fingers on his knuckles, briefly, and lifted his hand to transfer his palm from his left thigh to her right. Not in a sexual way, in her opinion. There was a certain area of space she considered utilitarian, and though Aldo had gone slightly rigid with uncertainty, she made a gesture she thought he'd recognize: *Continue,* she beckoned, and he frowned at her for a moment, then nodded.

He drew a hexagon carefully against the fabric of her skirt. Beneath his touch, she felt her skin pebble, a little chill settling around the cage of her ribs. She nodded again, dismissing it.

Then Aldo started writing numbers; she recognized the shape of the number two, then a five (he crossed the bridge of it at the end), then eventually recognized the letter z. He was one of those people who drew a horizontal line through his letters and numbers. He drew something like a sigma, more scribbles, then a broad horizontal line. He was definitely doing math, and she reveled in her possession of it; in being the instrument to channel his thoughts.

Then the shape of his formulas changed, his energy shifting along with it. He was drawing faster now, as if he'd caught onto something. She could see that his hesitation had faded; he was no longer concerned with the fact that he was touching her, which she wasn't sure whether to find exciting or insulting. The flame of his thoughts picked up and she rapidly lost track of what he was writing. Every now and then, she caught a number. A triangle. Once or twice she felt certain he'd drawn a question mark, as if reminding himself to come back later, only he wouldn't come back later. The medium of her skin—of her limb, in fact, which she was holding uncharacteristically still, not wanting to disrupt him—would likely not be there when he came back to it. His touch was quick and light. It fluttered over her and she fought the urge to grab his hand, to place it somewhere else that would benefit from this degree of frenetic concentration. Either it was cold in the church or something else had made her keenly aware of the warmth radiating from his touch.

He was left-handed, she realized belatedly, pondering the rarity of that for a moment. It occurred to her that Aldo Damiani was probably something of a rarity himself.

Then the homily ended and Aldo stopped scribbling, registering the shift in atmosphere and taking his cue from the people around him. He wasn't totally oblivious, then, though he hadn't seemed to notice that his leg was now pressing into hers. They were touching from hip to knee, a straight line of joint conjecture. He lifted his hand in the air, his fingers curling into his palm for a moment with indecision, and then he carefully retracted it.

Regan felt a spark go out of her, rising, ironically, to profess her faith.

Beside her, Aldo continued reciting things from memory. This was something he did every week, she recalled, so that made sense. This was part of his ritual. He had done it every Sunday before her, and he would do it every Sunday from this point on. She wondered how often he let other people in, considering for a moment that perhaps she was not the first, but then she dismissed it nearly as quickly. She knew, after all, which of his motions looked practiced and which of them did not. He wasn't accustomed to someone being this close to him. This was visibly unrehearsed.

She wasn't sure what to do with that revelation.

The priest blessed the body and blood of Christ and Regan thought nothing of it. In fairness, she thought little of vampirism, either. Nothing in her world was really grotesque. Her mind wandered elsewhere (a sin, surely, but the least of them), and it wasn't until Aldo reached for her hand that she remembered, suddenly, the way this usually went.

His palm was warm and dry, closing gently around her knuckles. This prayer she knew. This one even Marc probably knew, WASP that he was. Regan held Aldo's hand loosely, not quite breathing. She lamented not being able to take stock of him in further detail until she remembered there was no compelling reason to hold back.

She would have only one more conversation with Aldo Damiani after this one.

Regan slid her hand forward, traversing the peaks and valleys of his knuckles with her fingers. She felt him look at her, a little surprised, but she was looking at his hand. There were scars on his knuckles; faint ones. One or two on his fingers. She drew over them horizontally, then vertically, down each of his fingers and up to the beds of his nails, tracing the cuticles.

The prayer ended.

He didn't let go.

She turned his palm over, inspecting it. She ran her fingers over his life line, which curved from the side of his hand and branched off in two, possibly three, before ending around the tendon of his thumb. She closed her hand around his wrist, measuring it, and looked up to find his eyes, gauging his reaction.

He was watching her with curiosity, but not confusion.

She returned her attention to his hand.

Above the life line was the head line, then the heart line. She remembered this from a book she'd read as a girl, never removing it from the library. Her mother had Old World superstitions, but Regan hadn't been able to stop herself from seeking out whatever new ones she could find. Both lines stretched broadly across his palm, neat and orderly. Not like hers, all splintered and webbed. She always thought hers meant that she had two hearts, two heads, two faces. She stroked her thumb over his knuckles, an expression of gratitude-reassurance-apology.

Someone cleared their throat behind her. It was time for communion.

She moved to release Aldo's hand, about to trudge up to the altar, but he tightened his grip, stepping back to let the others pass. A slow trickle of four or so people slid by them, making their way to the center aisle, but Aldo sat down, not releasing her. She sat beside him, their joined hands floating between them for a moment before Regan decided to place them in the narrow vacancy between her leg and his, resting atop the wooden pew.

Then she swallowed, placing each of the tips of her fingers onto the raised calluses of his palm. They were more noticeable this way, when his hand was relaxed. She placed them one by one, index-middle-ring-pinky, and he curled his fingers around hers, drawing a slow circle along the knuckle of her forefinger.

They were both staring up at the altar, the rest of their respective pieces motionless and still, and she slid her fingers between his, interlacing them carefully.

His thumb stroked a hovering line over hers, journeying upward from first knuckle to second.

She drew hers along the crease of his wrist.

The music ended. Prayer resumed.

Aldo turned her hand over, this time twining the backs of their fingers together.

She gave him a single pulse of pressure, heart banging in her throat.

The priest announced something about canned foods.

Blessings, blessings, blessings. Their palms met up again. Aldo's fingers stretched out below her sleeve, running over her wrist. She grew increasingly conscious of her breath. She breathed in through her nose, swallowing, and breathed out. Her ribs expanded, stretching out to make room. She felt intensely aware of her breasts.

Around them, the congregation rose, and Aldo released her.

Her hand floated back to her side.

Shuffling out once the priest had gone was the most mundanely halted process. Regan felt mortal again; sapped of reverence, drained of any magnitude. She felt heavy, corporeal and dull, the sky outside no brighter than it had been when they arrived. She turned to face Aldo, opening her mouth to say something, and stopped when his eyes fell on hers.

He wasn't just unconventionally handsome, she realized.

He was uncommonly beautiful.

"What did you learn?" he asked neutrally.

That I could study you for a lifetime, carrying all of your peculiarities and discretions in the webs of my spidery palms, and still feel empty-handed.

"You do . . . martial arts," she said, clearing her throat, "or something. I thought maybe weight lifting at first," she explained, struggling with her grudging return to normalcy, "because of the calluses on your hands, but I don't think so." *Not after knowing you.* "Your knuckles are bruised."

If he was disappointed by her answer, he didn't show it. "They are," he confirmed, nodding.

"And you?" she asked, a little breathless. She couldn't remember the last time she'd felt this kind of apprehension, or possibly anticipation. "What did you learn about me?"

He reached forward wordlessly, taking her right hand and twisting her claddagh ring to the side.

She looked down, noting the paler skin revealed beneath it.

"You don't take this off," he said, not looking up.

"No," she agreed.

"Who gave it to you?"

It was a traditional piece of jewelry, usually passed down through generations.

Usually.

"Me," she said, and he nodded, releasing her hand and returning it to her.

"An unusual form of conversation," he remarked. "Does it count?"

If it wasn't a conversation then it was something else entirely, which Regan didn't want to think about yet.

"Yes," she said. "Only one more, then."

He nodded. "One more."

Someone nudged past them. Aldo glanced unhappily over his shoulder, then turned back to her.

"Should we have the last one now?" he asked.

Regan was briefly overcome with a surge of panic.

"No," she said. "No, and . . . I have to go, actually. I should go."

He seemed to understand, sparing a nod, and she turned to leave, then stopped.

"Aldo," she said.

"Regan," he replied.

"I—" Don't hold hands with anyone ever again.

"I'll see you," she said, and he nodded.

"Sure," he said, and she walked briskly away, relieved he hadn't tried to stop her.

———

"Oh, sorry—"

"It's fine," Aldo muttered, prepared to ignore the collision until he caught a flicker of bloodred from his periphery. "Regan," he said before he could stop himself, registering the familiar sight of her earrings, and the woman beside the man he'd just bumped into froze in place.

"Aldo," she said, her voice high and shiny and false as she drew the three of them away from the crowded sidewalk. "What are you doing here?"

"Aldo?" echoed the man, who progressed from an amorphous obstacle to a face paired with shoulders, hair and limbs. He was taller than Aldo, a little older, deeply Caucasian. "Don't tell me this is the math guy!"

"Yes, this is my friend Aldo," Regan confirmed. "This is my boyfriend Marc," she added with an apologetic glance, and Marc thrust out a hand for Aldo's, which he gave with some degree of reticence and shook.

"Nice to meet you," Aldo said.

"I thought you lived down in Hyde Park," Marc said, glancing at Regan for confirmation.

"No, no, Aldo *works* in Hyde Park," she corrected quickly. "He's a professor at UChicago."

"Doctoral student," Aldo said.

"Right, that," Regan confirmed, and Marc nodded.

"I'm just getting something," Aldo said, gesturing vaguely around. "For my dad's birthday."

"Oh," Regan said, softening slightly, but Marc merely nodded again.

"Cool," he said. "You know, I've been curious who Regan was talking to from the bathtub at five A.M.," he remarked with a laugh, shaking his head. "Nice to finally meet you, man. When Regan first mentioned you I was like, 'Aldo, really?'—but I get it now, it works."

"It's short for Rinaldo," Regan leapt to explain.

"Oh, interesting," Marc said, and briefly, Aldo thought about bees.

Specifically, drone bees.

"Well, we should go," Regan said. "Let you get back to it."

"Yeah, sure," Aldo said, relieved. "Have a good night."

"You, too," Marc said. "Hey, we should all get dinner sometime, right, babe?"

"Good idea!" Regan said.

"Sure," said Aldo, and turned away, continuing in the opposite direction.

He was inside of Crate & Barrel (Masso needed a new wine opener) when he got a text message, his phone buzzing in his pocket. He fished it out, turning away from the cheese boards, and glanced at Regan's name on his screen.

That doesn't count as one of the six.

No, he agreed, and put his phone back in his pocket before turning to the cutlery.

At home—on the kitchen counter, above the knife drawer—was the notebook Aldo usually carried with him. It was full, which tended to happen every six months or so, but this time it had only been about four. The drawings, more the consequence of impulse than anything, were usually the same; geometric patterns, usually hexagons, all shaded different ways and drawn in smaller or larger increments. Aldo didn't venture far from shapes, though he'd recently drawn a pair of lips. A regal, haughty chin. A set of eyes refracting a pattern of hexagonal beams. He'd left the notebook above the knife drawer, sitting out on the kitchen counter, and he would need to replace it while he was out.

He glanced up at the cutlery, frowning to himself.

It was about time for a new paring knife.

For this not-conversation, Regan wore jeans.

"Is this the Math-Stat Building?" she asked one of the students lingering outside, and they nodded distractedly. "The basement is . . . down, I guess?" she said, and the student pointed out the stairs. "Great, thanks."

She shivered a little. The weather had cooled considerably, and she hurried inside.

She'd arrived five minutes early, taking a seat at the back of the classroom. The other students were pulling out their laptops, preparing for class, groaning about their work. It was one of those tiny, cramped classrooms, no sunlight. The board sat vacant, waiting to be filled. She caught a few sidelong glances, one or two of them lasting several beats too long. She smiled politely in reply and the heads snapped forward, shamefully remorseful.

Aldo walked in at precisely three in the afternoon, striding up the center aisle. He pulled a textbook from his backpack, set it flat on the table at the head of the room, and glanced down. "The chain rule," he said, not bothering to greet anyone.

He looked up only to scan the room and then stopped short, catching sight of her.

He blinked.

"The chain rule," he said again, and turned back to the board without any adjustment in tone, writing out something that looked like total gibberish. "Used to find the derivative of two composite functions." He paused, and without glancing over his shoulder, prompted reluctantly, "I suppose you'd like an example?"

"Yes," said one of the people in the front row.

"Fine," Aldo sighed, as Regan struggled to smother her laughter. "Say someone jumps out of an airplane. You want to calculate a number of factors; velocity, atmospheric pressure, buoyant height."

He hadn't bothered to check, but from Regan's vantage point she caught a few heads nodding in comprehension.

"Simplifies it," Aldo said. "Takes all the relevant factors and applies a unified approach."

A few more heads.

"Anyway," Aldo said, and continued on, filling the board with Egyptian runes and demon-summoning witchcraft (or so Regan assumed) until 3:51 P.M., releasing the class with a stilted reminder that their midterm would take place next week.

Someone asked if Aldo planned to hold a study session. He confirmed that he would. His gaze slid to Regan and then back to the class. They rose, making their way out like a trail of industrious ants. Then Aldo erased the board, placed his textbook back in his bag, and retreated down the classroom's center aisle, pausing beside Regan's desk.

"Conversation number six?" he asked bracingly.

She shook her head. "Believe me," she said, "I learned absolutely nothing from that."

He smiled.

"Hungry?" he asked her.

"Yes and no," she replied, rising to her feet. "Well, yes," she corrected herself, "but I need to tell you first that this can't be one of the conversations."

"Why not?"

"Because it's primarily about logistics," she said, directing him toward the door. "I've decided I want you to come with me to my parents' anniversary party."

He froze for a second, the way he did when something wasn't computing properly. She gestured to the handle, wordlessly suggesting he open it, and he complied with a halted motion, stepping aside to let her pass before joining her in the corridor.

"When is it?" he managed upon recovery.

She stifled a laugh. "You're not going to ask me why I want you to go?"

"I'm focusing on logistics," he said. "I don't want this to be a conversation."

"Right," she said. An excellent point. "Well, it's on Saturday. And you'd probably have to stay the night."

He seemed to be struggling with something he didn't want to ask aloud.

"You're wondering if I've broken up with Marc?" she guessed, and he vigorously shook his head.

"Don't tell me," he said.

"Well, I'm going to talk to myself, then," she suggested.

That earned her a nod. "Okay," he said, and held the door again, gesturing her outside.

"Well," Regan exhaled, "the thing is, my parents don't like Marc, and I'm not in the mood for a lecture. I don't want to go alone because it's going to be horrible, but I also don't want them questioning me about, you know, real things. My future. My *plans*. I thought if I brought a—" She glanced at him. "Well, not a friend. But someone. They probably won't ask questions—so anyway, I'm just, again, thinking this out loud to myself," she mused, tightening her coat around her as he directed her to the left, "but *if* I were to bring someone, they'd have to be available early Saturday morning. It's about an hour's drive to Naperville, and—"

"You can say that part to me," he said. "It's logistical."

"Oh. Right." She paused, noticing she'd inadvertently permitted him to walk them to the motorcycle she had yet to see in real life. "Uh. What's this?"

"A 1969 Ducati Scrambler," he said. "You said you were hungry."

"They don't have food here on campus?"

"They do," he said, "but I don't want it." He handed her his helmet. "You can say no."

She let her eyes narrow, accepting the helmet. "You know I won't, though, don't you?"

His smile broadened. "Can neither confirm nor deny," he said, swinging a leg over the bike, "as that's not a logistic."

She climbed on after him with some degree of reluctance, though not as much as she'd expected. It wasn't the first time a boy on a motorcycle had offered her a ride, but it was certainly the first time she'd accepted. Implicitly trusting Aldo Damiani seemed to be a matter of personal curiosity that Regan consistently lacked the energy to deny.

"Careful," she warned him, strapping the helmet on. "Precious cargo."

He angled his head over his shoulder. "Hold on," he advised, and she moved to slide her arms around his ribs before stopping, noting an obstacle.

"You're wearing a backpack."

"Yes, and . . . ?"

"It's—" It'll come between us. "It's not comfortable."

He rolled his shoulders back, letting the straps fall and then sliding the backpack over to one side, offering it to her. "You want to wear it?"

It wasn't like there was another option. "Sure."

There was something vintage-ly charming about this, she thought. Very retro-chivalrous, and in reverse, too—*her* carrying *his* books— so it was even better. She slid his backpack on, tightening the straps to accommodate the textbook dragging her shoulders backward, and then contemplated the slope of Aldo's spine as he bent expectantly over his handlebars.

She wondered if he'd smell like leather.

She figured she was about to find out.

There was a moment where she grappled with her options, determining whether to lean first (and therefore subject herself, tits up, to instant intimacy) or to feel around the space preemptively, exploring the range of their combined edges before they met. She opted for the latter, placing her palms flat on his waist, first, and then permitting her arms to circle him. Finding that she was too far away to secure herself properly, Regan slid her hips forward on the bike, her legs cradling the outer edges of his thighs. He twisted around, glancing at her again.

"Ready?" he asked.

Only a logistical question, she reminded herself.

"Yes," she said.

He smelled like leather, she confirmed, and also something low and vaguely musky, plus a hint of sea breeze–adjacent laundry detergent. She took him in sense by sense: he felt certain, smelled permanent, sounded firm. The back of his neck was a travesty of wayward curls; someone needed to cut it. Wrapped around him like this, there was no mistaking the sharp breath he took as she locked her arms in place, waiting.

He wasn't an unsafe driver. He drove like he moved, like he thought, with evidence of calculation. For someone who paid attention to so little of his surroundings, he was extraordinarily careful on a bike, glancing around for obstacles with near paranoia. For Regan's part, once she'd dismissed her concerns about her hair, she could see why he preferred it. The lack of four doors and a steel frame around her altered her perception of her environment, freeing a new-old restlessness the further it and she began to blend. Regan felt some second self slip out from the cavity of her chest to revel in it, a pair of alternate arms tightening around Aldo's waist to whisper: *Faster, faster, faster.*

He didn't take her far, stopping at a diner somewhere in the southernmost portion of the Loop. The motions from there—her handing him the backpack, him holding the door for her to enter—were silent and vaguely awkward. Her feet hit the pavement with disappointment, bemoaning the indignity of being made to walk.

"What's good here?" she asked him.

"Everything," he said, "depending on your mood."

A logistical question, she reminded herself.

"Sweet?" she said.

"Cake," he suggested, gesturing to the glass displays of chocolate and red velvet. She laughed, for propriety's sake.

"Isn't it a little early for cake? Or late?"

He glanced at his watch. "It's 4:30," he said. "Kind of between meals, isn't it?"

When the waitress came around, seeming to recognize him, Aldo gestured to Regan.

"The red velvet cake, please," she said.

"The usual for you?" the waitress asked Aldo, who nodded.

"Yes, please."

The waitress gave him a motherly wink and disappeared.

Regan shifted, seeking out a comfortable position in the booth, and Aldo looked up at her from his glass of water.

"You could have just called," he noted. "Or texted."

"I thought it was fairer this way," she said. "Since you watched me work."

He seemed to find that an acceptable answer.

(Unrelatedly, the way he was looking at her made her throat itch. Like she needed to cough something up from the depths of it.)

"I'm not sure how to talk to you without it being, you know. A conversation," she said.

"We don't have to talk." He shrugged, leaning back in the booth. "Silence is fine with me."

"Okay." She supposed that was a relief, in some way. She'd done a lot of talking that day, and almost none of it had been helpful.

("Much as I love being spared a weekend with your parents," Marc had said to her that morning, "do I need to worry about you with this Aldo guy?"

Part of her had resented that he wasn't already worried.

"Of course not," she'd said. "He's my friend. Plus come on, you've met him—it'll be hilarious."

"Ah, I see." It was that easy; Marc had chuckled, shaking his head, not needing to question her further. "There she is. Queen of chaos."

Chaos for chaos' sake. Regan's staple, and what made her such a fucking laugh.

"So you don't mind?" she'd confirmed, and Marc had shrugged.

"We both know you're happiest when you're causing a scene," he said, turning back to the French press and letting that be that. It wasn't conflicted, and it certainly wasn't dramatic; he'd already seen every shade of Regan's highs and lows. Sometimes she was a marvel, brilliant, creative, witty; sometimes merely predictable, spoiled, manic, vain. It was never particularly cruel, but it was always honest. She loved Marc for his honesty. She was grateful, she reminded herself, for his candor.)

The cake arrived, a pile of whipped cream dousing the plate beside layers of cream cheese frosting. Regan lathered the fork in both, embracing the absurdity of excess (was anything more needlessly palatial than a diner?) and sliding it gluttonously into her mouth. It was rich, as velvety as its name suggested. The act of choosing it felt luxurious, extravagant in a reassuring way, and Regan slid down in the booth with satisfaction, her knee bumping into Aldo's.

"Good?" he asked.

"Divine," she said, leaning her head against the booth's vinyl cushion as she slouched down in a state of limp-limbed ecstasy, both legs fully outstretched.

He smiled knowingly, then dropped his gaze to his plate.

("How compulsive would you say you are?" her psychiatrist had asked her.

Enough to agree to six conversations with a stranger, Regan had thought.

"I don't know," she'd said, "maybe a little.")

The outer bone of her ankle brushed the inner bone of Aldo's, lingering there.

("And how are your moods?" the doctor had asked.

The thing about pills, Regan wanted to say to the doctor who had clearly never taken any, was that the ups and downs still happened; they were just different now, contained within brackets of limitation. Some inner lawlessness was still there, screeching for a higher high and clawing for a lower low, but ultimately the pills were loose restraints, a method of numbly shrinking.

Every time a pill sat in Regan's palm she suffered some new strangulation; a faint memory of some distant need to force her heart to race. She'd crave a senseless rage, a dried-up sob, a psychotic joy, but find only pulse after pulse of nothing.

Without the volatility of her extremes, what was she?

"Managed," she'd said.)

She blinked herself back to the moment at hand, taking another bite of cake and glancing up again at Aldo. His silence was less weighty than hers, or so she imagined. He seemed settled, or at least calm. He was considering something out of sight, gaze fixed on nothing.

His hair was falling into his eyes and it irked her, twitching between her scapulae.

"Do you live far?" Regan asked him, and Aldo looked up, dragging himself back to the present.

"No," he said, "just a couple of streets over."

Good. Perfect. Ideal.

"I'm going to cut your hair," she informed him.

("How compulsive would you say you are?" the doctor had asked. *I can't fucking remember!* Regan hadn't screamed.)

Aldo's gaze on hers intensified, a chatter somewhere in his mind rising visibly to the surface.

Then, abruptly, it went quiet. In his eyes, acquiescence was soft.

"Okay," he said, returning his attention to his sandwich.

———

Letting Regan into his apartment was precisely the sort of conundrum Aldo had never cared for, because it was difficult to quantify the projections involved. For example, would she think differently of him once she'd seen the way he lived? Presupposing he had any idea what she thought of him now, which he didn't. Still, would she find him dull? Dysfunctional? Would she ultimately wish to excise it from what she already knew of him, and would he be able to sleep there for any nights afterward, having witnessed in such detail all the places she had been?

Not that it mattered. He rarely slept, and she'd already been in all his other places, anyway.

He let her in, holding the door open for her, and she crept in quietly, carefully, as if she might disturb something. Don't worry, you'll fit perfectly, he thought. Don't worry, there's nothing here for you to break.

She straightened upon entry, glancing up. "High ceilings."

"Yes," he agreed.

She nodded, sparing a brief look around, then turned to him.

"Do you have, you know. A shaver?" she said. "Clippers? I don't know what they're called."

He arched a brow. "Should I be worried about what you're going to do to my head if you don't even know what the tool is called?"

"I really couldn't make it worse, believe me." She fixed her gaze on his again, surveying his hair. "It's really bad. And you haven't cut it since I met you, so . . ."

She trailed off.

"Bathroom," he said, gesturing her toward it, and she pulled her shoulders back, nodding. She had a distinct ability to take up space, he thought. She made her surroundings part of her dominion, her atmosphere bending to the strike of her stride. Aldo, on the other hand, was typically subjected to the laws and customs of the room.

She vaulted herself onto the counter upon entry, watching with her usual keen-eyed observation as he dug around for the hair-cutting set he'd gotten one year for Christmas and never touched. He half expected to blow a layer of dust off the case.

The moment he'd slid it out from one of the drawers, she leapt down again, reaching for it.

"Okay, now—" She glanced around, frowning. "Sit," she said, gesturing at first for him to straddle the toilet, but then she stopped herself. "No, wait. First your shirt."

He glanced down at it, then back at her. "What?"

"Well, I'm guessing you don't have one of those capes. Or whatever."

It took a moment to register that she wanted him to take it off.

He complied with a belated shiver, cold air meeting bare skin, then dropped it on the floor to sit as she'd requested. She, meanwhile, shifted around his bathroom, picking a blade length and scrutinizing a pair of scissors. She silently made her selection, plugging in the clippers, and then came up behind him, eyeing the back of his neck while he watched her in the mirror's reflection. She was frowning in concentration; her hands rested lightly above the scars on his shoulder (road rash, permanent) before running through his hair, measuring it out between her fingers. Her nails scraped lightly across his scalp and he allowed his eyes to close, soothed momentarily by her touch.

When his eyes opened, he found her watching him in the mirror. She didn't look away, her thumb drawing a line gingerly from the nape of his neck to the top of his spine.

Then she exhaled swiftly, glancing down to draw her attention back to his hair.

He wasn't sure what he'd expected. She seemed methodical, in a way, with a plan of attack, or at least some sort of sequential geography. She'd said art was precise, and he believed her. He was sure now that she was an artist, whether she believed herself to be or not. She was constantly in the midst of an underpainting, imagining things as they could be before steadily making them true.

Focus looked right on her, vibrant and bright. She had her lip caught between her teeth, pink tongue slipping out every now and then in concentration, and Aldo was so fixated on her that he didn't notice what she'd done to his hair until after she'd stepped back and looked up, meeting his eye in the mirror.

She'd cut it short enough that it was more tousled now than curly, trimmed safely away from his eyes and forehead. He hadn't necessarily cared about the outcome, but he found the results satisfactory; he'd been right to trust her eye, running his fingers over the subtle fade.

"There," she murmured to herself, mussing the cropped waves atop his head and smoothing them back to eye her handiwork. "Now it looks like somebody cares about you," she said, and her hand stilled, eyes rising up to his in the mirror again.

Aldo leaned his head back against her torso, resting it there for an experimental moment. In response, Regan ran the pad of her thumb over his temple; then lower, brushing the bone of his cheek. He slid a hand behind him, curling his fingers around the back of her knee; she ran her own through his hair again, her breath quickening beneath the weight of his head.

He let his eyes close, then open.

"What time?" he said.

She looked relieved. "Seven?" she suggested. "I'll drive."

"What do I need to bring?"

"Um." Her fingertips dropped to brush his clavicle, dancing along the narrow bone. "A jacket? Slacks? Do you have those?"

"I have a suit," he assured her, palm running down her calf to let his index finger brush her ankle. Then he slid his hand away, retreating to the safety of his own space. "I've had to interview for things, Chuck."

She blinked.

"Charlotte," she said, abruptly releasing him to set the clippers down on the sink. "You'll have to call me Charlotte."

He rose to his feet, turning to face her. "Sure," he agreed, and leaned against the doorframe while she wandered into the hallway, aiming herself uncertainly toward the door. "Anything else?"

"No. Not really." She half-laughed, coming to a stop. "Nothing that can't wait, anyway."

He nodded, glancing down at his watch; it was nearly six. "Want me to take you home?"

She shook her head. "It's fine, I'll take the train."

"You sure?" It was only a block or so to the Red Line, but still.

"Yes." She seemed fidgety, unsettled. Maybe she needed the solitude.

"Hope you didn't learn anything," he noted.

She cut her gaze away; when it returned, it was iron with certainty.

"Not a thing," she assured him. "See you Saturday?"

"Yes."

He did her the favor of not following her as she went, glancing instead at the lifeless curls that now spread across his bathroom floor and registering the vacancy of weight atop his head. He looked at himself in the mirror again, adjusting his hair as she had done.

Fascinating, really, to see what she saw. Bewildering that she could turn something in her mind into something real. Practical magic.

He wandered to the hall closet, noting the places she'd been.

Here. Here. There.

His mind retraced the shape of her touch, replicating its patterns and shapes; linking observations together. The speed of her hesitation. The force of her breath. He turned her over in his head, facts and details and observations, wrapping his mind around her the way his fingers had done.

Then he turned the vacuum on, permitting the sound to drown him out.

———

"You're actually serious about this?" Marc asked, chuckling a little as he watched her throw a pair of heels into her weekend bag. "I mean, I know you said you were going to, but—"

"I'm packing, aren't I?" she said. She swiped some hair from her forehead, wondering if she should bring the dress that always made her look good even if it meant her mother would berate her for wearing a funeral color to an anniversary party.

Madeline would be wearing red, probably. Red was Madeline's color, and coincidentally or not, it was a celebratory one, too. The color red meant good fortune in what little of Chinese culture Helen Regan (Yang in a past life) had retained, though Regan was fairly certain that element of tradition would have been cast out just as readily if it hadn't looked so stunning on her eldest daughter. When the Regan girls were children, both had been outfitted ubiquitously in matching red dresses, which eventually became red costumes for dance competitions and then a scarlet lip on Madeline for prom that became her signature well beyond college. The color, though, had never really belonged to Regan.

Minus the garnet earrings, but those didn't count.

"So, this guy," Marc said, interrupting her thoughts, and Regan glanced at him, already irritated. She detested having to read his mind.

"His name is Aldo."

"Fine, sure." Marc scraped a hand over the scruff on his cheeks. "What exactly are you doing, Regan?"

"I told you. Packing." Maybe the purple wrap dress, she thought. Still somber for her mother's taste, but Regan loved a jewel tone. Plus she'd never been to her mother's taste before, and she certainly wasn't going to manage it now.

"I meant what are you doing with *him,* Regan. Am I not paying you enough attention?"

"You're paying me plenty of attention." On second thought, the purple dress was stuffy. The blue silk was more flattering. Though, if her goal was flattery, then the obvious choice was the black, so she was back where she'd started. "I wish you'd pay less attention, actually, seeing as I'm busy."

"Regan," Marc sighed, catching her arm as she moved to survey her closet. "Just tell me if this is some sort of . . . episode."

She blinked with surprise, turning to look at him. "Excuse me?"

She'd used a *tone,* and he knew the warning signs. He considered her sudden shifts in mood to be part of the eccentric package, probably lamenting it over drinks in her absence.

Women, she imagined him saying, *am I right?*

"Don't be like that," he said. "I'm not accusing you of anything. I'm just asking."

Regan bristled; he hadn't asked *Have you taken your pills?* but she could hear it, the implication that she had not. "I'm fine," she said, returning her attention to the process of packing. She *was* fine, minus Marc's unwelcome hedging. She was *surprisingly* fine, actually. She was feeling something akin to excitement, in fact, which was an astounding but highly welcome alternative to the usual existential dread at the thought of facing her family. "Aldo's, you know. A friend," she reminded him. "A buffer, really."

With Aldo there, Regan doubted her parents would press her much about what she was up to. More likely they'd be stiff and formal, unwilling to venture anything beyond Midwestern politeness. Marc, who had a tendency to be fleeting in conversation, was never so reliable; he *mingled.* He was a *mingler.* Aldo, on the other hand, would be a fixture at her side.

"You like him," Marc observed.

"Is *that* an accusation?" she asked, glancing at him. He didn't answer.

In approximately the same moment, Regan suddenly remembered a dress she hadn't worn in years, turning to her closet to find it. She'd lost some weight in recent months but she figured it would still fit well enough. She'd been thinner in her criminal days; sleep had been something of a rarity at the time, and her tendency to focus on a given task meant she'd skipped a fair amount of meals.

"Regan," Marc said again, "if this guy is . . . I mean, if he's just something you need to get out of your system—"

He'd trailed off, and she turned to face him after pulling the dress free from the back of her closet, frowning. "What?"

"I wouldn't mind. I mean, I'd like to know," he amended with a dry laugh, "but, you know."

Something in her stomach twisted. This was happening entirely off schedule. Marc wasn't supposed to lose his possessiveness over her until at least a year into marriage.

"I hope this is some kind of weak attempt at reverse psychology," she opened testily.

He shook his head. "It's not. It's just, you know." A shrug. "I know you, Regan."

A nice sentiment, or it would have been, only it didn't sound intimate at all. It sounded like a taunt, and Regan folded her arms over her chest, facing him. "Would you give up speaking in riddles, Marcus? Just tell me whatever it is you want to say."

Probably a little too defensive.

"Yeah?" he said, his voice a little too mean. "Fine, Regan. Here it is, no bullshit: Fuck him if you want to." She tried not to flinch, though she was certain she'd recoiled to some degree. "You know why it doesn't matter? Because you'll come back to me," he said, and again, it was a disconcerting mismatch; soft words, hard intentions. "Because I know you. Because I *get* you. You think you want excitement, you think you want new and interesting, but babe—"

He stepped toward her, coolly brushing her hair away from her face.

"You know he'll see through you eventually," he murmured to her. "You'll put on an act for him, won't you, the way you do for everyone—but it just exhausts you in the end, doesn't it?"

She bristled, somewhere between slighted and caught.

There was nothing worse than being predictable. Nothing smaller than feeling ordinary.

Nothing more disappointing than being reminded she was both.

"We're the same, Regan," Marc reminded her. "It's not pretty underneath, is it? But you don't have to be anything else for me. You can be your fucked-up self," he said with a laugh in her ear, lips brushing her cheek, "and I'll still be there, even when everyone else turns away."

His sweetness was always moderately bitter. His candor was never without some bite. It was what she liked about him, really; his sense of power. Marc Waite was always prettily aloof.

There was a perpetual imbalance between them that she knew they both understood. She'd been so close to nothing when he'd found her that she would spend their entire relationship owing him something, or everything, just for staying when any reasonable person would have left. It wasn't wholly unromantic. Actually it was, perversely so. Even when the heat of sex died away there would still be some underlying sense of kinship; an understanding that Marc was shitty with his charming flaws of vice, but Regan would always be shittier, selfish and mercurial and vain. Complementary pieces in a perfect, shitty puzzle, where she was the broken one and he was normal. She would always be sick and he would always be fine.

"So you're satisfied with winning by default," she said, glancing up at him. "Is that it? I'm allowed to fuck Aldo because he'll leave me in the end?"

She wished he'd flinched, but he hadn't. She hadn't really expected him to. Do enough drugs and nothing could faze you; choose a woman who gambled on her shock value and eventually you went numb just to cope.

"That," Marc said, "or I love you." He released her, shrugging, and turned away. "Whatever works for you, Regan. However you have to justify it."

He left her holding the dress, the material folded over on itself in her hands; much as she might have preferred to throw something after him, instead she watched him go.

She hated the view of his back. It did something to her, diminishing her to inconsequence, insufficiency, insignificance. She could slip through the cracks in the floor like this, vanishing into nothing for her smallness, and he knew it. An old thud of hurt wrenched in her chest, and seeking reprieve, she glanced down at the dress, fingers tightening in the fabric.

Green was an interesting color. It had so many connotations, so many forms. Sometimes it was brilliant in emerald, sometimes muddied and dull. Sometimes green could be so dark it looked black at first glance, or at least like a shade far darker than it was. This dress was the latter. Difficult to place, though in certain rays of light it became intensely obvious; green, definitely green; so green it was incomprehensible that it might be perceived as something else, or that others could fail to notice. Green in the light of an armory. Green against the backdrop of a church. Green over drinks, over cake, over trivialities. Green in his reflection, staring back at her, his fingers penitently wrapped around her calf. The cut of the back was low and sleek, and a bra was out of the question. Underwear probably was, too. When he danced with her, *if* he danced—she had an odd suspicion he would if she asked him to—then his hands would have no place to rest without finding open skin. She remembered the feel of his fingers tracing patterns on her thigh, some indistinguishable sequence of calculation. Mentally, she rearranged her memories of him, taking the lightness of his touch and imagining it on the small of her back, rising up her spine.

Then she shuddered.

She placed the dress down on her suitcase, heading to the bathroom. Marc was somewhere in the living room, keeping safely out of range, but some things still required secret places, closed doors. She slid out of her leggings, pulled her sweater over her head, and lay down naked in the bathtub, shivering a little at the coldness of the porcelain.

She thought about calling him. A not-insignificant thrill ran through her at the prospect of it. *This isn't a conversation,* she imagined saying, *so don't speak. Just stay here with me, just breathe.* She wondered what he'd think of that, just listening to the sound of her. Marc, of course, would love that sort of thing. He was a lover of all things beautiful, all things sensual, though he loved them best as a caretaker, a keeper.

Aldo, Regan said behind closed eyes, did you learn anything about me?

(Haven't you been paying enough attention to run?)

Her palm slid down the parts of her that had been built from hours and hours of sweating through yoga and Pilates; consequences of "no desserts, thank you" and light dinners and whatever else it had taken to remain a flat, uninterrupted plane. Regan had worked hard enough on her body to appreciate her view of it; genetics hadn't done *all* of this, even if it had dealt her a favorable hand. The bones of her hips were shards like stalagmites, jutting up from the valley of her waist, and she loved them best for that. From this angle, she looked like a weapon. Or at least like a landscape that could provide some defense.

Her view of Aldo's chest and back, real and reflection both, was committed to memory by then. She'd always had a good eye for that sort of thing, and for inconsistencies, too. The muscles around his shoulders, the places where his wings would be, were too big. If his suit wasn't custom-tailored, which she felt certain it wasn't, she doubted it properly fit. Her mother would give him a scathing glance and oh, (cue a shiver) he wouldn't even notice. Aldo would be looking elsewhere, his mouth formed to the shape of her name, the whole of him tensed and uncertain and angled firmly and conclusively toward her.

The bastard, he'd been right. Not even six conversations and she knew him well enough to bring him to life. Green eyes, that cushion of muscle lining his spine, the sharp bone of his clavicle. That mouth. The bones of his cheeks and *that mouth*. Those eyes. Left-handed. *I need you to lie to me.* A little buzz that fluttered through her veins. His hands, long fingers laced through hers. Would sex be a math problem for him? An equation to solve? She'd always considered it fairly methodical herself. Penetration and friction, a plus b. So easy a hedge fund whatever on coke could do it.

Her phone buzzed and her eyes snapped open. She leaned over the lip of the tub, hand still between her legs, and glanced at the screen. It was Aldo; speak of the devil.

She reached over with her free hand, swiping to answer. "Hello?"

"A suit? Is that all?"

His voice was always a little dry, almost sharp. It reminded her of brut champagne.

"Something for the drive, if you want. And something to drive home in."

"You sound out of breath," he noted.

"I am. Kind of."

"Been running?"

"Sort of." She glanced down at herself, thighs clamped around her hand. "Sure." From his end of the call, she heard a siren. "Where are you?"

"My roof." She heard him take a drag of something. "Wanted to talk to you, but unfortunately I'm out of logistics."

"We can talk tomorrow," she said. "It's kind of a long car ride."

"Got a topic in particular?"

"We'll see what comes to us."

He exhaled slowly; a little gooseflesh broke out over her skin. "Alright."

Could have ended there.

Should have ended there.

"Aldo," she said. Fuck, fuck, fuck. "How do you like your coffee?"

"I don't drink coffee."

Of course he didn't. "Well, what can I bring you?"

These were logistics. "I don't need anything, Regan."

"You're doing me a favor, Aldo. I should bring you something."

He paused. "Am I?"

"Are you what?"

"Doing you a favor."

Fuck it. She leaned her ear against the bathtub, letting her fingers continue their wandering.

"Aren't you?"

"It's not much of a favor. You're doing most of the work, and I'm really not a very good party guest."

God, no, he'd be a disaster. "You'll be fine."

"Careful," he warned. "This is nearly a conversation."

He was probably stoned, wasn't he?

"Aldo."

"Regan?"

Even if he wasn't, he'd like it, she thought. Everyone did. I'm naked. I'm touching myself. I was thinking about you before, I'm thinking about you now, I'm going to come like this, thinking of you.

Men loved that. They were so fucking easy. The whole thing was so tragically primal.

"I'm glad you're going with me," she said, withering.

"I'm glad you asked me to. Logistically speaking, of course."

Speaking of.

"We should probably hang up," she said, closing her eyes.

She heard him take another drag.

"We don't have to talk," he said, exhaling again.

Perfect, she thought.

"Okay," she said.

By now she'd established the pace of his breathing; three pulses in, two or so out. In, out, with measured entrancement. She paced herself on his rhythm, seeing as her own had been lost to other pursuits.

She came after the pattern of ten more breaths; heart thudding, lip caught between her teeth to strangle the implication of sound.

"Aldo." It slipped out like a whispered sigh, half-unsaid; more a breath than anything, flooding through her bonelessly.

If he'd heard it, or anything else, he didn't comment.

"Tea would be nice," he said eventually, "if you want. Instead of coffee."

Logistics. She closed her eyes again.

"Do you want any cream or sugar? Lemon? Honey?"

"Just tea, please." She heard the sound of him rising to his feet. "I'll let you go."

That old reflex never died; the little pang of Don't go, just stay. Settle over me like the tide, cover me like a blanket, wrap around me like the sun.

Don't go, don't go, don't go.

"Okay," she said. "See you in the morning, Aldo."

"Bye, Regan," he said, and she hung up, letting the phone fall from her hand to settle on her bare torso, flat and still and lifeless.

This was no good, she thought dully. This wasn't even close to enough. She had a voracity she could never quite quench, a fear she couldn't stifle, a sense of dread lingering constantly overhead. She had a need, several needs, that she could never manage to extinguish. But people didn't like needy, so she'd learned to transform it. To bury it, cleverly disguised, in someone whose compulsions matched hers. Complementary shapes into fitting pieces.

Flaws, she thought, were just vacancies to be filled.

"Marc," she called, and heard his footsteps approaching, padding toward the bathroom door. He'd require no explanation, no invitation. She wouldn't ask forgiveness, and rightfully, he would offer none.

She closed her eyes as he stepped beside the bathtub, turning on the water just enough to let it drip down the soles of her feet. It caressed the shape of her heel where it met the cold porcelain below, and Marc smoothed a hand up her thigh.

"Better now?" he asked.

It was a relief, she reminded herself, not to be beholden to impossible expectations. Or even to meager ones.

"Will be," she said, letting out a breath.

However she had to justify it.

———

Aldo took another drag from the joint, letting it out on the breeze. It wasn't a particularly biting chill, which was good. He'd only have a few of these hospitable evenings left. One of them could have been the following evening, only he'd be busy then. At a party. With Regan.

He'd once asked his father what it had felt like to meet his mother. "Like jumping off a cliff," Masso had said, and not in a way that invited further questioning.

Aldo glanced down over the edge of his building, considering the length of the drop. He had a habit, carved into his affinity for heights, of looking down to determine the approximate point at which he would no longer be able to survive the fall. It was at moments like this, high enough to inhale the promise of risk, that the whittled lines of city streets brought out his lingering melancholy; that *l'appel du vide,* the call of the void.

In Aldo's experience, the void spoke many languages. Busy intersections, crashing waves, the too-still sounds in his apartment, the little plastic bottles he knew he could technically still get if he wanted to. Usually when the void spoke to him, Aldo countered with further contemplation of time. Time, and sometimes floods. Every ancient culture had a flood story. There must have been one, something to sweep them all away. The earth had been vengeful then.

He took another long drag, letting it out. They don't tell you how close smoking is to setting yourself on fire. Some days, he enjoyed the act of it more than the outcome. The sense that he could burn something, trap the smoldering of ash inside his chest, and then breathe it out like some sort of omnipotent god. Fires, floods. Plagues and locusts. He wondered whether Regan had given it any thought and considered calling again to ask her, then stopped himself.

He let out a puff of smoke, watching it drift away.

Sometimes Aldo thought a fall was precisely what he was waiting for.

––––––––

Regan was five minutes late, which Aldo would not have known (but possibly could have guessed) was really quite early for her. He was waiting outside his building, a duffel bag slung around his shoulders, and he was staring into nothing. His fingers were clamped together like he was holding an invisible cigarette.

"Hi," she said, rolling down the window, and he blinked, then refocused on her.

She'd done an excellent job with his haircut.

"Hi," he replied, pulling the door open and settling himself in the passenger seat of her S-Class, taking a moment to orient himself. He gave the space a scrutinizing glance, then permitted his shoulders to settle back, molding himself to his new surroundings. She wanted to laugh at his process of adaptation, but merely gestured to where she'd set his tea in the cupholder of the center console.

"Black tea okay?" she said.

He nodded. "Thank you," he said, and then looked momentarily distressed. "Really," he added slowly, as if he feared the initial acknowledgment of gratitude hadn't been enough, and she reached over to reassure him, patting his knee.

"Not a problem," she said.

His gaze fell to her hand.

She retracted it, placing it on the steering wheel, and shifted back into the lane, heading for the interstate as Aldo reached for his tea.

"So," Aldo said, leaning his head against the seat. "About that last conversation," he suggested, and Regan felt a small stirring of relief. "I think we should have it now."

"Yeah?"

"Yeah." He turned his head, looking at her. "Now that we know silence is perfectly fine," he pointed out, "there's really nothing wrong with this being our final one. We wouldn't technically have to speak again."

"True," she said. "You make an excellent point."

"Though, we never ruled out the option to renegotiate."

She nodded, satisfied that he'd been the one to suggest it. "Definitely true. Do you have any opposition to octagons?"

"Not my favorite of the geometric shapes, but they're certainly not invalid."

She smiled to herself, flicking her signal to merge onto the highway.

"What should we talk about?" he asked her.

"Personal information," she said. "Secrets."

"You know all my secrets."

She slid him an admonishing glance. "You told me *all* of your secrets over the span of five conversations?"

He shrugged. "I don't have a lot of them. Or any, really."

"Surely you have *some*."

"Is there something specific you want to know?"

Now that he mentioned it, yes.

"Let's talk about sex," she suggested neutrally.

He took a sip of tea.

"Okay," he said. "What do you want to know?"

"Who was the last person you had sex with?"

"A girl who goes to my gym," he said.

"Did you date, or . . . ?"

He glanced at her, smiling. "Her name is Andrea. She goes by Andie."

"With an i?"

"An i-e."

Regan made a face, and he laughed.

"She's a trainer. We went on two dates, slept together four times. Last time was about three months ago."

"What went wrong?"

"Nothing," he said. "She works odd hours, I wasn't around. Plus it wasn't really going to go anywhere."

"Why not?"

"Oddly," he said with another sidelong glance, "some people seem to have no interest in bees."

Regan suffered a rush of satisfaction she hurried to suppress.

"Did you tell her about the godless colonies?"

"I don't think those were technically my words, so no."

"Well, then you fucked up," she informed him, moving into the furthest left lane. "Anyone serious?"

He shook his head. "I don't really have a personality conducive to long-term relationships."

"Neither do I, but here we are." She frowned at him. "And who told you that?"

"Nobody," he said, "but I have my observations."

"Mm, it sounds very heteronormative," she commented, flashing him a glance. "A man who's allergic to commitment? Groundbreaking."

"Commitment is fine," he said. "Theoretically, anyway. But I find I have some difficulty understanding what other people want from me."

"Even though you're a genius?"

"I'm not that kind of genius," he said, "though I imagine you probably are."

He was obviously deflecting, but she figured that was fair.

"That," Regan said, "is an odd thing to say. Isn't it?"

"I just think you have a very clear understanding of how you fit with other people," Aldo said, adding, "It's a good thing."

"Doesn't sound like it."

"It doesn't?"

"Well, you've already told me I'm a liar," she pointed out. "Do you think I'm a fake, too?"

"Do *you* think you're a fake?"

She made a face at him. "Not what I asked."

He smiled.

"I think," he said, "that the inside of your head must require a specific set of keys."

"A whole set of them?"

"Oh, almost definitely," he replied. "I think that, for someone to get close to you, you must have to give them one key at a time. And even then, only one level can be opened at once."

Interesting. "Which keys in what order?"

"Not sure," he said. "Your history, I think, is a fairly straightforward key."

That was fair. "Anything else?"

She glanced at him, but he seemed to be concentrating very hard on something.

"What about sex?" she prompted. "Since that was the previously agreed upon topic."

"I think," he ventured, looking a bit strained, "for you, love and sex might be two different keys. Maybe even more than two."

"More than two?"

"Well, I wouldn't know," he said, shrugging. "I don't have the means to conduct a proper thought experiment."

She checked, but it wasn't a come-on. Fact, like anything else. "Missing some variables?"

Another shrug. "It's just a guess."

"Well, guesses are accepted currency here," she said blithely. "Along with theories, vague sensations, and counterfeit bills."

He tapped his fingers on the paper Starbucks cup. "I think you can be physically involved with someone before you need them," he said slowly. "And I think you can need them before you love them."

"And you're basing that on?"

"Five and a half conversations," he said.

There was something charming about his certainty.

"You missed one," she decided to confess. "I can sleep with someone before I want them, actually. And need them before I want them."

He glanced at her. "Always?"

"Historically, yeah," she said, "and you know how I feel about history."

He took a sip of his tea, leaning his head back again.

"What happened to the forgery boyfriend?" he asked.

"Nothing," Regan said, shrugging. "Not unusual. My relationships have a shelf life of about a year, sometimes two."

"You prefer being in a relationship?"

She thought about it. "I hadn't actually considered my preferences before, but yeah, probably. It's not like I ever look for anyone," she clarified, tapping her fingers on the steering wheel. "It's more like they manifest and I fall into it."

"Is that what happened with Marc?"

"Yeah."

She had the distinct feeling that anything she said about Marc would be a waste of a conversation.

"Sometimes," she said, "when I'm with someone else, I get this feeling like I'm asleep." She drummed her fingers on the steering wheel again, wondering if she could manage to make any sense of that or if she'd only wind up falling into a crevasse of repellant self-pity.

She kept talking anyway. "Sometimes it's like I'm there, but not really. Not fully. Like part of me is going to wake up a century later and everything will just be totally unidentifiable," she said with a gloomy laugh. "You know, like Rip Van Winkle or something."

Aldo was quiet for a moment.

"Time travel," he said.

She fought a smile, giving him an admonishing shake of her head. "I'm not trying to solve it, though."

"So?" he asked neutrally. "That probably means you'll solve it first."

"Because I'm a genius?"

"Because you're a genius," he confirmed, and then, without any transition, "I want to see your art."

She opened her mouth, then hesitated.

"That's a key," he noted, and she rolled her eyes.

"I just don't have any," she said. "I haven't done anything in ages. Years."

"Not even a sketch?"

"Not even a sketch," she said, shaking her head. "Haven't had time."

A lie.

"You're lying," he said.

She sighed. "You know, it's poor form to accuse a lady of lying all the time."

"Well, you can lie if you want," he assured her. "I just like to know when it's happening. You know, note it in the minutes, at least. Maybe know it in advance, if we can establish a system."

"Control issues," she observed aloud, brow arched.

He didn't seem to see a problem with that. "Do you prefer ignorance?"

"I should, probably," she admitted. "Ignorance really does seem to be bliss."

That, however, he *did* seem to take issue with. "I think I'd rather be informed than blissful."

"So you'd rather have knowledge than happiness?"

He thought about it. "Yes," he concluded, and then hesitated. "Sometimes," he began slowly, "doesn't happiness seem . . . fake? Like it might be something someone invented. An impossible goal we'll never reach," he clarified, "just to keep us all quiet."

"Almost certainly," she agreed.

They drove in silence for a few minutes.

"What's your mother's name?" she asked eventually.

"Ana," he said.

"Have you ever been curious about her?"

"Yes."

"Ever tried to meet her?"

"No. I don't think I could find her if I tried."

She spared him a sympathetic grimace. "Well, they say never to meet your heroes."

"She's not my hero," he said, "but I see your point."

"Was it just you and your dad, then?"

"And my nonna, yes."

"Are you close to her?"

"I was."

"Oh." She winced. "Sorry."

He shrugged. "You couldn't have known."

"Yeah, but still—"

"What about your mother?"

She chewed her lip.

"Another key," he observed, adding, "You don't have to answer."

"Well, you'll meet her," Regan said with a shrug, "so it probably won't take very long to figure out. I'm sort of a textbook case, you know. Narcissistic mother, high-achieving sister, work-obsessed father. So common it's nearly Freudian."

"I don't believe that. And Freud has been largely discredited."

"Well, I'm something along those lines, then," she said. "Every psychologist has seen some version of me before, I'm sure."

He gave her a long, searching look. "Who told you that?"

Her doctor. Her lawyer.

A judge. A jury of her peers.

Marc.

"No one." She met his glance briefly, then turned back to the road. "First kiss?"

"Sixth grade, Jenna Larson. Yours?"

"Ninth grade," she said. "Late bloomer."

"Probably best. Mine was terrible."

She laughed. "So was mine. First time?"

"I was sixteen," he said. "Under the bleachers. One of those anarchist stoner types."

"God, of course she was. I was sixteen, too," she said. "He was captain of the water polo team."

Aldo chuckled. "Of course he was."

"His name was Rafe," she said, and Aldo groaned.

"Of course it was," they said in unison.

When the laughter had died from her tongue, Regan felt something else take its place, filling the vacancy in her chest. Some other compulsion twitched at her limbs, and she reached over, placing her hand on his knee.

This time, Aldo didn't flinch. He rested his hand on hers, covering it briefly and running his thumb over her knuckles; satisfied, she retracted it, securing both hands on the wheel.

"How do you feel about dancing?" she asked him.

"My grandmother taught me when I was in high school," Aldo said. "I know how."

"That's not what I asked."

She caught the motion of him smiling.

"Ask me later," he suggested.

"Okay," she agreed.

Six conversations, she thought with another rush of palpable disbelief, and still, she couldn't wait to know.

PART THREE

KEYS.

One of Aldo's considerations when it came to time was how long it took, conceptually, before things became ordinary, unspecial. People were so easily desensitized, so helplessly numbed when it came to the repetitive nature of existence. He wondered, first, how long it had taken for Regan to lose her sense of wonder with her own life, but then secondly, whether she'd ever had any to begin with.

Aldo had never experienced an anniversary party, given that his own parents were never married and his nonno had died long before he was born, but he had been under the impression that such parties were generally reasonably-sized affairs. Not so for the Regan family, which consisted of the parents, John and Helen, and the two children, Madeline and Charlotte, along with Madeline's husband, Carter Easton, and their daughter Carissa. Aldo understood, logistically, why Regan had warned him to call her by her first name, and upon seeing her in context he proceeded to grasp it intuitively. Regan was her usual name for herself, but when she was here she was Charlotte, whom Aldo had begun to see as an entirely separate identity.

Charlotte, for example, was a dimmer Regan upon entering the house she'd grown up in; almost as if the effort of trying to fill this space, easily accomplished in every other place, had sapped her of the energy required for certain facets of her personality. Where Regan was typically poised in a languid way, Charlotte was tensed and strained, all her muscles tight, the pads of her fingers pressed white around her glass. It was all Aldo could do not to stare at her hands, repeatedly drawn back to them like something out of place. Her discomfort was, for him, an insurmountable distraction.

"—you do, Aldo?"

Aldo blinked, tearing his gaze from Regan as he registered that her mother had been speaking to him. She was a smaller woman (Regan's height was clearly inherited from her father—John, like his second daughter, was lean and almost reedy, while the other two women were petite and, for lack of a better word, woman-shaped) and Aldo was forced to look down, uncomfortably too-large by comparison.

"Sorry?" he said, grudgingly. He'd have preferred to speak to Regan, who in turn seemed to prefer to speak to Carissa, her niece. This, Aldo reminded himself, was something he probably should have anticipated. He hadn't formally modeled the party's events, but it was progressing as he could have (conceivably) predicted.

"What do you do?" Helen repeated, speaking with pained deliberation that time.

"Math," he said, and stopped for a moment, thinking there was something in his throat. There wasn't.

"Like a programmer?" Helen pressed.

"No. Theoretical math."

"Mom, I told you," Regan said, picking up Carissa and joining their conversation with the little girl's legs slung around her hips. "Aldo's a professor at UChicago."

"Adjunct," Aldo corrected. "Not tenured. I'm a doctoral student."

"Ah," said Helen. "Are you hoping to become tenured?"

"I don't especially love teaching," Aldo said.

"He's good though," Regan contributed. "Well, he's a genius, anyway."

She flashed him a smile and a wink as Carissa grabbed hold of her hair.

"Is there much of a job market for 'theoretical math'?" asked Helen.

"*Mom*," said Regan.

"I'm not sure," said Aldo, who had never really bothered to find out.

"Charlotte, I'm just asking questions. Are you from Chicago?"

It took him a moment to realize Helen was addressing him again.

"No. California," Aldo clarified. "Pasadena."

Regan, he noted, was glancing toward him with increasing frequency, so he guessed he was saying something wrong. Whether it was what he was saying or how he was saying it, he wasn't entirely sure.

"My father lives there still," he added. Perhaps he was permitting too much silence between words. "He owns a restaurant."

"Oh?" said Helen.

"Yes."

"Aldo's an excellent cook," Regan contributed.

Helen gave Aldo a sharpened glance, then turned to Regan. "When has he cooked for you?" she said, speaking exclusively to her daughter. Aldo had the distinct feeling he had abruptly disappeared, fighting the instinct to check for his hands and feet.

The answer to Helen's question was never, and that Regan had no evidence, qualitative or otherwise, to gauge Aldo's requisite skill. This, however, did not stop her from proceeding as if these were not relevant matters of consideration.

"We're friends, Mom. He cooked for me, I cut his hair. Looks good, doesn't it?"

It was a question, Aldo observed, but also somehow a threat.

"Since when are you friends?" Helen said. "I've never heard of him."

"You're meeting him right now, aren't you?"

"Charlotte. Please don't."

"Mom, you're being ridiculous."

Aldo sensed they were no longer discussing his cooking. He glanced at Regan's dress, which was a dark green that slid around her narrow waist to flare out slightly from her hips. He should tell her she looked pretty, he thought, though that was probably an underwhelming word.

"—all I ask is that you not be so irresponsible for once—"

"—not *being* irresponsible, *you're* the one who wanted me to come—"

On second thought, he considered that maybe he shouldn't use the word "pretty" at all. He guessed many people had told Charlotte she looked pretty, and that Regan had probably made a note never to forget. And perhaps it was merely a word used for children. It felt juvenile, at least slightly. Relatedly, Carissa, the toddler, was gone now. Regan had set the child down and turned away, facing her mother, and Aldo could see the lines of tension in her exposed back.

Pretty, he thought again, and forced himself to think about something else. The prospect of time seemed even foggier than usual. It seemed to have forgone its usual rate in favor of dragging moodily in place, traveling slowly down the notches of Regan's spine.

"Aldo, has anyone offered you a drink?" came a voice behind him.

It was Madeline, sister of Regan, mother of Carissa. Aldo had begun mapping all the relevant roles and characters, though it was a relatively small map. Charts, to him, were soothing. Corralling organisms of chaos into order was a pleasant (*more* pleasant) way to occupy his time.

"I don't need one," he said, and Madeline smiled broadly. Her smile was more practiced than either Regan's or Charlotte's, he noted. It had a look of frequent rehearsal.

"Maybe not a drink, then," she suggested. "Some air?"

There was a gentle urgency to her voice, which she paired with a motion that angled him away from Regan. Aldo followed reluctantly, a stiffening in Regan's posture his last glimpse before he turned.

Madeline was considerably smaller than Regan, in air and behavior in addition to physical design. She had a foxlike sort of face, a diminutive nose with liquid eyes and fine features. Her dark hair faded into something delicately golden, trailing over one shoulder. It was difficult to believe she was a woman who'd had a child, much less a medical degree. She looked as though she'd been plucked unsuspecting from her early twenties, or, alternatively, perhaps some sort of grove of woodland fairies. She was wearing a red dress and looked very, very pretty. She, Aldo guessed, would be more inclined to appreciate the compliment, but he suspected that if the younger Regan would find such a thing untrustworthy, the elder would tuck it away somewhere and use it to power her electricity.

"Out here looks nice," Madeline said, directing him onto the lawn. They'd ordered the same heat lamps Masso used on the small patio of his restaurant, though Aldo noticed Madeline still shivered a little in the October air.

"If you're cold—"

"Oh no, I'm fine," Madeline said quickly, flashing him a tight smile. There was a bartender set up outside, safely tucked away from the house. "Sure you don't want a drink?"

"No, thank you," Aldo said, and then, because he was thinking it, "It was a good idea to put the bar outside. Better queuing," he noted, observing that nobody was blocking any of the ingress or egress points of the party. "Smart."

Madeline's smile quirked. "Well, you learn a thing or two after doing this enough times, but thank you."

He glanced down at her. "You did this?"

That, he noted, prompted a different sort of smile. He guessed he'd said something more valuable than complimenting her looks.

"It's not that difficult, really," she said. "You wouldn't believe the party my parents insisted on hosting for Carissa's first birthday."

"I can imagine." He could, too, though it was mostly a line other people were fond of using. *I can imagine,* as if they'd lent their thoughts to it with frequency. Most people were really expressing their capacity for pattern recognition, for modeling data in their heads. He doubted many of them were using true imagination, except possibly for Regan. He made a point to ask her later: *Do you imagine things? Is your life a dream or a chart? Have you thought of this or this or this?*

He knew she would answer them and shivered prophetically.

"It is a bit cold," Madeline said, glancing over her shoulder. "I'd go back inside, but we should give them a minute. Sorry about my sister," she added.

Aldo didn't immediately see how the two thoughts were related.

"Why?" he asked, and Madeline blinked.

"Well, you know how she is, I'm sure," she said. "She's a bit difficult."

"Difficult," Aldo echoed, suffering an apprehensive twitch of misalignment at the word, and Madeline shrugged.

"She's always been this way. Very prone to picking fights, especially with my mother. I always tell her she's too defensive, and that Mom's way of showing she cares is, you know . . . overbearing, I guess, at times. But then she just accuses me of being on Mom's team, so it's really a bit of a lose-lose sit—"

"Of course she's difficult," Aldo said, still stuck on the initial verbiage. "She's more than difficult, actually. She's—" He paused, struggling to explain. "Well, within any equation, there's variables," he attempted, and Madeline, like many people he spoke with, gave him a look of amusement mixed with confusion. "You would know this, obviously," he recalled. "You're a scientist."

"Of sorts," Madeline permitted, and he nodded.

"Most people are relatively simple. A combination of environmental factors, genetic proclivities, inherent traits . . ."

He checked that she was with him. "I follow," she said, nodding as if she did.

"Right," he said. "So most people are fairly straightforward functions of x and y, behaving within constraints of expectation."

"Social constructs?" Madeline guessed.

"Presumably," Aldo confirmed. "So within those parameters, some people are exponential functions, but still largely predictable. Regan"—*Charlotte,* he reminded himself too late, but dismissed it as a foregone error—"isn't just difficult, she's convoluted. She's contradictory—honest even when she lies," he offered as an example, "and rarely the same version twice. She's confounding, really intricate. Infinite." That was the word, he thought, clinging to it once he found it. "She'd have to be measured infinitely in order to be calculated, which no one could ever do."

He glanced at Madeline, who was giving him a bemused half smile.

"Does that make sense?"

"Yes," Madeline said slowly, "it does."

Aldo decided he liked Madeline.

"Anyway," he said, figuring he'd gone on long enough. People typically didn't care for his theorizing, and though there was more he could say on the subject, he forced himself to summarize neatly with "You shouldn't apologize for her."

"No," Madeline agreed, "I suppose I shouldn't."

They were quiet for a moment, as it felt like her turn to speak. She seemed more interested in her own thoughts, though, and when she folded her arms over her chest, Aldo caught the evidence of raised gooseflesh on her arms. His phone buzzed in his pocket; probably his dad asking if he was behaving himself. *Try not to stare at the ceiling when other people talk,* Masso usually said, which Aldo found difficult. At the moment, his ceiling was a sky full of stars. If he'd had a joint and silence, it would be an evening like any other spent atop his roof.

Except that it wasn't, he remembered, because Regan was somewhere nearby.

"You're cold," he noted to Madeline, observing the way she'd curled around herself for warmth. "You should go back in. I'll be out here," he said, and then lied, "I'll get a drink."

She nodded, still thoughtful.

"It was nice to meet you," she said.

"You, too," he replied with a perfunctory lilt of his head, and then she smiled at him, heading back into the house.

Aldo rolled an invisible joint between his fingers, making his way to the edge of the lawn. When he'd arrived with Regan that morning, he'd noticed that her house overlooked a narrow creek, which he now wished he could see. Instead he could merely hear it, left to guess whether or not it was actually there or simply part of his imagination. Part of him considered leaping in, finding out by doing. Not every problem was best left to theory to explain.

"Brought you something," he heard behind him, jolting him from his thoughts, and he turned to find Regan approaching from the lawn, sidling up to him. The wind had whipped her hair around her shoulders and she smoothed it away from her eyes, offering him a glance of apology.

"Here," she said, holding out what remained of a blunt, and he looked down at it, skeptical. "Oh, come on," she said, rolling her eyes, "I can't help whatever shitty weed college me left in my old bedroom. It's still better than nothing," she reminded him, temptingly wiggling it between her fingers.

He reached out, taking it from her. The pads of her fingers were warm.

"Aren't you cold?" he asked her neutrally. She shrugged, holding up a plastic lighter and beckoning for him to place the blunt between his lips.

"Not especially," she said as he complied. She took his chin in one hand, flipping the lighter and holding it up to the end of the blunt, saturating the stunted tip in flames until it smoldered. "There," she said, obviously pleased with herself as he inhaled. "Better?"

She released his jaw, and he exhaled. It wasn't especially good weed, but he'd certainly had worse.

"Sure," he said, eyeing it. "Though it wasn't too terrible before."

She seemed to disagree, but dismissed her own feelings on the matter.

"I heard you talked to Madeline," she said, something of a challenge.

He shrugged. "A bit. Mostly about math."

"Not bees?"

"Not bees," he said, and handed her the blunt. "Bees are for you."

She smiled at him, accepting it.

"Thanks," she said, as if he'd told her she was pretty.

"You're welcome," he said as if he had.

She inhaled deeply, choking a little when it filled her mouth. "This stuff is stronger than I remember," she coughed up, and he chuckled, holding his hand out to take it back from her.

"Won't you get in trouble for this?"

She shrugged, glancing over her shoulder. "I'm an adult, Rinaldo. Or something like one."

"Mm." He took another drag, already more at ease. Above him were stars. Beneath him was grass. There was wonder here, even if Regan no longer saw it. Even if she no longer felt it, he would feel it for both of them. He would translate it for her later. He would learn to draw it for her, he thought, or to write it, or graph it. She seemed to appreciate things she could see. He thought of her gaze traveling over the scars on his shoulders, taking him in. Yes, he would draw it for her, and then she would see it. She would watch it take shape and he would know he'd said it in a way she could understand, and then she would know that even this, with its ordinary features, was wonder and glory, too.

He didn't blame her for not seeing it. He blamed everyone else for letting her forget.

She leaned over, guiding his hand to her mouth for another drag. Her fingers curved around his, brushing over his knuckles and sliding up to where he held the blunt, secured between the pads of his index finger and his thumb.

"What do you think about dancing?" she said, moistening her

lips and inhaling. She let it out smoothly this time, standing close enough to him that he could feel her breath as if he'd taken it himself.

"Yes," he said—he would have said it to anything, she could have suggested a mutiny and he'd have searched tirelessly for an axe, a pitchfork, Excalibur itself—and she smiled up at him, lifting her chin to permit him full view of her approval. The prospect of it, of anything, buzzed in his veins.

Then she was quiet as only she could be quiet, with every motion impossibly loud.

"Your hair looks good," she murmured, lifting her fingers to the roots near his temple. She brushed back the strands, nails raking lightly over his scalp.

He took another drag from the blunt as her fingers skated down, running lightly over his cheek and down to his mouth. The dark tips of her nails traveled the shape of his upper lip, curving with it, and in another version of this precise moment, he said, Regan, come closer, let's see what happens, let's see how the stars shine on your skin.

Instead he said, "Let's go," and licked the pads of his fingers, extinguishing the smoldering edge of the blunt between them. She watched, dark eyes solemnly following his motions, as he slid what remained into the breast pocket of his jacket, tucking it securely against his chest.

"Let's," she agreed, and slid her arm through his, leading him back to the house.

———

You're an adult, Charlotte, act like one.

Is it for attention? Haven't we given you enough of that by now?

Look at your sister, Charlotte, look at Madeline. She has a life, a family, a good job. You can't be irresponsible like this forever. What are you trying to prove? This man, whoever he is, did you bring him here to upset me? To upset us, is that it? He's rude, he's here in our home and hardly giving us the time of day, and where's Marc? Did you break up already? I keep telling you, Charlotte, you have to act like an adult if you want to be in an adult relationship. Not everything is about you, what you want, what you feel. That's what it means to grow up and realize there are other people in the world besides yourself.

Of course we don't like him. Why would we? He's weird, Charlotte, look how strange he is. Is he hanging around you for money? I hope you haven't promised him anything. No, don't get upset, don't get hysterical again, we're just trying to protect you. Which we've always done, haven't we? But you've kept this up long enough, Charlotte. Are you taking your medications, seeing your doctor like we asked?

I know you're not stupid. That's the worst part, Charlotte, I know how smart you are. I know what you could be, but you waste it, don't you? You waste your potential with tantrums like this, rebelling for no reason. Him? He's nothing, Charlotte! You want to settle down with someone with no goals, no nothing? I know you don't. I know you, and I know this game, and I'm tired of it.

He's your friend, yes, you said that. Okay fine, choose better friends then. Marc may not be our favorite person in the world but at least he takes care of you, he can support you and yet here you are, jeopardizing that as if it's nothing. Does he know you've brought some other man to this party? Does he even know this man? This . . . I don't care what his name is, he barely looks at us, Charlotte! It's as if we're not even here, and now you're making a scene—

You are, Charlotte. You *are.* You've always done this. You insist that you've changed and yet here you are, making the same mistakes. What was the name of that artist? Him, yes, another of your terrible ideas. This is what happens when you throw your life away for men who are lost, no ambition, no drive. At least Marc has a job, a *real* job. You can build a life with someone like him, Charlotte. I can see you're going to do something stupid now, aren't you, something reckless? Of course you are, see how well I know you? Fine. Ruin your life then, Charlotte, let your father throw money at your problems and see if it does anything for you. See how well I know you; how I know, even now, what you're thinking?

I know you, Charlotte. I know you so well that I can ring in your head even when I'm gone, even when you're smoking with your weird little mathematician in the backyard of this enormous fucking house, I know you can hear me. I know you can feel me, feel my disappointment in you, feel it all unfurling in your bones while you touch the blessed shape of his irreverent mouth and wonder if this voice in your head is crueler for being yours or mine. He doesn't behave like he should, Charlotte, you're doing yourself no favors, you're doing him no favors, fuck, don't even get me started on Marc. You're making a mess, you're flailing around like usual, did you take your pills? Did you hold them in your hands, cradle them between the lines of your palms, and let them remind you how ill you are, how sick, how desperate?

Not even the weed can possibly dull it, me, everything from your senses. You still hear me like the blood rushing in your ears, feel me like the buzzing of your fingers. Feel the sparseness of everything his lips have brushed, the vastness of everywhere his touch has never been. Oh, maybe I'm wrong about him, maybe you can comfort yourself with that, but I'm never wrong about you. You want him to want you, don't you? You want to feel him like an anchor, like a weight. You want all of him dragging you down, binding you to something. You want him to pull you close like this, like this dance that is not a dance but is more of a dance than anything you've ever done with anyone, but you don't even know the steps, do you, Charlotte? His hands are on your waist, and how many other hands have been there, or there, or there? Try to hide it, you can't, he'll see through you. Everyone sees through you. Everyone sees through you and on the other side of you is the way life looks without you, and inevitably they will run straight for it with relief.

You're going to make a mistake with him, Charlotte. I don't know what that mistake will be and neither do you, but it doesn't matter, you and I both know you will. Will it be worth it, just for his hands on your skin? Will it be worth him slipping through your fingers, bleeding through the cracks in your constitution, just to be reminded you're the kind of person people leave? Maybe it will, because look at his mouth, look at the shape it makes when his eyes are on you. You wouldn't make love with him, you'd make art. Maybe that would be worth it, but still, art is tragedy. Art is loss. It's the fleeting breath of a foregone moment, the intimacy of things undone, the summer season that passes. It's the peeled lemon and bony fish in the corner of a Dutch still life, rotten and dead and gone. It's him lying next to you, legs tangled with yours, only to know he'll be a specter in your thoughts by next month, next week, ten minutes from now. This is what makes it art, Charlotte, and you've always understood that. You've always understood, above everything, that what makes beauty is pain.

Grow up, Charlotte, and accept things as they are. You are not in love with Rinaldo Damiani whose hair smells like Sunday morning in the sun, you do not even know him, he doesn't know you. You can rest your hands on the scars of his shoulders and long to rid him of every breath of pain and still, you will not be in love with him, because this isn't love. Love is a home and a mortgage and the promise of permanence; love is measured and paced, and this, the too-hasty sprint of your pulse, that's drugs. You know drugs, don't you, Charlotte? Euphoria can be bottled, it can be smoked, it will dissolve on your tongue and burn through the vacant cavity of your empty fucking chest. His hands on you, that can be preserved, it can be painted, it can be committed to the canvas of your imagination, and it can stay in the vaults of your private longings, your little reveries, your twisted dreams.

Accept it, Charlotte. Accept it and grow up. You're an adult, Charlotte, act like one.

Charlotte Regan, you fool, you've been stuck inside a trance, wake up.

Wake up, Regan.

Regan, look at me. Wake up.

Tell the voice in your head to be quiet, would you? I know you're not here right now, I know you're lost somewhere that I can't go or touch or see, but look me in my green eyes and tell me what else matters. Bees, Regan, think of the bees, think about the implausibility of time and space, think of impossible things. Think about the stars in Babylon and tell me, Regan, all this time we've been talking and you've been syncopating your breath to mine and your pulse to mine and your thoughts to my thoughts, you've been learning how to love me, haven't you? If I am a lover of impossible problems then you will have loved me for my impossibilities, so tell me, Regan, what else matters but this, me, us?

Nothing.

Nothing.

Welcome back, Regan.

I missed you while you were away.

———

"Aldo?"

His eyes snapped open. He hadn't been sleeping, obviously—the weed had helped, but even so, he was in John and Helen Regan's guest room, which was too foreign a thought to lull him to even the vaguest approximation of sleep—but still, her voice in the dark was startling. She was half a dream as she carefully pushed open the door.

He sat up slightly, catching the motion of moonlight from the window falling on bare legs. She crept across the wooden floors with an air of practice, avoiding a spot near the door, and bounded lightly over to where he lay in the bed before perching on the edge of the mattress.

"Did I wake you?" she asked him. Her hair fell loose and half-dried around her face, parted like a curtain in the center.

"No," he said, "not really."

"Good." She nudged him over, sliding in next to him. "Did you have fun? Or, you know. Something like it."

"Something like it," he confirmed, turning on his side to face her. "Definitely something like it."

"Good." She was buzzing a little, almost vibrating with something indefinable. Excitement, maybe. She had, after all, snuck into his room, and perhaps not all elements of youthful rebellion faded with age. "You're a good dancer."

So was she. The rest of her family had mostly left them alone for the remainder of the evening and her mother, Helen, had looked deliberately at the wall behind his head. He could tell (he wasn't stupid) that it was a distasteful sort of apathy, something he should resent or, more helpfully, repair, but he wasn't entirely opposed to the idea of them communicating as little as possible.

Regan slid closer to him, propping her head up to look at him.

"I haven't done it in a while," he said. Dancing, he meant.

"Well, you're good. Very good."

Her fingers stretched out tentatively, finding the marks that State Street had left across his shoulders. The glow from the window illuminated pieces of their silhouettes, her right side and his left. With the way moonlight fell over them it seemed to him that they were each one half of a person, divided in two, each fraction left to be the other's reflection. He felt the echoes of her touch unfurling in gooseflesh down his arms, his legs, spreading to the soles of his feet.

"I'm sorry," Regan said. "About my parents."

"Why?"

He saw only half of her tiny half smile, a splintered crescent of amusement in the dark. "You didn't notice? No, of course you didn't," she sighed. "I shouldn't have said anything."

"Too late," he noted, and her smile tightened to a grimace.

"Well, it's no surprise they don't like you," she said. "They don't get you, and besides, they don't like anybody." She slid her thumb over his clavicle. "They hate Marc, too. Just for different reasons."

He had the distinct impression that she was drawing him, somewhere in her mind.

"Reasons like what?"

"Like, I don't know." She pulled away, her hand falling to the sheets, and he immediately regretted asking. "Marc's, you know, the normal kind of intolerable. Loud, flashy, all that."

"And I'm . . . abnormal?"

"Oh, extremely," she said, and then laughed. "You're the weirdest, Aldo."

She said it so sweetly he almost thanked her.

Then, on second thought (third, technically), he did. "Thank you."

"You're welcome," she replied, and rolled onto her back, closing her eyes. "Anyway, I'd say don't take it personally, but I guess you never do."

Not always, he wanted to say, but it was close enough to the truth that he didn't argue. "I'm the one who should be sorry."

That prompted one of her eyes to open. "What?"

"Well, you wanted me to make things easier for you," he said, "and I didn't."

"That's—" She sat up, bristling with a different energy now. One he couldn't identify. "Don't."

He sat up, too, mirroring her. "Don't what?"

"Don't . . . think that. I don't know." She was agitated, shaking her head. "They're the ones who are wrong, you know. And anyway, Madeline likes you." She smoothed her hand over the comforter, seeming to want to repair the damage her unexpected friction had caused.

She implored him, silently, and he took a long look at her, just looking. He had drawn her eyes a few more times than he'd planned to by then, and he was pleased to see his estimations were correct, geometrically speaking, if lacking in execution. Those eyes in real life were weapons, or possibly anti-weapons. They had kept her out of prison, he was sure of it. Wide-set and oversized, little picture-boxes of innocence. Frames that made a mockery of everything concealed within.

"And me," she said, so delayed he'd forgotten what they were talking about.

"And you what?"

"I like you." She rubbed her cheek. "I mean," she said, hurrying to obscure what she'd said with coquetry, "this *is* our seventh conversation, so that must mean something."

"Does it?"

She was quiet for a moment, wrestling with the truths she reserved for herself. He sensed she needed a push, a nudge. A mirror-motion. He leaned toward her, pausing before they touched, and left room for the reverberations inside her to echo in him. He could feel it again, the buzzing she'd come into the room with vibrating there in that empty space, now occupied by the tremors of possibility. She could fill it with herself, she could shove him away, she could pull him closer. She could pry apart his ribs and leave him there, gutted, doe eyes wide with *I didn't think it'd be so wet.*

He waited there, in the gruesome image of himself spilling crimson over her hands, seeping into the beds of her narrow fingernails and forever staining the sheets and the floors—and, if he were lucky, her conscience—when she matched the distance toward him that he'd already undertaken toward her. He could smell her hair, her skin, her lack of hesitation. The other half of her truths was a lie.

She said, "Am I imagining this?"

He shook his head, No, you aren't, or if you are then I am, too.

"Oh," she said.

She leaned forward. He matched her distance again, their foreheads meeting like old friends; Hello, how are you, been a long time, how nice it is to be here with you. Their hands, meanwhile, stayed back like tired captives, wary prisoners of war.

"These keys of mine," she said. "If you could have one of them."

It was an implied question: If you could open only one part of me for your consumption, for your delectation, for the whims of your carnivorous mind, which part would you wish to see?

The answer, or at least the answer she wanted, was more difficult to guess. On the one hand, there was quite obviously sex. There was no question she had it on the brain. So did he, now. More than now, though it was more unavoidable now, sitting close to her like this. He wasn't so oblivious that he could ignore how close she was, how tempting. She'd essentially teed up an answer for him, made it easy—Here, let me tell you what you want. In fact, let me show you. Let me be the one to decide for both of us. Let me be the one to want you in such a way as to make you acquiesce that you want me, and let me save us both the trouble of fumbling through the Do you want to?, Are you sure?, the tiresome little how-do-you-dos of intimacy.

He could imagine the softness of her cheek or feel it for himself, up to him. He could see the flutter of her lashes where her eyes were closed and his were open, he could watch her play the ingenue, he could let her have the starring role the way she wanted this to be. Her hair smelled like flowers because she'd washed it somewhere in this house, under this same roof. Somewhere in his proximity, somewhere within these very walls, she'd been naked; she'd let the stream of water spill down from the top of her scalp, cracking like an egg and dripping down her forehead—the same forehead now pressed to his—and then her lips. Those droplets would have slid along her nose the way he could now, with just an inch to make up the difference. Water might have fallen in the little cracks of her lips, the ones her teeth slid over now with anticipation, and then down from her chin to the floor while the rest of it draped over her shoulders, saturating her skin. Somewhere, she'd sighed amid steam that embraced her with comfort, washing away the tensions of the day, and massaged it free from her limbs—the way his hands could do now, if they wished to. He could slide away the strap of her shirt and discover what, until now, remained only hers.

(Hers, and whoever else had been given permission to see it. Hers, and whoever else possessed some version of this moment with her, touching and not-touching within the shelter of a darkened room.)

"Any key?" he asked.

"Any key," she said, in the kind of voice deliberately intended to make him shiver.

She turned her head slightly, her cheek meeting his. He could feel her breath on his skin, could sense her fingers tightening in the sheets, could taste the bitterness, the sweetness of her waiting, coiled and knotted and tensed.

How fragile the craving, he thought, and how delicate it was. How easy it would be to snap it between his fingers, to crush it between his palms. How effortlessly the wanting turned into the franticness of taking, and how very, very easy it was to take.

"I want," he began, his voice fighting its way through the dryness in his throat, and she pulled away a fraction of a degree; only enough so that if he wanted her mouth—if he wanted to match it with his—he could do it. He could find out what secrets she kept in her kiss.

"Yes?"

A thrill of opposition burst from the haze of her closeness.

"Your art," he said, and felt her stiffen.

"What?"

The tension snapped, striking them both.

"I want to see your art," he said, and she pulled away, staring at him.

"Aldo," she said. "You're kidding me."

He shook his head. "I'm not."

"But." She dragged her tongue over dry lips, mouth tightening. "Aldo, I have a boyfriend."

"Yes," he said, "I know."

"But I'm here. With you."

"Yes," he said.

She stared at him.

"You know what this means, don't you?"

"I have some idea."

"Of course you do, you're a genius." She sounded bitter about it that time, and though she didn't move, he could see her tightening inside herself, curling up and shrinking down. "I thought that you—"

"I do," he said.

"But then—"

"You said I could only have one key," he said.

She blinked.

"You realize this could be your only chance," she told him.

"Well, then I don't want it."

That information seemed to dizzy her.

"Why not?"

"This isn't the one I want."

"This key?"

"This chance."

"What's wrong with this chance?"

"Regan."

"Tell me, Aldo, I want to know."

Would he come back to this moment someday? Would he wish to? "You said one key," he reminded her, and from what he could see of her face in moonlight, she looked exasperated.

"Yes, but I thought—" She stopped.

"You aren't wrong," he told her.

She pulled her knees into her chest. "I feel wrong."

Rinaldo, where are we today? his father had asked him, and Aldo had said, We are somewhere in the depths of time, somewhere people only dare imagine in their dreams. We are floating in dark matter. We are trapped inside a star, which is locked inside a system, which is itself a galaxy we can't escape and we are lost to each other, to ourselves, and to the inconsequence of space.

He reached out, unthinking, and she sucked in a breath as his hand met her cheek, stroking along the bone, darting beneath the corner of her jaw. He shifted to his knees, facing her, and she did the same, a mirror game again, her hands floating up to brush a curl back from his forehead. Her thumb lingered beside his temple and he caught her fingers with relief.

"What key?" she asked again. A second chance.

He shook his head, lips still pressed to her knuckles. "Your art," he said.

Regan, he thought, Regan, this night is stolen, I want grand larceny and this is petty theft.

"I can't give you that," she said, but he only heard it after he felt it, the shutting of the doors and barring of the windows. Somewhere inside her she was triple-checking the locks, swallowing whatever keys remained, tossing them into flames and melting them down to be fashioned as jewelry, as armor, as chains. She was remaking herself as a vault and he felt it, the way she drifted away from him, even before she slid her hand from his.

"I don't have that key anymore," she said. "I probably never did."

I know, he thought, I know.

"If you find it," he told her, and didn't finish the sentence.

She stepped back from the bed, one long leg enough to brace her steadily against the floor, and he felt the steps she took away from him like aftershocks beneath her feet.

"Good night," she said.

He knew she would never forgive him. He had chosen his own end.

"Good night," he told her, and the door opened, and then it closed, and then she was gone from him.

Gone, as she had never been before.

———

The grandfather clock in the living room below informed Regan that the day had long since changed; one to another. That soon, another sun would rise, and she would still be dirtied by the choices of the night before. She held her hands around herself and shivered, newly frozen in Aldo's absence, and padded carefully down the hall, bare feet kissing the beams below.

She felt a mix of things, soft and hard. Things were compacting and expanding inside her. They'd been there before she'd entered the room, but now that she had left it, she felt exactly the same only worse. The same, only more so.

She snaked a path back to her bedroom, pausing beside the bathroom door. Inside her makeup bag was the Armani foundation, the Dior mascara, the Givenchy concealer she scarcely had reason to use. There was blush in there to mimic innocence, bronzer to imitate sun, gloss to postulate desire. It was a bag full of lies and somewhere at the base of it were orange translucent bottles calling for her attention, summoning the liar to her rightful place. I'll take them, she thought, I'll take them now, it'll be fine, I was going to anyway, and she was. She'd been standing here in her bathroom just a matter of minutes ago, eyeing the bottles and thinking: I'll take these pills right now, but then: No, I'll go see Aldo first, the beat of *you-and-me,* you and me together, *you-and-me-together* banging around the reckless channels of her veins.

She didn't really know what she'd expected to find when she came to see him. No, untrue, she knew what she'd expected, but she hadn't known what she *wanted,* and now all she knew was that she'd gotten nothing and was therefore more empty-handed than before. She'd wanted to assuage her curiosity, maybe; to have a taste of something so rushed and overwrought and lurid she'd have no choice but to deem it a disappointment and move on. She'd wanted to plead in his arms to be taken away from all this, from her pretense of a life. She'd wanted him to offer her his devotion, to transform into a nineteenth-century suitor and beg ardently for her hand. She'd wanted to fuck Rinaldo Damiani and then return to Marcus Waite and say: See, he wants me, I am valuable. See, I had a genius between my legs and held him inside me and swallowed him up, and then I made his brilliance mine.

Somewhere, a little voice reminded her that maybe what she'd wanted most of all was for Aldo to refuse her, to kiss her hand and say: Not tonight, Regan, not like this, not when you're not mine. But he hadn't even said that, not really, and now she felt nothing but loathing for the way she could only hate herself and still place no blame on him.

Her art. That was what he wanted.

She glanced down at her bag, contemplating the pills. She would take them, go to bed, and then tomorrow she would tell Aldo it was over between them, whatever it even was. It was done now, she had a boyfriend, she got swept up like she always got swept up; nothing they'd done was new or strange or even different. You asked too much of me, she thought to say. You wanted more from me than I am even worth.

Art. She'd never even been good at it, not really. Not in the way he would expect from her, and not in the way he would want. Her art would not satisfy him because it wasn't art at all, wasn't anything. Art was emotional truth and she had none of that, not one single truth, and this bag was proof of it along with everything else.

And anyway, it was one of her failures, and those were meant to belong exclusively to her.

Regan shook her head at her reflection—*speaking of failures,* a voice like her mother's whispered in her head—and left the bathroom, wandering to her father's office. She wasn't technically allowed inside, but for once he wouldn't be there. He would be sleeping soundly along with everyone else; except perhaps Aldo, but coincidentally the office was the room in her house that was farthest from where he was.

She cracked the door carefully and flicked on the light, wandering inside. Her father hadn't decorated it himself, so in terms of personality, it was indicative of extremely little. Revelations as to John Regan's private self were limited to the fact that he was neat, organized, and in possession of mass amounts of paper. He liked things in their place, as he always had.

Regan wandered over to the file cabinets, opening them and skimming the tops of her fingers over the tabs. Madeline, the good daughter. Charlotte, the problem. Somewhere in here he had probably actually filed them. There probably existed a folder to represent her, or at least the version of her that the paperwork could prove. Ladies and gentlemen of the jury, we have here an overprivileged child, a child with too much imagination, a child who never learned to submit herself to the authority of reality, a child who became a woman who still hadn't learned, and who would never learn, which gambles were worth it to take.

"This again," Helen had said that evening, dark eyes flicking to Aldo.

"This again," as if Rinaldo Damiani were simply a familiar antic. Just the latest piece of evidence in the file of what Regan was.

I tried to fuck him and he said no, Mom. He's different, he doesn't want me.

Of course he doesn't want you, Charlotte. Look at your behavior, it's reprehensible.

No, Regan thought, interrupting her own imagined conversation. No, you have it wrong, that's not what Helen would say. She would say it about Marc, maybe. Helen thought of Marc as elevated somehow, an impressive file, his value recognizable even with her dislike of its contents. But no, Regan's flaws were where Helen and Regan had always privately agreed, so what was more important was where they disagreed. "He's worthless, he's going nowhere, a bad influence on you"—as if Regan were still a child who could be influenced, a half-formed personality still vulnerable to change.

So no, Regan would say to her mother, *I tried to fuck him and he said no,* and Helen would say: *Good, you're better off, don't ruin things with Marc, you're only getting older and soon men will be looking for someone who isn't you. Someone who's maybe you, but younger, because wildness doesn't age with grace.*

Time, Regan thought suddenly, *you-and-me* still somewhere in the fumble of her pulse. Time had haunted Helen the same way it had bewitched Aldo. Time had made a mockery of them both, in different ways.

Amid the warps and stammers of her thoughts, Regan turned to find a painting beside her on the wall. It was a rare decorative item that John Regan had chosen for himself, having purchased it from a friend. He'd been attracted to the austerity of it, he said. Regan had been six or seven at the time, listening to her father praise the painting the same way he praised Madeline, with pride and conviction and surety. His voice had said: *This painting is good, this is an excellent painting,* and in response, Regan had thought: *Then I will be like that painting.*

Now, as an adult with a degree in art history, Regan could see that the painting wasn't anything especially impressive. It was by an artist who was quite famous now, which had been its appeal to begin with, who probably now earned a tidy sum for every commissioned work. This one, an early piece, would have only increased in value; John Regan, a master of investments, had somehow known enough to project what it could be worth.

Regan stepped toward it, eyeing the brush strokes. They weren't elementary, exactly, but neither were they particularly emotional. There was no frantic passion, no compulsive need. This wasn't a painting made to satisfy the heart, but rather to buy the groceries. It occurred to her that this was what her father had meant when he'd said "austere." Regan, with her art historian eye, understood upon viewing the painting that he had meant *severe, distant, emotionless.* Devoid of meaning, in her eyes.

Austere. It's a cold word, Aldo had said once, the memory of it igniting her with a chill.

The subject matter was an architectural landscape. All hard lines, soulless verticality. This was beauty? Of course it was, she knew that. She should take her pills. Lines like that would be incredibly easy to recreate. Replication, redundancy, recidivism. The whole painting was nothing special, take your pills, Regan (Are you happy with the space I took in your life?), it was nothing particularly impressive. How had her father loved that painting so much? How had he mistaken something so trite for brilliance? Take your pills, just take them, you've done it a million times, it means nothing and nothing will ache if you don't want it to. This was nothing. This painting was nothing. His approval was nothing. Take your pills. He would miss genius if it slapped him across the face, if it backhanded him with malice, if it tore free from its constraints to defenestrate itself from the window, if it lay awake in his guest room for the entirety of the night. Are you taking your pills, Charlotte? Of course, Mother, fucking of course I am, and if I weren't I would lie to you, because you already stole my capacity for truth. Because you needed me to be a lie, like you are. Of course you want everything to look tidy, you want everything in its place, you're a forgery, a fake. Your name isn't Helen. This painting isn't beautiful. You have never understood beauty and all the worse for you, you never will.

Regan turned and walked out, moving intently now, her footsteps less a kiss this time than a clap of thunder as she went. She dug through the drawers of her bedroom, furiously searching until she found her acrylics, her canvases, every scrap that still remained of her prior self. She hurried to grab it all, guessing at color values and tucking things under her arms. She raced back to her father's study, positioning herself across from the painting until Aldo's face had finally eased from her mind.

God, this probably wasn't even Europe; just a painting of a painting. A painting of a Google search, even, meant for nothing but to land in some rich white broker's house in a room that no one ever saw. The artist had probably tested paint swatches on the margins of a past due notice for his rent.

Good, Regan determined. Better that way. Better that the work was empty to begin with, better for it to stay hollowed out and vacant. The less there was of it, the better. Easier to cure its ills.

She glanced down at the canvas, taking hold of the brush, and for half a second, held her breath.

Then, for the first time in three years, four months, and fifteen days, Charlotte Regan began to paint.

———

"Do me a favor," she said, and Aldo looked up, surprised to find Regan in the doorway once again. This time, though, the sun was beginning to come in through the window, and he could see her clearly.

Could see clearly, too, that she hadn't slept.

"Yes," he said, "sure."

"Can you drive?" she asked him, swiping the back of her wrist against her forehead. Her hair was pulled back in a graceless ponytail, wisps escaping from her temples. "Like, you know how, right?"

"Yes," he said. Of course he did, he was from California where everyone drove, but she looked distracted. He didn't blame her for letting that escape her attention.

"Can we leave now?"

"You don't want to say goodbye?"

She shook her head. "I want to go back."

"Okay," he said.

They walked out to the garage, not saying another word. He got in the car. So did she. He glanced in the rearview mirror to notice the corner of something oversized and white poking up from where it had been placed inside a box, nestled in the backseat. He said nothing, and neither did she. She curled up in the passenger seat, resting her head against the window, and closed her eyes. Aldo started the ignition, pulling out of the drive and into the street, the little voice of her GPS instructing him. The sound of the turn signal was like a swinging pendulum, the silence emphatic and punctuated. He turned, she breathed. He thought about the cars on the road, the lines, and the precise moment he would go back to if he could.

She opened his door. He rose to his feet, took her in his arms, Don't say a word Regan, kissed her, she shoved him away, You're a pig, men are trash, it's over.

She opened his door. He waited, she slid into bed with him, Aldo, Regan, they kissed, he slid his hand under the exquisite softness of her matching pajama shorts to find the exquisite softness of her skin, he parted her legs and she sighed, I want this, Do you want this? Yes, I do, I really fucking do, she was gone in the morning, Can you drive me back?, back to her apartment, back to her boyfriend, back to her life, It was fun for a minute, Aldo, but now it's over.

She opened his door, he hurried to say, Not now, not tonight but definitely someday if you want me, she laughed in his face, Why would I ever choose you over him, over all of this, over anything?, still she fucked him with vengeful glee, with spiteful relish, she dug her fingers into his throat while she came, she tasted like cocktail bitters, You're an idiot, Aldo, it's over.

She opened his door, everything went wrong, he died in his sleep, it's over.

She opened his door, everything went right, he died in her arms, it's over.

She opened his door,

She opened his door,

She opened his door,

"Aldo," she said, and he snapped out of his reverie, glancing at her. Her eyes were still closed.

"Yeah?"

"Thanks for driving."

This, he realized with defeat, it's the getaway car. It's already done.

"You're welcome."

"I'm sorry I—" She stopped, eyes opening for a moment, and then she curled into a tighter ball around herself, closing them again. "Sorry."

"Don't be sorry," he said, and then, hoping she wouldn't ask him to explain, "I'm sorry, too."

She said nothing.

"Am I," he began, and trailed off. "Are we—?"

"I don't think we should see each other for a while," she confirmed.

His chest cracked open, spliced in half, and sealed shut.

He exhaled.

"A while?"

"Yeah, a while."

She opened his door and it was already over before she even walked in. He'd run it enough times to know. That moment would never have changed anything.

He presented his findings internally, and something heedless and desperate rejected them.

"Are you asking me to leave," he said, "or to wait?"

Her eyes opened. She stared blankly at the road.

"I don't know," she said.

She didn't close her eyes. He didn't reply.

Neither of them spoke again.

———

It didn't feel the way she thought it would. Not like it had in the past. This time it was more like live wire, electricity in her bones, catching fire. You and me together, you-and-me-together, you and me. It was a thought that woke her from slumber, like inspiration or a stomachache. It was a notion that could not be doused, couldn't be extinguished, except by the motion of her brush. She was painting to quiet her thoughts, the way they scribbled themselves in her mind, leaping and darting like insects, alighting on different planes.

Something is wrong, she thought, something is right. Something is definitely wrong but the something right is bigger, somehow, closer to truth. Wrong the way truth is when it's right.

"Have you been taking your pills?"

"No," Regan said, and the psychiatrist looked up, startled.

"Charlotte."

"I'm joking," she said, soothing her with a smile, and the doctor frowned.

"Charlotte, if there's something you'd like to discuss—"

"I'm fine," she said.

The doctor's eyes narrowed, doubtful.

Then, diplomatically, "You never told me how your weekend with your family went."

"Not well," Regan said. "My parents didn't like the friend I brought with me."

"The friend?"

"Yes, a friend." *You and me, you and me, you and me, Aldo, Aldo, Rinaldo, I am more addicted to the thought of your name on my tongue than I am to any other form of vice. The thought of having you is more dangerous than any cocktail of drugs, the idea of belonging to you endlessly destructive.* "He's a theoretical mathematician, one of those lost-in-his-head types. My mother thought he was rude."

"And your father?"

"Usually agrees with my mother."

"What about your sister?"

I like him, Madeline had said, murmuring it in Regan's ear and giving her arm a squeeze as she passed, saying nothing else.

"I don't know."

"Does it bother you? That they don't like him, I mean."

Regan cast a glance aside, impassive.

You cannot fathom the degree to which this bores me, she thought.

So she said, "I started painting again."

Regan watched the doctor go rigid with unasked questions, but reluctantly, she managed the effort to venture, "Oh?"

"Yes," Regan said, and didn't elaborate.

"Is it . . . going well, then?"

It's a fire. I used to burn out, now I just burn.

"Yes," she said.

The doctor's attention slid to the clock beside her.

"Well," the doctor said, clearing her throat. "How are things with Marcus?"

"He wants to know why I don't come to bed."

The doctor blinked, taken aback a second time. How mundane, Regan thought disdainfully. How small your concerns. How very little the scope of your understanding.

"And why don't you?"

"Because I'm painting." It's obvious, don't you see it, can't you hear it? His name is written on my skin, he scarred me, I've changed my entire shape for having fit within the enormity of his thoughts, and now the only words I know are lines and color.

"Are you—" The doctor looked tense. "Are you sleeping?"

Regan cast a listless glance out the window.

"It's getting cold fast this year," she observed, eyeing the grey streets, grey skies. Sensations of greyness, the onslaught of winter.

"It's not uncommon to experience symptoms of depression as the days get shorter."

These symptoms are, of course: sluggishness, detachment, loss of interest in the things that usually bring you joy, sensations of failure, worthlessness.

"I know," Regan said. "It's not like that," are you even listening?

"It's not?"

The grey of the sky outside was nearly blue. She could see the values in it now, again. She could look closely now, again.

"What's it like, then?" the doctor pressed, and Regan looked up, the word finding her at precisely the moment her tongue slid between her teeth.

"Incandescence," she said.

The doctor's expression struggled to contain both puzzlement and concern. "Charlotte, if something's changed, we should really discuss it."

"Yes, I know, and I told you, something has changed," Regan confirmed, rising to her feet. "I started painting again."

"Yes, that's wonderful, but Charlotte—"

"That's it," Regan said. "That's the only thing different."

"Yes, but if you're experiencing any . . . *disruption,* or if you're not responding to your medication—"

"See you in two weeks," Regan said, and slipped out of the office, pulling a pair of gloves from her purse and venturing back into the chill.

———

It was getting too cold for the motorbike to continue being a reasonable way to get places. Aldo shivered a little as he made his way to his usual spot by the tree, his phone ringing before he reached it.

"You're early," he said, and his father chuckled.

"By two minutes. How are you, Rinaldo?"

"Cold," he said.

"Those winters," Masso sighed. "You should come home."

"It's still technically fall and I will, at the end of term. After finals."

"You're missing Thanksgiving again."

"I know, I have to. Midterms to grade. Have to work on my dissertation."

"That thing I don't understand?"

"That thing you don't understand, yes."

"I understand very little."

"Nice of you to admit it. Most people in my department don't."

"Tell them to get a new hobby."

"I've been advised not to advise people."

"Probably best. Nobody likes to listen."

"No," Aldo agreed, and shivered.

Brief silence.

"Have you heard from her? The girl, the artist."

Aldo shook his head. "I don't expect to."

"Ah." A cleared throat. "Better that way. Focus on work and then come home."

"Yeah, I know."

"I have a regular here whose daughter goes to Stanford, you know. It's a good school."

"Yes, Dad, I've heard of Stanford. It's still not that close to you."

"Better Palo Alto than Chicago. Maybe try Caltech?"

"Maybe after I finish my dissertation I'll see if Caltech needs me."

"Of course they need you, Rinaldo."

"Right, sure, of course."

His phone beeped in his ear, indicating another caller. He ignored it.

"So, where are we today?"

"The Baltic," Aldo said. "No, industrial London. Dickensian London."

The beeping went away, and his father laughed. "You're just cold."

"We're slaving away in the—what's it called? Where they process sausages, the refrigerator room."

"It's all refrigerated, Rinaldo. It's meat."

"Right, well, we're there."

"I'd prefer somewhere else."

"Believe me, so would I."

The beeping started up again, and Aldo sighed.

"What is it?" asked Masso.

"Someone on the other line, hold on—"

He glanced down at his screen, teeth chattering now as he pulled his jacket tighter, and he blinked.

"Dad," he said, "I'll call you back."

"It's okay, we can talk tomorrow."

"Okay, thank you—"

His thumb shook as he hung up with his father.

"Hello?"

"Hi," said Regan.

She sounded breathless, almost frantic.

"Is everything alright?" he asked her, and she gave an apprehensive laugh.

"I need something," she said. "It's . . . an odd favor. But technically you asked me first."

"Okay," he said, uncertain. "You sure you're okay?"

"I'm fine. I'm just—" She was vibrating again. He could feel it through the phone. "I found it."

"Found what?"

"The key."

He blinked.

"Aldo?" she asked.

"Yes, I'm here."

"I need a favor."

"Yes, sure. What is it?"

"I need to see you," she said, and then, clearing her throat, "I want to, um. Draw you," she clarified, and the impulse to be startled faded, replaced instead by a steady thrum of curiosity.

"Me?" he echoed.

"Yes. Are you free today?"

He considered it, watching his breath unfurl in the biting chill.

"Yes," he said, after a moment.

"Oh, good."

He paused, and then, "Should I come to you?"

"No, no, I'll go to you. Your apartment is north facing, isn't it? Light will be good in there."

What a detail to remember, he thought. The single time she'd been there he'd been studying her, and all the while she'd been tucking away the direction his windows faced. "Yes. Okay." His breath was starting to hurt in his lungs, straining them inside the containment of his ribs. "Maybe around twelve, twelve thirty?"

"Twelve thirty, I think. I should finish what I'm doing here."

"Do you need me to . . . to do anything, or—?"

"No." She laughed. "No, Aldo, you don't need to do anything."

"Oh. Okay." He exhaled.

"Maybe smoke something," she suggested wryly. "You know, if you need to."

He shook his head. "I don't," he said.

"Alright, fine. See you at twelve thirty, then."

"You sure you're fine?"

"Yes, why wouldn't I be?"

"You sound," he began, and then stopped. "Good," he decided.

The word he'd meant was *bright*, perhaps even *blinding*, but it didn't make sense, and she laughed again.

"You sound good, too. I'll see you soon?"

"Yes. Bye, Regan."

"Bye, Aldo," she said, and was gone.

He glanced down at his phone awash in numbness, watching her name disappear from his screen.

Maybe he'd done it, he thought. Maybe some version of him had gone back in time, changed it, fixed it somehow, unlocked the door that she'd never ended up opening and that had somehow brought her back. Maybe he'd solved it, somewhere, and his current self would never even know.

Or maybe it wasn't done yet. Not yet.

He shivered in the cold, pulling his jacket tighter around him, and picked up his helmet.

That was enough thinking for one day.

————

Regan stared down at the storage space she'd rented, which was currently occupied by fifteen canvases of various sizes. One, the painting from her father's office, sat in the corner solemnly, staring out over the others it had spawned, all replicas of other peoples' originals. This, she reminded herself with a sigh, was the problem. It *had* been the problem, anyway, until yesterday afternoon when she'd been toying with the storage room key, thinking about nothing but the shape of it.

She used to dream like that, in nothing but lines and patterns and textures. Art was a language of both limitless vocabulary and limited syntax; endless concepts to express with boundless opportunities to express them, but only a finite number of ways to do it. Color, line, shape, space, texture, and value, six elements in total, which was newly revelatory to her until she realized why, running her finger along the edge of the key.

Bees.

She looked down at her forgeries, her elfin imitations.

"I'm going to make something today," she told them. "Something new."

They stared unsupportively back at her.

Why him? asked the mimicry from her father's study.

"Because," she said. Because I know he'll sit for me. Because I know he won't mock me, won't suffocate me, won't kill this fragile little thing I've found, this fledgling breath I've taken. Because he will know what it means, because he asked me to, because he asked. Because he's the thing I can't unsee. Because I don't know if I can get him right without looking, without proof, but also because I need to know, because I've already tried. Because either this is how everything changes, or this is how it ends.

She'd already called the museum and told them she needed the day. They weren't opposed. They told her to feel better soon, though she'd specifically never said she was unwell. That was the one thing she was not.

She'd already called Marc, too, shortly after the museum.

"It's cute you found a hobby, babe," he had said the previous evening, kissing her head while she pulled her sketchbook closer, surreptitiously blocking his view of her drawings with her arm. Would he recognize the hand, the shape of the palm, the angle of the fingers? Had he seen them reflected in her eyes the way she'd seen them in her mind? Probably not, but she wasn't ready for him to know the outlines of her thoughts, to see the geography of them.

That was all art was, wasn't it? The blatant exposition of the inside of her head.

"I have therapy today," she had told him. "Might go shopping for a bit afterward."

"Didn't you just see your psychiatrist?"

"Yes. I just have a lot on my mind."

She didn't actually know why she had bothered calling Marc to begin with. It wasn't as if she didn't do what she wanted most of the time, or rather, all of it. She supposed she'd wanted him to think: That's odd; maybe she'd wanted him to say: Are you fine? Possibly she'd wanted him to sense that something was systematically failing; to flag the relevant instincts that might suggest this conversation was not like any others they had had.

She dared him to ask: Are you lying?

What he said was: "Well, good that you're taking care of yourself," and then he told her he loved her, that he was heading into a meeting with a prospective client's firm, and then he promised he'd see her tonight before hanging up, the screen going black in her hand.

Regan eyed the painting from her father's office, replaying the mechanisms of its conception. She'd stayed up all night working on it, then spent days perfecting it when she got home, then stared at it for hours upon conclusion. The brushstrokes were precisely the artist's, not hers. It was thievery in every possible aspect of its creation. She had left nothing of herself in its reproduction, merely cloning the vacant starvation that had existed there before, and then she'd done the same another dozen times; proving to herself that, at the very least, she could still see, she could still think, she could still interpret.

But that wasn't enough, and she knew it. Art, a voice buzzed in her ear, was creation. It was dissecting a piece of herself and leaving it out for consumption, for speculation. For the possibility of misinterpretation and the inevitability of judgment. For the abandonment of fear the reward would have to be the possibility of ruin, and that was the inherent sacrifice. That, her mind whispered, was art, and she slid her finger along the edge of the storage room key, the jagged edges like teeth scraping over her skin. You and me, you-and-me, you and me, my heart will burn a hole through my chest until I know, and I am not done, I can't be done yet, this cannot be the ending.

Which was when she'd picked up the phone, choosing the contact that read *For When You've Found It*, and dialed Rinaldo Damiani.

————

She was at his door with a sketchbook and pencils, dressed in a boxy grey sweater and jeans. She was wearing her garnet earrings, he noted, but had foregone any other details. She looked determined, almost defiant, when she opened her mouth and said, still fidgeting, "I want to be clear. This is just me drawing you, nothing else."

"Okay," he said, and beckoned her inside.

His apartment had track lighting, a consequence of the owner's tastes. Upon entry, Regan began traversing the apartment, turning lights on, turning them off. "Do you have something to—?"

She gestured and he nodded, handing her the step stool that had been tucked into the corner of the kitchen. She clambered on top of it, angling the bulbs.

"Careful with the—"

"They're not hot yet," she assured him briskly, then pointed for him to stand by the window. "Wait over there," she said, and then, "I'll adjust you in a sec."

He obliged, positioning himself beside the window as she'd asked, and she frowned at nothing, arranging the empty space inside her head.

"Okay," she said, and then frowned again, at him this time. "Is that what you're wearing?"

It was his usual T-shirt and black jeans.

"I'm currently wearing it, yes," he said. "Conceptually, no. I could change."

Her frown transitioned from thoughtful to hesitant.

"Can I . . . ?" she asked, gesturing vaguely to his closet.

"You're the artist," he said, beckoning for her to go ahead.

She turned, riffling through his wardrobe, which was sparse to say the least. He watched her, noting her look of uncertainty, and cleared his throat.

"How have you been?" he attempted.

"Fine," she said. She paused, biting something back, and then turned over her shoulder to look at him. "I'm still with Marc," she said.

"Right," he said.

"Nothing's new, really."

He inadvertently made a low sound, something like a coughed-up laugh, and she turned sharply.

"What?" she demanded.

"Obviously something's new," he said, and amended, "Or, I don't know. Everything is."

"Something, or everything?"

"You tell me."

"Nothing's changed."

"Something's changed," he countered, and she spun back to his closet, directing her attention somewhere else, to the space between hangers.

"I'm painting again," she said, eyeing his shirts.

"But you wanted to draw me?"

He deliberately placed the emphasis on *draw,* not *me.*

"Yes," she said. "I'd paint you, but that's more things to carry around. Maybe another time."

So it had been impulsive, then. Or compulsive. "What are you going to draw?"

"I don't know. You, I guess. I figured you wouldn't mind."

"I don't."

"Well, there you go, other people would."

"Fair." He paused. "Are you doing some kind of anatomical study, or . . . ?"

She froze, pivoting to look at him.

"Yes," she said, so slowly he wasn't sure her brain and her mouth were actually in agreement. "Yes," she confirmed, more forcefully that time, and then, with a lift of her chin, "Yes. So you'll have to take off your clothes, probably."

He blinked. "Oh."

"Just your shirt," she assured him, and then grimaced. "Well, no, actually. All of it."

"All of it," he echoed slowly, and she nodded.

"I don't want to do fabrics right now," she said, stepping conclusively away from his closet. "They're an illusion, and besides, I don't like any of yours. I want to show how the shadows really fall."

"And you want me for a model?"

"Of course. Who else would do it?"

"How do you know I will? I haven't said yes."

"Well, I know," she said firmly, and he considered that for a moment.

"What are you going to do with the drawings?"

"Hang them in the Louvre" was delivered with perfect solemnity.

"They have higher standards," he said, "I presume. I hope."

"Well, maybe you underestimate me, hm? Besides, you said you wanted the art key," she informed him, shutting the door to his wardrobe and advancing in his direction. She'd made up her mind; clearly this was happening. "This is the closest thing to having it," she said, daring him to argue, "isn't it?"

"I picked the art key because I was almost positive you wouldn't give it to me," he said, which was true. He was capable of devoting his thoughts to any number of impossible problems. He was also, as it turned out, a seeker of unavailable things.

"Well, you were wrong," she said.

Then she flicked a glance over him that said, Go on, strip.

He relented, giving his T-shirt a tug over his head, then paused for "Where do you want me?"

She eyed his space again. "The bed, I guess."

It was as neatly made as a bed of its bare elements could be. She strode forward and pulled back the duvet, arranging the sheets, then propped his two pillows against the wall. "Here, sit here."

He slid out of his jeans, his boxers, folding them carefully and placing them on the floor before doing as she asked. That he was naked felt somehow much less relevant than the fact that she would be analyzing him, theorizing him in her own way, clothes or no clothes. He felt suddenly very conscious of what it was to be an equation.

He eased himself down on the bed, leaning back, but she quickly stopped him with a hand on his sternum, readjusting the pillows behind him. Her fingers on his skin were diligent and impassive, shifting to his shoulders, lean this way, chin up slightly, no down, okay now put your knee up like this, yes, bend it like that, good, perfect. She paused, eyeing him again, then took his elbow, resting it on his knee. Like this? Yes, like this, all their communication silent, him looking at her while she arranged the pieces of him. She glanced over at the window, up at the lights, back down at him. Should he look away? He turned his chin, angling it in the same direction as his outstretched arm, and she corrected the motion by dragging him back, taking his chin firmly in her hand.

"Look this way," she said aloud, and angled his chin over his shoulder, directing his gaze to her. "I'm going to do some studies on your hands," she explained, jiggling his fingers to make sure they were draped loosely, "and on your legs, but then I want to do your neck, too. And your face."

"Portraiture?" he asked.

"Only incidentally." Just like that he'd become an object, a feature in the room like a table or a lamp. She was looking at him the way she might look at a ring of condensation. "Will you be comfortable like this for a bit?"

"Yes, it's fine."

"Good." She slid one finger under his chin, holding it still. "Don't drop it."

"Should I look at you?"

"Look wherever you want, just don't drop your chin. Keep your fingers relaxed, and don't forget to breathe."

"Why would I forget to breathe?"

"I don't know, it's just what we tell people."

"We?"

"I was trained, Aldo. In a classroom. With other artists."

"Ah," he said, "so you *are* an artist."

She gave him an admonishing look.

"Hush," she said, and took a step back, pulling out one of the stools from his kitchen island. "I'm going to sit here and draw, okay?"

"Okay."

"You can talk, if you want. I'm just sketching."

"Talk about what?"

"Anything," she said, choosing a pencil and glancing down, motioning first in the air before he heard the low, scratchy sound of graphite on parchment. "Time, if you want."

Time.

Once upon a time.

Time to begin.

Time and time again.

Time after time.

Time is a function of lies, a trick of the light, a mistranslation.

"There's a group of about eight hundred people, a tribe in Brazil," Aldo said. "Called the Pirahã."

This amused her, it seemed. "Okay. Tell me about them."

"Well, they don't concern themselves with anything except what they've personally witnessed. Living memory, I guess you could say. They don't prepare for the future, and they don't store food. Just . . . whatever they have, they eat." He paused, listening to the scratching sound of her pencil, and then, "They have no religion—which makes sense, really, because what is religion except the vague promise of a reward nobody's ever seen?"

Regan glanced up. "What does this tribe have to do with time?"

"Well, presumably time is a completely different shape when you're only living in the immediate present," he said.

"Different shape," she echoed, returning her attention to the drawing. "Not hexagonal?"

"That's the direction of time," he reminded her, "not the shape of it."

"So what's the shape?"

"Well, I don't know. I can only understand time within my experience of it."

"Which is?"

"A little different from the Pirahã," he said drily. "As in, I expect to wake up in the morning. I need light, refrigeration, all that, so I pay the electricity bill every month. That sort of thing." She was looking at the bend of his knee, tilting her head to scrutinize the angle of it. "I can't possibly understand what time looks like because I'm inside my experience of it, but whatever version of time I'm inside has to be different than the version the Pirahã occupy."

"You say that like you're trapped," Regan noted. "Or they are."

"Well, aren't I? Aren't we? We can't speed it up or slow it down. We can't navigate it."

"Not yet," she said, sparing him half a smile.

"Well, we only know that time can't possibly exist within the Babylonian denominations of sixty. Not *actually*. A second is only a second within *our perception*. We try to standardize it, to make it useful, but we don't know the rules. We'll probably never know the rules."

"And how does that make you feel?" She was chuckling to herself, making a private joke.

"Trapped," he said, and she looked up.

"Does it?"

"Yes. From time to time."

"Like you're in a mortal prison?"

"You're being facetious," he observed, watching her mouth quirk with confirmation, "but yeah, kind of. Do people ever ask you what you're doing next?"

"Always. All the time."

"Right," he said. "So that's my point."

"Don't drop your chin," she told him.

"Right."

She turned her attention back to the parchment, continuing to draw.

"I don't mind being trapped," she murmured, the little strokes of her pencil like caresses to the page. "Sometimes I like it. Easier. Nothing to think about."

He drummed his fingers on his knee. She looked up warningly, telegraphing a glance that said, Stop that.

He obliged.

"You don't actually want things to be easy, do you?" he said.

"No, not really. But I wish I did."

"Why?"

"Well, if time really was a trap and I was on some sort of predetermined course, that would be a relief," she said. "The idea that I might have options or other time-spaces to occupy is a little overwhelming."

"Don't you like being overwhelmed?"

A blink. "Why would you say that?"

"I don't know," he said. "You just seem like you're looking for something to overwhelm you."

"I seem like I'm looking for something?"

"I think," Aldo said slowly, "that if you weren't, you wouldn't be here."

She looked up again, pausing the motion of her pencil this time.

It frustrated him immensely that he would never be able to prove that time didn't stop when she met his eye. Though, he reminded himself, maybe if he committed it to memory then he could return to it in another shape, with better understanding.

Eventually Regan cleared her throat. "I'm going to draw your mouth," she said, "so we probably shouldn't talk for a bit."

"Okay," he said, and as she dropped her attention back to her parchment, Aldo contemplated going back to live in that single second of time, when he and she had existed in perfect synchronicity.

———

His second toe was longer than his first, his feet were narrow, the arches were high and largely free of calluses. Had he been born to wear high heels he would have blistered unrelentingly, and Regan was relieved that he'd probably never know that pain. His calves were narrow and thin and so were his quadriceps. They were well-proportioned, though something had happened to his knee. There was a scar there, maybe surgery, maybe he'd fallen at some point. There had been no mother to kiss away the pain, and now the mark of inattention would remain.

His remarkable lines were, by chronology of looking: the one along the side of his thigh, the curve from his shoulder around his bicep, the ridge along his clavicle, the edge of his jaw. His color gradient was more saturated in his legs and then faded near his hips, then warmed again in his arms, his neck, his face. The most distinctive space was the one unseen between his eyes and thoughts, separated by what seemed to Regan to be a distance of miles, eons, light-years.

His fingers, which she already knew better than anything aside from his mouth and his eyes, started to move after only a few minutes of silence. His brain had gone somewhere else and his fingers danced along with his thoughts, almost swaying. He was drawing tiny shapes in the air, little letters, feverishly recounting his theories to empty space. The room felt full and perhaps even crowded with everything he'd injected into it, though his chin remained level in allegiance to where she'd placed it. There was no noticeable cleft there; the whole of him was smooth and uninterrupted, aside from the stubble of facial hair he was never fully rid of, and the natural shadow beneath the bones of his cheeks. He was breathing steadily, rhythmically, his pulse visible along his neck. Regan counted his heartbeats, tapping lightly and telling herself that was important for an accurate representation. Man at Rest, she'd thought to call the drawing, only he wasn't nearly at rest at all.

His fingers were moving; he'd caught onto something again. Something caught flame in his head and it showed in his limbs, disrupting them. His brow had furrowed; he'd pulled his knee in closer. She could see the lines on his stomach where his abdomen had been compressed. The slope of his torso to his hips was more obvious now, and everything was all wrong. He was himself again, precisely the way that she'd always known she would never be able to capture.

"Stop," she said, and his thoughts jolted back from wherever they'd gone, his attention snapping back to hers. "You're moving too much."

"Oh." He shifted, trying to adjust himself. "Like this?"

"No, Aldo, not—" She sighed, setting her sketchpad down and coming over to him, readjusting him. "Leg here, hands here. Relax your fingers," she said, shaking out his knuckles, and he gave her a look of amusement. "No, *relax* them, just—here, let me—"

She slid her fingers between his, curling and uncurling his hand with hers, and then let her fingers drape smoothly over his knee, silently beckoning for his to do the same. She waited, palm resting warmly over his knuckles, and then gradually, finger by finger, he relaxed.

She could feel the stillness in his torso; he wasn't breathing. She'd told him to breathe, and of course he hadn't listened. "Breathe," she instructed, and his fingers tensed again. "Aldo," she said, exasperated, and then, nudging him over, she sat beside him, fixing things as she went.

Knee like this, yes, thank you. Arm like this. *Curve* the hand, yes, like that, let it fall.

She turned, his eyes rising from where they'd been on her neck.

She couldn't prevent the urge to know his thoughts. She wanted to lace them between her fingers, to root them in her hands, to twine them around her limbs until he'd secured her within the invisible web of his carefully ordered madness.

"Time," she asked him, "or bees?"

"Just regular old quantum groups this time," he said, gently. She felt the words as if he'd placed them in her hands. "I don't actually think about bees as much as you think I do."

"What's it like," she murmured, "thinking so much that your whole body changes?"

"Fairly normal by now." He paused. "When I'm not in motion, I feel sort of . . . stagnant."

"Racing thoughts make the rest of you want to run, too?"

"Something like that, yeah."

She ran her fingers over his knuckles, flexing and unflexing them. You and me, she thought rhythmically, you-and-me.

"Can I tell you the truth?" she asked, not looking at him.

He leaned forward, his cheek brushing her shoulder, and nodded.

"I'm not taking my pills," she said. "I'm not sleeping." She exhaled raggedly, "I'm . . . I have problems. Like, diagnosed ones. Ones I should be treating somehow."

Then, regretfully, she added, "I suppose I should have told you that before."

He turned his head. She could feel his eyes on her, even if she refused to meet them.

"Do you feel like you have problems?" he asked.

"No." She turned to face him, grimacing, and he let his posture fall, abandoning the effort of posing. "I feel a bit like . . . I don't know. Like I did, or maybe I still do, but not the same. The roof's been patched but the shutters are still broken."

"And before?"

"Water got in everywhere. No floods, just a steady drip somewhere impossible to locate. Always about three degrees colder than I'd like to be."

"Ah. What changed?"

"I'm painting now." I can paint now, again. "I don't want to stop. I don't even want to fix the shutters, I just want to flood the damn house." She cleared her throat. "No, I'm lying. I don't want a flood, but I don't even want the house." A pause. "I want to light the house on fire and walk away while it burns."

"Okay," Aldo said, "then do it."

"I can't."

"Why not?"

"Because that's technically mania. Or hypomania."

"Well, I'm not a doctor."

His mouth was twisted up and if she looked down, she would see herself—she would see the way she had leaned into his arms—but she didn't. She couldn't look away from his face, which did not say: What's wrong with you? but instead, said: Hi. Hello. Nice to meet you.

"You haven't asked me if I'm lying," she said.

He shrugged. "Because I already know you're not."

"The drawing thing," she said, "it's not a ruse. I'm really going to draw you."

"I know."

"I mean it."

"I know, I believe you."

"But you said I seemed different."

"Yes, and you are. You sound different."

She grimaced. "That would be the racing thoughts, probably."

"Take your pills, then. If that's what you want."

She spread her fingers over his chest, possessing him.

"I don't want to," she confessed. "I can't go back, not anymore." You don't just unburn, she thought desperately, and in answer, Aldo smoothed a cool hand over hers, tracing the shapes of her fingers.

Her nose slid under his chin, grateful, as her lips brushed the motion of his swallow.

"Go back to what?" he asked.

The question smelled like him. His fingers were toying with her spine, skipping over her vertebrae like the motion of his formulas. What would they do, she thought, when they were put to work solving her?

She shivered, breath quickening, and his touch at her back rested where cashmere met skin, expectant.

"You can't fix me," she whispered to him, her mouth tracing his neck. Do you understand, do you know what you hold in your hands, do you know how readily it breaks?

"I don't see anything to fix," he said.

She dug her nails into his chest, a little violence to combat her own softness, to subvert the threats of her insecurity, and he had her in his arms in less than an instant, well before she could refuse, before she could even think to do it herself. She wrapped herself around him, raggedly compliant, and her fingers parsed through his hair with her lips on his scars, his hand curled around the back of her neck. You and me, thudded her pulse, You and me, and his answered, Yes, yes, yes, and she could feel it slither through her limbs. You and me together, Yes I know, I feel it too. Lean in and whisper it back to me; Come close and tell me again.

His mouth was warm against her throat, breath soft beside her jaw, and the sigh that left her lips escaped without permission, receding into hunger so powerful she wondered how she had failed to satisfy it before. This wasn't the answer, she thought desperately, and while her pulse said: You and me, her mind reminded her: This moment will always taste of filth, it will smell of dust, until you cleanse your palate.

She slithered away in a rapid moment, rising to her feet and picking up her sketchbook, her pencils, throwing them in her bag and heading for the door. He sat up but didn't move, didn't follow, didn't say a word. Her hands were shaking, and she darted out his door, into the hallway, *you you you* in the pace of her feet.

She had already hit the button on the elevator before she suddenly turned around, half-sprinting back.

He opened the door on the first knock, clad now in boxers. "Yes?"

"Aldo, I—"

She looked up at him, helpless.

"Do you want to see them?" she asked, lacking any better offering as she gripped her sketchbook in her unsteady hands, and Aldo slid his gaze over her in silence.

He let a moment stretch between them. "Are you ready to show me?"

Are you ready? his green eyes had asked, Because if I let you in, I will not let you go.

She exhaled, understanding.

"No," she said. "No. Not yet."

"Okay," he said.

She took a step back.

"Okay," she agreed, and left.

When she came back, as she inevitably would, he would open the door and she would open her arms, and for the rest of the night there would be no more questions. There would be some hours between those occurrences, though; perhaps a day or so.

First there would be Madeline, home for the holiday, saying: What are you doing with Dad's painting? and then there would be the usual between them: Don't tell Mom.

Jesus, Char, those look identical.

Yeah, yeah, I know.

Did you paint that?

Don't tell Mom.

Charlotte, what are you doing? Are you in trouble?

No, I'm not, just don't tell Mom, okay?

I won't, but Char—Wait a minute. Charlotte, are those my earrings?

Yes, do you want them back?

No, they look better on you.

I know, and then a hug goodbye, a kiss to the top of Carissa's head.

Then what, after Madeline?

Then the dealer, obviously, who would ask: Is this real?

Of course it's real. See the signature? Authenticate it however you like.

This is worth . . . Well, this is worth a tidy sum, to tell you the truth.

Tidy enough for you to want it?

Yes, definitely enough for that, let me make a phone call.

What next?

A bag, the bag that Regan had always known she'd one day pack, only this time when she stopped to place the things that mattered inside it she'd find that nothing here had mattered at all. Instead she'd throw nearly everything into garbage bags, countless balloons of bulging plastic to contain all her immaterial materials, and that would be another conversation. Two conversations, actually.

The first would be short: Regan, I'm walking into a meeting, what is it?

Nothing important, just letting you know I won't be there when you get home, thank you for the shape you took in my life but it's over now, it doesn't fit.

Then the second: May I help you?

Yes, how much is all this worth?

Well, I really don't know, this is an entire wardrobe.

Yes, I know. How soon will you know?

Maybe . . . maybe tomorrow? The next day?

That's fine, take your time, here's my phone number.

Where are you located? If we can't accept some things—

I don't know yet. If you can't accept it, just donate it.

Are you sure? This is a lot of stuff, most of it looks expensive.

Yes, I'm sure.

Then, when everything was gone, she'd find something, anything.

Three hundred square feet? Sure, fine, she didn't need space. What did she possess? As long as the light was good, it would do.

We'll need to run a standard credit check, obviously. You understand.

I can give you a year's rent upfront.

You . . . you can?

Yes. Cashier's check okay?

Well . . . all right, yes, fine.

(It's not the best neighborhood, but not the worst, either.)

She wouldn't throw her phone in the river or the lake. That was running away, which she wasn't doing.

She wasn't running away. She wasn't running at all. She was coming back, and it would only look and feel like running until she knocked on Aldo's door and he pulled it open, and then it would go like this:

Are you ready?

And she would say: Yes, I'm ready.

Come on, Rinaldo, let's start again.

PART FOUR

FIRSTS.

The first time with her is rushed, embarrassingly so, faster than he'd like. The first night is her at his door, saying words he can hardly hear through the effort of straining to recognize reality, to stop his head from saying, Is this a dream? Haven't we dreamt this?, and reminding himself that no, this was real, this was real because behind him the water will boil soon, the salt will go in and then the pasta, the oven will beep and dinner will come next. His brain is not thinking, Oh, she's here, I knew it, instead his brain is no use to him at all. It is thinking, What time is this? and it doesn't mean six o'clock, it doesn't mean evening, it doesn't even mean dinnertime, it just means, Where are we *in the cosmos,* because I have lived this so many times in fantasy that it has become six different forms of reality and now, tell me, which reality are we?

The first time, he doesn't ask any questions that would count as questions; nothing journalistic like when, how, where, what, and most importantly, why? As in, why him, why anyone at all, but most especially, *why him*? But he doesn't ask anything informative, he only steps aside, permits her through. She glances around at the simmering water and the pasta and the chicken in the oven; she recognizes she's entered a room that did not previously have plans to contain her and now has to expand. She opens her mouth to apologize and he, unthinking—thinking only that he doesn't want her to be sorry, that in fact "sorry" from her tongue should be reserved for only the most capital of offenses, such as disappearing from his life forever—he takes her hand and holds it, urgently. She looks down and closes her mouth, and maybe her heart beats faster. Maybe her breath quickens, maybe it stops. He can't hear the sounds of her physicalities over the loud rushing in his ears. He is a mathematician, a scientist, and he is precise in his waiting, so she is the one who graciously fumbles for him, toward him, on his behalf. He lifts her onto the kitchen island and they're both still mostly clothed when he fills her, right there next to the pasta that will soon be cooked. His forehead presses to hers as her hips lift from the countertop that might be marble, might not, he's never been an expert in materials but he knows that she feels soft and smooth, like velvet. He knows her tactility now and he can never go back to not knowing. The water boils and he comes, he doesn't know if she does, he asks her and she laughs. She pulls his mouth to hers, says to his tongue and his teeth and his shortness of breath, I'm hungry, what's for dinner?

The second time is slower, lazy even. This time they're both full, wine splashing on his shirt because they're drunk on each other, unstable. He doesn't taste the pasta at all, only watches her as she eats it, as she exclaims over it, Did you make this? Yes, yes I made it, Masso says Barilla is unacceptable, Well, good, all the better for me. Her blouse is unbuttoned, he can see her bra and the redness at her breasts where his lips and probably the stubble at his jaw have rudely marred her skin. He thinks, desperately, I should shave. She catches him looking and laughs, leans forward, points to the wine on his shirt and says, You're a mess. He thinks of the way her legs wrap around his hips. Yes, he is a mess. Put it in the wash before it stains, she says, and while he would happily sacrifice a T-shirt for evidence that any of this took place he says, Okay, okay fine, removes his shirt and places it in the washing machine (in-unit laundry, the most blessed of blessings) to be washed, only she's lingering in the hallway, looking at him. He was inside her, she liked his food, she came here for him. It washes over him in a wave, dawning, and it numbs him first before setting him alight; before he illuminates with it, resurrected. She wanders over to him and leans in, inspecting his handiwork, and closes the lid of the washing machine. He steps behind her as she pretends to scrutinize the dials. He rests his hand on her hips and she shivers.

This time, it will all be for her.

He places her hands flat on the washing machine as it starts to vibrate with effort, buzzing beneath her palms. From where he stands, lips on the nape of her neck, the whole thing quakes with waiting. This time, it's Barolo and her on his palate. This time he takes off her clothes slowly, strips her petals gently, waits until her knuckles go white on the machine and then threads his tongue between her lips, hands curled around her thighs. He will forget the pasta, he'll forget the color of the label, but he'll remember the wine. He will think of it every time he sees her bare legs, every time he finds himself at her back. Clean laundry, red wine, and her, from the first time he finds the little discolored freckle on the back of her knee and every time after, marking it like the north star. This time, she finishes with a gasp. It grits through her teeth and she leans back to tell him, raggedly, I knew you would feel like this. I knew I would feel you everywhere, in my whole body, I knew it. She's rocking against him slowly and whispering I knew it, I knew it, I knew it, in his ear until she sighs again, his hands tight on her hips.

The third time is shaky, full of little aftershocks that climb up his spine and descend again, free-falling toward a collision. They're on the roof, it's freezing, he tries to take her back downstairs to his apartment where it's warm but she says, No, no, let's stay up here, I feel alive like this, like I could die like this. He doesn't tell her how often he has the same thought but thinks that maybe she can see it, because somehow her palms find his cheeks. She's wearing his clothes, wrapped under a blanket with him when her hands wander, when they express their disinterest in being empty, when they fill themselves with him. He chokes out, I'm not a teenager anymore, she laughs, Aren't you? and yes, she's right, he's hard again, god damn it. There are rules about this, somewhere. Rules of physicality, rules of basic human exertion, rules about not fucking on the damn roof but she is adamant and he's still licking the taste of her from his lips. He has the unlit joint between his teeth, pretending he's capable of refusing. He isn't. She can see as much. She lowers her head to call his bluff and the joint falls from his mouth somewhere into the cracks in the concrete below, into the fissures of his constitution. He gives up, twists around, and both of them are shaking with cold and probably adrenaline and this is what he will remember, the way the muscles in his arms and in her legs are shaking while he's holding himself up; while she consumes him.

Consumption, that's what this is. He is being willingly eaten alive. He says, Good night, and she smiles, says, See you in the morning, she tangles her legs with his. She anchors him, then pulls away and orbits him. He moves, she moves. In sleep, she's different. Her hair is soft and smooth, and he doesn't touch it for fear of waking her, but he wants to. In sleep, she looks like she's floating, like he and she are somewhere underwater, both holding their respective breaths. She wakes around four and seems disoriented—How did we get here, down here in this ocean?—and then finds him and comforts herself aloud with "Oh, good." The fourth time he touches her, it's because of that: "Oh, good." What was she thinking, saying that? Was she thinking what he hopes—"Oh, good, it's still you, I didn't dream it"—or is she thinking something else? "Oh, good, you didn't leave." "Oh, good, I still feel the same as I did last night." "Oh, good, to-day is Sunday, I've woken up and didn't die in my sleep," what is it? He asks her silently while he fucks her, begs it with his lips pressed to hers. He hasn't even begun to think about her kiss, about the way it feels to kiss her, which is normally step one but with her is somewhere beyond intimacy. Being the thing on her tongue means something more to her, he can tell it does. It has required more per-mission to kiss her lips, to share her breath, than to slide inside her pussy, to occupy her cunt.

"Oh, good," she said when she woke to the sight of him, and that's what he thinks while he kisses her.

Oh, good. It's you.

There is a brief reprieve as she comes with him to church. This time she holds his hand while they enter, doesn't drop it. They should have showered, probably, but he likes that she's all over him. Makes him feel holier that way, shrouded in something that contains no doubt. He wears the smell of her draped over his shoulders, where her legs have been. No one else knows the lengths he has gone, the man he has become since touching her. He thinks of all the other versions of himself making love to all the other versions of her and resolves to pluck them out of their alternate realities, out of their alternate spaces and times, to place them in this one. He hopes she has not developed the ability to read his mind, that she isn't seeing herself bent over the pew or perched, queenly, atop the altar, with his rapturous head between her legs. He is especially worshipful this Sunday. This par-ticular Sunday, he willingly falls to his knees.

The fifth time is all newness and strangeness, unfamiliarity it-self. She shows him the studio she's rented. It's difficult to get to by public transportation but he prefers to walk, anyway. She shows him her paintings, her drawings of him. All of it is impossible, fuck, she's impossible. She took a blank page and turned it into something beautiful, how could she do that? She's a magician, of course she can read his mind, she knows exactly what he was doing to her for an hour in the Lord's house. She smiles. You're being awfully quiet, he says, Am I? She shrugs. We should shower. She is slippery, difficult to hold, but still he holds on tightly.

They part for a while, he has to work, though in truth he doesn't want to overwhelm her. What he wants to do is get on his bike and go somewhere he can scream into empty air, where he can take a breath that is not full of her just to prove it can still mean something, just in case. Just in case. She's elusive, impulsive, she wanted him yesterday and he was "Oh, good" today, but will he be something less tomorrow? Will he be "Oh, hm," and then eventually just "Oh." He writes down his thoughts, or tries to. What escapes him are shapes, organized ones, fitted cleanly together. Order, that's what he needs. His apartment is a mess, it has dirty dishes and the washing machine contains a stained shirt and she is everywhere. She is in all of his spaces and all of his thoughts. He contemplates formulas and degrees of rationality and they all turn into her. He thinks about time, which has only recently begun, or at least now feels different. He thinks: The Babylonians were wrong; time is made of her.

The sixth time, he notices paint flecks on her arms, a little on her cheek. He laughs, What were you painting? She says very seriously, You, always you, I can't help it. Only you these days. Jesus, he thinks, something is wrong with us, we are unwell, no one has ever felt any of this without destruction. Empires have fallen like this, he thinks, but it only makes him want her more, makes him look at his hands and think, My god, what a waste of time doing anything else but holding her. What a waste, and then he says aloud, JesusfuckingChrist what have you done to me? And she says, Kiss me.

He kisses her, thinks, Go on, ruin me. Wreck me, please.

She kisses him back and she does.

———

The first time they argue she is sure that she loves him. It's the first time she really knows it, because even though her thoughts have been telling her so for days and somewhere there is a burning for him that is impossible to extinguish, she doesn't really believe that love is anything more than science. Hormones, evolution, love, nuclear fusion, quantum theory, it's all just a theory. It's all just a sensation they tried to give an explanation to because humans are small, and stupid. Because people want to be romantic about everything, they want to give names to the stars, they want to tell stories. Love is a story, that's all, until she fights with him for the first time.

The first time they fight, she knows she loves him because she has never been worth the fight before. With others, with Marc, it was always Regan, please be reasonable, Regan, I don't want to do this right now, I'm tired. Regan, are you being difficult because you're bored? And for her, it was always Fine, fine, I'm sorry. Maybe not the I'm sorry part because she was almost never sorry, but the giving up was always there. The sense of resignation, it was inescapably tied to The Fight. Before Aldo, love was concession. Love was a withering Yes, dear, and the sensation of Don't fight, Be careful of the eggshells, You are not at home here and can easily be sent away. She had thought love meant being Reasonable, a proper noun for a proper effort, for the evasive toil of Love and Relationships, and it made her think, from time to time, of her briefest love story. Of the time in Istanbul when she'd been crossing the street, a train blocking her path, a boy standing inside the middle car, beautiful. His eyes found hers somehow (eyes always found hers) and he beckoned to her, Come, come. She shook her head, No, don't be crazy, he pouted and mouthed, Please. And for a second—for a moment—for a breath—she considered it. Considered boarding the train just to tell him: Is this destiny? She didn't and he disappeared, gone forever. She doesn't remember his face anymore but remembers the sensation: Am I the girl who stays while others leave?

Sometimes she hates that she didn't possess the requisite lunacy to board that train, and the itch to mend it, to do so in some other way, has always stayed with her. It festered into an impulsiveness that will not disappear. She thinks: I hate that I didn't get on that train, I hate that I watched him go and fade to nothing, and at first she thinks she loves Rinaldo Damiani the same way she loved the boy on the train. As if watching him go will haunt her for the rest of her life.

But then they fight and she thinks: Maybe this is different. It's not a very big fight, but the important thing is that they have it, that it happens. Surprisingly, this isn't how she knows he loves her. This isn't about him at all. She already knows his brain is something foreign to her, something that contains little pockets of mysticism that she will never understand, no matter how intently she can dig her greedy tendrils. So when he says, _____, she says, _____, mostly just to challenge him. Later she will forget what the argument was even about, only that it happened, and most importantly that when she said ???, he said !!!, and did not dismiss it. He didn't say, Regan, do you really want to do this now? Regan, I'm tired, let's not. Regan, go to bed, it's late and you're arguing just to argue. He doesn't do any of that, instead he !!s when she ??s and when she !!s he ??s, and she should be annoyed, she knows. She should be irritated or tired, the way people always are with her, but she isn't. Instead she thinks: I love him, and for a moment it doesn't matter whether he loves her back. It is enough to have known that the inside of her chest is more than a place for storage.

She knows better than to confuse apologies with affection. People are always sorry, so when he crawls toward her on the mattress she knows to wait for it, to sigh and say, It's fine, only instead he surprises her, says: I love your brain. She doesn't know what to deal with first, the use of "love" or the fact that it isn't what she was expecting, or the idea that anyone can possibly think fondly of her brain when she has put almost no effort into molding it. Her body, that's easy to love, and her personality, whichever version it is, is specially crafted for every occasion. She has always been studious of other people, despite what her mother thinks. Her mother believes she rebels just to rebel, just to provoke, but that, Regan thinks, is just another form of study. She understands what people want from her, knows when to give it or not. Isn't that the point? Isn't that the success of a rebellion, knowing what people want, so to vehemently deny what others so desperately desire?

Regan has always been good at that, at making people hate her or love her depending on her mood, but she has never given any thought to her thoughts. Then he says it, I love your brain, and she is so stunned she wants to fight with him all over again. She wants to fling things at him wildly—God is a myth! Time is a trap! Virginity is a construct! Love is a prison!—just to make him say it again, to make him prove it true. Oh, you love my brain? Well, do you love it when it does this thing, or this thing? Do you love it when it means I'm lifeless on the floor, curling my tongue around a pill or a stranger's dick? Can you love my brain even when it is small? When it is malevolent? When it's violent?

Can you love it when it doesn't love me?

She thinks so loudly that she wants to quiet her thoughts with sex, which nearly always works. Oh, she likes sex with Aldo, she craves it, the thought alone makes her entire body sing. The way he fits with her, inside her, she wants it in excess—she wants, as she always wants, to be smothered by it, to drown in it, for it to be so vast and devouring it swallows her whole—but she has felt that way about sex before, about men and boys before. She has already lost herself many times, many ways, so she wants to do it again and thinks it will be familiar. But with him nothing is familiar, and sex is the least of it. It isn't *nothing*—she sleeps with her hand wrapped around his cock just to comfort her subconscious with the shape of it—but this, I love your brain, is more. She already knows she is in love with him and now she suspects he is in love with her, too, in a way that makes her inclined to believe it. She yanks him up to her, ready to reward him with the places she can bend, but he laughs, slows her rushing hands. We can take breaks, you know, he says. She scoffs a little in her head—Oh, her brain, that's what he wants? Okay, then have it, all of it. She pulls his head to hers, bites his lip, says: I'm going to tell you my secrets.

He licks at her mouth. Tell me, then.

She starts small but moderately sinful, not quite convinced he's ready to hear the big things or worse, the meek. She tells him about how she flirted with a professor, got him to change a grade. She tells him about the neighbor boy, the first person to cup her breast in his hand and say, Nice. She tells him about the chemistry class she nearly failed except for the boy who sat next to her, who did her labs because she batted her eyes, sent a few dirty texts, okay fine, so there are pictures of her tits out there somewhere on someone's cloud account, probably, so what. Aldo listens with a smile, a smile that says, Mmhmm.

Before she knows it, she's confessing other things: I'm actually not very good at anything in particular. I'm not really very smart. People don't know it right away, but eventually they sort it out. Sometimes I think: No wait I'm lying, all the time I think: Everyone else is right about me. I am the common factor, aren't I? So that must mean everyone else is right.

He doesn't say anything at first, strokes her cheek the way he does when he's thinking about whatever it is he's thinking about (she doesn't expect to understand it, time or anything, nor does she want to; really, she's fine with mysteries) but then he says again: Why did you do it?

He means Why did you, a person with plenty of money and talent and by all accounts a promising future, decide to throw that away for a crime?

Her psychiatrist, the doctor, says it's because she wanted to fail. Because she was self-sabotaging.

Fine, that's a theory, but he didn't ask what her psychiatrist thought.

Well, who says she even knows herself? If she'd known she would eventually get caught, wouldn't she simply not have done it?

He thinks that's an excellent question.

Well, she's glad he thinks so.

He means she should answer the question, or try to.

She thinks he's commandeered secret time.

He has, but he's fine with it.

She wants him to kiss her. (She places his hand between her thighs.)

He's not letting her get away with that.

Well fine, maybe she'll just leave then, she has her own apartment, she hardly needs to sleep here, and besides, maybe he's being nosy.

Maybe he is but she started it, and she can leave any time if she wants to, so long as she comes back.

Fine, but only because he said that last bit. She's tired of people telling her she's free to leave, she hates it.

He doesn't want her to leave at all but there's a whole thing in the rule book about letting people have agency. "If it's meant to be" and all that.

She thinks that's bullshit, can't people just hold on?

He agrees.

Okay fine, she doesn't really know why exactly, but she thinks part of it was about taking hold of a sinking ship and steering it somewhere, anywhere. Even the prospect of a crash was better than floating aimlessly.

Why was her ship sinking?

She was just being needlessly metaphorical, it's a habit of hers.

He notes it, asks again: Why was her ship sinking?

Her ship? It's always sinking, she hates it, it's either sinking or it's exploding, either way it never seems to be going anywhere.

He doesn't think that's true.

Well, he doesn't really know her that well, does he? He's only had x amount of conversations with her and fucked her y times.

No no, he wants to be very clear: that's not how math works.

God, he's doing this now?

He's very interested in accuracy, he sits up to graph it for her: x is how long you know a person, y is how well. Maybe he has only known her for x, but look at all this exponential growth in y. Look how steep this curve is, does she see what he means?

Yes, grudgingly she sees it. What's his point?

He doesn't have a point, he just wanted to tell her.

She thinks he's incredibly weird.

He knows. Is she okay with it?

Okay with it? Fuck, he has no idea.

He reminds her they haven't talked about how she's doing, what with her pills and all that.

She doesn't want to take them anymore. She doesn't like what they do to her, how lost they make her feel. Maybe that's the big secret, that even though she hates her feelings, she'd still rather have them than not. Maybe the enormity of it all is that she hates the highs and the lows and she knows they're Bad, that they're Not Supposed To Happen, but she is not herself without them. She misses herself. She doesn't really know who she is but she *wants* to know, she wants to *find out,* and she can't do it with pills. She understands that might be hard for him.

Why does it matter what's hard for him? He has nothing to do with it.

Of course he does, he has to, because he's signing up to share her brain-space, her thought-space. Like it or not, the fight they just had? It's going to happen again, and he's going to get sick of her and then *she's* going to get sick of her but she'd rather get sick of all of her than get sick of the half-her the pills make her feel.

Of course he signed up for it.

What?

Of course he signed up for it, it's what he wants. Why should someone else get her highs and lows? He wants them all, selfishly, possessively. He wants to have them, he doesn't have any highs or lows himself, he's been . . . stuck.

Stuck? He isn't stuck, he's a genius.

He's been trying to solve the same problem for years. He's the definition of stuck.

That's the definition of insanity, which he definitely is. (This she says fondly.)

Okay fine, he's insane, is she happy now?

Immensely. (She is.)

The point is he doesn't need her to be anything, he doesn't need her to be on pills. He'd like her to be honest if she wants to be but if she's going to lie then he'd like to be in on it.

That doesn't make any sense.

Yes it does, he doesn't want to be the person she hides *from,* he wants to be the person she hides *with.* These are distinct, doesn't she realize? Does she have any idea how difficult he finds it to exist with other people? And then here she is, this mystery, this puzzle, does she even know how much he loves her unpredictability, her twists and turns? She thinks her brain is some sort of problem? Fine, good, he loves problems.

He keeps saying the word "love." Does he realize that?

Well, he hasn't exactly thought about it, but what is he supposed to say?

She doesn't expect him to say anything, she's just . . . commenting. They've never talked about love before, only sex.

That's because he has only loved people he's never fucked and fucked people he doesn't love, purely by coincidence. Sex has always been an afterthought.

Strange to think he has afterthoughts. That's too many thoughts. Besides, sex is about forgetting, about feeling.

He doesn't like to forget or to feel.

So he doesn't like sex with her?

No, he didn't say that, he loves sex with her.

"Love" again. He's doing it again.

Fine, he *likes* sex with her, is that better?

No, it isn't. He *likes* it?

See, that's why he said love.

He isn't very good at words.

No, he isn't, he knows that, people dislike his words and also, he can't explain anything. She's seen him teach, hasn't she? She knows that.

Why doesn't he just get better at it?

She should go to art school.

Okay, now he's deflecting.

No, he's thinking. She should be an artist and if she wants to go to art school, she should.

He doesn't know anything about art, he's just biased.

Toward what?

Her, obviously.

No, he would tell her if he thought she wasn't good at it. Or at least, he wouldn't tell her that it was good if it wasn't.

Well, he's still wrong. Maybe it's pleasing to his untrained eye but she can't exactly just *become* an artist, it doesn't work like that.

Right, that's why he said school, if she wants.

She needs something, first. An idea.

An impossible problem? (He's teasing, but she's serious.)

Yes, that. Something worth devoting all her thoughts to.

Can't she stumble on that?

Yes, conceivably she could, but she wants to find it first before she decides to invest in it.

How is she going to find it? Not like that, just to be clear. (He's shaking his head as she makes her way down his torso.)

She doesn't know. Jesus, can't he just be a normal guy, just take the blow job and say thank you?

He thanks her. But also he's serious, he wants her to find it, can he help?

He can help by being quiet.

She should know right now that the secrets of the universe aren't in his dick.

Has he checked?

He's familiar with the real estate.

That's not what she means.

He, genuinely, has no idea what she means.

(Silence.)

They should fight more often.

She was thinking the same thing. What were his reasons, just blow jobs? He can have those without fighting, it's part of the all-inclusive package.

No, not blow jobs, he thinks he can feel them (he-and-she them) changing their shapes a little. And he's been this-shaped for so long that he could do with some expansion.

Weird thing to say, but she isn't surprised.

She doesn't know what he means? He's pretty sure she knows what he means.

Well, fine, maybe she does. But she feels different all the time now, so who knows if it's him or something else or everything?

Could she have loved him if she'd kept up with her pills?

No, she couldn't have, she wouldn't have let herself, or the pills wouldn't have let her. And also, he said it again.

What, love? Probably because he's not as good a liar as she is.

She knows.

Does that mean she feels the same way?

Did she just blow him or not? (She's not going to admit it.)

She knows perfectly well that's not love.

She's surprised he even believes in love.

He doesn't, not really, but it's the closest thing to having a name for the concept. It's like how time only exists within their understanding of what time is, even though time is probably something else entirely. But they still call it time, because that's what everyone agreed to call it.

How . . . incredibly theoretical of him.

He *is* a theoretical mathematician.

Okay, well say there's no pre-established name for it, what does he feel?

She is asking some very difficult questions.

Good, she doesn't like easy.

He knows. He likes that.

Oh, so *that* he likes.

He wants to hold her but he can't.

He's holding her right now, see? (He is, loosely.)

Not like that, not physically.

He wants to . . . mentally hold her?

Kind of. Sure. If she can make sense of that. (She can't.)

Maybe they should talk about it another time. They have plenty of other times for conversations, he says, and this is when she knows—god, she *knows*—that she loves him so deeply and so passionately and so devastatingly that by the time she tells him, the words will inevitably feel empty and small.

The first time they argue, she is sure that she loves him.

But she doesn't tell him so, not really, not yet.

———

"Come home with me," he said.

She made a show of glancing around, stretching out languidly to brush the backs of her knuckles across his chest.

"I thought I was already home with you," she said, and he shook his head.

"Home home."

"*Home* home?"

"Home home."

She considered it. Which was perhaps a thing he should have done first, only it was getting increasingly difficult to do things without her, even in his head. She and his thoughts were inextricably linked now, to the point where even math, which had always been pleasing for being solitary, had become profoundly lonely. There were times when he imagined her there in his classroom, considering him from the back of the room: "Aldo, be patient, explain this, you haven't explained it." He saw her in his dissertation meetings, sitting beside him: "Aldo, are you sure?" with her brow furrowed in thought. "But have you considered this, or this, or this," things she said to him on a regular basis, like a speed bump to his internal narrative. She was always interrupting, stopping him to say in one way or another, That doesn't make sense. She always needed to look at things from every angle, turning them upside down, peering through keyholes to find the truth.

The Truth. She seemed to find it only by digging in with an obscene fascination, a close-to-perversity ravaging, no matter the subject. This type of pasta, why? Why this temperature? What happens if you put x here, no it doesn't work that way, why not? Even sex was a matter of experimentation, Try this, Aldo, talk to me like this, no no like this. Regan was always thinking but she called it feeling, and whatever it was, it was rapid and difficult to follow. He felt consistently lost, but he could feel himself changing. He could feel new paths of thought, those previously untraveled for self-preservation (things dismissed for reasons of: not a practical question, impossible, would never work this way) becoming worn beneath his feet. He could feel Regan twining her fingers with his and pulling him along—What about this, have you thought about it this way, Aldo? Aldo, make love to me and answer all my questions, placate me with answers!, with attention!, with your touch. Aldo, fuck me until my mind stands still; plummet with me, euphoric, over the edge of a fucking cliff.

The semester had ended, finally. He'd gone through the next round of oral arguments for his dissertation, had graded all his exams, had dealt with the muttered "Thanks, Damiani" from the students who'd narrowly passed, had submitted his end of term evaluations to the dean. Everything was as it was before, as it had been each semester prior, except for little, subtle differences. The extra helmet he kept strapped to his backpack, just in case. The checking of his phone more often, waiting for her name to appear on his screen. The extra key on the ring, freshly cut and polished, for when she was awake at three in the morning, her voice a hoarse whisper of "Aldo, you have to see this shade of blue *right now,* I want you to see it with me; I want to watch you see it for the first time."

He had never kept much from his father, and Regan was no secret. What is she, your girlfriend? Yes, he supposed so, though it seemed a silly word for her. Well, what was she, then? She's, I don't know. What do you mean you don't know, how can you not know? No, I know, I just don't think the word exists. Mm well then tell me, where are we in time, Rinaldo? Lost, Dad, lost, I no longer understand what time is, how it works, what it does, I give up. Ah, Masso said, okay, I see what she is. What does that mean, Dad, what is she? She's your . . . you know, your provocateur, she's your disturbance. Big words, Dad. Yes, Rinaldo, big words for a big concept, good luck, I love you, see you soon.

"Home," Regan echoed. He was playing with her hair, winding it around and around his finger, the thick silken strands glinting in a spiral. "You're sure you want to bring me? I know how much your dad means to you."

"Yes," exactly, that's the point.

"He might not like me."

"So? Your parents don't like me."

"That's different, they hate everyone and besides, they don't matter."

"I don't believe that's true."

"Well, believe it," she scoffed, rolling over to face him. Her eyes were oversized, vulnerable. She'd stopped wearing makeup around him and it was a beautiful, destructive thing, seeing her eyes so clearly. She looked younger, five years or lifetimes at least. It made something growl within him, something primitive that made him want to kill tigers for her, to beat other men with clubs. Marc had called at least twice. She hadn't made a secret of it, had even laughed and offered Aldo the phone, but he hadn't taken it. He no longer trusted himself.

"I don't always make a good first impression, Aldo. Especially not with fathers."

"Why not with fathers?"

"I don't know, I only know how to flirt. Older men make me uncomfortable."

Men, he thought. Men make you uncomfortable.

"My dad will like you. He likes, you know. Weirdness."

"Oh, so I'm weird now?"

"You spend all your free time with me, don't you?"

"Fair." She slid a nail down his chest, circling his sternum. "Did you tell him I'm an artist?"

"Yes."

"But I'm not."

He kissed the top of her head. "Okay. You're not, then."

"Don't patronize me," she grumbled, though she snaked an arm up to wrap around his neck, bringing his lips to hers. "I hate it," she whispered to him, her tongue grazing the edges of his teeth. She tasted like salt, like amatriciana, which always tasted salty to him.

"Come home with me," he said again, and she sighed, fingers twisting in his hair.

"And if your father hates me?"

"He won't. He doesn't hate anyone."

"He could hate me." Her voice was bitter, tasting like anise now. "Plenty of people do."

"Doesn't matter," he muttered, tipping her chin up.

Her hand circled his throat, experimental. Her thumb dragged over his Adam's apple, testing. He wondered what she was thinking. He wondered about her thoughts constantly, even in rare cases when he knew she had none. What did Regan think about quantum groups? Answer: Regan did not think about quantum groups, and yet his mind couldn't rest from wondering. She slid into his calculations and nudged him, pointing things out. What really happens in a superposition, Aldo? When particles are in two or more states at once, Aldo, what does that mean, what does it mean for us, what does it mean for time? Will we ever know *The Truth*? and he would think, unsatisfied, No, Regan, we won't, I can't do it, I've always known I'll never know, and she would express her disappointment with a bite, with the tightening of her fingers. Give me truth, Aldo, or be gone from my sight, get out.

The kiss progressed, as kisses typically did. He liked the way she changed direction, the way she chose her pace or else put her hands on his hands and told him, You choose, You tell me, You put me where you want me, Arrange me to your liking and let's see, let's see where this goes. He was in his head, always, even during sex, but she seemed to like that about him. Her hands were always drifting to his hair, to his neck or digging into his skull, as if she wanted to crack it open and lay claim to whatever was inside. He liked that. He liked it, how grabby she was, how selfishly insistent. He liked her even when she was stingy, when she was ungenerous. He liked her best when she was saying, with the twist of her fingers, You are already mine.

"I suppose," she sighed, "I should just do whatever you ask, shouldn't I?"

"Do I ask for much?"

"Oh, only everything," she said, half-smiling, and turned her head. "Will I disappoint you?" she asked, and her voice was hushed, the youth of her face playing tricks on him again, luring him into fallible safety. This was why it was so foolish, all his primal instincts. She was the hunter, not him.

"No," he said.

She thought about it for a moment, stroking her thumb over the bone of his cheek.

"Okay," she said, and kissed him. "Then I'll go."

————

Things Rinaldo Damiani knows:

Quantum physics, or something. Regan doesn't totally understand it, but whatever it is, Aldo knows it. He certainly knows calculus, algebra, most of the things that come after calculus and algebra, all of the things that come before. He knows some degree of physics, doesn't care for it; the fact that things work is less important to him than the idea of what he could *convince* to work if he thought about it hard enough. He knows about the scrapes, the scars on her body, he knows how often she eats and how much, he knows she dislikes goat cheese unless he pairs it with something sweet. He knows how to box, has shown her how, has known enough to stand still and say: Hit me here, it won't hurt, I'll block it if I need to. He knows how to defend himself, and here again is the irony: He hates physics, but he understands physicalities. He knows the angle to hold her hips. He knows how deeply he can fill her, how hard before it hurts. He knows this expression of hers means not now I'm thinking, he knows this one means yes now but one second, he knows this one means don't bother speaking, just take off your clothes, I don't know why you wear them. He knows her relationships are complicated. He knows whose calls she takes and which ones she ignores. He knows, as her doctor doesn't know, that she isn't taking her pills. He knows that she hears her mother's voice in her head and sometimes she loses her own voice inside it; he knows she finds it again when he takes her face in his hands and says: Are you in there? He knows so much; he knows almost everything. Likewise, she knows he is a genius.

Things Rinaldo Damiani doesn't know:

"Charlotte. Are you there? I called two weeks ago, you haven't called back, I called Marc and he told me you moved out. What are you thinking?" "Charlotte, just calling to check in, you missed your last appointment. Please do call to reschedule." "Char, Mom's freaking out, just call her back. Tell Aldo I say hi. Carissa's asking if you'll be here for Christmas? You'd better, or I think Mom's going to explode. Not joking." "Hello, this message is for Charlotte Regan from Dr. —'s office, please call us at your earliest convenience." "Regan, this is so you, honestly. If you've come to your senses, you know how to find me." "Regan! I'm in town until Christmas, want to get lunch? I know, I know, I haven't been the best at keeping in touch, but we should totally get a drink or something." "Wow, I can't believe you called back, a miracle. Sorry, I was working a long shift but listen, I really don't want to be the one who tells Mom. Is there any way you can like, you know, not? I'm happy you're happy with Aldo and that you're alive but Char, truly, you can't think this is the best way to go about this." "Charlotte, of course we can find a replacement while you're away—the holidays are a difficult time. Looking forward to seeing you upon your return! As for classes, I'll get in touch with someone at the Institute, I'm sure we can work something out." "Hi, this message is for Regan, the book you requested on figure drawing is in, you have five days to pick it up." "Regan, babe, ran into that sorority sister of yours—Sophie? Samantha? Whatever, she said she called to tell you she was in town and you never called back. I'm a little worried about you, not going to lie. Sorry about the text the other night, I was blasted out of my fucking mind, but look, I still care about you. Just tell me you're okay." "CHARLOTTE, WHY DO WE PAY FOR A PHONE IF YOU NEVER BOTHER TO ANSWER IT?"

"Hey," Aldo said, nudging her. "You alright?"

"Just thinking I should get a new phone," Regan said. "Or maybe just throw it away, live off the grid."

"Impractical, I suspect," Aldo said, shrugging. He gave her a second glance, maybe a third. She tucked her phone into her pocket, turning to him with a smile, and he shook his head. "You're lying."

"I didn't even say anything!"

"Yes, and it's a lie." He glanced over his shoulder, then pulled her into him, his arm looped around her neck; nearly a headlock, but that was Aldo. His version of proximity was restricting, and she liked it. She liked when he slid his hand around the back of her neck, led her around like that. Made her feel stable, secured. She leaned in, slid her lips up to his jaw, bit lightly.

"Ouch—"

"You called me a liar," she said. "That's what you get."

"Fine, you're not lying. But you're definitely thinking."

In answer (in retaliation) she slid her hand down to the lip of his black jeans. He gave her a look of admonishment.

"We're in the airport," he said.

She tugged the zipper, just to prove a point, and he sighed gruffly.

"Okay, fine, don't tell me," he said, and she tilted her chin up, locking eyes with him.

"I didn't tell my parents I wasn't coming home for Christmas," she said.

He lifted a brow.

"Didn't tell them anything, actually," she clarified.

He pulled her forward, advancing with the line.

"Because you don't want them to know about me?" he asked.

"No, I don't want them to know about *me.*"

"Okay." He kissed her forehead swiftly. "Well, that's your decision."

Ha, as if she'd let it end there. "You disapprove, I take it?"

"I don't pretend to understand your relationship with your parents."

"Why not? You understand everything else."

"One day," he sighed, "you'll discover that my understanding of math does not translate to a grasp of human behavior, and then it will occur to you that I am, in fact, an idiot."

"Oh, I already know that," she assured him, making his mouth quirk slightly. "You're entirely useless but still, be honest. You disapprove."

"I have no basis for approval or disapproval. I'm just, you know. Here for however long you want to keep me."

She looked up, startled. "You don't think I'm serious about you?"

"I didn't say that."

"You kind of did."

"Well, I didn't mean to 'kind of do' anything, I just meant to say it: I'm here for however long you want me."

"But that implies that you don't think it'll last."

"Does it?"

"Yes, of course, otherwise you wouldn't say it."

He said nothing.

She pushed him. "Do you think I'm not telling my parents about us because I'm not serious about you?"

"I didn't say that."

The line inched forward.

"It's not that," she said quietly. "I just . . . I like us like this, I like us how we are. I don't want them in it, around it. Near it, even."

"You don't want them to ruin it, you mean."

"No, I just—"

"It's okay. I'm trying to tell you, I don't have expectations."

"Well, why not?" The comment made her agitated, left her bristling. "What if I want you to have expectations?"

"Do you?"

"Do I want you to, or do I have them?"

"Both, I guess. Whichever you feel like answering."

"Well—" She cleared her throat. "I want you to have them."

"Which expectations should I have? Great ones?"

"Don't be cute," she growled, glaring at him. His uneven mouth meant he was laughing. "I just don't want you to think I'm not serious, Aldo. I'm serious."

"Okay."

"Like, really serious."

"Even if you weren't, Regan, that would be fine."

"Why?" she demanded, defensive again. "Because I can just flit in and out of your life and it wouldn't make a difference?"

He was quiet for a second.

"What do you want me to say?" he asked her.

He was really asking, not like Marc. Not Marc, who'd "You up?"-ed her just the other night, making her feel dirty again, like a relapse. Aldo wasn't Marc. He wasn't like her friends, either, who would have asked her the same thing, only they would have been sarcastic when they said it. He wasn't like anyone she'd known before, not like anyone who expected her to be a certain way. Not like all the people she'd been shielding him from, not for his sake but for hers, afraid he'd come to understand what she really was, what she'd been for years, what she'd always been. Afraid, always afraid, that this was still some splintered version of pretend, that she was only crafting a new version for him when she wanted to believe she was really herself. Afraid that now she was Aldo's Regan, which meant that Aldo's Regan could fade into obscurity; that her honesty with him was just another version of a lie.

"I want you to expect—no, I want you to *demand,*" she amended. "I want you to demand things from me, to tell me to make this work, to force me if you have to. I want you to bet on me, Aldo. I want you to make investments, I want your future." The last part slipped out. "I want your future, Aldo. I want it for me."

He glanced down at her, somewhere between surprise and understanding. The place that looked like amusement, but was really satisfaction.

"Okay," he said.

Then he stroked her hair once, gently, and she thought:

Rinaldo Damiani knows how to love me, and I didn't even think to put it on the list.

———

Aldo was never bothered by tedium, by the pained exit from LAX and the trudging and the monotony and the traffic, when he was doing it alone. Now, with Regan at his side, he was constantly making apologies, tripping over himself to reassure her—I'm sure our bags will be here soon, sorry the taxi line is so long, are you okay, are you hungry? My dad will feed us, I'm sure he won't even stop to breathe before he's shoving food at you, here taste this taste this— but thankfully she was in a good mood, smiling. Reassuring him; I don't mind waiting, Aldo, everything's fine, I can't wait to see where you grew up. Her gaze drifted out the window across unfamiliar streets and she was quiet, unusually so, but her fingers slid across the backseat to find his, squeezing his hand.

"Are you—?"

"I'm happy, Aldo, everything is great, don't worry about me. Don't think so much," and a kiss to his temple before she turned her gaze out the window again.

The drive seemed longer, the distance farther, the traffic noisier. Everyone was honking and it stung Aldo's ears. He checked Regan's expression frequently, constantly, relieved to find a placid, pensive smile on her face as she wondered out her window, but then check- ing again just to be sure he wouldn't miss it if it faded. Just to make sure he could fix it the moment an unpleasant thought crossed her mind, which it didn't, but just in case it did, he never left her. She must have felt his eyes on her; she turned and kissed him twice, then shoved his face away.

"What are you so worried about?"

"You," he said.

"Well, don't."

He didn't have any reason to, either. They went first to his house, which he worried would be cramped and diminutive compared to hers, but she exclaimed over the intimacy of it, How cozy, Aldo, I love it, I love this. You really grew up here, just you and your dad? Yes, me and Masso, and my nonna was here often. Sweet, Aldo, really sweet, I love it, another kiss to his cheek, to his mouth, a tug at his belt loops. Now? Yes, now, she whispered into his mouth, I already behaved myself so well, four entire hours on the plane I didn't touch you. She pulled him into his bed, the bed from his high school years, Did you sleep with anyone here? Yes, I wasn't the perfect son and I didn't always slink away behind the bleachers. The sun was stream- ing in, blinding him a little as she pulled off her shirt and twisted around to remove her bra. She climbed on top of him, pinned his shoulders down, whispered to him:

"I'm going to replace those memories, Aldo. I'm taking them back for me."

It was quick, rushed, like scratching an itch. He'd promised his father they'd be there for lunch and they hurried to re-dress themselves, him fixing her hair and her adjusting his collar, reapplying her lipstick. You sure Masso will like me? Masso will love you, come here.

His father, true to form, was ecstatic to see them, rushing around half-shouting, Remember my son, I told you about my son Rinaldo, the mathematician? Oh, the genius, actually, Regan corrected with a laugh, and Masso radiated with pleasure. I'm happy he has a smart girl, finally someone who can keep up with him. How do you know I'm smart? Oh, I know, I can tell, you have a look about you.

"Aldo, I have a *look* about me," Regan echoed, preening with her hand in his.

Yes, I know, I saw it first. "Dad," Aldo sighed, "you're going to spoil her, aren't you?"

"Regan, do you like mushrooms? Truffles?"

"Yes, I love it all, I'll eat anything—"

"She won't, Dad, she's lying, go easy on her—"

"Be quiet, Rinaldo, the adults are talking."

For nearly an hour Aldo was silent with relief, so enraptured and filled with satisfaction he could hardly say a word. Regan, by contrast, was chatty and exuberant, waving her fork around, telling Masso this and that and this.

"He's the worst model, really, he moves around all the time—"

"Same when he was a boy, always moving, impossible to tell him to sit still."

"Yes! But look at him." Her smile was bright, teasing. "I can't help it, I have to put him on paper, just to make sure he's really real."

They parted as Masso prepared for the dinner shift, promising to bring home more of the cheeses Regan had liked from lunch and telling her where to find the good wine. Don't let Aldo pick it out, his tastes are too sweet and also make him cook or take her out, make sure she didn't lift a finger. Aldo, who protested that of course he would never put her to work, was cheerfully ignored.

Outside, Regan was gleaming, buzzing. "It's so warm here, hardly even winter."

"Then let's walk."

"Is it a short walk?"

"No, like two miles, but it's a nice walk."

"Oh, that's short enough."

She held his hand while they walked. He ran his thumbs over her knuckles, pointing out this and this and this. She liked the trees, she said, how warm the sun is, how different it feels in the shade. How kind your father is. How nice the people at the restaurant are, they really love you.

"I worked in the restaurant for a long time," Aldo said. "They know me."

"How long is a long time?"

"I used to come to the restaurant right after school and do my homework in the kitchen, then in high school I was a busboy there. When I left college for a bit I was a waiter, then a bartender."

"So it's like home for you, then."

"Yeah, kind of."

"I'm so glad I came with you."

"So am I."

His father came home late, like always, but Regan wasn't tired, she insisted they stay up. Show me pictures, videos, I want to see it all. Masso didn't have to be told twice. He dug out the albums, showing Regan, See, here's Rinaldo's first bike, here's his first math competition, he was always so good, I had no idea. I assumed all the kids were like that, silly me, I never even helped him, I didn't know. Masso seemed sad at that and Regan leaned over, throwing an arm around his shoulders. You raised such a good man, Masso, she whispered to him, and Aldo felt heavy, felt like crying, only Masso turned and smiled. Thank you, Regan, it was only by accident, he was just made this way.

That night, Regan touched him like she had never touched him before, slow and sweet and syrupy with caresses. She lingered, persistent, taking her time. Time, they had so much of it here, and she seemed to feel it; seemed intent on making him feel it, too. His bed was so small, the room itself so small, but their needs were small, too, just each other. He opened his window and they stared out at the moon, contemplating it.

"What was it like, not having your mother?"

"Normal, I guess. I don't think about it much."

"Do you ever want to find her?"

"No, not really. She made my father sad, and my grandmother didn't like her. Maybe I thought about it once or twice, I don't know, but then I thought . . . if she wanted to find me, she could find me. She knew my name, and she knew my father's name. It wasn't like we ever moved."

"Oh," said Regan, softly.

He shifted, snaking his arm free to reach into his drawer for the picture of his mother and his father. "I have this," he said, handing it to Regan, who sat up, reaching for it like it was something fragile that might shatter in her hands. "It wasn't like I didn't know about her."

His mother was beautiful, dark-skinned and lovely, her hair precisely like Aldo's would be if he'd ever had the idea to grow it out. He liked seeing her that way, permanently young and in love with his father, which anyone could see. This, Aldo explained to Regan, was the only version of his mother that he needed.

Regan handed the picture back to him and he returned it to his drawer.

"I want to tell you something," Regan said, "but it's going to be so fucking stupid."

"I talk about stupid things all the time."

"No, you talk about interesting things, they're just weird. This, though, it's just . . . it's just so ridiculous. I shouldn't even bother."

"No, say it." I want you to say everything, anything. I want to have your thoughts, I want to bottle them, I want to put them in my drawer for safekeeping.

"Okay." She rested her head on his shoulder, then sat up again. "No wait, I should look at you, I think." The glow of moonlight was like a halo and she was in his T-shirt. She settled herself between his legs and looked at him, deathly serious. "Aldo," she said, and stopped.

"Regan?"

"No, never mind, it's stupid."

He laughed, reaching out, and slid his thumb over her cheek as she leant solemnly against his palm.

"Regan," he said after a moment, "I love you."

She closed her eyes, exhaling deeply.

"Why doesn't it sound stupid when you say it?" she muttered, shaking her head with an irritable sigh, and then she crawled into his arms again, curling around his torso.

"Probably because I say stupid things all the time," he said. "You're used to it."

He felt her smile twitch.

"Are you being like this because I don't have a mother?" he asked, feigning solemnity.

"Yes. I'm feeling very soft, like I need to nurture you."

"I'm fully formed, Regan, I don't require any nurturing."

"Don't you?"

He realized she was serious.

"Why did you do it?" she asked, pulling away to look up at him. "Try to hurt yourself."

"I wasn't trying to."

"Weren't you?"

This, too, was serious.

He sighed, "I don't know. Maybe."

"Why?"

"I just . . ." He thought of Masso's words. "I'm just made like that, I think. It wasn't anything that happened, not like I was sad or upset about something. I just—"

He quieted for a moment, considering the delicacy of what he could say and preferring the safety of silence, but she tapped his chest.

"Tell me," she said.

He lifted a brow, turning to her. "It's stupid," he said wryly, and she sighed.

"Fine, so I was going to tell you I love you," she said brusquely. "Now finish your thought."

Something ballooned in his ribs, cracking them. He felt himself fill up in the fractures, lifted, and since it had been an offering, he resigned himself to acceptance.

"Sometimes I feel like I'm just waiting for something that will never happen," he said. "Like I'm just existing from day to day but will never really matter. I get up in the morning because I have to, because I have to do something or I'm just wasting space, or because if I don't answer the phone my dad will be alone. But it's an effort, it takes work. I have to tell myself, every day, get up. Get up, do this, move like this, talk to people, be normal, try to be social, be nice, be patient. On the inside I just feel like, I don't know, nothing. Like I'm just an algorithm that someone put in place."

Regan was silent.

"Except," Aldo admitted, "when I have these . . . addictions. Obsessions, my father calls them."

She cleared her throat quietly. "Like time?"

"Yes, like time. Or—" He broke off. "Or you."

For a moment she said nothing, and immediately, even before her silence, he wanted to take it back. "I don't mean that you're an obsession, sorry, that sounded crazy, I just meant—"

"No, I understand," she said, cutting him off. "I get it, I do. I think maybe it might be unhealthy, but fuck it, I don't know, who even gets to decide what's healthy?" She sounded confident, coldly irreverent. "We don't even understand time, so how are we possibly supposed to understand health, which is a concept we made up? I don't just feel differently about you—I feel *more,* a lot more. It's like you woke up something inside me and it won't be quiet. It refuses to calm down, and why should it? It's not like 'Oh, you make me happy,' it's not something as clichéd as that. You make me feel like I'm alive for a fucking reason. Like for once I'm not just a goddamn waste of time."

She paused, slightly winded, with a glance up at him.

"If this is unhealthy or obsessive or whatever, who gives a fuck," she said. "You won't hurt me, will you? We're not hurting anyone, we're just—whatever, we're in love. Fuck it, we're in love, and why should we have to explain that to anyone?"

She sounded agitated, almost angry. "You let me be me, I like you when you're you. Why is that bad?"

"It's not bad," he said.

"Right, so don't apologize."

Her rant was over as quickly as it had begun. She slid back to his chest, settling herself there and said, serenely, "By the way, I said I love you. Did you hear it?"

She was most dangerous like that, when she was innocent.

"Yes," he said, smoothing her hair, "I heard it."

"That was the stupid thing."

"Yeah, I sorted that out."

"Jesus, we're fucked, aren't we?"

Yes, yeah, probably. "Who cares."

"Exactly." She sounded smug. "Besides, if we fuck it up, you can just go back in time and fix it, can't you? Promise me that, Aldo. If we fuck this up and it goes badly, then okay fine, you'll go back in time and make sure we never meet. Okay?"

He nodded. "Okay," he said, and finally, she seemed satisfied.

"Okay," she said again, and he leaned his cheek against her forehead, listening to the sound of her breathing as it slowed, then steadied.

When they woke up, Masso had already gone to the restaurant, leaving a note telling them he'd see them at the annual party for the restaurant that evening. Aldo made a strata while Regan sat on his kitchen counter, observing him with her dark eyes, and while it was in the oven he slid the T-shirt up her legs and they fucked quietly, her fingers tangled in his hair. She kissed his neck while he washed the dishes, telling him, You need another haircut. Her tongue slid over the lobe of his ear and he sighed, Stop, I'm just a human man, you'll have to wait until later.

"Fine, fine. What are we doing today?"

He didn't know. He'd never thought of logistics, like what to do with a day, until her.

"Nothing, I guess."

She smiled, licking Nutella from her finger and drawing it slowly across his lips.

"Perfect," she said, and he believed her.

PART FIVE

VARIABLES.

Every year, Aldo's father, Masso, hosted a party for his employees at the restaurant, inviting them and their families for an evening of sociability while he cooked and they mingled, like they were all his family. He said hello to each person individually, spoke to them at length; he opened the good bottles of wine, said a long toast about having a prosperous year, and invited them to have as much as they liked, to even take some home if they wanted. Masso, who for Aldo had been mother and father both, was friendly, warm, inviting. He was completely unlike his son in every conceivable way, and yet it was obvious to Regan where Aldo had gotten his heart, his attentive eyes, his good nature.

Watching Masso was, for Regan, like falling in love with Aldo all over again, piece by piece. There were Aldo's hands, there were his gestures, there was the way he stopped to look into space for a moment when he was trying to get the right words. Masso's pauses were shorter, his voice gentler—he was more accustomed to conversation, and his patience for others seemed unending where Aldo had a tendency to be clipped, halted, rushed—but still, amid this climate of affection, Regan could see the familiar elements belonging to the man who stood next to her, sheepish from his father's praise. Here, like this, she could fall for him anew; again and again and again.

Masso only called Aldo by his full name, Rinaldo, and he spoke of him as a man, not a child. As if they had always just been two friends stumbling together through life, one with his love of food and the other with his love of math. "My son," Masso would say, "he's always been in his head, too smart for his own good, nobody could ever understand him. So imagine my surprise, he brings home a girl—yes, I know, a *girl*, and a pretty one too, who knew?—and she came here to celebrate with us, isn't that wonderful?"

Regan, buzzed on wine and attention and the thrill of Aldo's hand in hers, spoke rapidly, with words dripping from her lips and spilling into the fluidity of mindless conversation, or not at all, thoughts popping and fizzing inside her head. Aldo spoke little, only introducing her to this person or that one and answering their questions: "Yes, I'm enjoying school," "We met at the art museum," "Yes, I like my job," "She's an artist, she insists that she isn't but she's very good, you should see her work." When Aldo spoke of Regan his voice had a tendency to change, illumination rising near his cheeks. "You should see her work," he would say the same way someone else might have said: Come outside, come look at the stars.

Eventually, filled to bursting, Regan pulled Aldo into the back corridor of the restaurant by his tie ("His *tie*! Imagine it," Masso had insisted in his toast, beaming with pride) and into the bathroom, which smelled like sweet basil and looked like Sorrento, and which felt like being near the sea.

"What are you doing?"

She answered by pulling him into her, feeling his smile against her lips.

"Here?" he asked.

Regan, always dressed appropriately for every occasion, slid his hand silently under her dress, feeling him shiver.

"Ah," he said, dazed, and kissed her firmly, getting that sleepy look of acquiescence. It was the one that meant he wasn't going to say no (the one that meant he didn't want to say no, and therefore wouldn't), and she thought to herself: This feeling, this flutter in my chest and this lightness in my bones and this flicker in my blood, this must be happiness. This must be what it feels like to be happy.

How many ways were there to feel sex, to suffer it, to describe it? She thought of the note in her phone filled with little glimpses of eroticism and laughed. How sad she had been, that Regan. How pathetic, thinking she could simply look at a gallery of intimacy and then approximate it for arousal in her head. Funny how desire had blended with closeness in her mind; how she'd confused pure physicality for the sensation of being whole. How positively laughable it was, now that she'd come this far.

She didn't feel whole with Aldo inside her. Instead, she felt splintered; like she became, in his hands, an infinite number of pieces, an entire infinity herself. Like she and eternity and omnipotence were the same, or like omniscience could be equated to the sound of his ragged breath in her ear. She wanted him to mess her up, deplete her, to deliver her to something lesser, something baser. Something less inclined to rational thought, and instead diminished only to sensations.

She thought of the last time she'd been sitting like this on the bathroom sink. She had thought: I wonder if I will ever feel anything again, and look at her now—now she was feeling everything. Was that growth? Of course it was growth, she was uncontainable now. She'd outgrown her container and yes, she still inhabited her body, and temporarily so did he, but they were more than that. This was vastness—and was it him? Was it her? Was it them? Maybe it was all of it, maybe it was everything, maybe he and she were a little speck of everything when they were touching like this, bound to tiny particles in the air. To things that science had yet to find or name or see.

She was colossal like this, the enormity of what she was now steadily irrepressible, ebullient for being in his arms; Kiss me again, please, don't stop, oh god don't stop. He would never, he wouldn't, but still, please don't, we'll shrink down to human-sized when we're done but for now, stay like this with me; see the magnitude of being, see existence through my eyes; don't blink or you might miss it. I am dwarfed, Aldo, by the happiness in that room, it's overwhelmed me. It has made me feel so infinitesimally small; I need you to help me remember what it feels like to be vast again.

Eventually he zipped his trousers, she fixed her hair, he kissed the back of her neck and slipped out after she wiped her lipstick from his cheek and said: See you soon.

She watched him go, then returned her attention to vanity, to her reflection above the bathroom sink. She stared at herself in the mirror and thought: My eyes are too big, everyone will know I've seen everything, they'll know I saw the universe itself. They will look at me and they'll think: This poor girl, she knows too much, she can't go back.

"I can't go back," she whispered to herself, refreshing a curl with a twist around her finger.

Okay, her wide eyes said, okay, fine.

Then get ready to move forward.

————

"Rinaldo," Masso said, half-smiling as Aldo wandered toward him. "And where have you been?"

Dad, you couldn't possibly imagine. I have been everywhere and everything, inside of her, out of body, finally understanding what it's like to exist outside of my own head.

"Bathroom," Aldo said, adjusting his tie, and Masso's smile faltered slightly, his fingers tightening around his glass as if whatever had tickled him just a moment earlier had sobered him now, slipping like a cloak from his shoulders.

"Rinaldo." Masso turned away, glancing out the window, and Aldo could see the silver in his father's hair. Tommaso Damiani was in his mid-fifties now, and he was aging well, like a fine wine. It was a joke Aldo had written into every birthday card, but it was true. Masso was well preserved, finely distilled. Masso Damiani was a rare vintage, one that Aldo had always admired, and it was for that reason that Aldo's chest tightened when his father said, "Are you sure?"

"Sure about what?"

"About, I don't know, everything."

Aldo, who had made a career out of wondering with only minimal promise of certainty, shook his head. "I don't know what you're talking about, Dad."

"Sorry, I know, I—" Masso scraped a hand over his cheeks. "I don't know myself."

"Well, try," Aldo suggested. "You're better at words than I am."

Masso's mouth quirked, shaking his head. "I worry about you, Rinaldo."

"You always worry about me. I keep telling you, you don't have to."

"Yes but I'm . . . a different kind of worried now."

Aldo tucked one hand into his trouser pocket. He understood the concept of change, of variables. There was an obvious, unmissable distinction between then and now.

"I thought you liked her," he said quietly, and Masso nodded.

"I do like her. I like her a lot, she's brilliant."

"But?"

"She's," Masso began, and stopped, turning to look squarely at Aldo. "She's too fast for you."

Evidently sex in the bathroom wasn't a great idea, which he might have guessed. "Dad, this isn't the fifties—"

"No, I don't mean—not like that." Masso grimaced. "Her mind, her nature, what she is. She's, I don't know." He shrugged. "She's moving faster than you are."

"But you said I'd finally found someone who could keep up with me."

"Yes, I know, and in many ways she is, but also she's moving too fast for you. I'm worried." Masso exhaled with reluctance; with reticence, as if he didn't want to be the one to have to pass on the message but hey, look around, there was no one else. "I worry that if you try to keep up with her, you'll burn out, Rinaldo."

"I don't understand."

Aldo's pulse now seemed too fast, his mouth too dry, and Masso turned to face him.

"Rinaldo, we both know you're not like everyone else," Masso said softly. "We don't talk about it often, but we know, don't we? That you're, I don't know. More fragile," he said, wincing slightly, and Aldo felt suddenly stiff, like his bones would splinter if he moved. "You need stability. You need someone reliable, predictable. Regan, she's impulsive."

Yes, Dad, I know. If she were any less impulsive, she wouldn't be with me and I would have never known what she was, or how it felt to hold her. I would never have known what it was to matter for once; for the first time, and for the only time that I have ever known.

"Maybe I need impulsive," Aldo said.

Masso shook his head. "Not this kind of impulsive."

"You can't know that."

"No, maybe I don't, maybe you're right." Masso's voice was grim. "I only know that I loved a woman once like her, who saw the world as she does: like a flame she can't hold between her fingers. I only know that a woman like that isn't afraid to burn, that she will drag you in with her, and I know she will come out laughing and you will not. I only know that I don't know what I'll do, Rinaldo, if something hurts you—"

"Dad, that's . . . You can't be serious."

But Masso was always serious. "Will she settle down, Rinaldo?" he pressed. "Will she want a life, a family, stability, what?"

"I don't know, Dad. I can't possibly know that."

"Yes, but someone has to know for you, someone has to ask you." He gripped Aldo's arm, tugging him into a more secluded corner. "Where are we in time, Rinaldo?"

"I—" He felt briefly dizzied. "Dad, I thought—"

"We are in the *now*, Aldo." His father was unusually insistent. "Look around, orient yourself. You're a grown man, she's a grown woman, and you have to protect yourself because she will not protect you. She's smart, she's beautiful, she's talented, yes. She's intuitive and kind, wonderful. So was your mother, and Regan is restless like her. I can see it in the way she moves, the way she looks at you, it's very familiar."

Immediately, Aldo's brain began rationalizing, compartmentalizing, placing things in boxes of like and unlike. "Regan isn't Mom."

"Of course not, no two people are the same. But I remember what it was to feel everything all at once, and I have to tell you," Masso said urgently, "I never pieced myself back together. And now, I don't know. I don't know if I can watch you do the same."

Elsewhere in the restaurant someone called out Masso's name, a burst of laughter ricocheting from where they stood. Aldo looked over his shoulder, catching Regan's silhouette; she'd emerged from the bathroom, smiling as someone took her hand and admired her, probably saying to her, How pretty you are, and Regan was probably saying, Oh, no, don't be silly, as if she hadn't heard the same thing every day, every hour, every minute of her life.

She looked up, caught his eye, smiled. She pointed to him, her lips parting to say something like, There he is.

There she is, Aldo thought.

Masso cleared his throat, following his son's line of sight. "Rinaldo, listen—"

"You're wrong about her," Aldo said, turning back to his father.

"I mean, you're right, she's impulsive," but it's an easy conclusion, too easy, it's not the sum of all her parts, "but she's not like Mom."

He was saying, in pleasant tones: Don't worry, Dad, I hear you, but it's different.

But he was thinking, with iron certainty: I have spent a lifetime encountering problems that ravaged my abilities before, Dad, and none have destroyed me yet. If I'm still here, then surely it's for something.

If I am still here, Dad, then please. Let it have been for something.

"I like her, Rinaldo, I do, I just—"

"You worry, I know," Aldo said, and beckoned for Regan from afar. "But don't."

She joined them; he slid an arm around her waist; she smiled and he kissed her cheek.

"What are you two talking about?"

If this is what it is to burn, he thought, then I will be worth more as scattered ash than any of my unscathed pieces.

"You," he said, and she smiled, leaning against his shoulder as if to say, Okay.

Okay, so let's do this, then.

————

Regan, always conscious of overstaying her welcome, came back to Chicago a week before Aldo did. She would resume the practice of normalcy, doing things like the laundering of clothes, the buying of groceries, the running of nameless errands. She would schedule her annual gynecological exam. She would return to the Art Institute, reconvene her usual tours. She thought perhaps she would return Marc's calls, grudgingly. She might return her mother's calls, impassively. Whatever tasks were required to begin approximating normal life activities, she would do them, responsibly.

In the end, she did only one of those things. The calls remained unanswered and the pap smear would have to wait. Without Aldo, Regan felt an uneasiness, a restlessness, something close to recklessness or, perhaps, far beyond it. She felt a vibrating sense of blankness, like the buzz of a fluorescent sign. Closed, open, vacancy, no vacancy.

She felt like a door swinging open and shut, things coming and going, and she was merely the operator saying, Hold please. She sat on the floor of her studio with her dearth of possessions and thought: I should get on a plane, I don't remember how to be without him, maybe if I ask him nicely he'll say yes.

Part of her thrilled with the idea of an *emergency*. Yes, an emergency, she thought, that would certainly bring him home. She thought about catching pneumonia; it would be easy. She'd only have to walk outside and stand in the snow for a few minutes until she turned blue. She imagined herself being found, unconscious, the emergency contact being dialed, Poor girl, Aldo sitting with his father and receiving the call, the phone falling from his hand as he shouted at his father: I have to go, I have to, she needs me and I need her!

Regan didn't want to *die,* obviously—nothing *that* emergent. She just wanted something reasonably compelling; something that would make him think about how precious time was, how every moment of it should be spent at her side, the two of them together. Eventually, though, her capacity for rational thought would return and she would remind herself that walking into traffic and getting hit by a car ("MASSO, I HAVE TO GO, SHE'S LYING IN A HOSPITAL BED AND IF I LOSE HER NOW WHAT WILL I DO, WHO WILL I BE?") would be an unpleasant experience, and probably not even worth it. No, maybe it would be worth it, but what kind of sex could she have with a broken leg? Just wait, she told herself, just wait.

Of the things she told herself she would do, returning to the Art Institute was the only one that seemed manageable, largely because she thought she could walk into the armory and see Aldo there, overlaying a hologram of him from her memory onto the empty floor. Sir, you can't sit there, she'd say in her thoughts, and he would turn to her and say, Can't I? And she would say, Sir, please, this is a museum, and he would take her in his arms and without hesitation he would take her standing up, holding her against the wall. He'd fuck her slowly, tormentingly, his eyes never straying from hers. He'd say: I came to look at art, to marvel at something, and here you are and so I will.

Reality, to her displeasure, left little time for fantasy. Many of her volunteer colleagues remained on vacation along with the tourists, which left Regan with larger groups, more tours, forced to chatter endlessly about this painting or that one. It was monotonous, which it had always been; it was a task she had chosen for the purpose of invoking monotony. That had been comforting to her once, though it was infected now by the bizarre and ill-founded hope that she would look out into the crowd and see Aldo standing there, a puzzled little frown furrowed into his brow. She started giving tours as if he actually *was* standing there, answering questions she thought he might want to ask. What does this painting show, how is one intended to feel, what makes this a masterpiece, why is it this size, why did they choose to set it off with this lighting, why this frame? She could feel herself pounding technicalities into her audience, who were largely uninterested. They wanted tidbits, morsels, postcard-sized facts to tell their friends and family, like did you know this artist painted nothing but haystacks for *months*? Karen, did you know this one was addicted to *drugs*? Truly, Jennifer, art is for the ill.

Meanwhile, all Regan could think of was Aldo; the things only he would see and only he would miss, the many things she longed to show him. No no, Monet didn't paint mundanity just for mundanity's sake, Aldo, it was to show the *transience of light,* don't you see? He painted wonder, he painted . . . fuck, Aldo, he painted TIME! She wanted to shout it, to dial him right then: Monet, he's obsessed with time, too, he just thinks of it like light, like color. Look at these fucking haystacks, Aldo! Who would do this??! Who would do this unless they, like you, were trying to grasp the way time passes; to put it in terms they would struggle for a lifetime to understand?

She felt different because of him, immensely changed, and therefore it frustrated her that her reflexes were the same. It enraged her that she still observed who was attractive in a crowd, or who in all likelihood had a dick worth temporarily considering. Every now and then she felt herself, distressingly, considering that the man who was not-so-secretly eyeing her across the wine aisle might be an acceptable way to pass the time, to calm the reverberations in her head. She had the same imaginings of herself pulling a nameless man somewhere cloistered and dark, only now she was whispering to him: You'd better make this good, don't disappoint me, you have no idea what it cost.

Now, in her post-Aldo fantasies, she was the rough one, the artless one. She was the one saying to them: You'd better make me feel it or this has been a waste of time. Then Aldo would burst in, he'd point a finger at her in disgust, he'd say, I knew it, I knew what you were, how dare you, Regan? And she'd chase after him; she'd cling to him, begging forgiveness. He'd push her away, merciless, and even that she would relish, perversely. He'd push and he'd flee and she, like a half-starved junkie, would only crave him all the more.

After a week, her fantasies, grotesque as they were, began to re-volve around him leaving her. Regan, how could you do this? Aldo, please, please I'm so sorry. Regan, you disgust me. Aldo, you can't mean that! Regan, you're toxic, you make me sick. Aldo, Aldo, if you go, what will happen to me?

She wanted to cry, needed compulsively to suffer. Jesus, she thought, you really have a fucking problem, and so she left all her madness out of her phone calls to Aldo. When she talked to him, she tried to make all her words beautiful, sensual, like she was painting for him with her voice. She didn't tell him the depravity of her imaginings, or the repulsion she felt with them, or with herself.

"I miss you," she said, as if missing were sexy. She spun her voice into the image of herself sprawled out on satin bedsheets, legs spread, inviting. She shaped her missing him into something far less ugly than it was. (She was lonely, needy, heartsick. It really wasn't cute.)

"I miss you too, I'll be home soon." His missing her was warm, like a golden retriever. *I'll be home soon.* Once he said that she could finally relax and sit upright, take off the imaginary silk robe she'd vocally donned and return to herself in her yoga pants, her cashmere sweater, the enormous socks because fuck, Chicago was cold in the winter.

She'd end her little astral projection with a grudging return to corporeality, and then she'd say, "Aldo, just send me a picture of your dick or something," and he'd laugh.

"Regan, I'm starting to feel a little used," he'd say, and she'd smile and ache and imagine him stabbing her heart with a dull pair of scissors.

She went out on New Year's Eve, mostly out of boredom, and ran into Marc. The problem with sharing the same portion of a city with someone for so long was that no places belonged exclusively to you anymore. You shared them, and then forgot to divvy them up after all was said and done. You knew the things he knew, he knew what you knew, so of course he's at the same bar, why did she even try.

He saw her and made a fucking coke line straight toward her.

"I see you're here alone."

"Yeah, but not really."

"You're really fucking that math guy?"

"I'm not fucking him, Marc, I'm with him."

"Then where is he?"

"In L.A., with his dad."

"He left you alone on New Year's?"

"Some things are more important than sex on the first day of the year."

"I disagree."

"Well, fuck you."

"Would you like to?"

"Jesus."

"Admit it, Regan, he can't give you the things I can."

"You think your dick is special, Marcus? Because it isn't, it's just a dick."

If Aldo were here, Regan thought, he'd say something about how sex was a simple formula. It wasn't even complex math, that crazy shit with functions. It was just penetration plus clitoral stimulation, easy. Nothing was easier. Marc babysat rich pricks for a living, Aldo solved the mysteries of the universe. Where the fuck was the comparison?

"I thought you wanted things to end amicably. Didn't you say you wanted to be friends?"

"That's just what people say, Marc. I've never been amicable in my entire life."

"Look how mad you are, it's adorable. Insecure about your relationship already, Regan?"

Great. Now he was psychoanalyzing her.

She said nothing.

"I told you, Regan, he only seems like a good idea. You just like the *idea* of him. But eventually you'll remember that we're not an idea, we're real. Eventually you'll get tired of working so hard at being whatever the professor wants you to be."

"He doesn't want me to be anything."

"Oh, sure." Marc laughed. "He loves you the way you are, of course. Because he doesn't fucking know what you are."

"And what am I?"

"I don't know, nobody knows, but he certainly doesn't fucking know."

She felt a rage she didn't understand; an anger she didn't know how to direct.

"Just wait, Regan, until he figures you out. You're complicated at first, unpredictable, exciting, but eventually you're just a pattern. You feel something, you lash out. You get soft again, you don't want to be alone, then you're Dream Girl all over again. You think you want sex? You don't *want* it, Regan, you *need* it. You need it to remind you that somebody loves you, and you won't believe that unless there's sex involved. That's it, that's everything there is to you, isn't there? You need to be loved, you need someone to believe you're perfect, you hate being reminded you have flaws. I already figured it out, so you needed someone else. Someone new. And when *he* figures you out, you'll just find someone else. You fucking love the con, Regan. You love the con, but the con doesn't love you, you're not good enough at it. Your game is a lot less fun when it's the same shit over and over."

Marc said all that, or she thought he said it. The words went in and out of her head and when he was gone, she still hadn't said anything. She went outside, fumbling for her phone, and she called Aldo.

"I'm not a game," she told him.

"I know you're not a game," he said, confused, and then, "Where are you?"

She'd created an emergency, she realized, abruptly shameful. She'd done it, she'd staged it, just like she said she would. Fuck, she really was predictable.

"I'm going home," she said. "I'm fine, I'm fine. I just wanted to hear your voice."

She'd defused the situation. Good job, Regan. Another day for him to believe you're something close to sane.

"I love you," Aldo said.

Marc used to say that, she thought.

"I love you. Come home soon."

"I'll come home tomorrow if you want. My dad's fine, and anyway he's busy with the restaurant."

"No, I'm . . . I'm fine, Aldo, it's okay."

Aldo, I cry when it rains, I pick fights sometimes, I don't know why. I look at the sky and feel this inexplicable sense of dread. I'm afraid that everything will end; are you ever afraid like that? No, you're never afraid, you have numbers and thoughts and your genius to keep you warm. You don't need me, I need you, and it will always be like that, unequal like that. I will always cling to you in gratitude and you will always be kind, you're just made that way. You'll let me do it but eventually I will make you unhappy, and then it will be on me to leave, because you are much too good to give me the ending we both know I deserve.

"Can I just come back there?" she asked, a little timidly, and he laughed.

"Of course. You miss Masso?"

"Yes, I miss Masso." He feels more like home than my home, he's kinder than my father. "I want cheese."

"I can pick out cheese for you."

"I could get on a plane right now."

"You could, but it's late. Are you sure you're okay?"

She was quiet for a moment.

"I don't think I really want to come back to L.A.," she said. "I think I just want to come back to last week."

"Ah." He considered it. "Okay, then we're in last week."

"Together?"

"Of course. It's last week, isn't it?"

"Which moment last week?"

"You tell me."

"Okay. Okay." She fidgeted, toying with the beads on her dress. It was cold outside, and she started walking, because getting a cab on New Year's Eve in River North wasn't fucking happening.

"It's that day you took me to the beach," she said. The ocean wasn't very close to Pasadena; it was a full day's activity just to go there and back, and the water wasn't particularly warm. Certainly not warm enough to get in, but she did, sort of. "I'm standing with my feet in the ocean, and you're smiling at me like I'm an idiot."

"I wasn't smiling like that."

"Yes, Rinaldo, you were."

"No, I meant—I was just trying to keep you there, prolong it in my head. I guess I didn't know I was smiling."

The idea that even he didn't recognize happiness when he felt it was comforting, in some way. She was comforted by knowing he was equally as stupid and hopeless as she was.

"You want to know what I was thinking?" she asked.

"Tell me."

"I was thinking that sex on the beach is probably overrated."

He laughed. "Yeah?"

"Yeah, the sand probably just gets everywhere, and besides, it was the first time I didn't want to have sex with you."

"Ouch."

"No, I mean . . . not like that." She pulled her coat tighter around her. "I was thinking about the way the water felt hitting my ankles, the way it could pull me away. I thought about how easy it would be to disappear, to get dragged under the waves and be lost forever, but you were standing right there, and I thought . . . all I'd have to do is reach out."

She could feel his silence. She imagined him tracing the shadow of something foreign and incomprehensible on her skin, ancient letters that stood for ancient concepts.

"I'm going to try to get a flight tomorrow," he said.

She exhaled swiftly, like a sob.

"You don't have to."

"Well, who knows if I'll be able to, but still, I want to. I miss you." Everything that had ever left Rinaldo Damiani's mouth was a fact, and with the same degree of factual authority, he said, "Stay on the phone with me until you get home."

Stay, stay, stay.

Regan stepped into the street, watching the streetlights glisten against the dampness of the asphalt. That day they'd suffered the sort of slushy, precipitous snowfall that left behind slickness and salt.

Every bar had muddied floors, caution signs, a slosh of weather and spilled drinks beneath the din of clamoring voices. The hazy sheen of red, yellow, green at her feet winked and glittered, reflections of headlights temporarily blinding her where she stood.

"Aldo," Regan said, "what's the ether?"

"It's what people used to believe the universe was filled with," he said. "They believed light needed to pass through something, only Einstein proved light can be particles, which don't need a medium to travel through. And before that," he added, "ether was what they called the air in the realm of the gods. A shining, fluid substance."

"So when people say we're alone in the ether . . . ?"

"Alone in everything. In time and space, in existence, in religion."

"But," she said, and stopped. "But the bees."

She felt certain she could feel him smile.

"Yeah," he said, "the bees," and she felt the weight in her chest ease a little, the sea that had risen to her ankles fading away with the tide.

That night, as the year was changing, Regan picked up a brush, tied her hair back and looked down at an untouched canvas, observing the blankness as if that were an object itself. She paced the floor, pushed the bed to the side; she rearranged things around the canvas, which sat in the center of everything.

Okay, she said to herself, what now?

(Just wait, Regan, until he figures you out.)

She closed her eyes.

I am not a game, she thought, breathing out and imploring time to slow.

Graciously, the night obliged.

———

Habits, Aldo had always thought, were the antithesis of linear time. As in, a habitual existence was to live time in circles, like chasing your tail, this time the same as this time the same as that one. Before Regan, each of Aldo's days had been precisely the same, as close to a carbon copy of the others as he could conceivably create. Monday layered over Tuesday layered over Wednesday; Thursday was a tracing of the others and so on, with only faint warps around the edges—where he ate something slightly different for breakfast or missed a traffic light on the way home from work—to acknowledge the passing of time. He could travel forward and backward merely by existing within the halo of habit. He lived each day over and over, with only his memory of rising each morning to prove that his existence followed the same rules of motion as everything else. He didn't know it was vacancy until his new life was overfull, bursting, his sense of stability lost to the effort of pacing himself to her. When she moved, he moved, and it was unsteadying; debilitating, at times.

Charlotte Regan, Aldo suspected, had never lived a day twice in her entire life.

He understood now why she'd agreed to six conversations with a stranger. It wasn't because she'd been curious about him the same way he'd been curious about her. It wasn't because of him at all, actually. It was because for her, life was careening into something for the reward of—of what? He wasn't entirely sure—*something.* He could look back on himself, time-traveling through retrospect, and see that he was in love with her right away, though he'd given it other names at the time: curiosity, interest, attraction. For her, though, he had been another break in habit, a disruption, and those were the things she craved like sustenance. She proved herself alive by proving this day had never been lived before, that this thing had never been felt or never tasted or never wanted, and now, because it existed, things were different; changed.

Charlotte Regan, Aldo realized, loved change, unhealthily. She loved it like an obsession, like infatuation. With change she had an ongoing affair, and perhaps it had been neutralized for a time with pills and psychotherapy but underneath it all, the little monster that was her soul was clawing for it, and it had been Aldo who'd hauled it out again. He'd unleashed a titan, he'd freed her, fallen in love with her, and as much as he'd hoped it would relent to something manageable, it did not.

"You know what I think?" Regan whispered to him one night. She didn't sleep regular hours. Neither did he, but he pretended to. He followed a schedule, even if his mind refused to rest within the parameters he prescribed. "I think you carry around a sadness from another life," she said. "From centuries ago." She traced his mouth, his cheeks, his eyes, practicing for something he would never understand. "You've just been carrying it around for so long that you can't put it down, can you? It's yours now. You've been tasked with looking after it. You're like Atlas," she said with a laugh. "Aldo, you poor thing, what a curse. I wonder which god you angered."

His mouth was dry, and not purely because she'd slid her fingers into it, hooking one behind the backs of his front teeth. She did that, loved him invasively, exploring him like the depths of the sea.

"I don't really believe in reincarnation," he said.

"Well, neither do I, but it's a hypothesis," she replied. "Sometimes," she added, with a mournful little twist of confession, "sometimes I think it's so pointless that we'll never know anything. We'll never *test* anything because we can't, it's impossible to be around long enough." She hummed to herself, something unrecognizable, probably the melodic nature of her thoughts; he wished he could commit the full score to paper, to see what the violins were up to when she was busy channeling the upright bass. "I guess we just have to believe what feels right, don't we?"

"So, I'm . . . cursed?" he asked her, and she laughed again, then sobered quickly.

"You have to take back your life, Aldo," she said, suddenly admonishing. "You can't just live in your past lives."

"I wasn't aware that I was."

"Of course you are. Don't you see, if you make the trajectory even a little bit longer, everything's a little different? Happiness," she told him, "maybe it's something you've been earning slowly, over several lifetimes, and now it's something you get to have. Maybe all this math you know, maybe it was a little seed of something before and now it's finally bearing fruit. Maybe you weren't made this way, you *became* this way," she finished triumphantly, and then he understood.

I'm made like this, he had told her before, and so now she was setting him free, casting off the restrictions of a dull reality. She made his life magic as a favor to him, without his asking, and he understood now, too, what she'd meant: I don't believe it, but maybe I do.

It isn't real, but maybe it is. Because maybe she needed to relinquish him from something and maybe she didn't, but wasn't his burden lighter now, either way?

He loved her fiercely for that.

He didn't see the problem in loving her that way, with a savagery that felt as ancient as his sorrows, until he realized that he could no longer recall a life without her. It was as if the older versions of him had been erased and could no longer exist. He realized that his relationship with time, whatever it was before, was now forever altered.

It brought him back to memories of his grandmother, his nonna, who had died of a blood clot when Aldo was in his early twenties. He and his father had sat there through the night, silent except for the prayers she requested. I hope she'll wake up, Masso said hoarsely, his eyes red-rimmed and swollen, and Aldo, a scientist—a *mathematician*—pondered how to explain it to him. You see, Dad, he said gently, she's lost so much blood already, irreparable damage has been done, the human body is fragile. Even a minute, even a second without that which it needs to survive leaves it crippled, weak, uncertain how to proceed as it has always done. Yes, she could open her eyes, she could begin breathing on her own, miracles are not unheard of. But the body cannot come back, it cannot rebuild itself. It cannot suffer a loss and become what it was before, no, it doesn't work that way. If she comes back, Aldo told his father, she will be different. Will she be less? Who's to say (yes, definitely, but this was his nonna, and Masso wouldn't want to hear it) but either way, she will not be the person you remember. She cannot be, even in resurrection, what she was in life.

This was what Regan did to Aldo: irreparable damage to his former self. Regan was Regan, but she was also the loss of a former life to which he could never return. Of course he didn't wish to, but that wasn't the point. It could never exist a second time. He considered what she'd said—*if it all fails, Aldo, go back and erase us, make it like we never happened*—and he understood that while it would be a cruelty, it would be a kindness in equal measure. Because the old him was dead, and what existed of him now could die, too, a painful death, if he were capable of doing what she asked. What he was now, some toddler of a man learning how to breathe again, would be gone. His life before her, his life without her, the Parthenon, they would all be ancient rubble. Only stories would remain to give them value. Charlotte Regan had killed him once and she could kill him again, easily. She could kill him, and that was what Masso had feared, even if he didn't know it. She could kill him, and now Aldo understood.

So this is what it is to love something you cannot control, he thought. It felt precisely like terror.

He studied her, as that was in his nature. For Aldo, to love something was to study it; to devote every spare thought to understanding it. He knew how to study and he'd been doing it for years; learning was more at the core of his being than teaching. He researched her, trying to identify her laws and constants, starting with how she looked at relationships.

"Why don't you like your sister's husband?"

"I don't know, they're just so conventional together."

"That sounds like a dirty word for normal."

"No, normal is a nice word for boring."

"I suppose you're better at words than I am."

"Well, that's part of it, isn't it? Carter is so unspecial and Madeline isn't. It seems like a waste."

"What does that have to do with me and words?"

"Oh, only that you're so terrible with them but so good with numbers. Sorry, I guess I didn't explain that."

(Regan explained very little. Half of what she said existed in silences that Aldo tried and struggled to interpret.)

"So I'm not unspecial?" he asked.

"Of course not."

"And you're certainly not unspecial."

"Sweet of you."

"So should unspecial people only deserve each other, then?"

"I don't know," she said listlessly, "I just don't like him. But Madeline does, so why do I have to?"

"You don't, I just wanted to know why."

He was worried she'd become agitated, but she seemed to settle instead.

"Ah," she said, smoothing out the furrow in his brow. "Trying to solve me again?"

"What makes you think that?"

"Oh, only that I know your equation face so well by now."

He felt desperately uninformed. "Equation face?"

"No, you know what it is? It's the little moan you make," she said, as if that was as unremarkable a detail about him as the color of his hair. "That sound has a face, and that face is very similar to your equation-solving face. It's frustration and restraint," she clarified, surer now after having built some momentum, "like you want the satisfaction of the end result, but not too quickly, not too easily. If it comes too easily, it's not worth doing. You know how good it'll feel to figure it out, but you don't want it yet so you're pushing it away. It's like that," she said.

Regan always spoke about sex with an incredible, incomprehensible ease. For Aldo, sex had always been a little dirty, a little taboo, certainly not something to discuss. She brought it up easily, without batting an eye. For her, sex was part of her humanity. It was part of how she experienced the world.

"I don't think you can ever really know a person without fucking them," she said once, which was a moderately disturbing thing to hear. "I don't need to know *everyone*," she said, watching his face change and laughing a little to herself. "Not everyone is worth knowing in full, I'm just saying, you can't know someone until you've had sex with them. I mean, look at all the kinks a person can have, the things they can be attracted to, whether they have to feel love or not feel it. Whether they enjoy it or not. It's all so comprehensive to who a person is. Can you really understand someone without knowing what brings them pleasure? No, you really can't, so we have to resign ourselves to knowing that we won't know most of the people in our lives at all." Then she added, conspiratorially, "But that doesn't mean I can't make guesses."

She confessed to him that her relationships with men, which he'd already understood in an abstract way to be flawed, were like that because she was constantly thinking of herself as a sexual object.

"I think it was just like that, from so early on," she told him. "For boys, sex is a part of life, a rite of passage. Boys look at porn when they're twelve, thirteen! Boys get to have sex just as it is, just sex. Girls are taught fairy tales, they're taught *happily ever after,* they're taught sex as a consequence of marriage. Imagine seeing the world that way, as if sex isn't a right but a rung on a ladder. We have to withhold it, can you imagine that? Because it's so brainless and simple that if men get it too easily, they'll just leave. Because really, how the fuck is my vagina different from any other woman's? No, the thing that makes me different is somewhere else, literally anywhere else, but I can't enjoy sex without some archaic sociological risk. And if you think about that it's even worse, because look at the vagina, Aldo. It can have *infinite* orgasms. It doesn't require any recovery time. It can come and come and come and what, maybe it gets dry? Lube it up again, easy. If any sexual organ is omnipotent it's the fucking cunt but no, penises are the ones who get to decide whether a woman has value. Who let that happen? Really, Aldo, who? Maybe this is why men rule the world, because they were clever enough to convince women that virginity is precious, that sex itself should be secret, that being *penetrated* was sacrosanct. It's idiotic, it's even dumber than it is cruel and that's the worst part. The idea that I should want sex less than you, why does that exist?"

Not that her relationships with women were much better. In fact, Regan had told him right away that she didn't have many friends, and gradually, Aldo discovered that she had been right, or at least honest. That, of course, was the interesting part. Regan didn't have a lot of time or energy for the sort of love that required openness, and it made Aldo realize that the best thing he could have done to win Regan over was to immediately identify her primary truth: that she was most comfortable when she was at her falsest. Regan did not enjoy honesty. She hated it, was repulsed by it, and by her own truths especially. With other people's truths she merely collected them like shiny things, tucking them away or else carrying them around, wondering where to put them.

With Aldo's, though, she hoarded them. What did he think about this, why did he love this thing, why was sex best for him like this, why did he choose her? Her compulsion to know was familiar—physically, mentally, procedurally—but it was also a significant break in what he understood about her. Why was she truthful with him and not with others? Why did she wish to know his truths while immediately rejecting them from other people in her life? She wasn't uncaring in the slightest. She spoke highly of a number of people, but detested possessing any realities of what they were.

Perhaps it was because people were naturally inclined to be honest with her. She had an innocent look; those wide eyes were tricky. She had a deceptive way of making attentiveness look like interest. She was like a magician, down to the quick of it. She measured silences, she used physical cues to guide them to the outcome she wanted; Pick a card, any card, only she was subtly planting with the tilt of her head or with the open motion of her hands: Choose this one. Tell me about your weaknesses, your insecurities, your sex life; yes, tell me, don't you want me to know? They fell for it every time, not recognizing her for what she was.

It only occurred to Aldo later why he was different.

"Because I love you," she said.

He had watched her ignore a phone call, silencing the vibration, and asked her why she didn't care to know what her parents and sister and friends were up to but always wanted to know the most meager details about his day. She hungered for them, the unremarkable crumbs of him. What did you teach today? Who's your favorite student? What did your advisor say about your dissertation? Did you box today or run or both? For how long, how was it, which muscles hurt? What was your favorite thing that happened today? Why? What do you want to happen tomorrow? He answered all of her questions, amused, but wanted to understand: Why ask me this when you haven't seen me for ten hours, but you don't care how your mother filled up the last ten days?

"Because I love you."

As simple and uncomplicated and wildly unimaginable as that.

It was around that time when, knowing Charlotte Regan was capable of murder, Aldo made a decision. He would have to possess her, all of her, the way he did not currently possess anything and had never possessed anything before. He would have to be able to look at everything she was all at once; to open all the doors she kept locked inside herself and then run through the house, laying claim to the whole of it. How long would that take? Surely ages, eons, several different lifetimes and fuck, he would have to start soon, start imme-diately. She was right—wasn't she?—that humans were inherently flawed, hindered by their insubstantial life expectancies, by mortal-ity itself. He would never have enough time, but still, he would have to have all of it, most of it. He couldn't get back the time that he'd missed, but if not him, then who would have all the rest?

He would have to keep her, somehow, and that would mean solv-ing her. That would mean making her his impossible problem. Time travel no longer held any interest for him, only Regan and whatever it would take to make her a fixture in his life. Knowing her would mean knowing everything, not just her thoughts or her truths or the way she liked to be fucked. Knowing her would mean knowing her future, having it for himself. It was knowing what her children would look like, and what *she* would look like someday, when the youth was gone from her face and replaced by something else; by what? A mystery. It was a fucking mystery and Aldo couldn't sit idly by while there were mysteries afoot. Uncertainty was something he lived with, yes, but not anymore. Frustration and restraint, she had said, equating his love of math with his love of her.

I am Atlas, he thought, holding up the heavens. I will be endur-ance, I will have to endure.

"What are you thinking about?" she asked him.

"I think we should move in together," he said.

She smiled.

"Hm," she said. "And here I thought you'd be sick of me by now."

––––––

In early February, Aldo and Regan walked hand in hand into her lit-tle studio apartment, put things in boxes, summoned a cab outside and then stepped into it, laden down with possessions that smelled of her perfume. They spent two hours shifting pieces of Aldo's life aside to make room for hers: a toothbrush beside his, her makeup in his medicine cabinet, her dresses hanging beside his suit. He shrank down to make room for her, lent her the corners of his sanity. They had unhurried sex in the bed, which had once been his but was now theirs; she slid her palm across the sheets and thought of changing things. She would implant herself in Aldo over time, whether she intended to or not. She would buy him nicer sheets, give him a taste for her softness that he could never unfulfill. She would occupy his fridge with the foods she liked, the things she loved that she would say: Come here and taste this, and then he would and he would enjoy it, too. He would come to share her joys until he could no longer separate them from his own, and then one day, maybe turning to her at a party or rushing to ask in a text message, he would say: What's that thing I like? And she would know the answer. She would know everything. Eventually, all the answers to all that he was would be cradled in the palms of her hands.

How dangerous! What a fool he was, how shortsighted, how little-lived he'd been not to feel her fear as she felt it. For her it was an informed terror, reentering a haunted house, replaying an old and frequent death. She kissed him; Sorry about your stupidity. She wanted to tell him, to teach him: Every time you love, pieces of you break off and get replaced by something you steal from someone else. It seems like it's the right shape but it's slightly different every time, so that eventually, very very quietly and over days and days and days, you are transformed into something unrecognizable, and it happens so slowly you don't even notice, like shedding scales and making new ones.

He smiled at her like: Isn't it great?

Yes, she thought, pained. Yes, it is perilously wonderful to suffer so sweetly with you.

She had thought of him as a sort of nomad-adjacent person with meandering habits, but that wasn't true, not really. He worked hard, worked diligently, worked often. He went to class to learn and to teach, had meetings constantly with professors and colleagues, worked tirelessly on his dissertation. His work, unlike hers (hers was the opposite) was almost entirely inside his head. She came to understand that he could sit relatively still for an hour and only write down one, maybe two things when he was done.

She joined him in his rituals, sitting next to him with her shoulder pressed to his, coaxing him to tell her what he was thinking about as he toyed with a joint between his teeth.

"What's your dissertation about?"

His response was practiced. "The math behind quantum physics."

"Which is?"

"Dimensions, functions of reality. Time. Uncertainty; the math behind Heisenberg, Schrödinger—"

"The cat?"

"Not so much that. But sure, also the cat."

"Is it dead or alive?"

"Both."

"And that makes sense to you?"

"It's just a thought experiment. And my job is to make things make sense."

Said playfully, "Well, you're not doing a very good job."

Said with agreement, "Probably why they haven't given me a degree yet."

"What does any of this have to do with time travel?"

"Everything—most things—fit within the parameters of time. If we understood how time worked, then maybe we could use it."

"Do you love it?"

"Love what?"

"What you do, what you study."

He paused for a moment before answering.

"Math comes very easily to me," he eventually said.

"What if it didn't?"

"What?"

"What if it didn't come easily? Would you still do it?"

Only then did he seem to understand the question.

"Math is a difficult thing to love," he said. "It's precise and unforgiving, it's evasive and it will never love me back, but I don't have much of a choice, do I? It's the thing that I can do that other people can't, or that other people lack the patience for. Are there worthier things, more rewarding things? Yes, probably. But I don't know what they are, they never showed themselves to me. Only math did."

"How unromantic," Regan said, and it was meant to be a joke, but she thought for a moment she meant it.

"Not entirely," he said, and she recalled suddenly that while he believed himself securely fixed, it was really math that saved his life. His answer, which had not seemed like an answer at all at first, was that he had devoted himself to math because it had found him. He couldn't imagine another life for himself because for him, this was not choice, it was simply destiny.

Ah, so fate, Regan thought. So it is romance, after all.

"Charlotte," the doctor said, "are you listening?"

Regan dragged her attention back to the doctor, who was sitting across from her.

"Sorry," she said, and the doctor's expression tightened.

"You realize these sessions are court-ordered," the doctor said. "If I reported to the judge that you were no longer complying with the terms of your sentence—"

"I'm here, aren't I?"

"You aren't here in any way that matters," the doctor said. "You do not participate in our sessions."

"What exactly do you want from me?"

"Something, Charlotte, anything."

Regan glanced moodily at her hands.

"I moved in with my boyfriend," she said.

"Marc? I thought you lived with him already."

"No, not Marc, Aldo. Rinaldo."

The doctor's brow furrowed in puzzlement. "The . . . mathematician?"

"The genius, yes."

"Why do you call him that?"

"Because he is." And he was. She'd seen the proof several times over. She was positive he only had so much time for her because he could do the work faster than his colleagues. He rarely had to do things twice, and as far as she could tell, he never struggled. He was a genius and she, lamentably human, regularly marveled.

"What about your painting?"

"I still do it." Aldo was usually busy during the day, and she'd kept her studio. It was littered wall to wall with paint supplies and canvases now, things left out to dry while she slept at home with Aldo. "I'm working on something new. A collection."

"What are you working on?"

"I don't know yet."

"Charlotte."

"I don't know yet," she repeated, irritated. "I'm not not telling you or anything. I just don't know what it is."

The doctor stared at her for a moment.

Then, "I called your pharmacy expecting that you would need a refill authorization, Charlotte. They told me you still had three refills remaining."

Regan said nothing.

"I wrote you a six-month prescription," the doctor said, "and it's been nine."

Regan knew enough about guilt and innocence not to fidget.

"You're not taking your pills," the doctor finally deduced, and Regan crossed her arms over her chest, annoyed.

"No, I'm not. I don't want to," she said. "I don't like them, I don't like what they do to me, and I can't paint when I'm on them. I'm happier now."

"Are you?"

"Yes, things are different. Very different."

"Because you're not with Marc?"

"Because I'm with someone better than Marc."

"I thought he was a friend?"

"I don't have friends," Regan said, with a laugh that sounded hollow, even to her. "Aldo was never just a friend. I just didn't want to admit it."

"Did you cheat on Marc?"

"What does it matter?"

"I'm just asking."

"No, I didn't. Aldo isn't the bad guy in all this. And Marc certainly isn't the good guy."

"Then who is? The bad guy, I mean."

Regan laughed again. "Me, I guess. I'm the criminal, aren't I?"

She could see the red flags in the psychiatrist's mind; surely this had been a subject on all the psychiatry exams. Surely this doctor had once convinced a board of established professionals that this was something she could handle. Oh, a recalcitrant patient says they will no longer medicate, they self-identify as a problem or an illness, what do you do?

"I don't like the idea of you not being on pills, Charlotte."

Excellent, Regan imagined a professor saying in response: gentle yet tactful, harsh but fair. Human, but not excessively so. Let us not forget our roles in this office. Let us not forget the parts we've all agreed to play.

"I hate being called Charlotte," Regan said, suddenly feeling her edges start to fray, "and you don't know me. You don't know anything about me. You only know my prescriptions, my diagnosis, things you've written in your notes. Why should I do what you think is best," she scoffed, "just because you went to Harvard? Because my family wants me quiet, they want me numb, is that why you don't like it?"

The doctor was silent a moment. "If I don't know anything about you, it's because you've never told me anything. You've told me the barest, least informative details about your life, and I have no way of knowing who you are, or how you feel, unless you tell me. If you're not participating in therapy, you're wasting both our time."

Regan's voice was bitter, coarsely mean. "So should I go to prison, then? Is that what you think I deserve?"

"Is it what *you* think you deserve?" the doctor countered, and Regan wanted badly to break something. A window, an elbow, anything.

"Before I met Aldo," Regan said tightly, "I was a forger."

"Yes. I know."

No, Regan thought, you don't. "Forgery isn't art," she said, "it's precision. It's a process of labor more than it is a craft. It's interpretation, translation. But it is a talent, and it is the one I had. There really is nothing more to who I was than that."

"It's not your only talent, Char—"

The doctor broke off, catching Regan's preemptive flinch.

"But now?" the doctor asked instead, and Regan turned away, grimacing.

She felt, suddenly, entirely detached from everything, including herself.

"Aldo believed I was an artist, so I made it true," Regan said. "He believed I was an honest person who lied from time to time instead of a liar who sometimes told the truth, so I was. He believed I could love him and so I did, I do."

He woke me up, she wanted to scream; he woke me, and for that I will always rely on him, I will be to him what he is to math, and can't you see how fragile that is? Can't you see how intangibly I exist, and how perilously? Can't you see that I—the me that I am right now, sitting here with you at this moment—am a figment of his imagination? He dreamt me into being. He can always undream me, unbelieve me. He can unmask me, and then what will be left? Will I always fear him as much as I love him? Will I always be only one half of his whole? What are soulmates, and am I one, or am I just a parasite, a leech, a cancer that spreads and takes hold and takes pleasure in choking us both?

The doctor uncrossed her legs, thinking, and crossed them again.

"Tell me," the doctor said, "why you shouldn't be on medication. Convince me."

Regan lifted her gaze warily to the doctor's.

"How about this," Regan said. "We'll have six real conversations. If, at the end of them, you still believe I need to be medicated, then fine, I'll take my pills. But if not, I won't ever take them again. You can watch me if you want to, and I'll still come in every two weeks, but if after six conversations you believe me, then we're done with the pills." She stopped, watching for a reaction, but found none. "Okay?"

"Why six conversations?" the doctor asked.

Regan cleared her throat, recognizing that this would be a very long, highly revelatory answer. Surely the cracks would show.

But it had worked once, hadn't it?

"It has to do with," Regan began, and paused. "Bees."

The doctor leaned back in her chair, nodding.

"Alright, then," she said. "Tell me about the bees."

PART SIX

PART SIX

TURNS.

Aldo wasn't sure which moment he would have to return to in order to fix everything that had gone wrong.

Typically, identifying the nexus of any event was a skill of his. He could plot almost anything once he could identify the sequences, the order in which things went from fine to bad to worse. Despite this, or perhaps because of it, he would struggle to piece the night together temporally. Instead, he would experience it as if it were happening all over again, only in bits and fragments all at once.

There was Marc's voice, saying, "You really don't see it, do you? And here I thought you were supposed to be some sort of genius. See, she picks people her parents don't approve of—just your standard run-of-the-mill daddy problems, nothing new or even exciting about it—and then they lose their appeal, and suddenly she gets mysterious. She starts doing fuck-knows-what all the time, something about finding herself or some shit, and oh, so now she's not happy, but she twists it all, somehow, she twists it so it's your fault, and you fucking believe her, but here's the thing: *She doesn't want to be happy.* You can't make her happy, you know why? Because some people know how to fucking coexist and Regan doesn't, she doesn't want to, she never will. I don't know why I came here, honestly, I think I just had to see it for myself. I had to see her stand there and pretend like you're the new best thing in her life, and you know what? Maybe you'll last longer than I did, because her parents hate you so much they asked me to be here and I know for a fact they can't stand me. Fuck," Marc says in Aldo's mind with a laugh, "you poor bastard, I don't even blame you for any of it. You're just the latest thing she'll step on to get wherever she goes next."

From there it's only lines, colors, textures. A party, and requisite party scenes. Nothing remarkable—until his eye settles on something surprising, that is. A golden hexagon, tiny in the corner of a painting, with the same sort of metallic glint made famous by

Klimt, which is an artist he knows she loves. She once told him that she could stare at *The Kiss* for hours, just looking at the woman's face and imagining what it was to be her, to be held like that, to be touched like that.

Why does she turn her face away from her lover? Aldo had asked. Regan thought it was to show the woman's expression, to capture her emotion by the blissful contortion of her face, but Aldo thought otherwise. He thought: To give into something all at once was to lose yourself completely, and therefore to resist was to exchange one fleeting moment of pleasure for a more exquisite, abounding pain.

Relatedly, there was Regan. "No, not here," he had said, catching her hands. She'd already had his pants unzipped, her dress hiked up, but he had his face turned away. "Not here, not now," followed by pain or anger, he didn't know which. What had come first, the warp of rage when he'd pushed her away, or the one when her mother betrayed her? Had Regan felt a compulsive need for sex to be reminded that she was loved, or had she simply craved the love she had never received inside the house where she had never received it? Aldo had thoughts about compulsion and craving, about the differences between them, and now, he thought, Which was he?

Was it love between them, or was it need?

Lines, colors, and textures. The little hexagon, and then the yellow-not-yellow of Regan's dress.

Where would he undo it, if he could undo it?

"Where's the real one?" he had asked her, and was that the thing that had done it?

(Undone it?)

No, not there. Not yet. Close, but not quite—

She was full of innocence, softly murmuring, "What do you mean?"

"You're lying." He'd already done the research. He'd learned her right away.

"Aldo, listen—"

Wait for it, he thought, replaying it again. Wait for the blood to boil in his sad, pathetic veins. Wait for his confusion, his sense of loss. Wait for her to stare at him, lying like only she could lie, and wait for him to think, for the first time, about the way she's never really answered a question. It was charming at first, wasn't it? An eccentricity, an artistic detail, a golden little hexagon on the mark of what she was. It was infatuating, learning to read her, only she's not just a problem without a solution, she's a broken loop that can't be fixed. Wait for him to realize it, to place things into categories in his head, and then wait for him to wonder if, while he was experiencing something special, she had ever really felt the same?

Wait for him to think, My god, she's a forger. She's a thief, she replicates things. Wait for him to say to himself: I am not only the same as Marc, but Marc is the same as the man before him, and the men who are the same as the men before that, and perhaps we are all counterfeit bills, recreated over and over while she cheapens our value, drains us of meaning, spends us like currency and throws us away. Wait for him to think, It's too fast, everything is too fast—and surely he doesn't really *believe* this, but how could he not, when the signs are all there? He is supposed to recognize the patterns. He is the one who calls things that are always true by their names, he understands the difference between constants and variables, he assigns logic to exceptions and rules. Wait for him to look at her as if he has no idea who she is, or who he is, or what they are.

Wait for it—

"You really haven't changed, have you?" he asks her.

Eventually, a later version of Aldo will recognize the detail for what it is. There it is, he thinks, and the thought is unsatisfactory, but final.

There it is. That's the moment.

That's the one.

THIS IS WHAT HAPPENED TO ALDO.

The spring preceding that particular evening was both familiar and unfamiliar, the way spring in Chicago always was. One day it was winter and the next the ice had thawed, and gradually buttons were loosened on coats, or perhaps coats were forgotten altogether on the way to normal, unremarkable errands down the block. Let's get coffee, Yes yes let's, is it cold out? Surprisingly no, let's go; and then outside the sun would shine, and so the relevant parties would say, Sunglasses?, Yes, sunglasses; and thusly, spring would creep into their constitutions. People would begin to crawl out from wherever they'd been hiding through the winter months, filling the streets again and reminding the rest of the city's inhabitants that people *did,* in fact, live there. Every year it was a surprise how long and desolate a winter could be, and thus, every year spring was a welcome champion. It was like a collective breath of relief, the exhalation of monochrome dreariness. Even for Aldo and Regan, who had been warmer that winter for having been in each other's arms, the arrival of spring was its usual reminder that all things have a season.

For Aldo in particular, the spring was much as it always was. His students always did better in the second half of the year; the approach of longer days and warmer weather was enough to motivate even the most ambivalent of learners. He typically did his best work in the spring as well, finally able to return to his usual patterns of park visitation, his pursuit of open space. He took his motorbike, mostly cleaned of salt and rust, to the usual park, making his way to the usual bench and letting the sun's rays, old but new, drift again over his shoulders.

It was much the same as it always was, his thinking. It was constant and frantic and dull and stagnant, as his thoughts had always been, and put to work for an impossible problem, as it usually was. On that particular day, he withdrew a newly rolled joint from his pocket and spun it between his fingers, much as he often did.

Only this spring, things were slightly different. For one thing, Aldo's hair, which usually fell into his eyes until he scraped it carelessly back, was freshly cut. His clothes were clean, and he no longer smelled faintly of weed. He smelled, instead, a little like acrylic paint, spilled wine, and honeysuckle. The T-shirt he wore was new, purchased on his behalf and then slipped into his closet without ceremony.

The problem, too, was slightly different than it had been.

"You seem a little distracted," said Aldo's advisor.

"Is there a problem with my dissertation?"

"No, nothing like that, your work is fine, and, well, you've always been . . ."

(People were usually too polite to finish that sentence.)

"Distant," the professor continued, clearing his throat, "But still, is everything quite all right?"

"With me? Yes, of course," said Aldo, who unlike Regan, could only lie selectively.

His problem was this: Beginning in late March, Regan had stopped sleeping. Her sleep patterns had always been erratic, often easily disrupted, but that had been the difference: the predictability of her unpredictability. During the winter, she had occasionally been loath to leave their bed, still nestled in the sheets until Aldo returned from class in the afternoon, or else she would be inclined to stay up all night, postulating wildly about the universe. Regan didn't often cook, but when she did it was a production, a spectacle; she used every pot and pan in the cupboards and produced multiple courses of varying quality. On those days, Aldo would spy the glasses of wine upon entry and observe, drawing from his shallow but reliable well of experience, that it would be another night of sex and conversation.

His days were a process of recognizing subtle cues: Had Regan gotten out of bed willingly or sluggishly? Had she leapt or dragged? Had she purchased something, many things, and had she been gone for several hours, or had she never left the house? Was Regan smiling, was she crying, was she shouting? Regan's tears were almost never of sadness and, instead, usually of rage or frustration, little of which was directed at him. More often she was at war with something entirely different; someone she'd seen that day, or a thought of injustice she'd recently had. She could spark to passion about almost anything, and Aldo learned to recognize the signs, the patterns: What films had she been watching? She had happy films, sad films, cathartic ones, and same with books. She read voraciously, several books at once, or not at all. She consumed music like it was a conversation with her soul; Did you hear that, Aldo, were you listening? How can you stand there as if nothing has changed when either you are not alive at all or all of what you are is now inconceivably different?

He grew accustomed to the turbulence until, abruptly, it stopped. March rolled around, the first day of spring came and went, and by April, Regan had begun to assimilate herself to regularity. Whose regularity that was, Aldo couldn't say. He knew that when he came home in the evenings, she was gone; she would creep in late at night and kiss his neck, or climb into his lap and say things—Regan things—like Aldo, I've been thinking about you all day, Rinaldo I'd like to put my fingers in the slats of your ribs, I want to shape my teeth to the ridges of your stomach, I'd like to kiss the tip of your cock and hold you inside me until we both see stars.

He didn't ask what she'd been doing, because he had already learned that she didn't like to be asked much of anything. Don't pry, she would say, I'll tell you when I'm ready, and he would listen to her because he trusted her, because he was afraid of her, because he loved her.

"I love her," he told Masso, who sighed.

"I know, I know you do, Rinaldo, but everything is too fast. First you like her, then you love her, then you live with her, then what?"

Flames licked at Aldo's thoughts, dancing in the shape of Regan's hips.

"So? Sometimes things move fast, Dad. It happens."

He didn't tell Masso that he had been right; that by May, Aldo was sure Regan was too fast for him. Much too fast, and he struggled to take in air, because even one breath to clear his head would mean faltering and falling behind. Aldo did not tell Masso that he was gripped with terror, understanding now what it really meant to love something. That to love a person was to forfeit the need to place limits on them, and therefore to love was to exist in a constant, paralyzing threat.

Secretly, Aldo believed that if he slowed down at all, Regan would run out of sight. He would never see anything of her but the back of her head. Perhaps there might be a glimpse over her shoulder, perhaps a regretful smile of Aldo, oh Aldo, thank you for your time, it was fun while it lasted—but then she would slip out, fall away, through his fingers and into the cracks of the sidewalk into some upside-down world where she belonged and where he could never, ever follow.

His thoughts of time persisted, though he no longer wished to transport himself through it and instead felt desperate to stop it, to drag it to a halt. He would suspend the hexagon of time at one edge and say, See, Regan? See, you're still alive even if things don't move in a blur, and then maybe she'd stroke his hair and touch his cheek with the pads of her fingers and say, Rinaldo, you're a genius.

People thought addiction was a craving. People were always saying they were addicted to things like chocolate or reality television, and as a result Aldo felt lexically homeless. That isn't it, he wanted to insist to them. He wanted to say, You don't understand, because now *he* understood. There was a difference between craving and compulsion. He knew this because of the pills, *his* pills, which had once been prescribed and dutifully followed. But the problem with pain existing in the mind is that it is easy to trick the mind into almost anything—placebos, opinion polls, skewed data; the list of what the brain could be taught to believe was endless—and likewise, the body will do almost anything to feel nothing. The extent to which Aldo aspired to be numb had once been vast, and his desperation for silence hardly much smaller. What omnipotence his medication had possessed until it hadn't; how obediently his mind would quiet until it had fallen out of love with the quiet and fought back.

People thought addiction was a craving, but the difference was this: Cravings were wishes that could be satisfied, but compulsions were needs that must be met.

He had once told Madeline that Regan was infinite, and she was. There was no way to tell where she began and where she ended. Aldo could think: Where has she been? What has she been doing? And she could answer him and he would still not understand, because where she was at any given time wasn't necessarily where she *was*, and what she'd been doing was another matter entirely. For example: Was she cooking, or filling a void? Was she painting, or summoning demons? Was she sleeping or was she dreaming, was she transporting through realms, what was it?

What was any of it, and would he ever understand?

He twirled the joint between his fingers, shaking his head. Why had he chosen the theoretical side of math? Because math had no stake in the consequences. Math was about explanation, not application. He had never cared to see whether anything really worked, only whether he could solve it, fix it, make it into something possible to understand. Let someone else *create* the particles; let others be the ones to discover what the universe was made of and then rebuild it, molding life out of proverbial clay. He only wanted to take something that no one had ever solved and transform it into something that could be viewed on a page, just so that someday, someone would say, Oh. Oh okay, I see it now—and then they would do with that knowledge whatever they wished, which was not a matter of concern for Aldo.

He had never taken responsibility for anything before Regan, and now it seemed that taking responsibility was all he could do.

His phone buzzed in his pocket. He pulled it out, bringing it to his ear.

"Ready for this?"

He glanced down at the joint, contemplating it. "Almost."

"You're in the park, aren't you?"

"Well, the museum's your space."

"It's yours, too." She liked to think of things as being shared. It was one of her virtues.

"Yeah, but it's nice out."

"It is, isn't it? But you'll have to come home, we need to get going."

"Okay. Now?"

"Yes, now." Patience, on the other hand, was not. "I've been assured it won't be terrible."

"By Madeline?"

"Yes, by Madeline."

"She's lying, isn't she?"

"Yes, almost certainly. But I think it's probably for the best."

Yes, he thought, it probably was.

"Okay, I'm on my way."

"I'll make it worth it, I promise."

She always did. "You always do."

"See you in five?"

"See you in five."

He put the joint in his pocket with his cell phone, looked out over the blossoming greenery of the park, and held his breath, fleetingly prolonging the length of a second.

Then he picked up his helmet and headed home, fulfilling the promises he'd made.

———

Last week, Madeline Regan had called not her sister Charlotte, but Aldo.

"Sorry," she said, "but I'm going to have to ask you to do something extremely unpleasant."

"Yes?"

"I need you to convince my sister to come home for our dad's birthday party. You won't have to stay the whole weekend," Madeline added quickly, before he could reply, "but at least come for the night, okay? He's turning seventy. It's a big one."

"How'd you get my number?"

"Charlotte gave it to me for emergencies."

"She did?"

"Yes."

"And this is an emergency?"

"Yes. As in, I *very emergently* do not want to explain to my mother why my sister won't come."

"Did you try asking her?"

"Aldo," Madeline said with a scoff, "are we talking about the same Charlotte Regan?"

To his surprise, though, Regan had been quick to agree. She'd seemed almost eager, in fact, as if this visit could somehow salvage the last one. She had picked out a tie for Aldo; had bought herself a new dress. She spoke of it as a normal event—"My dad's birthday party is next week, don't forget"—and did not seem to imbue it with any prophetic discomfort. Despite acknowledging that this event ("like every event my parents host") would likely be disastrous, she dismissed it with a flippant "You'll be there."

As in, "Everything will be fine, you'll be there."

Or, "I'm not worried, you'll be there."

She'd chosen a dress that was a yellow so pale it almost looked white, and she'd left her hair down, wearing it in waves that brushed romantically over her shoulders. It was an unusual choice in that it was soft, and Regan was not typically given to softness. She had costumed herself as Charlotte and had done so with apparent ease. She smiled at Aldo as she drove through metropolitan Chicago traffic, chattering to him the way she always did.

"I think it's my opportunity to mend things," she was saying, possibly trying to convince him, herself, or both of them, "and besides, they should meet you again."

He was less certain. "Do they know about me? Us, I mean."

"I assume Madeline told them," she said, shrugging. "They do know you're coming."

(Masso had been largely unhelpful: Of course they like you, Rinaldo, what's not to like? Dad, I really don't think so, Oh well all the poorer for them, never mind but I still say you're wrong. Dad, I think you overestimate how much people like me, my students hate me and most of my colleagues do, too. Well what do they know, only what you teach them, hm? Just show them something else, he'd said, as if that were so easily done, and it probably was. For Masso.)

Aldo was mostly silent while Regan drove, thinking about other things. About how, possibly, probably, her parents both hated him and also did not hate him, and how he could easily believe both were true until he arrived and opened the box. She reached over mindlessly, with the surety of frequent rehearsal, and laced her fingers with his. He brushed his lips across her knuckles, squeezed them once. He looked for omens and didn't find any, aside from the usual.

"Why did you bring me last time?" he asked.

"Instead of Marc, you mean?" she said offhandedly, and then, "Because I wanted you there instead."

He shook his head. She was misremembering. "It was because they didn't like Marc," he reminded her, meaning *and now they don't like me.*

A cycle. A pattern. (You should know what comes next, said his troublesome brain.)

She glanced briefly at him.

"That was an excuse," she said.

It was, he thought, and it wasn't. A lie and a truth contained paradoxically within a still-closed box that perhaps not even Regan had any interest in opening.

"I don't care if they like you or not," she informed him.

For a moment, his heart raced, stomach plummeting. His momentary loss of breath was acutely sharp, everything abruptly too fast.

"Okay," said Aldo, opting not to file it under *SIGNS.*

———

"You really haven't changed at all, have you?" Aldo had said in his usual matter-of-fact way.

Later, Regan would replay the evening in her head, running backward through time to identify her errors, but in that precise moment she felt trapped, unable to move.

She only saw Aldo with his back to her, his green eyes on her painting.

"Where's the real one?" he said stiffly.

Her first thought: He really was a genius. She'd left the original artist's signature, forged it perfectly, but out of something ill-advised—hubris, maybe, or some unexamined need to leave her mark on something, anything, just to prove she'd been part of the art in some small, insignificant way that her father would never possibly notice—she had added one tiny embellishment. One nearly invisible mark; a little flaw, just to prove her existence in the world. To prove to herself her location in time, in consequence.

And Aldo had seen it.

Telling the truth seemed too vulnerable; old habits. "What do you mean?" she said, hoping he would drop it, but she wasn't surprised when he didn't.

"You're lying," he said, only this time, for the first time, it was an accusation, not an observation.

"Aldo, listen—"

"You really haven't changed at all, have you?"

It stung, knowing what he meant even before he said it. "What's that supposed to mean?"

"This, the painting, it's a forgery. You called yourself a thief when we met," he reminded her, and she felt something seize her.

Maybe panic. Maybe the fear she'd been waiting so long to feel.

(*He can always undream me, unbelieve me—*)

"Why did you do it?" he asked her, and she shook her head.

"I told you, I don't know. Because I was good at it, because the idea stuck in my head, because—"

"Because you needed to?"

She suddenly felt too exhausted to argue with him, or to re-explain something that her mother had asked countless times; that a judge had asked; that her psychiatrist had asked; that they had all asked and never sorted out, but that Aldo, only Aldo, had always willingly trusted.

"Yes," she said, realizing the moment she said it that it was the answer he'd been dreading all along.

"And you still need to?"

That question was slightly different, but still, the same.

"No, Aldo," she sighed, "I was just—"

"You're not okay, Regan," he said, suddenly agitated, and she blinked. "This isn't normal."

"What isn't?"

"Any of it." He rubbed at his temple like she was a headache, a formula that wouldn't obey, and it stung her. She, like his thoughts, had drained him, and the pain of knowing it festered in her chest.

It felt unfair, unjust, that the things that had so easily been shared between them—I'm strange, no I'm strange, okay we're both strange, nobody understands us except for us—were now hers to bear alone.

"*I'm* not okay?"

He looked at her blankly.

"You've *never* been okay," she flung at him, and Aldo turned his head away, neither surprised nor unsurprised by her tone, which made things infinitely worse. "You think you fixed yourself, Aldo?" she snapped, desperately seeking higher ground and only managing to shrink inside it. "You didn't. When I met you, you were empty, not fixed. You were trying to find meaning in nothing!"

"You think I don't know that there's something wrong with me?" He looked strangely disenchanted, like he'd woken from something. (*He can always undream me, unbelieve me.*) "It's all my father ever tells me, Regan. My brain is broken," Aldo said robotically, "and your brain is broken, but we can't both be broken. One of us has to be fixable—no, one of us has to be *fixed*, or else—"

"Or else what?" It came out sharply escalated. "What happens, Aldo, if you can't fix me?"

He looked at her for a long time without answering.

"I'm not an overdose you can undo with a PhD," she said, hurt where she'd wanted to be angry. "I'm not a problem you can solve. I thought you understood that."

"I did. I do."

"Well, it seems like you don't. It seems like you have conditions for being with me."

"It's not . . . it's not that. It's not conditions."

Her pulse faltered. "But it's something."

"I just don't know," he said, sounding as if he might say more, but then he spread his hands helplessly. "I just don't know."

She stared at him in silence. She felt the floorboards giving way beneath her like sand, some tide in the distance turning.

"I used to have this theory that I could save myself with time," Aldo said. "That I'd solve it, and then I'd turn a corner one day, and then everything would be different. One hundred and twenty degrees from what it had been." He paused. "Now, of course," he mumbled, more to himself than to her, "I realize I can't actually save anything."

Tears pricked at the back of her eyes. "Why? Just because I forged a painting?"

He seemed sorry, but he didn't say it.

"Because," he exhaled wearily. "Because I think you need me more than you want me, Regan, and I think maybe—"

There was a dull drone in her ear, temporarily deafening.

"—I think maybe that means that I should go."

Reaction flooded her in waves, in surges.

First, like an electrical socket she'd shoved herself into, she sparked with panic, angry and lost without knowing which to suffer most. She felt stricken and empty and vacant with rage. Then it was doused, drenched, plunged. In a wash of desperation, chilling her to a shiver, she felt like falling to her knees, like grabbing him around the ankles. She felt like kissing his feet, like slapping his face.

Next, it was violence. She wanted to take the words and force them back into his mouth—the shape of which she knew like the God she'd never believed in—and shove them back down to his liver. She wanted to stab him and stab herself and stab her mother and especially to stab Marc; she couldn't stop the images of herself, stabbing and stabbing and stabbing until her hands were soaked with tears and blood.

She would do all of it, she thought, and then use the carnage to paint something new, something brilliant, and with Aldo's blood especially—from the vessels of his lovely wounds—she would paint a sky mixed with gold, dotted with constellations. Then she would say: See what I did, what I made? She would make a promise to him, kissing each of his lifeless eyes with reverence, and the promise would be this: Now, you and I will live forever.

But after the violence had been the numbness, the unfeeling calm. "Maybe you should go, then," she said dully, and Aldo froze, hesitating for a moment.

Then he nodded, tucked his hands in his pockets, and headed for the door.

––––––––––

For a long time afterward Regan would think about what had gone wrong, turning it over and over in her mind. She couldn't escape the feeling that she had misjudged something in the framework, somewhere in the landscape of The Fight, and that perhaps it had been something not of her making, but of theirs. She had thought, since their love had been red—had been fiery and passionate and untamed, magnetic and disruptive—The Fight was meant to be red as well, but the more she thought about it, the more it became clear that they—neither of them—truly knew what it was to fight like that for anything. They could have only fought in blue, in melancholy tones of it, because relationships, for them, were blue. Life was, for Regan, a cycle of arriving and leaving, passing through a revolving door. When she left, which she always did, she left quietly; not even a gust of wind but a little breeze, hardly a disturbance at all. Aldo had told her himself that he was a master of outlasting his friendships, enduring until there was nothing, and then he simply faded away. Should she have screamed, should she have made demands? Yes, probably, but she was out of practice, untrained. Too many people had refused when she had wished that they would beg her to stay, and now, because of them, she had let him go so easily, unclenching all her fingers at once.

THIS IS WHAT HAPPENED TO REGAN.

"So," the doctor had said the week prior, "how are things?"

"They're actually really good," Regan said.

"Classes at the Institute still going well?"

"Yes, very. They picked my work for the student showcase, did I tell you that?"

"You didn't! But I'm not surprised, you're very talented."

Regan scoffed. "You've only seen one painting."

"Take the compliment," suggested the doctor. "It's better for both of us if you do."

"Is that doctor's orders?"

"Call it a professional assessment," the doctor said, though she moved on quickly. "How are your moods?"

"Fine, mostly. I've been working a lot, trying to finish up my piece for the showcase."

"So, your sleep patterns . . . ?"

"Not much sleep. But by choice," Regan said quickly. "Only until the piece is finished. Which it is, nearly."

"Ah, I see. And how about this birthday party for your father? Any concerns about that?"

"Nothing new," Regan said, shuddering. "I'm really trying to be positive about it, just to keep Aldo calm. Besides," she added, deciding to shrug on a casual optimism, like a coat that matched her blouse, "I think you're right. Having him there will be helpful."

"And why do you think that is?"

Regan had spent months adjusting to those questions, finding them less obtrusive now.

"Well, when he's there, I feel more . . . like me, I guess. Like I finally have something to be proud of. I'm in love with someone I think highly of, and I have my work in an actual art show. A real one, not one my daddy bought me." She exhaled swiftly. "It just feels new, I guess. In a good way."

The doctor half-smiled. "Do you like new things?"

"Yes, almost always, but not like this. This feels like a new-old thing."

"Oh? Explain that."

"Well, it's not new in a *shocking* way. Does that make sense? I think I used to crave newness—No, wait," she corrected herself, shaking her head, "no, not crave it. Aldo says there's a difference between cravings and compulsions, and I think he's right. I used to have this compulsion for newness," she explained, and the doctor nodded, "but this particular newness is slower, steadier. I actually worked on my technique, you know?" A shrug. "I created something I'm proud of. I'm with someone who makes me feel, I don't know. Good."

"Makes sense," the doctor said. "When is the party?"

"Next week."

"Oh, soon. And the art show is . . . ?"

"The Monday after, actually."

"And have you told Aldo yet?"

"No, not yet, I want to surprise him." Regan paused for a moment, half-smiling, and said, "You know, this is the first time in my life that I actually feel like an artist."

"Oh?" asked the doctor.

"Yeah. I mean, Aldo tells me I am all the time," she said with a laugh, "but it really doesn't mean anything when he says it. Well, no," she amended quickly, "that's not true. I don't think I would have started if he hadn't said it."

"Then why keep it a surprise?"

"Well, because—" She grimaced. "Honestly, I don't know if I'm ready to tell him. For as long as I keep it a secret, it's mine, you know? My thing to accomplish or fail."

"And are you afraid of failing?"

"I'm . . . not exactly. I think—"

She paused for a moment.

"I think it's the idea of an ending," Regan said. "I feel like I've been going in circles for most of my life, just repeating the same patterns. This is the first time it feels different, and it's not like I'm *afraid,* exactly, it's just that I don't know how it will feel. I've never done it before," she admitted, "and it's scary, I guess, but I'm not afraid."

"Do you think Aldo knows that?"

Regan considered it for several long moments.

"Maybe," she said.

She would remember that she said it because it was the only lie she told that day. She used them, her lies, sparingly these days. She found they were like old coping mechanisms, like the old pair of crutches she'd had when she was eight; something she'd kept around, just in case, until her mother had cleaned the basement and decided to throw them away.

———

It had been Regan's mother who invited Marc to her father's birthday party, which was a typical Helen move. The more Regan thought about it, the more she realized she should have known it would happen. She shouldn't have brought Aldo to the dinner at all. The longer she went about replaying her choices, the more selfish a decision it seemed. She knew, for example, that Aldo disliked crowds. His introversion was fiercer than her extroversion, which was something she'd learned quickly and should therefore theoretically understand. He disliked conflict and confrontation because of course he did—he had been raised by *Masso*, who was gentle and soft-spoken and kind. Regan wondered if anyone had ever shouted at Aldo, or even raised their voice at him. She doubted it, and that, like everything else, was something she should have known.

She also knew that Aldo had been worried about something. He was incredibly transparent, and by now she understood that when he was thinking—*really* thinking—he was doing it so rapidly that his thoughts outpaced his lips. When Aldo was quiet, it was because something was pressing on the inside of his brain like a tumor, rotting him from the inside. Regan noticed that it was easy to keep her art show a secret because if she didn't present Aldo with all the information, he didn't bully her with further questions. He merely seemed relieved when she walked in. She would press him about his work—how was his dissertation, how was teaching, was everything okay?—and he always answered factually. Yes, it's fine, and No, there's nothing wrong. It took her longer than it should have to realize that she was probably asking the wrong questions.

She should never have let Marc talk to him. Marc was slippery like that, getting into people's heads. His skill set was distinctly different from Aldo's in that he was persuasive, self-interested in a way that seemed self-actualized; possibly even kind, at first. He never seemed to have an agenda behind his obsession with hard truths, only he very definitely did. Regan had spared Aldo the trauma of knowing the things Marc had said to her since they'd broken up, all meanness and incivility that had felt like honesty and even love while they had been together. She hadn't thought Aldo would want to know, but she hadn't thought to protect him from it, either.

"What did you do?" she hissed to Marc after she saw them talking, but he shrugged.

"Nothing you wouldn't have eventually ruined on your own," he said.

She decided it would be the last time they ever spoke to one another, and it was.

Regan also routinely forgot that while Aldo enjoyed sex, he didn't think much about it when he wasn't having it. Sometimes it seemed like he was going so far as to placate her with it, giving her what she wanted as easily as if she'd asked for a glass of water, or for him to pass the salt. She'd shouted at her mother and then pulled Aldo into the bathroom, guiding his fingers to tug at her seamless thong, but he'd been listless, impassive, even resistant. The rejection she'd felt from his disinterest was an old one, more hers than his, with her mother's voice fresh in her head: You see, Charlotte? Nobody wants you, nobody has ever wanted you, you're irresponsible with the love of others and so they lose interest in you, they always will.

It was a mistake she only registered in retrospect, seeing things more clearly once her mother's voice had faded from her thoughts.

"Where is he?" Regan had pleaded with her sister, chasing Madeline down where she held a struggling Carissa. "I need to apologize to him," she said, and added grudgingly, "I did something really stupid."

"Yeah, you really do need to," Madeline agreed, straightening from her attempt to wrangle her daughter. "Char, look, I don't know what Mom was thinking—"

"She was thinking she doesn't give a shit about whether I'm happy or not," Regan muttered. "Not like she ever has before."

"Well, I don't know if that's true, but—" Madeline sighed. "The point is, Aldo's really upset." Carissa had wriggled out of her mother's hold, flashing Regan a toothless grin, and Madeline shook her head before adding, "I sent him to Dad's office."

Regan blinked. "Dad's office? Why?"

"I don't know, it's quiet? He wanted to be alone, I think."

The idea sent a little tremor of concern through Regan's spine. "I don't want him to be alone. I'm worried." I've been worried about him for months, she didn't say aloud, but Madeline didn't seem to need her to.

"Go find him, then."

Regan had raced up the stairs to find the door ajar with Aldo inside, one hand curled mournfully around his mouth, his green eyes staring at her painting.

———

Was it over? It wasn't not over, and for Regan, this was typically how things met their ends. It wasn't broken, but it had a fissure of pain, a crevice that could swallow them up if either of them weren't careful. She wasn't surprised that he'd left—he usually respected her wishes, and she had been the one to suggest that he should—but was that the end of it, then? Say she did not come home the next day, or on Monday, either. Say Aldo left for class and for work as he had always done; should he return home to find her side of the closet empty, leaving a vacancy for him to try to fill? Perhaps he was thinking: Maybe today I'll come home and it will be like she never existed, and then I won't even know where I am in time.

The thought dazed Regan, arresting her in a state of half-awake, half-asleep. If she reclaimed all her things—snuck in like the thief that she was and stole back the life that she'd shared with him— would Aldo wake to feel relief? Would he recognize it as a favor? On the one hand, she wanted to bear his entire sadness for him; to hurt herself doubly, just to keep it from him, and was that illness or love? Was she really so broken that she wanted to suffer to spare him, and if that was true, then had he been right all along? Did she want him to forget (did *she* want to forget?) or was his pain something that she had earned, that she deserved, purely by virtue of existing? Was it fairer for him to come home to an emptiness he could trace like the scars along his shoulders? Should the echoes of her still linger for him beyond the pain?

It was something new to curate, Regan thought: the possibility that she could haunt him or free him, and that whatever she did or did not do was entirely up to her. The immensity of it was crippling. Bearing the responsibility for what happened when two people fractured and bled was not something she'd ever attempted before, and she felt weakened by the prospect of it now. She'd given him arrows and he'd shot, and now parts of her were gaping holes, flayed and filleted and left behind as open wounds. Why hadn't she run after him, why hadn't she stopped him, why hadn't she told him the truth? Why had he left, why hadn't he said to her this time, "I love your brain even when I fear it," why why why? The effort of asking herself felt like the loneliest thing of all, and the silence that followed was deafening.

Regan imagined cradling the pieces of her broken brain in her palms and staring at them, molding them together and then shaking them like a Magic 8 Ball. *Ask again later,* it said, and obediently, she shook again. Have I already destroyed this little fledgling thing I tried to nurture? *It is certain. Reply hazy, try again.* Perhaps he would return? *It is decidedly so. Outlook not so good.* Maybe she should find him? *You may rely on it. Very doubtful.*

So it turned out divination was useless. The future was uncertain, and the past was a series of cycles that she could only see once she had passed. She thought of Aldo, of time, and how time wasn't the thing that couldn't be fixed, it was *them*—it was humanity in general—because time was what gave shapes to things. They could not see themselves unless they could exist outside themselves; ipso facto, without time passing, they could never really know what they had been.

The multiverse is impossible to understand, Aldo had once said, because we can't know where we are inside it—and if we don't know where we are, then what is our basis for understanding anything else?

You're right, Rinaldo, Regan thought, soothed by his mind in retrospect; by a past Aldo who had left her something with which to comfort herself now.

Give it time, she told herself. Let it breathe, take the space to find the outlines.

An ending is only an ending, she thought, when both parties agree they've reached the end.

———

Shortly after their fight, Aldo noticed that Regan had left him something. He couldn't tell if it had been a recent Regan who'd entered while he was away or if a past Regan had left it for future Aldo to find or not find. Either way, he noticed one of her dresses in his closet as if it had been deliberately placed in his line of sight, slightly withdrawn from the other articles of clothing for the purpose of catching his eye. It was the sort of thing she typically wore to work, and it reminded him of that sacred space in their Venn diagram of existence: The Museum.

Aldo had already considered the possibility that perhaps they had done the right thing; the smart thing; the best thing. In some way, he was quite certain they were safer now, better protected. He was free to be devout about some other thing, to find some new, less fragile theology for survival. There was an ease in that, a simplicity, and was there not some value in such stability? They could easily revert to ancient cultures of themselves, carrying nothing, resuming their mindless worship of the stars.

The Art Institute was much as it always was, quiet on a Monday except for an exhibition that would have normally repulsed Aldo, because it was surrounded by a crowd. He had no intention to observe its contents, noticing the chatter that meant it concerned other people; but then he paused unwillingly when something caught his eye.

It was a view that was both familiar and not. It was new in that he had never seen it before, but also, it was recognizable in that it seemed to have previously existed inside his brain. The colors, he thought, looked like something he'd seen once or twice amid the fabric of his musings, and so he gravitated toward it, slipping through the crowd.

From afar it had been one painting, but upon closer inspection he could see it was actually a triptych of three, individual segments comprising one comprehensive landscape that was smaller upon approach. Up close, Aldo could see the tiny hexagonal lines, fissures of gold so delicate they made the painting look as if it had scales, splintering its content into smaller pieces.

It didn't appear at first to have a subject. Nothing in it was strictly identifiable, either as a scene or as an object, only Aldo felt very strongly as if he'd been transported in time and space. He was no longer inside of a bright white museum looking at a painting, but instead he was on top of his roof, looking at the sky.

"I think it's incredibly human what you do," Regan had said, turning her head to look at him. (He'd been smoking and mumbling about Euclidean space.)

"Is it?" he asked, doubtful, "because as far as I know, other humans seem to disagree."

She made a noise she often made, usually to indicate that he was being ridiculous, hush, stop. "You look for explanations," she said. "It's part of our fundamental code to wonder, don't you think? The Babylonians did it, and so do you."

"Yes, and yet," Aldo exhaled, "Zeus' affairs are more common knowledge than Babylonian math."

"Well, sex is human, too," Regan said. "But they're still both ways of telling stories about existence. You just happen to use a language that only you and—" She paused to estimate it. "Maybe ten other people understand."

"What about art?" he countered. "Isn't that storytelling?"

"No, not really." She leaned over, taking a puff from the spliff between his fingers. "Art isn't about explaining shit," she said, coughing once. "It's about sharing things—experiences, feelings. Art is something we do to *feel* human, not because we are."

"Do you feel human?"

"In some interconnected way, like I'm part of a common species? Not often. You?"

"Almost never."

"Well, it was a good try."

She'd taken another hit, leaning her cheek against his shoulder, and he'd thought with a sudden, sparkling clarity: Whatever you are made of, Charlotte Regan, I am made of it, too.

"What is this used for?" someone had asked him later in class. It was a variant of questioning that he was, by then, beyond sick of, but which he deigned to answer that day, about linear partial differential equations. Perhaps because he was tired and his defenses were weak; or, perhaps, because he had laid his head down the previous night next to a woman whose thoughts and matter he wanted desperately to know, and who, if she had been there, would have asked him some variation of the same thing.

Aldo, what's The Truth?

The easy answer, and the one he would have given had he not been tired or in love, was simply that linear partial differential equations were used for describing changes over time within the scope of quantum mechanics. The answer he gave, however, was something like this:

"We map things," he said, "and chart things, observing and modeling and predicting, because we have no other choice, and this is the language we have agreed, collectively, to use. Because we have agreed, collectively, that to proceed without knowledge or understanding is a stupid kind of bravery, an impulsive kind of blindness, but that to be alone without wonder or curiosity is to chip away any possible value we might discover in existing."

She, the student doing the asking, was later the only one to give his class a five-star rating, saying, "I really don't understand what Damiani's talking about most of the time, but I feel like he actually cares and that's pretty cool. Nobody cares anymore. Anyway I probably failed this class but I liked it, sort of. As much as you can like differential equations."

In the present, Aldo felt a tap on his shoulder; someone wanted to get by to look at another painting. He snapped to attention, nodding quickly and stepping closer to read the plaque below the triptych.

Alone with You in the Ether, it said, followed by *Oils and acrylics.*

Below, in smaller letters: *C. Regan.*

"Oh, this is pretty," remarked someone beside him, pointing to Regan's work, and Aldo turned his head, suddenly irritated.

It isn't pretty, he wanted to say, it's lonely, it's desolate, it's a chilling portrait of vastness. How ignorant are you to look at this and diminish it to some kind of trinket, are you dead? It's the human condition! It's the entire universe itself! It's the depths of space-time you utter fucking philistine and how dare you, how fucking *dare* you stand there and fail to weep? What kind of sad, unremarkable nothingness have you so callously lived that you can witness the splendor of her existence and not fall to your knees for having missed it, for having misunderstood it all this time? Pretty, that's what you think this is? You think that's all she's capable of? You fool, she's done the impossible. She has explained everything there is to know about the world in less than the time it took for your eyes to fully focus, and do you realize that I will spend a lifetime trying to do the same and never come close? This is an opus!, this is a triumph!, this is the meaning of life and you would think the answer would be satire, but it isn't, it's Truth. She told The Truth like you could never dream of telling it, and I pity you, that you could see the inside of your own soul and reduce it like this, so carelessly. With the vacuous deficiency of,

Oh, this is pretty.

But Aldo didn't say that, or say anything. Instead, he nodded and turned, pulling his phone out of his pocket and racing outside, faster and faster the closer he got to the doors.

"Dad," he said, the moment Masso answered the phone. He wanted to scream, primally, or to tear at his hair, hysterical with understanding. "She's nothing like Mom."

"Rinaldo, I haven't heard from you in two days, where have you b—"

"You're wrong and you're right," Aldo said again, pacing the stairs outside the museum. "She does burn me, she ignites me, you're right. But it's different, they're different things." He was thinking more than he was saying, unsure what was even coming out of his mouth. Science without faith is crippled, Masso, and life without it is soulless. She is my hope and for that she is dangerous, unequivocally, but she is also alive, unreservedly. It took this long for me to finally understand.

Masso was silent for a long moment.

"So then what will you do, Rinaldo?"

Aldo laughed, startling the stranger sitting peacefully on the steps who was witnessing, unknowingly, a bit of existential decay. It's you and me right now, Stranger! Aldo wanted to tell him. It's you and me alone in the ether and you don't even know it, you don't even care, but still you are tied to this, and to me, and so be it, really.

So be it. This is what it means to live.

"I'll do whatever she wants me to do," Aldo said to his father, who contemplated this in three beats of silence on the other side of the phone.

"Okay, Rinaldo," said Masso. "Sounds like a plan."

———

Aldo had stared at her paintings, alone, for over fifteen minutes.

Throughout that time, Regan had been crafting imaginary scenarios of what came next. At first it was very simple, perhaps even boring, a little scripted. For the first minute or so she imagined herself walking up to him and tapping his shoulder, casually saying: How did you know?

Between minutes three and five, her projections went a bit further. She imagined herself apologizing to him, saying: I should have stopped you, I shouldn't have let you go, this is my love letter to you and I hope that you like it, goodbye now if that's what you want. It would be sweet, and also masochistically generous. She could probably live with herself if she said that.

But Regan had never martyred herself with grace before, so somewhere around minute six—which felt borderline ungodly—she grew angry. You see that it's my work! she wanted to shout at him. Why are you still looking, come find me! By minute ten she was infuriated, considering kicking him in the shins and then storming away, saying nothing at all. Wouldn't that serve him right? He couldn't just stand there and stare like that, judging her work. When had he ever made himself that vulnerable? Never, probably, and now look at him, just standing there, staring. He hadn't even noticed how many people had jostled him; nor had he noticed the girl in Regan's anatomical figure drawing class who had the spot right below hers, which the girl and her grandfather were presently struggling to see because Aldo was standing in the way and hadn't moved.

By minute twelve Regan had abandoned her sanctimonious posturing and begun thinking Aldo, oh, Rinaldo, I miss you; only you would look for so long and so closely; only you would bother trying to see what others don't. She wanted to creep up behind him, press her chest to the blades of his shoulders and her lips to the back of his neck: Thank you. Because of you, she would whisper in his ear, I made the very first real thing I have ever made, can you believe it? I'm an artist for the first time—yes, an artist, I said it, you heard me!—and it is only because I painted the world as you saw it, so it was theft, sort of, but no, it wasn't, because we made it together. This is our love, do you see it? This is what it looks like to love you; it looks like an abyss, but it isn't, do you understand? All falls come with danger, Aldo, but not us. Not us, we float.

By minute fourteen she wanted to drag him somewhere private. She was alight with a desperate need to feel close to him, to feel connected, beatifically vulgar and harmoniously obscene. Alone *with you,* she would gasp when she came, do you understand why I called it that, what it means? Because you and I, we are so different, aren't we, and yet we are more like each other than the rest of the world is like us, and for that I bless you, I condemn you, I sanctify you, I sustain you. This painting, Aldo, it's about God. They cannot hang it in the Louvre, they will have to put it in the Vatican, because what we are is holy, and this, you and me as one together, is transubstantiation of the highest degree. This is you and me becoming the consecration of us; amen, above everything, I believe.

By minute fifteen she began seeing flashes of their lives in snippets, apart and together, playing side by side like a film. A wedding, maybe, probably. Aldo wouldn't want one but Masso probably would, and Regan would invite Madeline happily and her parents less happily. But they could be there, because she had taken away their ability to hold any power over her happiness (okay it was an ongoing effort, but she had started it and that counted for something), and they could watch as she said to Aldo: I do. In another frame, they break up and she moves to Italy or something. She fucks a series of younger and younger twenty-year-olds until they exhaust her, and then she comes back with her life in pieces to find that Professor Damiani is busy, can I take a message? and she says, No, no, never mind, this was a mistake. In another frame she turns to Aldo and says, You know, one of the little quirks of this mortal prison of mine is it can make other humans if you want it to, and he smiles in a way that means: Yes. In another frame she watches him leave her on a loop, on repeat, and her feet are trapped in place like it's a nightmare—and it is, isn't it?—so she thinks, No, not this one, next. The next frame has her sleeping beside him; that's it, just sleeping. He leans over and kisses her forehead while she sleeps on, ignorant and stupidly peaceful. It is free of time entirely, belonging to no special hour. This, she thinks, this is the one.

Somewhere in the universe a star exploded or someone was born or they died or time passed while Regan stood there and missed him, while she mourned him, and then she thought with an equally quiet violence: Maybe I do not have to do it alone.

By the end of minute fifteen he was finally gone, turning abruptly and half-sprinting for the doors, and in his absence Regan emptied, watching all their alternate lives begin to wilt. She mourned them like her children, holding their lifeless corpses to her chest, and then she forgot them, slowly, each one vanishing without a trace, until she held nothing at all.

Eventually she looked down at her empty hands and thought: Damn it.

Damn it, I love him.

Then, after the smoke cleared, she could see nothing else.

THIS IS WHAT HAPPENS NEXT.

He answers the phone on the second ring; he didn't think she would call.

She hadn't planned to, but here she was.

(Silence.)

For what it's worth he'd hoped she would. But then again it's not strictly within his skill set to hope.

She disagrees. His profession is built on hope, isn't it?

Funny she should say that. He was just starting to think she might be right.

(Silence.)

Well, anyway, they didn't need to get into that again. Not yet.

Yet?

No. Actually, she called to tell him something.

Oh?

Well, more accurately, she called to talk to him about something. She wants to have (and here, another breath of pause): A Conversation.

Okay. (Is he smiling? He is.) Okay, he's free, he can talk. What does she want to talk about?

She wants to talk about time.

Time?

Yes, time.

He thought time was his thing.

Well, it's about his thoughts on time, so yeah, it is.

Okay, tell him.

Well, she was thinking about what he said; about how he could turn a corner and walk into some other situation that was nearly the same but different. What exactly did he mean by that?

(A pause.)

Well, he thinks time is some sort of cycle or loop, right? But seeing as it's more likely to be a hexagon than a circle, because of nature etc. etc., that means time must have corners.

So, she could turn a corner and end up as . . . what, exactly?

She'd still be herself, only she'd be herself as she would have been in the direction time was moving *at that point*.

Okay, so say she turned a corner and she was . . . maybe eighteen years old or something, but say she carried with her some vague memory of who she'd been before. Could she do that?

She can do anything she wants. (He sounds like he means it.)

Okay, cool, so she turns a corner, she's eighteen, it's a past that isn't her *actual* past, so she's in love with him but she doesn't know it yet.

If she's eighteen, then they don't know each other at all.

Right—not *yet*, but maybe they meet a different way that time. Say they meet at a party, for example.

A party? (He's skeptical.)

Yes, she knows, just go with her here—

Okay, okay, if she says so . . .

She's holding a beer and looking around like, Fuck this shit, and naturally he sees her.

Because she has an energy?

Yes, exactly, because she has an energy and he recognizes it. He's seen it before.

In the past which is also the future, you mean?

Right.

Okay, so what next?

Well, that's the thing. He sees her, and now he has to say something so she'll know it's really him.

Like a time loop situation?

Sure.

But how can she possibly know it's him?

She'll just know. But that's not the point; the point is, she wants him to say something very specific.

Okay, like what?

Maybe she wants him to say: He's been waiting a long time for her.

But she'll hate that. She'll think it's a line.

No, no, she'll know he means it. She knows him, remember?

But she doesn't.

But she does.

How?

She just does. So anyway he'll say it, and she'll know he wouldn't just say that. He doesn't just say things like that.

He really doesn't, but still. Seems a little corny, doesn't it?

Okay, okay fine. Then he should also bring up bees, probably.

Bees? First thing?

Of course. Remember? She already knows about the bees, even though she doesn't.

This is getting complicated, he thinks.

No, it isn't, it's . . . Fuck, she knows what it is. It's a fucking perfect circle.

There are no perfect circles, Regan.

Yes, there's one, and it's this one: They fall in love because they're always in love.

That's circular, not a circle.

He can believe whatever he wants; she knows it's a perfect circle.

Okay, but still. Say he accepts her premise—what does that actually mean?

(Triumphantly:) It means that they, as they are right now, could be their *future selves' pasts*.

(A pause.)

He is beyond lost.

Okay, look. She's trying to say that maybe an older version of them has *already* turned a corner, and so they met again in the armory of the Art Institute, knowing but not knowing that the moment they met was something they've done before. Does that make sense?

(He makes a humming sound, like, Maybe.) How many times?

What?

How many times have they done this before?

She can't possibly know that, Aldo, and besides, that's not the point. The point is, maybe it works or maybe it doesn't, but they just keep trying and doing it over until it does. Right?

That sounds like a lot of uncertainty.

Of course it is! *Everything* is uncertain, he and she both know that by now, but there is a smaller certainty within all of the uncertainty, which is: The Truth.

And what, he asks, is The Truth?

That she will keep turning corners until she finds him.

(He is quiet for a moment before he says:) Okay.

Okay what?

Okay, he accepts her premise.

And?

And what?

And how does he feel about it?

He's glad she said it. She explained it better than he could have. He would have tried to graph it.

As a reminder: if he graphs it, it'll just be a perfect circle.

Cycle.

It's a circle, Aldo.

Okay fine, she's poked enough holes in his theories for one day, he accepts.

He concedes, just like that?

He *accepts,* yes. Just like that.

Okay good, she's too tired to keep explaining anyway. It's been a long day.

Has it? For him, too. Oh and he saw her art, by the way.

What did he think?

He thinks he always knew she was an artist.

(Groan. But fondly.) First of all, she's only an artist because he said she was an artist.

Does that mean he's a genius because she said he was a genius?

Look, whatever they are, it's irreversible. She is this version of herself because of him, and vice versa. There's no changing that now.

Yeah?

Yeah.

You're sure?

Yes.

Okay, good.

Really?

Yes.

(Silence.)

(The wind screams in the background while a driver shouts at a pedestrian. The Cubs have won and the L is delayed, the Red Line packed tight like sardines; a city beginning to sweat looks up at the sun overhead and rejoices.)

So anyway, is she hungry?

God yes, she's starving. Is he going home now?

Yes, he's going home, will he see her there?

(She waits for a second, half a heartbeat; the time it takes to let a smile flicker.)

Yes. She'll see him at home.

THE NARRATOR, THE AUTHOR: Aldo and Regan hang up in the same moment without saying goodbye, because they do not need to. They have each unlocked a hidden door today, and though hers is different from his and vice versa, the contents within it are no less valuable from one to the next.

It is unfortunately worth noting that he remains not a particularly good teacher. He will shortly choose to shift his research to something with more math and fewer people. Her showcase triptych, ultimately reviewed as "visually pleasing if a bit lacking in narrative clarity or substance," is not nearly as good or as valuable as either of them is willing to believe. Her clinical mood disorder does not disappear because it can't and "healthy" for them will always be a relative term. There are still bills to be paid and things to be said and they will argue in shades of purple as early as tomorrow, but they are different now; changed. After they hang up the phone and he wipes a bead of early summer from his forehead while she adjusts the slightly sticky strap of her purse, he will take a right onto Harrison Street while she takes a left onto Michigan

Avenue and both of them will opt to walk briskly, as if they have places to be, which they do.

Because when they embark, they will have each turned a corner. And everything will be as it was, only very slightly different.

ACKNOWLEDGMENTS

Let me begin by saying that while this story is about a woman with a mood disorder who learns to live without medication, that is not intended to be prescriptive. Being a person with a mood disorder myself, I can assure you that I would not have had the stability to exist within the constraints of a "normal" job without medication, nor am I able to function now without regular therapy. This is not a book about how pills are bad, but about finding the acceptance we need to feel both well and alive.

I was diagnosed with bipolar disorder during my first month of law school; I had known something was wrong since I was a teenager but, as a method of survival, I had chosen to turn a blind eye. Everyone has bad days, I told myself. Then I met the man who would become my husband, who did not deserve my bad days, and suddenly my broken brain had to become someone's problem. I made it my own, but only superficially: Just give me some pills until I'm fixed. I had received no treatment before then, though my symptoms had long been medically identifiable. I self-medicated to soothe my raging disquiet, suffered through days of bedridden depression, called it all coping. But once I met the man who would be my husband, it wasn't enough to live by putting out my own fires. I needed a version of myself that could withstand life with the rest of the world.

The fundamental truth about mental illness, however manageable or grave, is that it is difficult to coexist. People often ask me how I know the difference between what's in my head (between whatever chemical imbalance might be lying to me on any given day) and what's real, but the truth is that I have no choice but to accept that what's in my head *is* what's real. My clients' pain was my pain. Everyone's pain was mine, and I lacked the proficiency to carry it. Eventually I left law school, and due to some fluke administrative error, my pills ran out. I wouldn't be writing this if not for the fact that my psychiatrist did not refill my pills, nor did his receptionist answer their office line. Panicked, I stared at the empty bottles. I went to bed. I stared at the ceiling. I got out of bed. I sat at my desk and opened my computer. I wrote a short story, and then another. For four nights, I didn't sleep. I started writing obsessively, compulsively. I wrote because it was something I could do, because the pills were gone, because I couldn't sleep.

Then something happened. I stopped having violent mood swings. Now I was constantly thinking of stories, worlds, characters, plotlines. I would write eight hours a day, then ten or twelve. I wrote like my life depended on it, and I think maybe that was instinctual, atavistic, because it did. I found a therapist and told her sternly, perhaps fearfully, to watch me; to let me know if I ever needed pills again, and she agreed. I relaxed a little bit. I wrote book after book after book, four million words of fan fiction, graphic novels, film scripts, anthologies of stories. For the first time in my life I wasn't manic or depressed, I wasn't bracing myself for the next up or down, I was just telling the truth in the shape of fiction. I was using my stories to help other people understand their own.

Eventually I thought: I can't go back to an office, I can't go back to pills. Maybe I can do this instead.

And because so many of you have picked up my stories, I was able to write this book.

Which is of course to say thank you, which I will continue to say many times. Thank you to Aurora and Stacie, beloved CPs and editors, for being early readers and supporters of this manuscript. Thank you to Mr. Blake, who lets me use and reuse our love story to write new ones, and who sat through my rambling hypotheses on quantum theory. (My husband is not Aldo, nor am I Regan—he is an incredible and gifted teacher, and he is *also* the artist in our household.)

Thank you to Nacho, more important with every book, for saying the right things, and for occasionally pushing me outside my comfort zone. To Elaine and Kidaan, for embracing not only my fiction, but my voice. To Little Chmura, who is forever bringing my stories to life in a way no one else will ever understand. To my family, whose support should probably not be surprising, but who always seem to pop up to cheer me on when I least expect it. To my mom, my sisters KMS, my mother-in-law, for letting me fill your bookshelves, for always making me feel my stories find a home in your hearts. For distant toasts and reassuring messages; for believing that I will make it, even when I'm not so sure. To my therapist, who did not react adversely when I said, "Uh, so there's a guy in my head fake-smoking and he's been sitting in there for like, a week." You helped me find Aldo, and health.

Thank you to my husband, whose birthday it is today, who let me into his world one September in Chicago and told me I could stay. Thank you for changing my life, and for giving me one. Thank you for teaching me about time, and for loving my mind enough that I could learn to love it, too. If one day I have found the right words, know that I couldn't have managed it without you.

To you, my fellow mortals with your gorgeous little fractures: Your crazy is your magic. Your wildness is what makes you. Resilience is your talent. Burn, but don't burn out. As always, it has been my honor to put these words down for you. I hope you enjoyed the story, and above all else, I hope it brought you something true.

xx, Olivie

Turn the page for a sneak peek
of more from Olivie Blake

ONE
FOR MY
ENEMY

Available Winter 2023 from Tor

THE PROLOGUE

Many things are not what they appear to be. Some things, though, try harder.

Baba Yaga's Artisan Apothecary was a small store in Lower Manhattan that had excellent (mostly feminine) Yelp reviews and an appealing, enticing storefront. The sign, itself a bit of a marvel in that it was not an elegantly backlit sans serif, carried with it a fanciful sense of whimsy, not unlike the brightly colored bath bombs and luxury serums inside. The words "Baba Yaga" were written in sprawling script over the carved shape of a mortar and pestle, in an effort to mimic the Old World character herself.

In this case, to say the store was not what it appeared was an understatement.

I just love it here, one of the Yelp reviews exclaimed. *The products are all wonderful. The store itself is small and its products change regularly, but all of them are excellent. Duane Reade has more if you're looking for the typical drugstore products, but if you're looking for the perfect handmade scented candle or a unique gift for a friend or coworker, this would be the place to go.*

The hair and nails supplements made my pitiful strands twice as long in less than a year! one reviewer crooned. *I swear, this place is magic!*

Customer service is lovely, which is such a rarity in Manhattan, one reviewer contributed. *I've never met the owner but her daughters (one or two of which are usually around to answer questions) are just the most beautiful and helpful young women you'll ever meet.*

The store is never very full, one reviewer commented blithely, *which is odd, considering it seems to do fairly well…*

This store is an absolute gem, said another, *and a well-kept secret.*

And it *was* a secret.

A secret within a secret, in fact.

Elsewhere, southeast of Yaga's apothecary on Bowery, there was an antique furniture store called Koschei's. This store, unlike Baba Yaga's, was by appointment only.

The storefront always looks so cool, but the place is never open, one reviewer complained, giving the store three stars. *On a whim, I tried calling to arrange a time to see one of the items in the window but couldn't get in touch with anyone for weeks. Finally, a young guy (one of the owner's sons, I believe) brought me in for about twenty minutes, but almost everything in the store was already reserved for private clients. That's fine, obviously, but still, it would have been nice to know in advance. I fell in love with a small vintage chest but was told it wasn't for sale.*

REALLY EXPENSIVE, contributed another reviewer. *You're better off going to Ikea or CB2.*

This store is sort of creepy-looking, another reviewer added. *There always seem to be weirdos moving things in and out of it, too. All the stuff looks really cool, but the store itself could use a facelift.*

It's almost like they don't want customers, groused a more recent review.

And they were right; Koschei did not want customers.

At least, not the kind of customer who was looking for him on Yelp.

ACT I:
MADNESS MOST DISCREET

"Love is a smoke raised with the fume of sighs;
Being purged, a fire sparkling in lovers' eyes;
Being vexed, a sea nourished with loving tears.
What is it else? A madness most discreet,
A choking gall, and a preserving sweet."

Romeo to Benvolio,
Romeo and Juliet (1.1.181–185)

I. 1
(Enter the Fedorov Sons.)

The Fedorov sons had a habit of standing like the points of an isosceles triangle.

At the furthest point forward there was Dimitri, the eldest, who was the uncontested heir; the crown prince who'd spent a lifetime serving a dynasty of commerce and fortune. He typically stood with his chin raised, the weight of his invisible crown borne aloft, and had a habit of rolling his shoulders back and baring his chest, unthreatened. After all, who would threaten him? None who wished to live a long life, that was for certain. The line of Dimitri's neck was steady and unflinching, Dimitri himself having never possessed a reason to turn warily over his shoulder. Dimitri Fedorov fixed his gaze on the enemy and let the world carry on at his back.

Behind Dimitri, on his right: the second of the Fedorov brothers, Roman, called Roma. If Dimitri was the Fedorov sun, Roman was the moon in orbit, his dark eyes carving a perimeter of warning around his elder brother. It was enough to make a man step back in hesitation, in disquietude, in fear. Roman had a spine like lightning, footfall like thunder. He was the edge of a sharp, bloodied knife.

Next to Roman stood Lev, the youngest. If his brothers were planetary bodies, Lev was an ocean wave. He was in constant motion, a tide that pulsed and waned. Even now, standing behind Dimitri, his fingers curled and uncurled reflexively at his sides, his thumb beating percussively against his thigh. Lev had a keen sense of danger, and he perceived it now, sniffing it out in the air and letting it creep between the sharp blades of his shoulders. It got under his skin, under his bones, and gifted him a shiver.

Lev had a keen sense of danger, and he was certain it had just walked in the room.

"Dimitri Fedorov," the woman said, a name which, from her lips, might have been equally threatening aimed across enemy lines or whispered between silken sheets. "You still know who I am, don't you?"

Lev watched his brother fail to flinch, as always.

"Of course I know you, Marya," Dimitri said. "And you know me, don't you? Even now."

"I certainly thought I did," Marya said.

She was a year older than Dimitri, or so Lev foggily recalled, which would have placed her just over the age of thirty. Flatteringly put, she didn't remotely look it. Marya Antonova, whom none of the Fedorov brothers had seen since Lev was a child, had retained her set of youthful, pouty lips, as fitting to the Maybelline billboard outside their Tribeca loft as to her expression of measured interest, and the facial geography typically left victim to age—lines that might have expelled around her eyes or mouth, furrowed valleys that might have emerged along her forehead—had escaped even the subtlest indications of time. Every detail of Marya's appearance, from the tailored lines of her dress to the polished leather of her shoes, had been marked by intention, pressed and spotless and neat, and her dark hair fell in meticulous 1940s waves, landing just below the sharp line of her collarbone.

She removed her coat in yet another episode of deliberation, establishing her dominion over the room and its contents via the simple handing of the garment to the man beside her.

"Ivan," she said to him, "will you hold this while I visit with my old friend Dima?"

"Dima," Dimitri echoed, toying with the endearment as the large man beside Marya Antonova carefully folded her coat over his arm, as fastidious as his employer. "Is this a friendly visit, then, Masha?"

"Depends," Marya replied, unfazed by Dimitri's use of her own diminutive and clearly in no hurry to elaborate. Instead, she obliged herself a lengthy, scrutinizing glance around the room, her attention skating dismissively over Roman before landing, with some degree of surprise, on Lev.

"My, my," she murmured. "Little Lev has grown, hasn't he?"

There was no doubt that the twist of her coquette's lips, however misleadingly soft, was meant to disparage him.

"I have," Lev warned, but Dimitri held up a hand, calling for silence.

"Sit, Masha." He beckoned, gesturing her to a chair, and she rewarded him with a smile, smoothing down her skirt before settling herself at the chair's edge. Dimitri, meanwhile, took the seat opposite her on the leather sofa, while Roman and Lev, after exchanging a wary glance, each stood behind it, leaving the two heirs to mediate the interests of their respective sides.

Dimitri spoke first. "Can I get you anything?"

"Nothing, thank you," from Marya.

"It's been a while," Dimitri noted.

The brief pause that passed between them was loaded with things neither expressed aloud nor requiring explanation. That time had passed was obvious, even to Lev.

There was a quiet exchange of cleared throats.

"How's Stas?" Dimitri asked casually, or with a tone that might have been casual to some other observer. To Lev, his brother's uneasy small talk was about as ill-fitting as the idea that Marya Antonova would waste her time with the pretense of saccharinity.

"Handsome and well-hung, just as he was twelve years ago," Marya replied. She looked up and smiled pointedly at Roman, who slid Lev a discomfiting glance. Stas Maksimov, a Borough witch and apparent subject of discussion, seemed about as out of place in the conversation as the Borough witches ever were. Generally speaking, none of the three Fedorovs ever lent much thought to the Witches' Boroughs at all, considering their father's occupation meant most of them had already been in the family's pocket for decades.

Before Lev could make any sense of it, Marya asked, "How's business, Dima?"

"Ah, come on, Masha," Dimitri sighed, leaning back against the sofa cushions. If she was bothered by the continued use of her childhood name (or by anything at all, really) she didn't show it. "Surely you didn't come all the way here just to talk business, did you?"

She seemed to find the question pleasing, or at least inoffensive. "You're right," she said after a moment. "I didn't come exclusively to talk business, no. Ivan." She beckoned to her associate, gesturing over her shoulder. "The package I brought with me, if you would?"

Ivan stepped forward, handing her a slim, neatly-packaged rectangle that wouldn't have struck Lev as suspicious in the slightest had it not been handled with such conspicuous care. Marya glanced over it once herself, ascertaining something unknowable, before turning back to Dimitri, extending her slender arm.

Roman twitched forward, about to stop her, but Dimitri held up a hand again, waving Roman away as he leaned forward to accept it.

Dimitri's thumb brushed briefly over Marya's fingers, then retracted.

"What's this?" he asked, eyeing the package, and her smile curled upward.

"A new product," Marya said, as Dimitri slid open the thick parchment to reveal a set of narrow tablets in plastic casing, each one like a vibrantly-colored aspirin. "Intended for euphoria. Not unlike our other offerings, but this one is something a bit less delicate; a little sharper than pure delusion. Still, it's a hallucinatory with a hint of... novelty, if you will. Befitting the nature of our existing products, of course. Branding," she half-explained with a shrug. "You know how it goes."

Dimitri eyed the tablet in his hand for a long moment before speaking.

"I don't, actually," he replied, and Lev watched a muscle jump near his brother's jaw; another uncharacteristic twitch of unease, along with the resignation in his tone. "You know Koschei doesn't involve himself in any magical intoxicants unless he's specifically commissioned to do so. This isn't our business."

"Interesting," Marya said softly, "very interesting."

"Is it?"

"Oh, yes, very. In fact, I'm relieved to hear you say that, Dima," Marya said. "You see, I'd heard some things, some very terrible rumors about your family's latest ventures"—Lev blinked, surprised, and glanced at Roman, who replied with a warning head shake—"but if you say this isn't your business, then I'm more than happy to believe you. After all, our two families have so wisely kept to our own lanes in the past, haven't we? Better for everyone that way, I think."

"Yes," Dimitri replied simply, setting the tablets down. "So, is that all, Masha? Just wanted to boast a bit about your mother's latest accomplishments, then?"

"Boast, Dima, really? Never," Marya said. "Though, while I'm here, I'd like you to be the first to try it, of course. Naturally. A show of good faith. I can share my products with you without fear, can't I? If you're to be believed, that is," she mused, daring him to contradict her. "After all, you and I are old friends. Aren't we?"

Dimitri's jaw tightened again; Roman and Lev exchanged another glance. "Masha—"

"Aren't we?" Marya repeated, sharper this time, and now, again, Lev saw the look in her eyes he remembered fearing as a young boy; that icy, distant look her gaze had sometimes held on the rare occasions when he'd seen her. She'd clearly learned to conceal her sharper edges with whatever mimicry of innocence she had at her disposal, but that look, unlike her falser faces, could never be disguised. For Lev, it had the same effect as a bird of prey circling overhead.

"Try it, Dima," Marya invited, in a voice that had no exit; no room to refuse. "I presume you know how to consume it?"

"Masha," Dimitri said again, lowering his voice to its most diplomatic iteration. "Masha, be reasonable. Listen to me—"

"Now, Dima," she cut in flatly, the pretense of blithe civility vanishing from the room.

It seemed that, for both of them, the playacting had finally ceased, the consequences of something unsaid dragging the conversation to a sudden détente, and Lev waited impatiently for his brother to refuse. Refusal seemed the preferable choice, and the rational one; Dimitri did not typically partake in intoxicants, after all, and such a thing would have been easy to decline. *Should* have been easy to decline, even, as there was no obvious reason to be afraid.

(No reason, Lev thought grimly, aside from the woman who sat across from them, some invisible threat contained within each of her stiffened hands.)

Eventually, though—to Lev's stifled dismay—Dimitri nodded his assent, taking up a lilac-colored tablet and eyeing it for a moment between his fingers. Beside Lev, Roman twitched forward almost imperceptibly and then forced himself still, dark eyes falling apprehensively on the line of their brother's neck.

"Do it," Marya said, and Dimitri's posture visibly stiffened.

"Masha, give me a chance to explain," he said, voice low with what Lev might have called a plea had he believed his brother capable of pleading. "After everything, don't you owe me that much? I understand you must be angry—"

"Angry? What's to be angry about? Just try it, Dima. What would you possibly have to fear? You already assured me we were friends, didn't you?"

The words, paired with a smile so false it was really more of a grimace, rang with causticity from Marya's tongue. Dimitri's mouth opened, hesitation catching in his throat, and Marya leaned forward. "Didn't you?" she repeated, and this time, Dimitri openly flinched.

"Perhaps you should go," Lev blurted thoughtlessly, stepping forward from his position flanking his brother behind the sofa, and at that, Marya looked up, her gaze falling curiously on him as she proceeded to morph and change, resuming her sweeter disposition as if just recalling Lev's presence in the room.

"You know, Dima," she said, eyes still inescapably on Lev, "if the Fedorov brothers are anything like the Antonova sisters, then it would be very wrong of me to not reward them equally for our friendship. Perhaps we should include Lev and Roma in this," she mused, slowly returning her gaze to Dimitri's, "don't you think?"

"No," Dimitri said, so firmly it halted Lev in place. "No, they have nothing to do with this. Stay back," he said to Lev, turning around to deliver the message clearly. "Stay where you are, Lev. Roma, keep him there," he commanded in his deepened crown-prince voice, and Roman nodded, cutting Lev a cautioning glare.

"Dima," Lev said, senses all but flaring with danger now. "Dima, really, you don't have to—"

"Quiet," Marya said, and then, save for her voice, the room fell absent of sound. "You assured me," she said, eyes locked on Dimitri's now. It was clear that, for her, no other person of consequence existed in the room. "Spare me the indignity of recounting the reasons we both know you'll do as I ask."

Dimitri looked at her, and she back at him.

And then, slowly, Dimitri resigned himself to parting his lips, placing the tablet on the center of his tongue and tilting his head back to swallow as Lev let out a shout no one could hear.

"It's a new product, as I said," Marya informed the room, brushing off her skirt. "Nothing any different from what will eventually come to market. The interesting thing, though, about our intoxicants," she said, observing with quiet indifference as Dimitri shook himself slightly, dazed, "is that there are certain prerequisites for enjoyment. Obviously we have to build in some sort of precautionary measures to be certain who we're dealing with, so there are some possible side effects. Thieves, for example," she murmured softly, her eyes still on Dimitri's face, "will suffer some unsavory reactions. Liars, too. In fact, anyone who touches our products without the exchange of currency from an Antonova witch's hands will find them . . . slightly less pleasant to consume."

Dimitri raised a hand to his mouth, retching sharply into his palm for several seconds. After a moment spent collecting himself, he lifted his head with as much composure as he could muster, shakily dragging the back of his hand across his nose.

A bit of blood leaked out, smearing across the knuckle of his index finger.

"Understandably, our dealers wish to partake at times, so to protect them, we give them a charm they wear in secret. Of course, you likely wouldn't know that," Marya remarked, still narrating something with a relevance Lev failed to grasp. "Trade secret, isn't it? That it's quite dangerous to try to sell our products without our express permission, I mean. Wouldn't want someone to know that in advance, obviously, or our system would very well collapse."

Dimitri coughed again, the reverberation of it still silent. Steadily, blood began to pour freely from his nose, dripping into his hands and coating them in a viscous, muddied scarlet streaked with black. He sputtered without a sound, struggling to keep fluid from dripping into his throat while his chest wrenched with coughs.

"We have a number of informants, you know. They're very clever, and very well concealed. Unfortunately, according to one of them, *someone*," Marya murmured, "has been selling our intoxicants. Buying them from us, actually, and then turning around to sell them at nearly quadruple the price. Who would do that, I wonder, Dima?"

Dimitri choked out a word that might have been Marya's name, falling forward onto his hands and knees and colliding with the floor. He convulsed once, then twice, hitting his head on the corner of the table and stumbling, and Lev called out to his brother with dismay, the sound of it still lost to the effects of Marya's spell. She was the better witch by far—their father had always said so, speaking of Marya Antonova even from her youth as if she were some sort of Old World demon, the kind of villainess children were warned to look for in the dark. Still, Lev rushed forward, panicked, only to feel his brother Roman's iron grip at the back of his collar, pinning him in place as Dimitri struggled to rise and then collapsed forward again, blood pooling beneath his cheek where he'd fallen to the floor.

"This hurts me, Dima, it really does." Marya sighed, expressionless. "I really did think we were friends, you know. I certainly thought you could be trusted. You were always so upstanding when we were children—and yes, true, a lot can happen in a decade, but still, I really never thought we'd be . . . here." She sighed again, shaking her head. "It pains me, truly, as much as it pains you. Though perhaps that's insensitive of me," she amended softly, watching Dimitri gasp for air; her gaze never dropped, not even when he began to jerk in violent tremors. "Since it does seem to be paining you a great deal."

Lev felt his brother's name tear from his lungs again, the pain of it raking at his throat until finally, finally, Dimitri fell rigidly still. By then, the whole scene was like a portrait, gruesomely Baroque; from the crumpled malformation of his torso, one of Dimitri's arms was left outstretched, his fingers unfurled toward Marya's feet.

"Well," exhaled Marya, rising from the chair. "I suppose that's that. Ivan, my coat, please?"

At last, with their brother's orders fulfilled, Roman released Lev, who in turn flung himself toward Dimitri. Roman looked on, helpless and tensed, as Lev checked for a pulse, frantically layering spells to keep what was left of his brother's blood unspilled, to compel his princely lungs to motion. Dimitri's breathing was shallow, the effort of his chest rapidly fading, and in a moment of hopelessness, Lev looked blearily up at Marya, who was pulling on a pair of black leather gloves.

"Why?" he choked out, abandoning the effort of forethought. He hadn't even bothered with surprise that his voice had finally been granted to him, and she, similarly, spared none at the question, carefully removing a smudge from her oversized sunglasses before replacing them on her face.

"Tell Koschei that Baba Yaga sends her love," she said simply.

Translation: *Your move.*

Then Marya Antonova turned, beckoning Ivan along with her, and let the door slam in her wake.